Fiona Barton trains and works with journalists all over the world. Previously, she was a senior writer for the *Daily Mail*, news editor for the *Daily Telegraph*, and chief reporter for the *Mail on Sunday*, where she won Reporter of the Year at the British Press Awards. Her first novel, *The Widow*, was a *Sunday Times* and *New York Times* bestseller. Born in Cambridge, she currently lives in southwest France.

THE CHILD

When a paragraph in an evening newspaper reveals a decades-old tragedy, most readers barely give it a glance. But for three strangers, it's impossible to ignore.

For one woman, it's a reminder of the worst thing that ever happened to her.

For another, it reveals the dangerous possibility that her darkest secret is about to be discovered.

And for the third, a journalist, it's the first clue in a hunt to uncover the truth.

The child's story will be told.

Books by Fiona Barton
Published by Ulverscroft:

THE WIDOW

FIONA BARTON

◆

THE
CHILD

Complete and Unabridged

CHARNWOOD
Leicester

First published in Great Britain in 2017 by
Bantam Press
an imprint of Transworld Publishers
London

First Charnwood Edition
published 2018
by arrangement with
Transworld Publishers
Penguin Random House
London

A catalogue record for this book is available
from the British Library.

ISBN 978–1–4448–3673–8

Published by
F. A. Thorpe (Publishing)
Anstey, Leicestershire

Set by Words & Graphics Ltd.
Anstey, Leicestershire
Printed and bound in Great Britain by
T. J. International Ltd., Padstow, Cornwall

This book is printed on acid-free paper

For M & D

'When truth is replaced by silence, the silence is a lie.'

Yevgeny Yevtushenko

1

Emma

My computer is winking at me knowingly as I sit down at my desk. I touch the keyboard and a photo of Paul appears on my screen. It's the one I took of him in Rome on our honeymoon, eyes full of love across a table in the Campo de' Fiori. I try to smile back at him, but as I lean in I catch a glimpse of my reflection in the screen and stop. I hate seeing myself without warning. Don't recognize myself, sometimes. You think you know what you look like and there is this stranger looking at you. It can frighten me.

But today, I study the stranger's face. The brown hair half pulled up on top of the head in a frantic work bun, naked skin, shadows and lines creeping towards the eyes like subsidence cracks.

Christ, you look awful, I tell the woman on the screen. The movement of her mouth mesmerizes me and I make her speak some more.

Come on, Emma, get some work done, she says. I smile palely at her and she smiles back.

This is mad behaviour, she tells me in my own voice and I stop.

Thank God Paul can't see me now, I think.

1

★　★　★

When Paul gets home tonight, he's tired and a bit grumpy after a day of 'bone-headed' undergraduates and another row with his head of department over the timetable.

Maybe it's an age thing, but it seems to really shake Paul to be challenged at work these days. I think he must be starting to doubt himself, see threats to his position everywhere. University departments are like prides of lions, really. Lots of males preening and screwing around and hanging on to their superiority by their dew-claws. I say all the right things and make him a gin and tonic.

When I move his briefcase off the sofa, I see he's brought home a copy of the *Evening Standard*. He must've picked it up on the Tube.

I sit and read it while he showers away the cares of the day, and it's then I see the paragraph about the baby.

'BABY'S BODY FOUND,' it says. Just a few lines about how a baby's skeleton has been discovered on a building site in Woolwich and police are investigating. I keep reading it over and over. I can't take it in properly, as if it's in a foreign language.

But I know what it says and terror is coiling round me. Squeezing the air out of my lungs. Making it hard to breathe.

I am still sitting here when Paul comes down, all damp and pink and shouting that something is burning.

The pork chops are black. Incinerated. I throw

2

them in the bin and open the window to let out the smoke. I fetch a frozen pizza out of the freezer and put it in the microwave while Paul sits quietly at the table.

'We ought to get a smoke alarm,' he says, instead of shouting at me for almost setting the house on fire. 'Easy to forget things when you're reading.' He is such a lovely man. I don't deserve him.

Standing in front of the microwave, watching the pizza revolve and bubble, I wonder for the millionth time if he'll leave me. He should have done years ago. I would if I'd been in his place, having to deal with my stuff, my worries, on a daily basis. But he shows no sign of packing his bags. Instead he hovers over me like an anxious parent protecting me from harm. He talks me down when I get in a state, invents reasons to be cheerful, holds me close to calm me when I cry, and tells me I am a brilliant, funny, wonderful woman.

It is the illness making you like this, he says. *This isn't you.*

Except it is. He doesn't know me really. I've made sure of that. And he respects my privacy when I shy from any mention of my past. 'You don't have to tell me,' he says. 'I love you just the way you are.'

St Paul — I call him that when he's pretending I'm not a burden to him, but he usually shushes me.

'Hardly,' he says.

Well, not a saint, then. But who is? Anyway, his sins are my sins. What do old couples say? What's

3

yours is mine. But my sins . . . well, they're my own.

'Why aren't you eating, Em?' he says when I put his plate on the table.

'I had a late lunch, busy with work. I'm not hungry now — I'll have something later,' I lie. I know I would choke if I put anything in my mouth.

I give my brightest smile — the one I use for photos. 'I'm fine, Paul. Now eat up.'

On my side of the table, I nurse a glass of wine and pretend to listen to his account of the day. His voice rises and falls, pauses while he chews the disgusting meal I've served, and resumes.

I nod periodically but I hear nothing. I wonder if Jude has seen the article.

4

2

Kate

Kate Waters was bored. It wasn't a word she normally associated with her job, but today she was stuck in the office under the nose of her boss with nothing to do but re-writes.

'Put it through your golden typewriter,' Terry, the news editor, had shouted across, waving someone else's badly written story at her. 'Sprinkle a bit of fairy dust on it.'

And so she did.

'It's like Mike Baldwin's knicker factory in here,' she complained to the Crime man, sitting opposite. 'Churning out the same old rubbish with a few frills. What are you working on?'

Gordon Willis, always referred to by the editor by his job title — as in 'Get the Crime man on this story ... ' — lifted his head from a newspaper and shrugged. 'Going down to the Old Bailey this afternoon — want to have a chat with the DCI in the crossbow murder. Nothing doing yet, but hoping I might get a talk with the victim's sister when it finishes. Looks like she was sleeping with the killer. It'll be a great multi-deck headline: THE WIFE, THE SISTER AND THE KILLER THEY BOTH LOVED.' He

5

grinned at the thought. 'Why? What have you got on?'

'Nothing. Unpicking a story one of the online slaves has done.' Kate indicated a pubescent nymph typing furiously at a desk across the room. 'Straight out of sixth form.'

She realized how bitter — and old — she must sound and stopped herself. The tsunami of online news had washed her and those like her to a distant shore. The reporters who once sat on the top table — the newspaper equivalent of the winner's podium — now perched at the edge of the newsroom, pushed further and further towards the exit by the growing ranks of online operatives who wrote 24/7 to fill the hungry maw of rolling news.

New media stopped being new a long time ago, the editor had lectured his staff at the Christmas party. It was the norm. It was the future. And Kate knew she had to stop bitching about it.

Hard, she told herself, when the most viewed stories on the paper's slick website were about Madonna's hands being veiny or an *EastEnders* star putting on weight. 'Hate a Celebrity' dressed as news. Horror.

'Anyway,' she said out loud, 'it can wait. I'll go and get us a coffee.'

Also gone were the days of the CQ — the Conference Quickie — once enjoyed by Fleet Street's finest in the nearest pubs while the executives were in the editor's morning meeting. The CQ was traditionally followed by red-faced, drunken rows with the news editor — one of which, legend had it, ended with a reporter, too drunk to stand, biting his boss's ankle and another reporter throwing a typewriter through a window into the street below.

These days the newsroom, now in offices above a shopping mall, had windows hermetically sealed by double-glazing and alcohol was banned. Coffee was the new addiction of choice.

'What do you want?' Kate asked.

'Double macchiato with hazelnut syrup, please,' Gordon said. 'Or some brown liquid. Whichever comes first.'

Kate took the lift down, pinching a first edition of the *Evening Standard* from the security desk in the marble lobby. As she waited for the barista to work his magic with the steamer, she flicked idly through the pages, checking for the by-lines of friends.

The paper was wall-to-wall with preparations for the London Olympics and she almost missed the paragraph at the bottom of the News in Brief column.

Headlined BABY'S BODY FOUND, two sentences told how an infant's skeleton had been unearthed on a building site in Woolwich, not a million miles from Kate's east London home. Police were investigating. No other details. She tore it out for later. The bottom of her bag was lined with crumpled scraps of newspaper — 'It's like a budgie cage,' her eldest son, Jake, teased her about the shreds of paper waiting for life to be breathed into them. Sometimes whole stories to be followed up or, more often, just a line or a quote that made her ask, 'What's the story?'

7

Kate re-read the thirty words and wondered about the person missing from the story. The mother. As she walked back with the coffee cups, she ticked off her questions: *Who is the baby? How did it die? Who would bury a baby?*

'Poor little thing,' she said out loud. Her head was suddenly full of her own babies — Jake and Freddie, born two years apart but known as 'the boys' in family shorthand — as sturdy toddlers, schoolboys in football kit, surly teenagers and now adults. *Well, almost.* She smiled to herself. Kate could remember the moment she saw each of them for the first time: red, slippery bodies; crumpled, too-big skin; blinking eyes staring up from her chest, and her feeling that she had known their faces for ever. *How could anyone kill a baby?*

When she got back to the newsroom, she put the cups down and walked over to the news desk.

'Do you mind if I have a look at this?' she asked Terry, waving the tiny cutting in front of him as he tried to make sense of a feature on foreign royals. He didn't look up, so she assumed he didn't.

★   ★   ★

Her first call was to the Scotland Yard press office. When she'd started in journalism, as a trainee on a local paper in East Anglia, she used to call in at the local police station every day to lean on the front desk and look at the logbook while the sergeant chatted her up. Now, if she

8

contacted the police, she rarely spoke to a human being. And if she did, it was likely to be a fleeting experience.

'Have you listened to the tape?' a civilian press officer would ask, in the full knowledge that she hadn't, and she would find herself quickly re-routed to a tinny recorded message that took her through every stolen lawnmower and pub punch-up in the area.

But this time she hit the jackpot. Not only did she get through to a real person, it was someone she knew. The voice on the end of the phone belonged to a former colleague from her first job on a national newspaper. He was one of the poachers turned game-keepers who'd recently joined the safer, some said saner, world of Public Relations.

'Hello, Kate. How are you? Long time . . . '

Colin Stubbs wanted to chat. He'd done well as a reporter, but his wife, Sue, had grown tired of his rackety life on the road and he'd finally given in to the war of attrition at home. But he was hungry for details about the world he'd left, asking for gossip about other reporters and telling her — and himself — over and over that leaving newspapers was the best thing he'd ever done.

'That's great. Lucky you,' Kate said, determinedly upbeat. 'I'm still slogging along at the *Post*. Look, Colin, I saw something in the *Standard* about a baby's body being found in Woolwich. Any idea how long it'd been there?'

'Oh, that. Hang on, I'll pull up the details on the computer . . . Here we are. Not much to go on and a bit grim, really. A workman was clearing a demolition site and moved an old urn and underneath was this tiny skeleton. Newborn, they say. Forensics are having a look, but it says here that early indications are it's been there a while — could be historic, even. It's a road in student land, towards Greenwich, I think. Don't you live round there?'

'North of the river and a bit further east, actually. Hackney. And still waiting for the gentrification train to stop. What else have you got? Any leads on identification?'

'No, newborns are tricky when it comes to DNA, says here. Especially if they've been underground for years. And the area is a warren of rented flats and bedsits. Tenants changing every five minutes, so the copper in charge isn't optimistic about it. And we've all got our hands full with the Olympics stuff . . .'

'Yeah, of course,' Kate said. 'The security must be a nightmare — I hear you're having to bus in officers from other forces to cope. And this baby story sounds like a needle-in-a-haystack job. Look, thanks, Colin. It's been good to catch up. Give my love to Sue. And will you give me a call if anything else comes up on this?'

She smiled as she put down the phone. Kate Waters loved a needle-in-a-haystack job. The glint of something in the dark. Something to absorb her totally. Something to sink her teeth into. Something to get her out of the office.

She put on her coat and started the long walk to the lift. She didn't get far.

'Kate, are you off somewhere?' Terry shouted.

10

'Before you go, you couldn't untangle this stuff about the Norwegian royals, could you? It's making my eyes bleed.'

3

Tuesday, 20 March 2012

Angela

She knew she was going to cry. She could feel it welling up, thickening her throat so she couldn't speak, and went to sit on the bed for a minute to postpone the moment. Angela needed to be on her own when it came. She'd tried to fight it over the years — she never cried, normally. She wasn't the sentimental sort. Nursing and living the army life had trained that out of her a long time ago.

But every year, March 20th was the exception. It was Alice's birthday and she would cry. A private moment. She wouldn't dream of doing it in front of anyone, like the people who stood there and wept in front of cameras. She couldn't imagine what it felt like to be on show like that. And the television people kept on filming, as though it was some sort of entertainment.

'They should turn off the camera,' she'd said to Nick, but he'd just grunted and kept on watching.

It made her feel uncomfortable, but apparently lots of people liked it. The sort of people who tried to be part of the news.

Anyway, she didn't think anyone would

understand why she was still crying all these years later. Decades later. They'd probably say she'd hardly known the baby. She'd had less than twenty-four hours with her.

But she was part of me. Flesh of my flesh, she told the sceptics in her head. *I've tried to let go, but . . .*

The dread would begin in the days before the baby's birthday and she'd get flashbacks to the silence — that bone-chilling silence in an empty room.

Then, on the day, she would usually wake up with a headache, would make breakfast and try to act normally until she was alone. This year, she was talking to Nick in the kitchen about the day ahead. He'd been complaining about the mountain of paperwork he'd got to deal with and about one of the new lads, who kept taking days off sick.

He ought to retire, she thought as she listened. He could have done it two or three years ago. But he couldn't let go of the business. He said he needed a purpose, a routine.

He doesn't give any sign that he knows what day this is.

He used to remember — in the early days. Of course he did. It was never far from anyone's thoughts.

People in the street used to ask about their baby. People they didn't know from Adam would come up to them, squeeze their hands and look tearful. But that was then. Nick was hopeless with dates — deliberately, Angela thought. He couldn't even remember their other children's

13

birthdays, let alone Alice's. And she'd stopped reminding him. She couldn't bear the flash of panic in his eyes as he was forced to revisit that day. It was kinder if she did the remembering on her own.

Nick kissed her on the top of her head as he left for work. And when the door closed behind him, Angela sat on the sofa and let herself cry.

★ ★ ★

She'd tried to train herself to put the memories away. There wasn't much help at the beginning. Just the family doctor — poor old Dr Earnley — who'd patted her shoulder or knee and said, 'You will get through this, my dear.'

Then, later, there were support groups, but she'd got tired of hearing her own and other people's misery. She felt they were just circling the pain, prodding it, inflaming it and then crying together. She upset the group when she announced that she'd discovered it didn't help to know other people hurt too. It didn't take away her own grief — just added layers to it, somehow. She'd felt guilty, because when she'd been a nurse and someone had died, she used to give the grieving family a leaflet on bereavement.

I hope it helped them more than it did me, she said to herself as she got off the sofa. *Mustn't be bitter. Everyone did what they could.*

In the kitchen she filled the sink with water and started preparing vegetables for a casserole. The cold water numbed her hands so she found it hard to hold the knife, but she continued to scrape mechanically at the carrots.

She tried to summon up an image of what Alice would be like now, but it was too hard. She only had one photograph of her. Of Alice and her. Nick had taken it on his little Instamatic but it was blurred. He'd taken it too quickly. Angela braced herself against the kitchen counter, as if physical effort could help her see her lost baby's little face. But it wouldn't come.

She knew from the photo that Alice had a fuzz of dark hair, like her brother, Patrick, but Angela had lost a lot of blood during the delivery and she was still high from the Pethidine when they put her baby in her arms. She'd asked Nick afterwards — after Alice was gone — but he couldn't tell her much more. He hadn't studied her as Angela would've done, memorizing every feature. He'd said she looked lovely, but had no details.

Angela didn't think Alice looked like Patrick. He'd been a big baby and Alice had been so fragile. Barely five pounds. But still she'd studied Paddy's baby photos, and the pictures they took when their second daughter, Louise, came along ten years later — 'Our surprise bonus baby, I call her,' Angela told people — willing herself to see Alice in them. But she wasn't there. Louise was blonde — she took after Nick's side.

Angela felt the familiar dull ache of grief round her ribs and in her chest and she tried to think happy thoughts, like the self-help books had told her. She thought about Louise and Patrick.

'At least I have them,' she said to the carrot

tops bobbing in the dirty water. She wondered if Lou would ring her that night when she got in from work. Her youngest knew the story — of course she did — but she didn't talk about it.

And she hates it when I cry, Angela said to herself, wiping her eyes with a piece of kitchen roll. *They all do. They like to pretend that everything is fine. I understand that. I should stop now. Put Alice away.*

'Happy birthday, my darling girl,' she murmured under her breath.

4

Wednesday, 21 March 2012

Emma

The baby has kept me awake most of the night. I tore the story out of the paper and went to put it in the bin, but ended up stuffing it in the pocket of my cardigan. I don't know why. I'd decided I wasn't going to do anything about it. I hoped it would go away.

A small voice inside me whispered, *Not like last time, then.*

And today the baby is still here. Insistent. Demanding to be acknowledged.

Paul is dozing, almost awake and beginning to move his legs, as if he's testing whether they're still there. I wait for his eyes to open.

I dread it. I dread the disappointment and exhaustion I'll see when he realizes my bad days are back.

It's what we used to call them, so it sounded like it wasn't my fault. It has been so long since the last episode and I know he thought it was all over. He'll try hard not to show it when he sees me, but I'll have to carry his anxiety, too. Sometimes I feel as though I'll shatter under the weight.

People say what doesn't kill you makes you

17

stronger. They say that when you've been through something terrible. My mum Jude used to say it. But it doesn't. It breaks your bones, leaving everything splintered and held together with grubby bandages and yellowing sticky tape. Creaking along the fault lines. Fragile and exhausting to hold together. Sometimes you wish it *had* killed you.

Paul wakes and fetches my pills and a glass of water from the bathroom without a word. Then he strokes my hair and sits on the bed, while I take them. He hums under his breath as if everything is normal.

I try to think *All things will pass,* but *This will never end* slips past my defences.

The problem is that a secret takes on a life of its own over time. I used to believe that if I didn't think about what had happened, it would shrivel and die. But it didn't. It sits in the middle of a growing tangle of lies and fabrications, like a fat fly trapped in a spider's web. If I say anything now it will mean ripping everything apart. So I must say nothing. I have to protect it. The secret, that is. It's what I've done for as long as I can remember. Kept it safe.

★ ★ ★

Paul is talking to me at the breakfast table and I've missed what he was saying.

'Sorry, darling, what was that?' I try to focus on him across the table.

'I said we're almost out of toilet paper.'

I can't concentrate. Something about paper.

18

Oh God, has he read it?

'What?' I say, too loudly.

'Toilet paper, Emma,' he says quietly. 'Just reminding you, that's all.'

'Right, right. Don't worry, I'll do it. You get yourself ready for work while I finish my coffee.'

He smiles at me, kisses me as he passes and rustles around in his study for ten minutes while I throw away my breakfast and wipe the surfaces. I find myself cleaning more lately. *Out, damned spot.*

'Right,' he says at the kitchen door. 'Are you sure you are all right? You still look very pale.'

'I'm fine,' I say and get up. *Come on, Paul. Just go.* 'Have a good day, darling. Remember to be nice to the Head of Department. You know it makes sense.' I brush some fluff off the shoulder of his overcoat.

He sighs and picks up his briefcase. 'I'll try. Look, I can call in sick and stay with you,' he says.

'Don't be silly, Paul. I'll have an easy day. Promise.'

'OK, but I'll ring at lunchtime. Love you,' he says.

I wave from the window, as I always do. He closes the gate and turns away, then I sink to my knees on the carpet. It's the first time I have been alone since I read the story and pretending that everything is fine has been shattering. The headline from the paper is like a neon sign everywhere I look. I just need five minutes to pull myself together. And I cry. Frightening crying. Uncontrollable. Not like English crying,

19

where you fight it and try to swallow it. It goes on until there is nothing left and I sit quietly on the floor.

When the phone rings, I realize an hour has passed, and my legs are cramped and tingle with pins and needles when I try to pull myself up. I must've drifted off. I love the image that creates in my head, of lying in a boat and being carried by the current. Like Ophelia in the painting. But she was mad, or dead. *Stop it. Answer the phone*.

'Hello, Emma, it's Lynda. Are you busy? Can I come for coffee?'

I want to say no to the appalling Lynda, but 'Yes' comes out instead. Ingrained politeness wins out again.

'Lovely. Be there in ten minutes.'

'I'll put the kettle on,' I hear myself say, as if I am in a play.

I rub my knees to get the feeling back and get a hairbrush out of my bag. Must look presentable or she'll know.

Lynda's husband teaches at the same university as Paul — different departments, but our two men often catch the same train in the morning. That, apparently, makes Lynda and me sisters under the skin.

But I don't like her. She has those teeth that slope backwards, like a shark, and an insistent manner. She and the other WOTAs — Wives of the Academics, as I christened them when I joined their ranks — gossip about me. I know they do. But there's nothing I can do about it. Ignore them. Keep calm and carry on.

20

Lynda breezes in as soon as I open the door. High energy this morning. Must be good news about Derek. I want her to leave immediately.

'You look tired, Emma. Didn't you have a good night?' she says, my attempt at grooming totally wasted, and takes over the coffee-making process. She leaves me standing like a spare part in my own kitchen.

'Hmmm. Tossed and turned a bit. Trying to work out a difficult bit in the book I'm editing,' I say.

She bristles. She hates the fact that I have a job. Sees it as a personal insult if I mention it. Lynda doesn't work. 'I have too much to do at home to need a job,' she says when asked. Usually with a brittle laugh.

Anyway, she decides to ignore the implied slight and plunges in with her news. Derek is getting a new title — with brackets, apparently. It will mean more importance and a bit of extra money. She is thrilled, the self-satisfaction coming off her in waves.

'The HoD wants him to take on more responsibility. He'll be Assistant Director of Student Welfare (Undergraduate) from next term,' she says, as if reading from a press release.

'Student Welfare? Goodness, he'll be knee deep in drugs and sexually transmitted diseases,' I say, relishing the idea of Derek, the most pompous man on earth, dealing with condom machines.

She stiffens at the mention of sex and I

21

disguise my enjoyment of this tiny triumph.

'That's great, Lynda,' I say. 'The milk's already out — on the draining board.'

We sit at the kitchen table and I listen to her chatter about the goings-on in the department. I know she will eventually broach the subject of Paul's 'little difficulty' — his clashes with the head of department — but I'm not going to help her get there. I keep going off on tangents — world news, train delays, the price of coffee — in the hope it will exhaust her. But she is, apparently, inexhaustible.

'So, is Paul getting on any better with the HoD?' she says, trying to smile kindly.

'Oh, it's just a storm in a teacup,' I say.

'Oh? I heard Dr Beecham was taking it to the next level,' she says.

'It's all a bit silly. Dr Beecham wants to cut Paul's most popular course to make way for one of his own. He's being a bit of an arse, to be honest.'

Lynda's eyes widen at the word. Clearly not what she calls the HoD.

'Well, you have to make compromises sometimes. Perhaps Paul's course was getting a bit tired.'

'I'm sure that's not true, Lynda. Would you like a Ginger Nut?'

Placated, she munches through the plateful. We are now on her daughter, Joy — 'She is our pride and joy, so that's what we named her' — and Joy's children. They are a handful, it seems. I notice Lynda doesn't refer to them as her grandchildren when she is listing their faults and misdemeanours. They are 'too independent', apparently, which in her closely fenced world is a terrible sin.

'Josie told me to mind my own business the other day,' she says, the outrage still rankling. 'Nine years old and telling her grandmother to mind her own business!'

Go, Josie, I think, and say, 'Poor you.' Default position.

'Of course, you haven't got that worry,' Lynda says, 'not having any children.'

I gulp and cannot trust myself to reply. Instead, I look at my watch and mutter, 'Sorry, Lynda, it's been lovely catching up, but I'm on a deadline so must get back to work.'

'Well, you working women,' she says gracelessly. She looks disappointed, but smiles her Great White smile and puts her hands on my shoulders to kiss me goodbye. When she steps back, she says in an exaggeratedly caring voice, 'You should go back to bed, Emma.'

I bat her and her faux concern away.

'Tell the new Assistant Director of Student Welfare brackets Undergraduate congratulations from us,' I say as I usher her out. 'Have a good day,' I add.

Stop it, I think. *You sound like a shop assistant pretending to care.*

I go upstairs to my office and sit with the baby in the paper in my head, in my lap and on my back.

5

Kate

Howard Street on the edge of Woolwich was not looking its best. A herd of heavy machinery blotted out the houses, heaving clouds of smoke and dust into the air as it forced the transformation of this area of London.

Kate stood at one end, an escapee from the office.

She concentrated on picking out the houses that were still occupied. It looked as if there were only two or three left. She knew from the local free newspaper that the homes had been compulsorily purchased after a long planning battle. Now work had begun to tear them down, leaving the street looking like a retouched photograph from the Blitz. Kate counted herself lucky that her own corner of east London had largely escaped the notice of planners determined to re-imagine the capital as a series of villages, and her terrace remained untouched.

She and Steve had bought their ex-council house in Hackney in the early nineties, the first professional newcomers to the street. The night they moved in, next-door Bet had brought round a liver casserole in a flowered Pyrex dish, like the

24

one Kate's gran used to have. Bet had hovered in the kitchen, taking it all in — their matching kettle and toaster, the witty magnets on the fridge — and asking all sorts of nosey questions, but their worlds rarely collided after that, beyond a warm 'Hello, how are you doing?'

When they'd invited their friends to noisy barbecues or boozy dinner parties and popped corks in the garden, they felt rather than heard the sucking in of the neighbours' breath. But, gradually, others of their kind had arrived, lured by the affordable prices, and the street saw its first glossy black front door with a bay tree in a pot on the doorstep. The bay tree was nicked the second night, but its message remained.

Now, only next-door Bet and an old couple at the end of the street survived, surrounded by a rising tide of topiary and roman blinds. The recent arrival of a Marks and Spencer food emporium, on the corner where the video rental shop used to be, seemed to be the final straw for the old neighbourhood.

Thank goodness we don't have to put up with this, Kate thought as she surveyed the scene. Here, the interiors of three-storey houses gaped like life-sized dolls' houses, curtains flapping miserably. The only sign of human habitation was a light in a front kitchen, shining through the industrial gloom.

Kate walked up to the door and rang the bottom bell of three. The name written in biro beside it was Walker.

An older woman opened the door, peering round it nervously. 'Hello. Mrs Walker?' Kate

25

said, in performance mode. 'Sorry to bother you, but I'm doing a piece for the *Daily Post* on the changes around here.' She'd decided not to bring up the baby immediately. *Easy does it.*

The woman looked at her carefully, weighing her up, and then pulled the door open.

'It's Miss. Come in then. Quickly. I don't want to let all that dust in.' She led the way into her ground-floor flat, shifted a moth-eaten Jack Russell off the sofa and nodded at Kate to sit down.

'Sorry about Shorty. He's shedding,' she said, brushing the hair off the cushion. 'Which paper is it, again?'

'The *Daily Post.*'

'Oh, I buy that one. That's nice.'

Kate relaxed. A reader. Home and dry.

The two women chatted about the work going on just outside the window, raising their voices when a lorry thundered past, revving hard to get up the incline.

Kate nodded her sympathy and gently led Miss Walker round to the subject of the building-site grave.

'I heard the workmen found a body where they're working,' she said.

The older woman closed her eyes. 'Yes, a baby. What an awful thing.'

'Awful,' Kate echoed, and shook her head in sync with Miss Walker. 'Poor man who found it. He won't get over that for a while.'

'No,' Miss Walker agreed.

'It makes me wonder about the mother,' Kate went on. 'Who she was, I mean.' She'd put her notebook down beside her, to signal to Miss Walker that they were 'just talking'.

The woman was not as old as Kate had first thought. About sixty, she guessed, but she looked worn down by life. There was something of the fairground about her: bright colours distracting from a tired face. Kate noted the ginger patina of home-dyed hair and the make-up pooling in the creases of her eyelids.

'Do you have children?' she asked.

'No,' Miss Walker said. 'No kids. Just Shorty and me. We keep each other company.'

She stroked her pet in silence, the dog shivering with pleasure.

'He's a lovely dog,' Kate lied. She loathed dogs. She'd had too many confrontations on doorsteps with ravening beasts, snapping and lunging against their collars as their owners restrained them. They always said the same thing: 'Don't worry. He won't bite.' But the look in the animals' eyes said they would if they got the chance. This one was eyeing her up, but she tried to ignore it.

'Well, they don't know when it was buried, do they?' Miss Walker said. 'Could be hundreds of years old, I've heard. We might never know.'

Kate hmmed and nodded, head on one side. Not what she wanted to hear. 'When did you hear about it? You're only over the road — you must notice everything,' she said.

'I'm not some old busybody,' Miss Walker replied, her voice rising. 'I don't poke my nose in where it's not wanted.'

'Course not,' Kate soothed. 'But it must have

been hard to miss the police cars and things. I know I'd have been dying to know what was going on if it happened across from my house.'

The older woman was suitably mollified. 'Well, I saw the police come, and later, one of the workmen, John, who runs the site, told me what they'd found. He was very upset. Terrible to find something like that. A horrible shock. I made him a sweet tea.'

'That was nice of you,' Kate said. 'Perhaps your friend John will know more about when the baby was buried. Maybe the police said something?'

'I couldn't say. John saw it — the baby, I mean. He said it was just tiny bones. Nothing else left. Terrible.'

Kate picked up her notebook while Miss Walker went to make a cup of tea and wrote down the name of the workman and the quote about the tiny bones.

★ ★ ★

Twenty minutes and a tea with two sugars later, she was walking down to the site office, a first-floor Portakabin in a stack, with a panoramic view over the mayhem.

A stocky man in jeans cut her off at the door. 'Can I help you?'

'Hi. Are you John? I've just been talking to Miss Walker down the road and she suggested I come to see you.'

The foreman's face softened slightly. 'She's a lovely woman. She used to be a model or

28

something, you know. Long time ago now, obviously. She walks past with her dog every day and has a chat. Sometimes she brings me a cake or something else nice. Must be a bit lonely for her with pretty much everyone else gone.'

Kate nodded. 'Must be,' she said. 'Hard to be old these days, when everything is changing around you.'

The chitchat had gone on long enough and Kate thought the foreman might make his excuses and leave.

'Sorry,' she said. 'I didn't introduce myself. I'm Kate Waters.' She stuck out her hand to shake his. Difficult for people to be rude if they've shaken your hand.

'John Davies,' he said back automatically. 'What can I do for you?'

'I'm a reporter, doing a piece on the body found on your building site,' Kate went on and the foreman started to turn away. 'It must have been a terrible shock for you, you poor thing,' she added quickly.

He turned back. 'It was. Sorry to be rude, but we've had the police coming and going on the site. Taping off their crime scene, stopping us working. The men are all spooked and we're falling behind schedule.'

'Must be a nightmare,' Kate said.

'It is,' Davies agreed. 'Look, I shouldn't be talking to the press. The boss would have my balls if he knew.'

Kate smiled at him. 'I've got a boss like that. Come on, I'll buy you a pint in the pub up the road — it's lunchtime and it's just for a bit of

29

background. I don't have to quote you.'

Davies looked doubtful.

'I just want to get to the bottom of who the baby is. Awful for a child to be buried without a name. Like some Victorian pauper.'

'OK. But just one drink,' he said, and padlocked the site gates behind him.

'Brilliant,' Kate said, turning on a full-beam smile.

He walked awkwardly beside her past Miss Walker's and Kate waved to her new friend, standing watching at the kitchen window.

6

Wednesday, 21 March 2012

Kate

The pub was already full of site workers, the sharp smell of wet cement mixing with last night's beer slops, and Kate fought her way to the bar with a ten-pound note already waving in her hand.

'White-wine spritzer,' she ordered. 'What are you drinking, John?'

'Pint of bitter shandy, please.'

The landlord, his eyes hidden behind heavy-rimmed spectacles, pushed the full glasses forward and gave Kate a handful of change without a word.

'He should get a refund from the charm school he went to,' she said, plonking the drinks down on a ring-stained table.

'He's all right,' John said gruffly, taking the first long gulp of his pint. 'His pub is next to go if the second phase is approved. Must be hard, serving us, the forces of destruction.'

'Yeah, must be. How long has the work been going on?'

'Months. Feels like years.'

Kate sipped her drink. The bastard landlord had used lemonade instead of soda and its

31

sweetness was setting her teeth on edge. 'It sounds like hard work all round.'

'And last week didn't help. Awful thing.' John put down his glass and looked into its depths.

'It must've been. Was it you who found the body?'

'No, one of the labourers. Poor lad. He's only nineteen. Been off since.'

'What happened?'

John Davies emptied his glass.

'I'll get you another,' Kate said.

When she returned, he was peeling the design off his beer mat, in a world of his own.

'Peter was clearing rubble behind where the houses were so the machines could get in there,' John said without looking up. 'He was trying to move one of those old concrete urn things. That they plant flowers in. He said he disturbed the ground shifting it back and forth. And he saw this little bone. It was so small, he thought it was part of an animal and went to pick it up to see. But there was more. When he realized what it might be, he screamed. I thought he'd cut his leg off or something. Never heard a scream like it.'

'He must have been so shocked. You all must,' Kate murmured, encouragingly.

Her companion nodded wearily. 'He's very religious, Peter. Eastern European, you know. Always going on about spirits and things. Anyway, I went and looked. It was so small. Looked like a bird. It'd been wrapped in something and there were bits of paper and plastic stuck to it. I called the police and they came out.'

32

'Where was this?' Kate asked.

'Behind the terrace we pulled down a couple of months ago. Big, run-down old houses — four floors, some of them. Bedsits and flats. The whole terrace looked like it would fall down by itself if we hadn't given it a shove.'

He stood up. 'Anyway, back to work. Thanks for the drink, Miss. Remember, no quoting me.'

She smiled and shook his hand. 'Of course. Thanks for the chat, John. It's been a big help. Do you think Peter would talk to me? I just want to check some details.'

'Doubt it,' John said.

'Look, could you give him my number in case he wants to contact me?' she said, offering her business card.

John Davies put the card in his trouser pocket and nodded his goodbye. The rest of the workers followed him out.

Kate sat in the suddenly hushed bar and began writing up her notes. The peace and quiet didn't last long; the landlord ambled over to collect the glasses and interrupted her thoughts.

'Heard you were a reporter,' he said.

She looked up at him and smiled. 'Yes, I'm Kate, from the *Daily Post*,' she said.

'Graham,' he said, suddenly matey now the lunchtime crowd had gone. 'What are you reporting on, then?'

'The baby's body found on the building site.'

The pub landlord straddled the leatherette stool opposite her. 'Oh. I see. Shocking thing, burying a baby in the garden,' he said. 'Makes you wonder what happened to the poor little

33

thing. I mean, did someone murder it?'

Kate put down her pen and looked at him. 'Exactly what I thought,' she said. 'Who could kill a baby? It doesn't bear thinking about.'

They sat for a moment in silence.

'Did you know the people who lived in those houses?' Kate asked. 'The police must be busy tracking them down.'

'They'll have a job. Tenants mostly and they changed every five minutes,' he said. 'The usual story: the owner didn't live here — he had loads of property round here, rented out cheap. Those rooms were revolting inside. The sort of places people leave as soon as they can. Anyway, the baby wasn't buried recently. A copper told me when he was asking around. It could have been put there forty or fifty years ago.'

'Really? I wonder how they know that? Long before your time, then?'

The landlord smiled, trying not to be flattered by the outrageous compliment. 'Hardly,' he said. 'Do you want another one of those?' He pointed to the sticky remains in Kate's glass.

'Thanks. Can I have a soda straight up, this time? I'm driving.

'Anyway,' she added as she followed him back to the bar, nose to the trail, determined to keep his attention, 'who was running the pub back then? In the seventies and eighties? They'd have known the people living in the street, wouldn't they?'

'Actually, it was my better half's mum and dad,' he said. 'We took over from them. Toni might be able to help, but she's at work.'

'Don't worry, I can come back,' Kate said.

7

Thursday, 22 March 2012

Emma

It's lunchtime and I'm still in bed, where Paul left me this morning. The happy pills are working their magic and I am beginning to feel comfortably numb, so I force myself up. I can smell the stink of stale sheets on me so I stand in the shower until my fingertips start to prune, then pull on a loose jumper dress to hide my body.

I've put the tranquillizers back in the bathroom cabinet and closed the door on them. I hate the pills — they mean I'm failing. I'd like to put them in the bin, but what if I can't cope without them?

Maybe I'll try to get a different sort of help this time — look beyond the chemical route. I almost laugh as I think it. It would mean talking, wouldn't it? Telling someone my thoughts. Why I'm such a mess. What lies at the bottom of it all. It would mean brushing the loose dirt away and then excavating the thick clay packed deep around my memories.

My mum Jude once suggested talking therapy — back when the bad days had only just begun — but I refused to get in the car when she tried to take me to see a counsellor. There was a terrible scene in the street, with her screaming at me to get in and me bracing myself against the car door. God, was that me? The thing was, I knew then that silence was — is — the only option.

I know I won't do anything different now. It's too late. I'll just put it all away, take the pills until I get everything back under control, and get on with my work. Fill my life with other things to blot out the dread, like I normally do.

My normal.

Anyway, I'm going to go to the butcher's to get some meat for Paul's dinner — to make up for the burnt offerings and frozen food. The word 'meat' sticks in my head. Flesh and blood. I want to throw up.

Stop it, I tell myself, twisting the skin of my stomach through the dress.

At the butcher's, I can smell blood as soon as I enter the shop, metallic and coating my throat. I can feel panic rising so I stand quietly in the queue practising the breathing technique from yoga. In through the right nostril, out through the mouth. Or is it out through the left nostril?

'Mrs Simmonds,' the butcher says quite loudly. 'What can I get for you today?'

Startled out of my meditation, I blurt, 'Er, steak, please. A sirloin steak.' *I'll have a salad.*

He looks unimpressed. 'Just the one? Eating alone tonight?' he laughs, all red-faced under his stupid straw boater.

I give him a look, then try to laugh it off to show the other women in the shop that I'm in on the joke. But it sounds fake. 'Yes, George Clooney's let me down again,' I say.

I shove the parcel in my carrier bag, pay the king's ransom demanded and go home to try to get some work done.

★ ★ ★

It's five o'clock and Paul will be home soon. The thought makes me type faster. I'll carry on for another hour then resume domestic duties. Can't stop yet. Must keep going. If I stop I'll be back with the baby. Distract, distract, distract.

I thank God for work most days. I got into editing about ten years ago. A good friend was working at a publishing house and one weekend, when she was landed with an emergency re-write, she asked me to help. I'd always written for myself — and at college — but this was sleeves-rolled-up writing, translating some fairly adolescent scribblings by a footballer into heart-wrenching prose. It appeared I had a talent and she got me more work.

Today, I'm in the midst of a marriage break-up, navigating the sorrow, guilt and relief of a young actress over her parting from her 'childhood' husband and her optimism (mis-placed, as it turns out) for her first 'industry' marriage. I never meet the subjects. That's the ghost writer's job. If it's a big star, they spend hours — sometimes weeks — with them, teasing out their stories and feelings. I'm not in that league. I'm more X Factor winners, that sort of thing. From what I gather, most of it is based on cuttings about them from magazines and newspapers, and I tinker and polish until it reads like a fairy story. It's never very satisfactory, but when it's a rush job for an unexpected news hook — death, scandal, success — it has to be done that way.

It's hard work and sometimes, when I'm sweating over every word, I curse the millions of people who buy celebrity memoirs just to look at the photos.

But it pays well enough and it's my own money. Paul thinks the work is beneath my talents, but I can do it from home and I am anonymous.

No one knows who Emma Simmonds is, even though my words are sold all over the world, in dozens of languages. My name never appears on the cover of the book. And that's how I want it to stay. Paul says I ought to be acknowledged, but I just laugh it off.

It always works. He's got enough on his plate, what with Dr Beecham and his scheming. Paul is more worried than he lets on and I try to boost his confidence. I tell him what a great teacher he is and how much his students love his classes.

And when that doesn't work, I tell him he saved my life when he took me on and that always makes him smile. I wonder if he is remembering those early days, in the 1990s, when I was trying to get my life together. I was too old and too different from the other students to join in their games. And there was Paul. I made a pitch for him in my first term, but it was only in my final year that he fell in love with me.

It was complicated, him being my personal tutor, but that didn't matter to me at the time. I thought Dr Paul Simmonds had all the answers to my problems.

He was twenty years older than me and wonderfully clever and funny in that dry, academic way. A bachelor, in un-ironed shirts and odd socks — and completely absorbed in his work.

'You mesmerized me,' I tell him and he laughs.

'Me? I couldn't mesmerize anyone,' he says.

But it's true. When he talked about things, he could captivate you. Me, anyway. And it felt like he was talking directly to me. His lectures on the psychology of Shakespeare's tragic heroines were all about me. And I would sit there and feel that he understood me and my jumbled head. I actually thought he might be able to make me better. Poor Paul. What a responsibility.

He says he fell for me immediately, but I think we both know he has romanticized the whole thing. The truth is that he was flattered at first by my interest in his lectures, and then sympathetic to my struggles with essays and college life. He took me under his wing, the department's problem child. Poor Paul. He didn't have a clue what he was getting into.

I began following him around the campus, sitting at the back of all his lectures just so I could be near him. The students in my year picked up on it immediately, nudging each other when they spotted me, whispering their catty remarks.

In the end, even Paul realized it was getting

39

out of hand and tried to talk to me about my behaviour, pointing out his professional respon- sibilities and urging me to find a boyfriend my own age. Sweet.

'Emma,' he said, 'I am old enough to be your father.'

Jude would have said that that was the point, if I'd told her. But I didn't. My mother wasn't part of my life back then. I didn't have to tell anyone that I saw Paul as my safe harbour and I wasn't about to let him go. He told me later it was my vulnerability that clinched it. He said I needed him more than any woman he'd ever known.

So romantic. Not like our first clandestine date in a dingy curry house with loud wallpaper and sitar music to drown out our declarations of love. Paul almost had to shout.

We had to wait until I'd finished my degree before we could go public but everyone knew anyway. We kept the department in scandalized whispers for two terms, and Paul suggested he apply for other jobs, so we could have a fresh start together.

'And we won't mention how you were still a student when we fell in love,' he said. 'Best not. *Mea culpa*, but sleeping dogs and all that . . .'

I've always thought that's a funny saying. Let sleeping dogs lie. Because sleeping dogs always wake up eventually, don't they?

8

Thursday, 22 March 2012

Kate

Peter, the labourer, rang the next morning, his voice hesitant, struggling to express himself in a foreign language.

'Miss Waters?' he said. 'I am Peter. John said you want to speak with me.'

Kate gripped the phone a little tighter. She hadn't thought he would actually get in touch.

'Peter, thank you so much for calling. I know you must be so shocked by what happened.'

'Yes, very shocked,' he said. 'How do you know about me?'

'Well, the police gave me some information about the investigation,' Kate said quickly. The man on the end of the phone was clearly nervous and she was anxious not to alarm him. It would be easier if they met. She could work her charms better face to face. 'Look, it's difficult to talk on the phone,' she said. 'Difficult to talk about something as sensitive as this. Could we meet, Peter? I could come to you.'

He hesitated. 'Well, OK,' he said. 'But just for a little time. I am staying with a friend just now. In Shepherd's Bush. Can we meet there? In the café by the station, perhaps?'

41

'Of course. I'm not that far from there. I can be there in half an hour. Is that OK?'

Kate was already pulling her bag off the arm of her chair when Gordon Willis looked up. He earwigged every conversation. It was a given. And she'd mentioned the police — his jealously guarded patch.

'What are you up to?' he said. 'Something I should know about?'

'No. Just a dead baby in Woolwich. It was in the *Standard*, Gordon,' she said, carefully underselling the story to head off any interference. The Crime man was a renowned by-line bandit, always looking for a chance to get his name on other people's work.

'Yeah, saw that,' he said. 'Cops think it's old — historic, probably.'

'Well, I thought I'd have a look at it. Could be a good human-interest story behind it.'

'Girls' stuff,' he said and resumed his crossword puzzle.

★ ★ ★

Peter had a coke in front of him when Kate walked across to his table. He was stick thin and his skin was so pale she could see the veins beneath. He looked up as she approached, stood and shook her hand. His was cold and she felt it tremble.

'Thanks very much for seeing me, Peter. I really appreciate it,' she said warmly as they sat down. 'I'm just trying to make sure I get my story right — for the baby's sake.'

It struck the right chord. His eyes filled with tears and he looked down at his lap.

'It was so small. Almost not there at all in the dirt,' he said to his drink. 'I didn't know what I was looking at. Then I saw . . . '

Kate memorized his words automatically, an intro already playing in her head.

'What made you dig there?' she said, moving him on from his sticking point and opening up the conversation. 'Tell me about that day.'

Peter spoke haltingly, occasionally looking up, about how he'd been told to clear a route through the gardens for a digger. 'It was a hard place to dig. There had been buildings a long time ago, John said, and concrete was left in the ground. Foundations. Underneath the gardens. It was raining and I was slipping in the mud. I remember I was laughing with the digger driver because we both fell over. It was funny . . . ' he said, then looked stricken at his flippancy.

'It's all right, Peter,' Kate said. 'You're not being disrespectful. It was what happened. It was funny at the time. You can't change that.'

The labourer nodded his thanks and leant forward on his elbows to get to the climax of his story. 'I was moving a big concrete pot and the driver went back to his cab to get ready to pass through the gap. And there it was. It was buried deep, but I had made a hole when I dragged the flower pot. I put my hand down — '

His voice failed and he started to cry into his red, cracked hands.

Kate reached across with a cheap napkin too thin and shiny to absorb anything. She touched his hand lightly. 'Please don't upset yourself, Peter. None of this is your fault. And perhaps the baby can be buried properly now.'

Peter looked up. 'That is what my priest said. That would be good.'

'Was there anything with the body? Clothes, toys?' she asked, praying for more details to make the baby seem real for her readers. People found it hard to care about skeletons, she'd learnt.

'No, I didn't see anything. Some bits of paper. Small like confetti, my boss said. I couldn't look after I pulled the first little bone out.'

'It must have been terrible for you,' Kate said, sneaking a quick look at her watch as she picked up her tea. 'How are you getting home? Can I put you in a cab?'

Peter shook his head and stood up. 'I prefer to walk, thank you. It helps clear my head.'

★ ★ ★

On her way back to the office, having checked the spelling of Peter's surname and paid the bill, she wondered if she'd get the story in the paper. It would take some careful selling to the news desk. There wasn't much to it yet — just a body and a sobbing workman. She'd write it up and see what Terry said.

★ ★ ★

The piece ran — down page, back of the book — the following Saturday. Kate had managed to

44

squeeze five hundred words out of the bare facts, ramping up Peter's tearful testimony with some colour from Howard Street and an anodyne quote from the police about 'continuing inquiries'. She ended it with a haunting question to get the readers involved. The sub-editor had pinched it to use as the headline: 'WHO IS THE BUILDING-SITE BABY?'

But Kate wasn't happy with the story. A question as a headline was an admission of failure, as far as she was concerned. Meant you hadn't nailed down the facts if you had to ask. She was sure there was more to get, but she needed the police forensics team to do their stuff to get a sniff of a follow-up.

And she knew she needed to look for other stories to keep her name in the paper so the editor didn't forget she existed.

But she couldn't get the image of the baby, wrapped in paper as if it was rubbish, out of her head.

She wouldn't let it go.

9

Saturday, 24 March 2012

Angela

She didn't really know why she'd picked up the paper. Nick had flicked straight to the Sports pages when he'd brought it back from the garage that morning and then abandoned it on the table. Angela had had her morning all planned — supermarket shop, then a coffee with Louise on the way home — but she reached out and turned the pages of the paper while she waited for the washing machine to finish spinning. She wanted to put the washing straight into the dryer before she went out. She wasn't even really reading, just looking at the photographs. But the word 'BABY' stopped her in her tracks.

'WHO IS THE BUILDING-SITE BABY?' the headline asked.

She read on, her flesh prickling beneath her clothes. A baby's body found. It was the word 'found' that made her cry out. Nick came running through.

'What is it, Angie?' he said. 'What's happened?'

She couldn't speak. She just thrust the paper at him, jabbing at the headline with her finger.

He looked where she was pointing and Angela

46

saw the weariness in his face as he took in what it meant.

'Angie, love, this doesn't mean anything. You know that, don't you? We've been here too many times, haven't we?'

She refused to look at him and carried on reading and re-reading the article. Memorizing it.

'But it's just after her birthday. That could be a sign,' she said.

'Angie,' he said, louder this time. 'It will be more heartbreak if you get your hopes up. It'll make you ill, like before.'

She nodded. There'd been a body found in Staffordshire in 1999 and she'd been sure then that it was Alice. Had felt it in her bones. But it wasn't. It turned out to be a boy — the child of some poor, sad woman who used smothering babies as a form of contraception. The police had found two others in the freezer.

'The police would've contacted us if there was any chance this was Alice. Wouldn't they?' Nick said, finally using their daughter's name.

'They've forgotten about her,' his wife said. They had. Everyone had. And they wanted her to forget, too, she knew. The police had got tired of her calls.

'We will be in touch as soon as we have news, Mrs Irving,' the last officer she'd spoken to had said. He'd sounded bored and irritated and she knew she had become a nuisance caller. Angela hadn't rung in since, and now, thirteen years on, she didn't know who to call.

She folded the paper and pushed it down the

side of the chair. She'd come and get it later.

'Shall I take you to Asda?' Nick said. 'I can give you a hand with carrying the bags. Save your back.'

★ ★ ★

Angela didn't manage to look at the story again until Nick had gone up to bed that night. She pulled it out of its hiding place and smoothed it with her hand. She let herself read it through two or three more times and then wrote down the name of the reporter in her diary and folded the story into a tiny square of paper. Maybe she'd ring this Kate Waters, she thought. Just to ask a few questions. Where would be the harm in that?

10

Emma

I've created a Google alert for the baby story. I know I said I wasn't going to do anything about it, but I need to know what everyone else knows, don't I? Just in case. To be prepared.

And this morning, I find the next instalment in my inbox: 'WHO IS THE BUILDING-SITE BABY?'

A reporter has been poking around, making the story grow bigger, talking to the poor man who found the body. And the police. *The police.*

I can feel the drum of my heart making my fingers vibrate on the keyboard. *Who else will she talk to? I* write her name — Kate Waters — on a pad beside my computer and read the story, over and over again.

When the phone rings, I let it go to answerphone. But I hear Jude leave a message, her voice echoing up the stairwell from the machine in the hall, as if she's in the house. As if we're back in Howard Street and she's calling me to get up for school.

I knew my mum would ring today. It's my birthday — one of the days she gets in touch

49

since we started talking again. It's only been a couple of years since we had the big reunion and we are more like distant cousins now, feeling for common ground when we speak.

'Do you remember that terrible bathroom suite your grandmother had?' Jude will say and I'll chime in with 'Yes, thank God avocado went out of fashion.' And we'll laugh and feel close for a few minutes. But it doesn't hold us together, this 'Do you remember?' game. Because too much is out of bounds.

So we ring each other on birthdays and at Christmas, that sort of thing. It's a routine that allows us to stay in touch with the aid of a calendar, not our emotions.

The thing is, I have done without a mother for so long I find I don't need her, and I'm sure Jude feels the same about me.

It's bizarre, really. None of my relationships are quite like other people's. My mum is like a cousin, my husband is like my dad, and my baby . . . Well, there is no baby. I can't think about that now. Stop it.

Today, the sound of my mother's voice makes me shiver. I wait until she stops speaking before I get up and go downstairs to listen to the message.

'Emma, it's Jude,' she says. She never calls herself Mum. She made me call her Jude from when I was ten — 'Mum is so ageing, Em,' she said. 'It's much more grown-up to call me Jude, anyway.' I didn't like it. It was as if she was ashamed I was her daughter, but I did it. To please her.

50

'Umm, are you there?' my mother's voice says. 'Pick up if you are. Umm, OK, just ringing to wish you happy birthday and see how things are. Umm, I need to talk to you, Emma. Please ring me . . .'

I need to talk to you. I sink down on a chair. *She must have seen the stories. What does she know?* I ask myself, almost automatically. It is a question I have tortured myself with for years.

I listen again, in case I've misheard. But I haven't. Of course I haven't. There is the same quaver in her voice as she searches for me. *Are you there?*

Am I? Am I here? I sit quietly, eyes closed, breathing deeply, trying to clear my mind. But when I open my eyes, the message light is still blinking. Winking at me as if it knows.

The phone suddenly bursts into life, its ring filling the hall, and I leap up from the chair as if to flee. But I pick up the receiver.

'Emma? It's me,' Jude says. 'Where were you earlier? I've been trying to get you . . .'

'Sorry. Busy with work.'

'On your birthday? I thought Paul might be taking you somewhere for lunch. Did he forget?'

'He's having to work this weekend, but we're going to celebrate tonight.'

'Good. Well, sorry I didn't send a card. I forgot to post it. It's sitting here on the desk. I'd forget my head if it wasn't screwed on . . . Anyway, how are you?'

I pause, wrong-footed by this chitchat. 'Er, so-so.'

'Oh dear,' she murmurs.

51

'How are *you*?' I ask. *Keep to safe subjects.* 'How's your hip?'

'Er, aching,' she says. 'I'm all right. Emma? Are you still there?'

The tension in my throat is making me gag and I don't speak for a second or two. I retreat to the secret place inside my head, where everything is known, where I am safe.

'Yes,' I croak eventually. And wait. I should say something, preempt it. Say, all casually, that I've seen they've dug up the body of a baby in our old street. *Fancy that . . .*

But I'm not sure I can have a pretend conversation about it. I might break down and cry. And she'd start asking questions. She used to put me to bed with a hot-water bottle — her panacea for all that ailed me — when I was a teenager and say, 'You are getting yourself all upset again, Emma. Have a little sleep and things will look better.'

But of course they didn't. It must have been terrible for her, having to cope with my moods, but she said a lot of teenagers went through the same thing. 'Hormones. It's all part of growing up,' she said. At first. But the excuses started to pall. And patience never was her virtue. I stopped crying when she stopped reacting. Tough love, she called it. It didn't solve anything for either of us. I started shouting and breaking things instead. Until she threw me out.

I try not to blame her. Not now — I might have done the same if I'd been the mother. But then . . .

'There's someone at the door, Jude,' I say

suddenly, wrapping my fist in my sleeve and rapping on the table to support my lie. 'Sorry, I'll call you back later.'

'Oh, Emma,' she says.

'I'm expecting a parcel,' I say desperately, tangling myself in the fabrication.

'Oh, go then,' she says. 'I'll call back.'

I put down the phone and the relief makes me giddy. But I know I've only postponed the inevitable.

The phone rings again five minutes later and for a split second I consider not picking up. But I must. She'll only keep ringing until she gets me.

'Why don't you come over?' Jude says, as if there has been no break in the conversation. 'You've never seen my flat and it's been months since we saw each other.'

I react immediately. Guilt and Shame — the Catholic twins, and my Pavlovian response to my mother's passive-aggressive parry.

'It's a bit difficult. I'm trying to finish this book by my deadline.'

'Well, if you're too busy. You must prioritize, I suppose.'

'That's not fair,' I say. 'Of course my work is important to me, but so are you.'

'Right,' she says. 'But not enough to spend some time with me. Never mind. There's a new Sunday serial starting on the radio. I won't be bored on my own.'

'I'll come, I'll come,' I say, back to being a sulky teenager.

'Lovely!' Jude says. 'I'll cook a birthday lunch

tomorrow then. Will Paul be coming? He's always welcome, of course, but it might be nice to just be the two of us.'

I'm silently furious on Paul's behalf, but he wouldn't want to be there anyway. He has tried his best to like Jude, but he struggles.

'I admire your mother's intellect,' he said after meeting her for the first time at a particularly sticky Sunday lunch in Covent Garden. 'But she is determined to be the cleverest person in the room, isn't she?'

His tiny revenge is to call her Judith — a name she detests.

'Actually, Paul's busy with an open day, so it will only be me anyway,' I say.

'See you at twelve, then. Don't be late,' she says. 'Lots to talk about.'

11

Sunday, 25 March 2012

Jude

She'd put the food on to cook far too early in her eager anticipation of Emma's arrival, and she could smell it beginning to catch.

The fug of simmering lentils had fogged up the window when Jude went into the kitchen. She whipped the saucepan off the electric ring and put it on the draining board, ready to reheat once Emma arrived.

She went to look out of the sitting-room window, again. Hovering. Restless. She hadn't realized how much she'd been looking forward to seeing her scratchy only child. It had been at least six months since the last time — maybe nine. She didn't know why she bothered. Emma clearly didn't.

From the moment she'd brought Emma home, she'd been determined to have a completely different bond with her daughter from the tense relationship she had had with her own mother. She'd played the big-sister card, treating Emma as an adult instead of a child, but it had exploded in her face.

The terrible teens. Jude leant her forehead on the cool window-pane as her mind filled with the vision of Emma screaming and slamming doors. And the silence as she'd trudged away from her, up Howard Street, two bulging carrier bags pulling her shoulders down. Her own shoulders drooped and she closed her eyes. She could still taste the dry, sour fear she'd felt as she watched her child disappear.

She'd had to throw her out. Well, hadn't she? 'The monster in our midst,' her boyfriend Will had said.

But that was then, she told herself firmly as the doubts threatened to overwhelm her again. *Emma's an adult now. We have both moved on.*

She focused on the lovely time they were going to have and put on a Leonard Cohen CD to give herself something to do, singing along to the well-worn lyrics and pushing books and papers into more pleasing piles.

But five minutes later, she was back at the window to watch the street for her child.

'I wish she'd just get here,' Jude suddenly said out loud. She was talking to herself more and more lately. An unattractive habit, she felt. It made her sound a bit mad and old, but the words just spilled out of her before she could stop them.

Funny how things change.

There'd been a time when she would have paid money to get rid of Emma for an afternoon. She was a little chatterbox, going on and on about things until Jude's head hurt. And she never stopped talking about her father. Her bastard father. *Ironic how absence makes the heart grow fonder,* Jude thought. *The unknowing heart.*

She remembered how Emma used to invent stories about him. He was always the hero, of course. Brave, kind to animals, handsome, and once, at the age of eight, in a piece of homework entitled 'My Family', even a member of royalty.

Jude had been called in by the teacher to be told her daughter had an impressive imagination but they needed to be careful this imagination didn't spill over into telling lies. The teacher had called her Mrs Massingham, even though she knew she was unmarried.

Jude's face darkened at the memory of how she'd slunk away, admonished. She'd wanted to tear the teacher's head off, but she didn't want to draw more attention to herself. Or to Emma. But she remembered very clearly her anger when she got home. Emma was down the street at Mrs Speering's, doing her homework.

She'd snapped at her child about calling her father a prince and Mrs Speering had laughed, thinking it was a joke, but she'd shut up when she realized it was serious.

Emma had looked up, cool as a cucumber, Jude recalled, and said, 'I heard you say he was called Charlie. That's the name of a prince.'

Jude had wanted to shake her. Instead she'd told Emma her father wasn't a prince. He was nothing.

Emma had been devastated and Jude always suspected that it was at that moment that her daughter became determined to find out the truth.

As far as Jude was concerned, the truth was greatly over-rated. It could be so many things to different people, she'd said to Emma. But she'd ended up fuelling her daughter's mission. Her obsession.

Jude hadn't wanted her to even think about her father. He had done nothing for her, literally nothing. He'd left as soon as he could.

But as Emma got older, she'd latched on to any male figure in their lives — the man at the corner shop, one of her teachers at school, her best friend Harry's dad. And Jude's boyfriends. She invented stories about them, fantasizing about them being her father, and Jude had had to stamp on that and later silly lies.

★   ★   ★

The fierce buzz of the doorbell made the cat run under the sofa. Jude pushed the button to release the front door for Emma and felt a clutch of nerves as she waited for her to appear.

'Hello, Jude,' Emma said loudly, trying to be heard above Leonard Cohen's mournful growl, and kissed her cheek.

'Sorry, I'll turn it down,' Jude said. 'I was listening to it while I waited. You took your time.'

'It's only ten past twelve,' Emma said quietly.

'Oh, right, I thought it was later,' Jude said.

She could hear the irritation in her voice and tried to stop herself. This wasn't how she'd planned it. She'd imagined them sitting and chatting over a glass of wine, laughing, even, about some silly shared joke. Like friends. But here she was, snapping at Emma straight away, as usual. Their dialogue seemed to run along

58

well-worn grooves, with a gaping hole between them.

Her frustration exhausted her and, for a moment, she wished Emma hadn't come. But she handed her daughter her present. It was a biography of David Bowie that she'd chosen specially.

'This is lovely. Thank you,' Emma said and hugged her. Jude held on for a second too long and felt her child let go first.

'Thought you'd like it. Do you remember that poster in your room? You used to kiss him goodnight. Do you remember?'

'Yes,' Emma said and laughed. 'My first love. I've still got that poster.'

'No! It must be in shreds by now,' Jude said.

'There is a bit of sticky tape involved,' Emma said.

This is lovely, Jude thought, hoisting herself out of her seat to pour the wine chilling in the fridge.

'Shall I put lunch on the table while I'm up?' she asked and Emma nodded as she looked at the photographs in the book.

In the kitchen, Jude heated up the food and dished it out on to two plates. 'Lentil casserole,' she said. 'Used to be your favourite.'

Emma smiled and murmured, 'Thanks.'

Jude watched as Emma pushed the food around the plate, rearranging it to make it look like she was eating. *Back to your old tricks*, she thought. But she decided not to say anything.

She was about to speak when Emma suddenly said, 'Did you see that a baby's skeleton has been found in Howard Street?'

'Really?' Jude said. 'Howard Street, of all places? What a horrible thing to happen. Where was it found? I bet it was one of the heroin addicts from the end of the street. Do you remember them?'

'No,' Emma said. 'Oh, was that the house with all the rubbish and empty milk bottles outside?'

'That's it. How did you hear about it?' Jude asked, pouring herself another glass of wine.

'It was in the paper.'

'But what happened? Was it murdered?'

'They don't know,' Emma said, and put some lentils in her mouth.

Jude did the same. When she finished her mouthful, she said, 'Well, we don't want to talk about dead babies, do we?' and moved the conversation on to Emma's work.

'Are you still in touch with Will?' Emma said, cutting her off mid-sentence.

'Will?' Jude was caught completely off-guard. 'Er, well, yes. On and off. Actually, he rang me a few weeks ago. Out of the blue, about some university fund-raiser. We had a bit of a chat.' She looked at Emma's face for clues, but there was nothing. 'Why are you asking about Will?' she said nervously. She wouldn't have dreamed of telling Emma that Will had been back in touch. She knew it would have been taboo. But her daughter had been the one to mention him.

'I just wondered,' Emma said, and there was silence at the table apart from the scrape of spoons on plates.

'He was an important part of my life for nearly

60

ten years, Emma,' Jude said defensively, her face flushed by the alcohol. 'An important part of yours, as well. For a couple of those years, at least.'

Emma's face froze.

'Well, I know you had your differences . . . ' Jude said. 'But that was so long ago. Surely you're not still sulking about that?'

Emma looked up from her plate, but said nothing.

She's jealous, Jude thought. *She always had a crush on him.*

The subject appeared to be closed and Jude's disappointment sucked all the energy out of the room. Her daughter stood wearily to help with the washing up. They both knew she would leave as soon as was decent.

At the sink, Emma dried while Jude washed. They'd turned the radio on to have voices in the room.

'I ought to get back — Paul will be home soon,' Emma said to her mother's back. 'Thanks for the lovely book and lunch.'

'You didn't eat it,' Jude said over her shoulder. 'Don't think I don't know. You can't hide anything from me, Emma.'

Emma kissed her mother's cheek once more and walked out, closing the door quietly behind her, the only sound the click of the latch.

12

Sunday, 25 March 2012

Emma

The walk back to the Tube seems to take twice as long because my legs are so shaky.

I'd got it all wrong. I'd steeled myself for the baby conversation, had my responses ready for possible interrogation, but I'd had to ask her that last question. About Will. To reassure myself that he was no longer in the picture. But of course he is. How could it be otherwise?

I try to do my breathing, but my heart is still bumping against my ribs when I finally sit down on the Central Line train.

I sit in a daze. In between stations, I can see myself reflected in the window opposite.

★　★　★

When I finally get home, hours later, Paul has cooked his chicken thing — I can smell it; it smells of home — and is waiting patiently when I turn the key in the lock. I'd remembered to call him earlier to tell him I'd decided to have a look round the shops while I was in town.

'Darling, you look frozen,' he says. 'Come in and get warm. Shall I run you a bath?'

'I'm fine, Paul,' I say, and sidetrack him with how the lunch went.

'Jude cooked lentil casserole,' I say and he laughs. He knows I've always hated it.

'Of course she did,' he says. ' 'What was her flat like?'

And I have to think.

'Wall hangings and scarves over the lamps,' I say. 'She'd probably describe it as shabby chic but it's more shabby shit.'

Paul smiles. 'Did you have far to walk?' he says and pulls my feet into his lap to warm them.

'It's miles from the Tube — in the land of shops selling second-hand fridges. Actually, I felt a bit nervous walking down her road. I don't know why she chose to live there.'

Jude moved north of the river years ago. She'd felt like a change, she told me later, when I got back in touch, when I made the first move to make the peace. It had been years since we'd spoken, but you know how things reach a stage when decisions get stuck in stone. My own anger about being chucked out would probably have cooled down pretty quickly if I'd been left to myself, but I went to live with my grandparents for a bit and Granny loved the opportunity to be proved right about her daughter's shortcomings as a mother. She ramped up all the ill-feeling, putting the phone down on Jude so she couldn't talk to me — 'It's for your own good,' she told me. And by the time I left to fend for myself, the silence was total.

Of course, I wondered about Jude, over the years, and sometimes fantasized about a reunion.

I thought I'd see her when my grandfather died, but the conflict between her and her parents was too deep-rooted to be negotiated by then, I suppose. She didn't come to his funeral — or Granny's a year later. She probably hadn't guessed that they'd left her some money and I wondered if she'd felt guilty when she got the executor's letter.

I kept putting the idea of getting in touch aside for later. I was busy, finding jobs and bedsits, shifting around and rootless for a few years. Then university and Paul. Life got in the way, I suppose. And I didn't know what I'd say to her.

It was my fortieth birthday that made me want to get in touch. A landmark birthday, Paul said.

I sat for ages worrying about what to write — how to say hello after twenty-four years? In the end I put, *Dear Jude, How are you? I have been thinking about you — about us — and I would like to see you again. I am married now and living in Pinner. I will understand if you decide not to, but if you would like to contact me, please write or phone. Love Emma.* I still sounded like a child.

I waited and waited for a response, hurt at first, then angry, and then I panicked that she was dead and I'd left it too late.

I rang our old number at Howard Street — for the first time since I was sixteen — to find out, shaking and hanging on to the phone. But when I finally got an answer it was another woman's voice.

'Who?' she said. 'Oh, her. She's long gone.

Blimey, must be ten years since I moved in. Funny, there was a letter for her a couple of weeks ago.'

'I sent it,' I said. 'She's my mum. Do you know where she is now?'

'No, don't know where she moved to. Sorry.' The woman sounded sad for me. 'What shall I do with the letter?'

'Throw it away,' I said.

I rang her old office the next day — more strangers — but they told me that, according to their records, Jude was still alive and agreed to forward my details to her.

She kept me dangling another three months, and I began to believe that I might never hear from her again. To be honest, I didn't know how I felt about that. Some days, I was devastated — I felt abandoned all over again — and other days, I felt a sense of relief. I'd tried. I could put it away now. Get on with my life.

Then her short note came through the letterbox. I remember smelling the paper as if I could catch a scent of her and I rang her new number immediately to tell her how glad I was to hear from her.

I'm not sure what I was expecting, but Jude didn't scream with excitement when she realized it was me. Not her style. Nor did she apologize for the rupture in our relationship, for throwing me out, for choosing Will over me.

'I needed to put myself first for a change,' she said. 'I needed to find myself. After Will left me — those were difficult years, Emma. But I think you and I can put it all behind us now. We're different people now.'

And I agreed.

'I think we should meet somewhere neutral,' she said. 'Have a cup of tea somewhere. What do you think?'

Her terms, her territory, I suppose. She's never been to our home. Jude calls it 'Paul's house' and says it's too far for her to travel — 'Pinner — it's about to fall off the edge of London, Emma.'

The first time, she chose a café in Covent Garden and I took Paul with me, holding his hand tightly. Jude didn't bother to hide her shock at the age gap between us and there was an awkward silence while we pretended to study the menus and I waited with a clenched stomach for the inevitable remark. But she held back. Nothing was said. And it had been all right in the end. No big emotional reunion, but then, no row either.

'Well, that wasn't too bad,' Paul had said as we walked away.

'What did you buy? Anything nice?' Paul says now as he gets up to set the table, and for a moment I don't know what he's talking about.

'Oh, no, nothing in the end,' I say when I realize. 'I just had a look.' And I sit quietly for a moment. I haven't been shopping.

I should have taken the Central Line west to get back to Pinner, but I didn't. I went in the opposite direction. I remember thinking, *I'm not going home.* Well, I was in a way. I was going back to Howard Street.

The journey passed in a blur, stations coming

into bright focus and then flashing back into the darkness, walking up and down concrete steps with the crowds to change to the Jubilee Line and then up into the daylight again at Greenwich. The 472 bus to Woolwich took a long time to come — *It's Sunday*, I kept telling myself. I watched the digital display count down the minutes until I could board. *Three mins. One min. Due.*

But when I got there, it had all gone. The rubble of 63 Howard Street was behind a steel mesh fence and I could only stand and re-create it in my head. When I walked further on, I could see behind the builders' huts to what was our garden, once. I could see the police tape, a loose end fluttering, and the dirt. But there was nothing else to see. And I walked away. A face at a window in one of the houses opposite watched me. I pushed my fists into my coat pockets and kept my head down.

13

Monday, 26 March 2012

Kate

It was Monday — 'Another day at the coal face,' the Crime man had announced to no one in particular as Kate arrived late. Not a good start to the week.

Terry had given her the *What time do you call this?* eyebrow tilt but she'd decided to ignore it and not offer an excuse. Instead, she went to sit at her 'work station', as the management now called their desks.

Kate looked around the newsroom to see who else was in and saw the political editor was already deep in conversation with Simon, the editor. There was loud, laddish laughter as the political editor told an off-colour story about one of the cabinet and his boss clapped him on the shoulder. He looked pleased with himself. Master of his universe, Kate noted.

All quiet, otherwise. The muted clatter of keys and the hunched shoulders of the online slaves would keep Terry happy — and off her back, she hoped. She logged on to her computer and scanned her inbox. She'd already looked at the messages on her phone, but she hoped that in the ten minutes since she'd last glanced at them there'd have been some reaction to the baby story. A bit of information, maybe, to give her a leg up. But nothing.

She didn't bother with her voicemail. People used to phone her with stories and tip-offs and they'd bounce ideas around and pass the time of day. Now it was all online. She didn't need to physically speak to another person all day, sometimes.

Kate yawned. The Crime man yawned back companionably from across the desk.

'By the way, Nina's had a word with me about Terry's latest crackdown on expenses,' he said quietly.

Nina, the news desk secretary, was the fount of all knowledge and was loved universally by the reporters. She'd been around 'since Moses published his commandments', she told everyone, and knew how to get four-star hotel receipts past the managing editor, how to cover for 'her boys' when there was trouble at home or at work — 'I'm sure he's on his way,' she'd purr down the phone to an angry wife or Terry. She could also get you into a war zone with a hire car and no visa without batting an eyelid.

'She says that Terry is ringing restaurants to make sure the staff ate there and that the total on the receipt matches their records. Death to the *blanko* is his goal this month. It won't last.'

The war on reporters' expenses erupted periodically, usually when the news desk budget ran out. The *blanko* — a blank receipt from a hotel or restaurant that could be filled in by the reporter, rather like a blank cheque — was the usual target.

Producing receipts used to be an art form in the old days — rumours abounded of children's John Bull printing sets being used to make whole books of receipts. Coffee stains and insects were then added to give them foreign credentials.

'Oh dear,' Kate said.

They both stared at their screens.

Kate wondered what an alien would make of the scene. Dozens of people sitting in isolation in front of computers, not speaking or looking at each other. It was a bit like the lost souls in Las Vegas casinos, perched for hours at the slot machines with dead eyes, mechanically pressing buttons in the hope of a jackpot. *Alert! News editor approaching*, she thought.

Terry had a winning smile on his face. He obviously wanted a favour. Kate pretended to be absorbed by something on her screen.

'See you managed to get in this morning, then.' He attempted a light touch but his banter clanged to the floor.

'Sorry, bad traffic, Terry,' she said, her fingers resting on the keys as though in mid-sentence.

'Yeah, yeah. Terrible out there. Anyway . . . '

Here it comes, she thought. *The task of death*.

'Kate, the editor has got his eye on one of the new young reporters and he wants you to take him under your wing.'

She looked at him and raised an eyebrow. 'My wing?' she said tartly.

'He's very bright,' Terry said. Her heart sank. 'Very bright' was code for 'extremely irritating'. 'And you're the best reporter on the paper.'

The Crime man cleared his throat in a

warning growl at the slight.

Kate felt herself soften, despite herself. Compliments had been thin on the ground lately. Her star billing after the Widow Taylor exclusive had begun to wane. It was two years since she'd broken the story of what really happened to little Bella Elliott, the toddler who vanished from her garden. The story, with its twists and setbacks, had consumed her, and when the truth finally emerged in the pages of her newspaper, there'd been lunch with the editor, an award and a pay rise.

But that moment had passed, as they always do. The paper's focus had moved relentlessly from investigative journalism to the sort of instant news that got the online community clicking and commenting. She now found herself evermore redundant in this new world order. She could write a picture caption with the best of them, but it was hardly a job for a grown-up, she told herself, as she tried to hold on to her dignity.

And she felt a growing paranoia every time Terry sent one of the kids on a story instead of her.

'Saving you for the big one,' he'd say when he caught her eye. But the big one hadn't come for a while. Now she was being put in charge of the office crèche.

'I'm too busy for work experience, Terry,' she said.

'He won't get in your way. He'll be learning on the job and you've got so much to share, Kate. Simon says — '

Put your hands on your head, she thought, back in her primary-school playground.

'Where is he, then?'

'Joe, can you come over?' Terry called across the room and a short lad with a floppy fringe and his shirt hanging out of his trousers leapt up and bounded over.

'Hi, Kate. It's an honour,' he said without a hint of sarcasm.

Oh my God, he's going to say he loves my work.

'I love your work,' Joe said.

'I'll leave you two to it,' Terry said, his work apparently done.

'But . . . ' Kate spluttered.

'Sorry, Kate. Got a call waiting,' Terry said and scuttled back to the safety of his news desk.

Kate swallowed an expletive, indicated the chair next to her and tried not to catch the eye of the Crime man.

'When did you join us, Joe?' she said.

'A month ago. Straight from uni. I've always wanted to be a journalist — it's in the blood.'

'How do you mean?'

'My mum's a journo.'

'Oh?'

He named the editor of the *Herald on Sunday*, a woman with a reputation for coarseness and brutality — 'the tyrant in knickers', the old guard called her. The male old guard, Kate reminded herself. Mandy Jackson had embraced the nickname, hoisting it like a war trophy as she scaled the career ladder. Any woman who rose beyond features editor was popularly deemed to have

72

either slept her way to the top or broken balls. Kate wasn't sure which route Mandy had taken but she was still there, queen of the dunghill.

And this was her little boy.

She looked closely at Joe Jackson — his mother had clearly already been thinking about his by-line when she named him — as he busied himself setting up his laptop at her right hand. He looked as if his voice hadn't broken yet, but maybe he could be useful — she wouldn't mind a job on the *Herald on Sunday*.

'What story are you doing, Kate?' he asked, sitting up expectantly with a notebook in hand to capture her golden words.

'I'm looking at emails, Joe. Give me ten minutes. Why don't you go and get us a coffee?'

She dug in her handbag and gave him a handful of change.

'The chief reporter's bitch,' the Crime man snorted after Joe had disappeared through the swing doors.

'Shut up, Gordon. You're just jealous you haven't got one. What the hell am I going to do with him?'

'Well, don't sleep with him or Mandy will tear your head off.'

The crassness of his remark made Kate burn but she laughed with him, a survival technique learnt early on in a world dominated by men and drink.

'*Just go along with it. You don't have to mean it,*' an older woman colleague had advised her many years ago. '*The sexist jokes will never stop. You need to show them you're as good a reporter as them. That'll shut them up.'*

And they hadn't all been woman-haters. She'd worked with some brilliant men, but there remained the occasional dinosaur lurking in the primeval swamp. One night-news editor liked to tell female reporters to 'break up the knitting circle' if they were discussing a story. Another executive would ask 'On the rag?' if a woman challenged an idea and would laugh uproariously as if he were the new Oscar Wilde.

The Crime man was pretty harmless and she knew his wife. He was on a short leash at home, so Kate allowed him the occasional burst for freedom.

'Have you worked with Mandy?' she asked.

'Yeah. She was a ball-breaker.'

Joe arrived back with the drinks and a cake for her. 'Thought you might like one,' he said.

'You have it,' Kate muttered irritably. 'You'll burn off a double chocolate muffin faster than me.'

He laughed and unpeeled the paper.

The editor appeared behind them — Simon Pearson had an unnerving ability to materialize without warning; Kate suspected he'd been a cat burglar in another life — and clapped Joe on the shoulder, sending a shower of crumbs over the desk.

'Don't make our new protégé too comfortable, Kate. He won't find any stories eating muffins. Need to keep him hungry and get him out there.'

Joe looked stricken as Simon left to continue his silent patrol.

'Take no notice. It's his way of being friendly,'

she said. 'You're very privileged to have been singled out for any kind of notice at all. Anyway, let's look busy. Have you got any story ideas? We've got a news meeting in half an hour and we need to come up with three good ones.'

His face was non-committal as if he were considering his answer, but his eyes said no.

'Well, you read the papers and see if there's a follow-up we can do, and I'll ring a contact who's emailed me. These news meetings are bollocks, really. Bit of grandstanding for the specialists and a chance for the news editor to tell us all we're rubbish. Welcome to journalism.'

14

Emma

My yoga teacher is doing a guided relaxation, her voice purring over the tinkling of finger cymbals, lulling us into a coma. I love this bit of the class normally, but today I'm lying on my mat trying not to think about the ghosts of Howard Street. About the baby. About Professor Will.

My head refuses to clear, despite Chloe's exhortation, and Will materializes and fills my brain.

He appeared in our lives in the eighties. Well, 'appeared' doesn't really describe it. He stormed our castle and swept Jude off her feet. It was a huge event in our lives. She didn't normally have boyfriends when I was growing up. She used to say she'd taken a vow of celibacy and was living like a nun. And laugh. I remember looking up 'celibacy' when I was about twelve and being quite shocked. I thought Jude was talking about religion but she was talking about sex. Of course, her friends howled with laughter and started calling her Sister Jude. I wasn't included in the joke. I was still just a kid. But I knew Jude wasn't happy being celibate. For a nun, she spent a lot of time talking about men. But it was talking, not

76

doing. My best friend Harry said Jude needed a bloke, but I didn't pass this on. *Unwanted advice*, Jude would've said.

I knew something had changed, though, when I heard her singing in the bath one night. Singing 'You Are the Sunshine of my Life' at the top of her voice with all the harmonies and 'yeah, yeahs'. She sounded so unlike Jude that I knocked on the door and shouted through, 'You sound happy!'

'I am! Come in!' she shouted back.

I didn't really like seeing Jude naked — it didn't feel right — but she said I was being a ridiculous prude and how did a child of hers grow up to be embarrassed by the human body?

I remember sitting on the loo seat so I didn't have to look straight at her while she told me that a man from her past — a man she really liked when she was younger — had reappeared. I felt all hot because I thought she must mean my dad. The man we were not allowed to talk about.

I didn't know who he was, my dad, and I used to think that she didn't either. When I was little, and there were dads in the books she read to me, I'd ask. I'd point at the pictures and say, 'Is that my daddy?' and she'd laugh and say, 'No. That's the daddy in the book.'

'Where's my daddy?'

'You haven't got one, Emma. It's just us.'

I think she weeded out books with fathers in them after a while, because we never seemed to read about them again.

Of course, when I got a bit older I realized that everyone had a dad, but I understood from

Jude's silence on the matter that I shouldn't ask. So I daydreamed one up. He was tall and good looking and fun and clever, and some days he played the guitar and others he wrote books, and he took me on holiday to faraway places. Hilarious, really, because no one I knew had a dad like that. Harry's dad was old and wore cardigans. He looked like Captain Mainwaring in *Dad's Army*.

But as I got better at eavesdropping, I began picking up bits and pieces about my real father. I listened in when Jude told a neighbour over a bottle of wine about her struggle to bring up a child alone, earn a living and pass her law exams. 'No time for men for ages,' Sister Jude complained. 'Emma's dad is long gone — he couldn't wait to leave. Charlie was much younger — well, he was still a baby himself.'

I stashed away the information — I now had a name and a baby face to feed my imagination.

Anyway, Jude sat in her bath and told me the man she'd met again was coming to the house. She said she'd spotted him on the telly news — he'd been speaking at an anti-nuclear demonstration — and had recognized him immediately.

'After all these years, I've never forgotten him,' she said. She chattered on about how they knew each other at college — Jude went to Cambridge and did History. Jude was and is super clever. She's retired now, but she used to be a lawyer specializing in human-rights cases. She always used the word 'lawyer' — 'Solicitors are middle-aged men with tummies, doing conveyancing,' she told me. Anyway, the law wasn't her

78

first choice. When she left university, she joined a publishing house and was rushing round London, lunching with 'the Beautiful People'. She always sounded as though she was using italics when she said it.

But I happened, and we had to live with Granny and Grandpa for a while. When we left, she said she needed to do something more solid, more nine to five, instead. She got a job in an office while she studied. I remember she spent hours with her head in her books and court papers. Her bedroom had that sharp, inky, papery smell. She had to concentrate, she would tell me if I tried to ask a question about my homework or tell her about how mean Mr Lawson was in assembly. She had to concentrate or she might miss the tiny detail that could get her client out of prison. So I went back to David Bowie in my room and talked to his poster on the wall.

I liked this new Jude, singing in the bath. She wanted to tell me about things and she sounded young and excited. I stayed in the steamy bathroom, listening and giggling with her until my clothes felt damp and my mother was ready to emerge from the water.

I didn't say the 'dad' word. I knew it would kill the mood so I decided to wait and see.

When the love object came to the house, I smiled my welcome as instructed earlier by Jude.

She'd been jumpy and nervous the whole morning, changing her clothes at least three times.

'You look really nice,' I'd said each time she

appeared in a new outfit, but she kept disappearing back upstairs to change. I was so pleased that she was wearing the pretty turquoise earrings I'd bought for her birthday out of my pocket money.

When 'Professor Will', as she insisted on calling him, finally knocked on the door, I thought Jude would pass out with the excitement.

'You go, chick,' she said, taking one last look in the mirror. 'And smile!'

I loved it when she used to call me chick, my pet name from when I was a little girl. She'd all but abandoned it as I'd got older, but it still had the power to make me feel warm inside.

Anyway, I'd only just got the door open to let him in when she wafted past me and took over.

'Hello, Will. How lovely to see you! Will, meet Emma — my baby. Darling, this is Professor Will, my old friend from uni.'

Will flashed me a sympathetic smile and held out his hand. 'Hardly a baby, Jude. She's a young woman.'

It's funny the things you remember. His hand felt dry and warm and a gold ring on his thumb brushed my knuckles.

I risked a closer look at him to check if there was any family resemblance. There wasn't. He was all corners. Sharp nose, sharp cheekbones. Nothing like me and my pudding face. Jude used to tell me I was pretty sometimes, when we were on our own. But I wasn't — I'm not. Pretty was shiny hair and long eyelashes and pink cheeks — like Jude. I had brown curly hair that wouldn't lie flat and a pudding face. I hated my face. I used to stand in front of the mirror, pulling at my flesh like it was made of plasticine until my cheeks stung. Jude said all teenage girls went through this.

Will must've caught me staring at him and smiled. Jude didn't see, she was too busy closing the front door, so it was a smile just between us and it made me feel a bit tingly. He might be my friend too. Or my dad.

'Tea?' Jude said as she led him into the sitting room.

'Lovely,' he said. 'What a great house.'

In the kitchen, filling the kettle and searching for two matching mugs, I remember wondering what sort of man wears a ring on his thumb.

He must be nearly forty, I thought, spooning the tea into the pot. *It's like your granddad wearing platforms.* I laughed to myself at the idea and carried the tray through.

The professor had kicked off his sandals to sit cross-legged on the sofa and his feet looked soft and white like bread against the cushions.

'I can't quite believe you're here,' my mother gushed.

Very unlike her. Very un-lawyer like, I thought, crossly crashing the tray down, spilling the milk into the sugar.

'Sorry,' I said, not meaning it. Jude looked furious but Will swooped forward, nearly toppling from his guru pose, to help steady the table.

'No damage done,' he said. 'Just ready mixed.' And he and Jude laughed.

I felt left out of the joke, but when Jude was mopping up, he winked at me.

15

Monday, 26 March 2012

Jude

There was still a trace of lentils on the plate she picked up off the draining board for her toast and she plonked it straight into the sink.

Her daughter had hardly touched the meal yesterday. It used to be her favourite, back in the day, when Emma was eight or nine and they first moved into their rented Victorian villa in Howard Street. The late seventies had been tough for Jude, trying to forge a new career with a child to look after, but the rent was cheap because of the area. And it didn't seem to matter to Emma where she lived. She was always caught up in her own little world, anyway.

If she closed her eyes, Jude could almost smell the house at Howard Street: a pervading mixture of damp plaster and her favourite perfumes. It hadn't been a palace, but it had had character. The house had a hall paved with cracked black and white tiles — 'They're antique, not old,' Jude had told her mother when she turned her nose up.

Will had liked it straight away.

'Oh, Emma!' Jude said out loud now as she banged about in the cupboard, looking for another plate. 'Why can't you let things go? It was you who brought Will up.'

Jude had never intended to tell her daughter all the details of the telephone call that had come out of the blue, how she'd recognized Will's voice straight away, even though it'd been nearly ten years since she'd last heard it. He'd slammed out of the house with his bag in 1992, calling over his shoulder that he'd be in touch when she'd calmed down. But she knew he wouldn't. There'd been a row too far.

His attention had begun to wander again. She'd hit her fifties by then and he'd lost interest in her, preferring to flirt openly with waitresses during supposedly romantic dinners.

'Oh Jude,' he'd laughed when she finally decided to confront him. 'I just appreciate a pretty face — I'm only looking.'

But he wasn't. He was doing as well as looking. Jude knew. She smelt it on him and lay awake worrying that he would leave her. She tried to keep cool, telling herself it was a mid-life crisis and he'd grow out of it. But when she caught him groping one of her friends at a party, there had been a flaming row and he'd packed his bags.

There had been complete silence after that, even when she made the first move. His phone went straight to voicemail and he didn't ring back. Or reply to her emails. Or her letters. And gradually, she stopped trying.

But he'd rung when he read her father's obituary in 2003, in a Cambridge University newsletter. She had recognized the voice but not the tone. He was quietly polite as he offered his condolences, but there had been no small talk. Good of him to bother, she'd thought, but it had been horribly awkward and hadn't led to any more contact.

Until now. This time he'd called her 'my lady' like in the old days and flirted with her. And how good — and young — it had made her feel. But telling Emma about wanting to see Will again after all this time, she knew she had the wrong audience. And Em had sat there, her face frozen, as if she'd just vomited on the table.

Like the day I told her she had to leave, Jude thought.

It had been different when Will had made his first appearance — when Emma was thirteen. *She liked him then,* she thought. *Adored him. Like I did.*

Will had been so special when she met him at Cambridge. A boy born to succeed. She'd joked with friends later that genius oozed out of his every pore and if she licked his skin she would be able to taste it.

She remembered telling a colleague in the office that once — and the way her face had twisted with disgust.

'Sounds revolting. You are a handmaiden, then?' Erica, the senior clerk at Bowen and Bailey Solicitors, had said. Erica was no handmaiden. She was a feminist. It said so on a sign on her desk — 'SEXISM IS A SOCIAL DISEASE' — and she never missed an opportunity to put her views forward. The partners were all very right on with their long hair and ironic,

84

second-hand pinstriped suits, but they still called her the Dyke out of earshot. Jude was sure Erica knew — she knew everything — but she didn't object. She probably saw it as fair exchange for being in charge.

Jude had laughed off the handmaiden barb and pretended to get on with her work. But little Barbara Walker, the office junior, wouldn't let it drop. She'd wanted to hear all about it.

All this talk of Howard Street from Emma had awakened old memories and Jude wondered where Barbara was now. She'd been a close friend of Jude's once. She could picture Barbara — annoyingly pretty, she recalled, but hopeless with money. She'd moved into Howard Street — *the room on the middle landing, that's right* — in 1983, to help Jude pay the rent, but she kept getting behind and the landlord had to keep coming round.

Al Soames, she remembered. A former public schoolboy who used to turn up uninvited and sit in the kitchen. He'd ladled on the charm, talking about all the important people he knew and the parties he went to. She'd been impressed when she first moved in, but she began to wonder if he was a bit of a Walter Mitty. And he made Barbara very nervous. Will had liked him, though. Said he was good company.

Jude licked her finger and dabbed at the crumbs on her plate.

Poor Barbara had moved out quite quickly really — less than a year, Jude thought. She'd been a bit fed up — it was more money to find each month — but Will had been pleased.

'Nice to have you to myself without the Barbie doll hanging around, making eyes at me,' he'd said. Jude hadn't noticed that, but Barbara was gone now anyway and she hoped that Will would think he had met his match — intellectually and sexually — and would settle down. At university, their affair had lasted just three weeks, but this time it would be different. Then, there had been other women in the queue for his attention and they had grown impatient for their turn. Jude had found him ministering to the next girl late one Friday morning when she skipped a lecture to call on him.

She glossed over this now in her head. Along with the retribution she'd taken on the next girl: breaking into her room and smearing dog shit on her bed the following day. People got that kind of thing out of proportion, didn't they?

Anyway, the next girl hadn't complained. Jude imagined she'd simply taken the bedspread to the launderette. Will hadn't found out — at least, he'd never mentioned it and he'd stayed friendly, having the occasional coffee with Jude when they bumped into each other in King's Parade. But he'd vanished from her world when she left Cambridge.

And she'd met someone else. 'The total bastard', as she always referred to him now. But he'd been Charlie until he left Jude and Emma. She'd been forced to return home to her parents with a newborn baby so they could torture her with guilt.

She could feel the bitterness darkening her day, even after all this time. It wasn't good for her to revisit past hurts. People said you shouldn't bottle things up, but she could never be this open with anyone else. People jumped to conclusions, rushed to judgement. Better to keep things to herself. She'd been too open with Will, she knew that now. She'd let him know how desperate she was to keep him. She'd gone along with everything — changed her clothes, her hair, her friends, everything. She'd even taken his advice to push Emma 'out of the nest' when she got too difficult.

He'd made it sound caring and responsible: 'Tough love will help her, Jude. You'll see. It's what she needs.'

She'd done it. Told her child she had to go. Helped her pack. Closed the door on her.

And with Emma gone, Jude had poured all her energies into Will, running after him, trying to anticipate his every wish. At first, he'd loved it. Loved having his favourite meals on the table every evening, the sexy underwear she bought to please him, the phone calls at work 'Just to say I love you'.

But he grew to see it as needy.

'Men hate needy,' Jude told herself as she cleared the breakfast things. 'It's a big turn-off.' Will had told her so the day he left.

16

Wednesday, 28 March 2012

Kate

She'd had enough of the day already when she emerged from the lift at work. Her foul mood had soured her eyes and lined her forehead, but Joe Jackson still hadn't got the hang of people.

'Hi, Kate, how are you?' he'd chirped like a friendly budgie.

Kate had given him a look that would have made a Rottweiler hesitate. She threw her computer bag on the desk, the laptop making an unhealthy clunk, and stalked off to the Ladies to give herself breathing space.

Steve had brought her 'bed tea' half an hour earlier than usual that morning and stood over her until she surfaced from sleep.

'Sorry it's so early, love, but I need to leave for work at eight — I've got ward rounds this morning — and Jake is downstairs already,' he'd said, a warning note in his voice. They both knew there was trouble coming.

Jake, their eldest, had appeared unexpectedly the night before, in the middle of his university term. It had been too late to talk — Steve was already in bed, exhausted by the day's appointments with his cancer patients, and Kate couldn't face tackling Jake's latest crisis alone. She'd packed him off to bed with the promise that they'd talk in the morning. That moment had clearly come.

Kate had stumbled out of bed and hardly had time to sit down at the kitchen table before Jake announced he was dropping out of his Law degree and going travelling.

Well, 'announced' was probably overstating it. Jake had mentioned it in that irritatingly casual way he had as he swirled two poached eggs in a pan of water. He was a boy who 'took everything in his stride', according to his senior school reports. *Rolling over* is what Kate called it, but Steve had always counselled against confronting their son.

'It'll just make things worse. He'll grow out of it,' he said.

But he hadn't.

'He just gives up when things get difficult,' Kate had said when Jake decided to stop playing the saxophone after three months, despite having begged them to buy him the instrument. 'He's so clever, but he can't be bothered to put in the effort,' she'd complained. 'Poor old Freddie has to work his socks off to get the grades. It must be infuriating for him to see his brother flick through a book and get an A.'

And it infuriated her, too. She'd been just like Freddie. And she couldn't see where Jake's lack of motivation came from. Both she and Steve had the work ethic in spades, but Jake just stood at the foot of the ladder, looking up and shrugging at the idea of climbing.

It was Steve who had broken the silence that followed their son's latest news.

'Where are you thinking of travelling to?' Nice and neutral. *Very Steve*, Kate thought.

'Not sure really,' Jake had said, smiling his beautiful smile. 'Thailand maybe?'

'Couldn't you do that when you finish your degree?' Kate had said as he put his plate of food down on the table. 'You've only got one more year to go.'

'I'm not sure I'm doing the right subject, Mum,' Jake said, tackling his eggs, tea towel over one shoulder.

'But, you've always wanted to do Law,' she said, sinking down further into her chair. 'What's changed?'

'I think *I* have,' he said, mopping the yolk with a crust of bread. 'I think I want other things now.'

Kate and Steve exchanged a look over their son's bent head.

'Well, best not to make any hasty decisions, Jakey,' Steve said. 'Why don't you finish this year and then take stock? Give yourself a chance to think it through.'

'Actually, I've told college I'm not going back,' their son had said. 'They were very nice about it. It's all sorted.'

There'd been stunned silence and then raised voices — Kate's mainly, with Jake patiently munching his way through his food — followed by pleas, recriminations and slammed doors. Breakfast had ended as an ugly showdown. Steve had stormed off to the hospital, Jake had gone back to bed and Kate had stood in the kitchen and sworn.

'It isn't even bloody eight a.m. yet and the day is a nightmare,' she'd said.

Later, as she'd driven across London to the office, Kate had ground her teeth and practised what she would say to Jake later, cursing the black cab drivers and white van men who dared to cut her up.

* * *

The stress had taken its toll. She looked at herself in the mirror and saw the bags under her eyes, her mascara already smudging and her hair escaping from a collapsing ponytail.

'Christ, what a sight,' she muttered. She looked like she'd just stumbled up the embankment after a train crash. She pulled the elastic band off her hair and got a brush out of her handbag to repair the damage.

'Oh, get a grip,' she told her reflection.

You can do this played in her head as she brushed her hair into submission. It was a mantra she'd picked up from her dad, a man who was not at home to negativity.

'Come on, Katie,' he'd say as she struggled to ride a bike, pass maths O level or get a job interview. 'You can do anything.'

It was wonderful to have your own personal cheerleader, but the constant pressure for her to succeed was exhausting. *OK, Dad, I'm on it,* she thought, and gripped the sink to still her hands.

17

Wednesday, 28 March 2012

Kate

When she emerged from the Ladies, there was a strange silence in the office. No one was speaking, no one was clattering on a keyboard — not even the online crew — and no one was making eye contact. Kate's 'Morning all' petered out halfway, the 'all' abandoned as she sat down at her desk.

'What's going on? Has somebody died?' she hissed across at the Crime man.

He looked up, eyes pouchy and bloodshot. 'Not yet,' he said.

'God, you look awful,' she said. 'What were you up to last night?'

'Out with the Major. He looks worse than me.'

Kate whirled round to look at the defence correspondent — 'the Major' to his workmates — and laughed at the sight. 'Has he been to bed?' she asked.

'Mind your own bloody business, Kate. You haven't looked at your emails, then?'

'No, I was late leaving home. Why?'

'There's another round of redundos. The bloody bean counters are at it again,' he said. 'Costs are being cut. Again. They say we've got to lose fifty-two people across the titles — seven from our newsroom.'

'Seven? Christ! That's half the reporters,' she said, looking round the room, ticking off her colleagues in her head.

'Don't be stupid. There are at least thirty of us,' he said.

She looked blank.

'The online staff, Kate.'

'Oh yes,' she replied. 'Well, it won't be them getting the boot. Bloody hell. Who is going from our lot?'

The Crime man shook his head. 'Two subs, but no one has been invited for the coffee of death from our side yet. We're all just waiting.'

They both knew he was a prime candidate. Gordon Willis was old, difficult to manage, a Luddite when it came to technology and, perhaps most importantly, highly paid. Kate cast about for something positive to say.

'Spoke to Colin Stubbs the other day, sent his best,' she said. The Crime man nodded, preoccupied. 'Says leaving journalism was the best thing he ever did.'

'Did he? Haven't seen him in months. Thought his witch of a wife had locked him in a cellar. Look, I'm going to the Yard for the daily briefing. Can't sit around here waiting for bad news. Give me a shout if anything happens.'

'Sure,' she said. 'You'll be fine. You're way too valuable to them.'

He tried to smile. 'Thanks, Kate. See you later.'

She watched him shamble out of the door, the

collar of his jacket half up, a bed-hair rosette on the back of his head and his notebook poking out of his pocket. He nodded at the news desk as he passed. Terry didn't nod back. *Bad sign*, she thought. *The pack abandoning its own.*

Kate considered her own position. She reckoned she was on the list somewhere — age and size of salary would count against her — but she crossed her fingers that others would volunteer to take the money before they got to her name. She didn't want to go. She didn't know what else was out there, job-wise, and life without work wasn't worth thinking about. What would she do all day? Watch telly and do Sudokus in those big puzzle books? She'd rather die. She'd rather write up celebrity nonsense. What she needed was a big story.

Terry walked over and Kate glanced up.

'All right, Kate?' he asked. 'You look terrible.'

'Thanks, Terry. Sweet of you to say. I'm fine. Just got a bit of a domestic going on. My eldest.'

'What's Jake got up to?' Terry asked. 'I'm sick of my kids. All they want is money and lifts to parties.'

'Bit of a wobble at university. It'll sort itself out,' she said.

★ ★ ★

The news that the Crime man was going came at about six thirty. Late enough that he could be ushered out of the building with minimum fuss if things got nasty. He'd been called into the managing editor's office and fifteen minutes later emerged as an *ex-Post* reporter.

'They've given me a shed load of money,' he said to Kate as he started dumping his belongings into a black bin bag. 'I'll be fine. Time for a change. Been here too long.'

They both knew there would be no more jobs. Too old. Too old school.

'The worst bit is telling her indoors,' he said. 'Don't know whether to phone Maggie or wait until I get home. God knows what she'll say. But it's likely to be at full volume.'

'Oh come on, Maggie'll understand,' Kate said. Actually, she had no confidence that 'the Iron Lady', as she was known in the office, would be sympathetic — it was a side of her nobody had ever witnessed — but Kate was trying not to dwell on the negatives.

'We'll see,' he said and shook his head wearily.

'Anyway, where will you have your leaving do? Everyone will want to come and give you a proper Fleet Street send-off,' Kate said, picking up a stray envelope off the floor.

'Yeah. I'll sort something out. I'd like it at the Cheshire Cheese — it's where I was taken on my first day as a national newspaper reporter. Back in the Stone Age. We used to go there when the presses started up. Whole building used to vibrate. And the noise . . . ' His voice had begun to crack and he shut up, pretending to check his drawers.

'I'll probably do it on Friday,' he said eventually. 'Get it over and done with. I'll let the Major know and he can send an email to everyone.'

He looked round at the office and his shoulders drooped. 'Better go then.'

Terry walked over and the other reporters began to stand up.

'Good luck, mate,' the Major called across as the Crime man picked up the bin bag containing the evidence of his career. Kate picked up her notebook and began banging the desk with it. The other reporters did the same and the subs and back bench joined in the cacophony, thumping the tables with their fists and whatever else came to hand. They banged the Crime man out as tradition required. It was a roar of emotion in a grey new world and he wept as he left for the last time.

When the door closed behind him and the noise stopped, everyone looked shaken and teary.

'I'm going for a drink,' the Major said. 'I need one.'

18

Friday, 30 March 2012

Kate

The Cheshire Cheese was a labyrinth of wood-panelled hidey holes and snugs in Fleet Street. It had been the haunt of journalists — the scene of punch-ups, celebrations and wakes — until the papers scattered to the four corners of the capital in the 1990s. Now, the Cheese sold itself as a colourful relic of those days. The new owners peddled anecdotes of historic scoops and back-slapping camaraderie to the tourists and city workers who had moved in. As if journalism belonged to another age.

But it still smelt the same, Kate thought, as she shook the never-ending rain off her umbrella and threaded her way through the standing drinkers to the private room upstairs. Stale-beer-and-crisp breath.

The noise grew as she climbed the stairs and burst over her when she walked into the party. The Crime man was centre stage, handing pints over the heads of his former colleagues, red-faced, shouting and sweating already.

She looked round quickly, a reporter's scan. *Who's here? Who's interesting? Who do I want to avoid?*

Her eyes lit on the coppers in the corner. It was a real gathering of the clans. She could see the Met Press Office almost in its entirety — even Colin Stubbs on a late pass — and what looked like detectives from every big story the *Post* had covered.

'Bob,' she shouted above the din, working her way through the crowd. He hadn't heard her.

DI Bob Sparkes was deep in conversation with another officer. She hadn't seen him since the Bella Elliott case. They'd spoken on the phone a few times, but Kate hadn't been on a story on his patch in Hampshire since.

He suddenly caught sight of her and smiled. Kate felt a bit goose-bumpy. *Ridiculous. How old are you?* she told herself crossly. She suddenly wasn't sure how to greet him. Handshake or kiss on the cheek?

DI Sparkes clearly had no such dilemma. The detective stuck out his hand immediately and she shook it warmly.

'Hello, Bob,' she said. 'Great to see you.'

'Lovely to see you, too, Kate,' he said, still smiling. 'Must be over a year.'

'More like two years,' she corrected him. She hadn't let go of his hand yet. She gave it a final squeeze.

'This is Kate Waters, the reporter I was telling you about,' DI Sparkes said to a younger colleague. 'Kate, this is DS Chris Butler.'

'Oh, I've heard all about you,' the young detective sergeant said. 'The boss is your number-one fan.'

Kate and Bob reddened and the DS grinned.

98

Both started to talk at the same time, stumbling over each other's words, and then stopped. It was Bob who steered the conversation into calmer waters.

'What are you up to then, Kate? What have you got your teeth into now?'

She signalled her gratitude with her eyes and ploughed on, grabbing at the details of the baby story for cover. She'd actually been working on a story about an MP's expenses claim for the last couple of days — 'an editor's must,' Terry had said — but the baby had popped straight into her head. It seemed to be playing in the back of her mind like an annoying tune. Her ear worm.

She started to change the subject to the MP's sordid claims for 'entertaining constituents', but Bob stopped her, going back to the baby, asking about the progress of the forensics and the history of the area. The young DS began to glaze over and Kate could see he was looking for a getaway. Bob clocked it too.

'Why don't you get Kate a drink, Chris? She's going to die of thirst, standing here with us.'

DS Butler nodded, took her order and was sucked into the crowd.

They looked at each other. 'It's so noisy, Kate, I can hardly hear you. Old age . . . ' Sparkes said. 'Chris won't be back for ages once Gordon gets hold of him. Let's go downstairs and have a quiet drink.'

She followed him out, noting the grey hairs and growing bald patch on his retreating head. He was still sexy, though.

They sat at a small, sticky table, he with a diet

coke, she with a warm white wine.

'So — this baby. Do they have any idea who it might be?' he said, immediately picking up the thread of their discussion.

Still not up for small talk, then, she thought, abandoning any idea of a cosy tête-à-tête.

'Not as far as I know, Bob. It's not a recent burial, they say. Maybe historic, even, but tests are still going on. It was newborn and I've heard, unofficially, that the copper on the case thinks it was probably a desperate single mother back in the dim and distant past when illegitimacy mattered. I don't think he's that interested, really. They're all up to their ears in the Olympics, the Queen's Diamond Jubilee and terrorism threats.'

Sparkes nodded. 'Course they are.'

'I've written about the discovery of the body — it was in the paper last Saturday,' Kate added. 'So small, you probably wouldn't have seen it. Anyway, I'm not sure how much further I can take it as a story. If it's a domestic, it'll have limited news value as far as my lot are concerned. Might make a page lead, but I'm not sure it's worth too much running around.'

She waited for a response. She felt she had wittered on long enough. Didn't want to bore the man.

'What about you? What are you up to?' she said when the silence grew.

Bob put down his glass and smiled at her. 'Sorry, Kate. Just thinking. I'm doing some policy revision for the force at the moment. Apparently that's also police work. Anyway, have the Met looked at missing persons? They must have done.'

'I expect so, but it's hard when they don't know what era to start with. Why?'

'It's not a long list, wherever they start looking. Abducting babies is an unusual crime anyway, but the number not found is tiny.'

Kate nodded. She was trying to think of any cases where a missing baby hadn't been found and reunited with its parents within weeks, if not days. She remembered the disappearance of a baby who was reported stolen from a car. But all the other headline cases had ended happily.

'I can think of three cases,' Bob said. 'Baby taken from back seat of a car in London.'

'Just thinking about that one,' Kate said. 'Must be twenty years ago.'

'Yes, and then one taken from a pram outside the Co-op in Portsmouth just after — possibly a copycat crime — and a newborn taken from a maternity hospital in Hampshire in the seventies. Alice, she was called. Never seen again.'

'Don't know either of those. Were you involved in the Hampshire case?' Kate said.

Sparkes laughed. 'Hardly, Kate. I'm not that old. I was about thirteen at the time.'

'Sorry,' she said and laughed with him. 'Hadn't done the maths . . . '

'I remember the case because one of my aunties had a baby around then,' Sparkes said. 'And she called my cousin Alice. So she and my mum talked of little else for a while. It was a big story — not 24/7 like it would be now, but it made an impression and I've never forgotten her name.'

'Another of your lost children, Bob?' Kate

said. She knew the list from their previous entanglement: Bella Elliott, of course; Laura Simpson, taken by her paedophile uncle; Baby W, shaken to death by his stepfather; Ricky Voules, drowned in a park. Bob Sparkes carried them all with him — those he'd rescued and those he felt he'd failed during his career. And little Alice was tucked away there, too, apparently.

'Have a look at your cuttings files on missing children, Kate, if you're interested. I might have a quick look at the files our end,' he said, and she knew he would. Sparkes was the sort of detective who could never let anything go.

'May be nothing, but . . . ' His thought was interrupted by DS Butler putting his head round a pillar.

'Speeches, boss. Hurry up or you'll miss them,' the young officer said, his face flushed and excited.

'Coming,' Sparkes said. 'He doesn't get out of Southampton much,' he muttered to Kate and they grinned at each other.

'Bring your wine — we ought to get back up there,' he said, but she knew he was all about the building-site baby. And now, so was she.

19

Monday, 2 April 2012

Kate

The remnants of the Reference Library staff dwelt in the bowels of the newspaper, troglodyte survivors of the Google revolution. They were reduced to a handful of oddbods and nerds — a low-budget version of the *Star Wars* bar, the Crime man said (*used to say*, she reminded herself). Their heyday had come and gone with the advent of internet search engines, but they were still there, sorting and filing every story published and holding on to their expert knowledge of news items of the past century until the last paper cutting was digitalized.

Kate always enjoyed challenging them with bizarre requests: Have you got anything on widows who married their husband's brother? There would be a pause while the librarian disappeared down the corridors of filing cabinets and he or she would appear with a brown envelope of cuttings marked 'Marriages: women who married brothers-in-law'. Never failed to amaze.

The library smelt of paper and silverfish when Kate pushed open the swing door and she breathed it in deeply. It was the scent of her past:

103

the days of running down the stairs to the library when a story broke, racing through telephone directories at the counter in search of a name, leafing through cuttings and spotting the vital link that would make a tip-off work.

Geoff Bridges, a man who wore the sort of jumpers normally favoured by Portuguese tractor drivers and seemed to have been on the brink of retirement for decades, looked up from his table.

'Hello, Kate. What can we do for you?'

'I'm looking at old missing-children cases from around 1970 to the mid 1990s,' she said.

'Well, you've come to the right place,' he laughed. 'We do old. Do you have a name? Or shall I get 'missing children, general' for the period?'

'I've only got one — Alice, I think — so I'd better take all the folders,' she said.

'Alice Irving,' Geoff said quietly, mentally flicking through his internal filing system. 'The baby who disappeared from a hospital, right?' His knowledge and recall of news stories was legendary.

Kate nodded.

'Hmmm. Army family. Based in Hampshire. Aldershot, was it? Or Basingstoke? Mother suspected, I seem to remember.'

'The mother? Really?' Kate said, her pulse quickening. 'Well, let's have her folder too, please.'

★　★　★

Upstairs, she and Joe unpacked the bulging envelopes. The cuttings were yellowing and starting to crumble and Joe looked doubtful as he carefully unfolded the first one in the 'missing children, general' folder.

'You're looking for the mother of a baby who went missing between twenty and forty years ago?' he asked, his brow puckering. 'Why?'

'Because I want to know what happened, Joe. It's called human interest. Not all news is about soap stars or politicians. This has got the makings of a good story. I can feel it in my waters.'

Joe looked slightly squeamish.

'It's a saying, dear. Nothing gynae about it.'

He looked mortified and she felt terrible. She was turning into one of the dinosaurs.

She could see he was disappointed. He had probably expected to be part of an investigations team blowing the lid off some international conspiracy when he joined the *Post*.

'Come on, it'll be fun,' she heard herself say, as if to a recalcitrant child. *Why does everything have to be fun to matter, these days?* 'We're looking for babies who disappeared without trace. A contact has suggested three possibilities, but we've only got years and one name.'

She looked at Joe's drooping mouth and sighed.

'You take Alice Irving, then. We are looking for clues to the whereabouts of her mother, Angela Irving.' *Oh God, I sound like a policeman.* 'Anyway, we need to find her now and there may be leads in the stories at the time.'

105

'Leads?' he said.

'Clues, Joe. Things like relatives' names, old addresses, places where she used to work. We can go back to them and ask where she moved to. She might have stayed in touch. Do you see?'

Joe nodded glumly. No keywords or search engines. He looked lost.

'OK, how about if you search for her birth and marriage certificates online first,' Kate said.

Joe looked a bit more interested.

'The more info we have on her — middle name, date of birth, that sort of thing, the easier it will be to track her down now,' she said. 'Look for the marriage first — it'll be easier. We've got the husband's name — Nick, probably Nicholas Irving — from the cuttings, and Angela's first name. It says they had a two-year-old son when Alice was taken, so they probably married at least a year before he was born. Look for everyone called Irving who married in 1967 — it's done alphabetically — and work backwards through the sixties and then forwards if you don't find them there. The marriage register will have Angela's maiden name and then you can search for her parents and siblings. OK?'

She noticed he was looking at her in a worryingly wide-eyed way and wasn't writing anything down.

'Make a note, Joe. Reporters make notes. Make that your first golden rule.'

Joe picked up his pen and scribbled down the names while Kate logged into the Births, Deaths and Marriages website on his computer and left him to fill in the boxes and press enter.

'Actually, start with a search of Deaths, in case she's died,' she added. 'We don't want to waste time looking for a corpse.'

While Joe clicked, Kate speed read the cuttings files from the nineties. She quickly found the abductions — one was a six-month-old girl, the other practically a toddler. Neither had been found, but it didn't seem likely they would ever fit the description of a newborn. She dutifully noted down names and dates, in case.

When she picked up Alice's file, there were at least fifty stories — the last in 1999 when three babies' bodies had been found in Staffordshire. She remembered the case — there was some talk of incest and the mother/murderer had been sent to a psychiatric hospital. It was an investigation that was over before it had got going and the *Post's* man in the Midlands had covered the trial, but Kate had been sent to try to get a talk with the family. They'd told her to piss off. She'd been glad. They looked like the cast of *Deliverance*.

She went back to March 1970, when Alice had been taken, and stared at the photographs of Angela and Nick Irving leaving the hospital in Basingstoke, their arms empty. Kate studied the grainy black and white images of the young couple. The mother looked devastated, her arms wrapped round herself as if cradling her grief. *Instead of her baby*, Kate thought and carefully unfolded the next story.

Geoff had been spot on. The initial coverage of the disappearance of Alice was swiftly followed

107

by articles hinting in a heavy-handed way at the mother's possible involvement. These seemed to stem from a police search of the Irving's house, three weeks after Alice disappeared.

'Routine police work' was the official comment, but the papers printed pictures of officers carrying items from the house. And Angela Irving being led to a police car. Those arms wrapped tightly around her stomach again.

Was it guilt she was holding in? Kate wondered, and wrote down the name of the officer in the case. She'd see if he was still around.

Kate raced ahead, scanning headlines for the outcome of the questioning, but it wasn't mentioned again. Mrs Irving hadn't been charged with anything as far as she could see, and the stories about Alice got smaller as 1970 came to an end. The last few cuttings were anniversary stories — *Whatever Happened to Baby Alice?* etc. — or she featured as a name in round-ups of missing children written as backgrounders to new abduction cases.

Kate noted that Angela wasn't quoted in the later anniversary stories. The reports said she and her husband had moved abroad. She, too, had disappeared, then.

The online Electoral Register had more than a dozen current listings for Angela and Nicholas Irvings. They were scattered all over the country, but there were none in Basingstoke.

Kate was looking at her notes when Joe announced he'd established that Angela Alice Irving was not dead, had found her marriage to

Nick and the births of their two other children — Patrick and Louise — one married and both living in Hampshire.

Kate smiled. They were on the trail of where Angela was now. And she had an Angela Alice and Nicholas Irving listed in Winchester.

She rang Bob Sparkes immediately.

'Hi, think I'm going to be heading down your way on the building-site-baby case. The baby Alice you mentioned is called Alice Irving and her mum, Angela, is living in Winchester.'

'Is she now?' Sparkes said.

He sounded pleased. Not a man to go overboard, he added, 'Good work, Kate. Will be interesting to hear what she says. What about the other cases? The girl in the car and the one in the pram?'

'Found them, but I think they are too old. Definitely not newborns.'

'Right, well. Is there anything more from the Met about their investigation?'

'No, nothing. There's a big anti-terror operation going on at the moment. I'm keeping out of their hair. I'm also looking for the officer who led the original hunt for Alice — DI Len Rigby. You don't happen to know if he's still alive, do you?'

'I'll have a look and call you back if I find him. He'll be long retired by now.'

'Yes, bit of a long shot.'

'Well, let me know when you're coming down,' he said.

She grinned to herself. 'Sure. I'm going to give Mrs Irving a call now.'

20

Monday, 2 April 2012

Angela

She'd had a feeling that morning that something
would happen. A buzz in her head. Nick was
quiet, checking an order for the plumbing
wholesaler while he ate his cornflakes, but she
felt surrounded by noise. She hardly heard him
say goodbye when he left.

She'd sat with the number for Kate Waters in
front of her while she finished her coffee and
promised herself she'd make the call at
lunchtime.

But the phone rang just before midday.

'Hello, I'm sorry to bother you, but I'm trying
to contact Angela Irving,' a woman said. Nice
voice, she thought. Polite. Warm.

'That's me,' she said. 'How can I help?'

'Oh, I'm so glad to have found you, Mrs
Irving. I'm Kate Waters from the *Daily Post*. I
wondered if I could talk to you about a story I've
been working on . . . '

Angela said: 'I hoped you'd call.'

There was a sliver of silence as Kate Waters
found herself second-guessed. 'Oh?' she said
quickly. 'Did you see the story I wrote last week,
then, Mrs Irving?'

'Yes,' Angela said. 'Do you think the baby is Alice?'

'Do you?' the reporter said.

'I don't know. I hope . . . ' And Angela burst into tears.

Kate Waters waited for her to gather herself, murmuring down the phone that she hadn't meant to upset her, that she understood how emotional this must be, even after all these years.

When Angela finally spoke again, she just said, 'You'd better come round, then. Have you got my address?'

Kate Waters said she'd be there in a couple of hours and the two women said goodbye.

Angela sat in the same place until she heard the knock on the door. Her head was full of Alice. Of the day she went. Of the days that followed.

She hadn't been able to go back to nursing afterwards. Couldn't be in a hospital. The smell of the wards, the starched aprons, the laced-up shoes, took her straight back to her loss. Instead she fought the overwhelming grief at home, privately. They both did. Their son Patrick had gone to stay with his grandma and the house echoed with his absence.

She and Nick would be sitting, watching television, or reading a paper, or listening to the radio, and something would come on. A silly song she'd liked when she was pregnant, the mention of the name Alice, or the word 'baby', or 'pregnancy' or 'hospital' — or anything, really — and she'd cry. Nick would hold her hand and talk her through it. Tell her it wasn't her fault.

111

She'd been in a hospital. She should have been safe.

But she hadn't been.

By the time the nurses had arrived, skittering down the linoleum of the corridor at the sound of her howl, the cot was cold.

21

Monday, 2 April 2012

Kate

The drive down to Winchester had been easier than she'd expected, with little traffic on the normally busy M3, but Joe's excitement about 'actually' going on a story — he used the word 'actually' at least a hundred times a day, she noticed — had started to get on her nerves. She almost expected him to ask, 'Are we nearly there yet?'

'What are we going to ask her?' he'd said as soon as his bottom touched the car seat.

'Will she cry?' as he did up the seatbelt.

'Do you think it's her baby?' as she turned the key in the ignition.

'Did she kill her baby?' had made Kate forget what gear she was in for a moment.

'For God's sake, Joe, shut up,' she said, moving from second to third and back to second. 'If you barge in asking questions like that, she'll throw us out immediately. We are going to let Angela Irving talk. A Paxman-style grilling doesn't work in this sort of situation. She's not a politician. She's a mother whose baby was stolen. Can you imagine what that feels like?'

Joe cleared his throat. 'Actually, I wouldn't have asked that question,' he said.

Kate smiled to herself.

'OK, when you arrive at a doorstep, what is the first thing you do?' she asked.

'Knock?' he ventured nervously.

'After that, you noodle.'

He looked as if he was flicking back through college notes in his head. Deep concentration.

'Tell her who we are? That we're reporters . . .'

'OK. And then?'

'Ask our first question.'

'At the door? Not if you're hoping to be asked in. You need to build some trust, make a human connection.'

Joe fished his notebook out of his bag and started writing. Kate glanced at the page at the traffic lights. He'd spelt 'connection' wrong. She sighed and turned up the radio.

The news was talking about a demonstration in Bangkok about something or other — she hadn't really been listening — but the word 'Thailand' stopped her random thoughts.

All she could think about was Jake and his wasted opportunities. *Thailand is for losers*, she told herself and felt tears pricking her eyes. *Stop it, you're at work.* She tensed her shoulders and then let them relax. She would have done some deep breathing, but Joe was in the car. *Mustn't show out to the junior.*

Joe showed no sign of noticing her distress. He wittered on about the Olympics, his favourite football team, and who would be playing at the Queen's Diamond Jubilee concert, in a stream of

114

consciousness that washed over her.

'Have you been to Thailand, Joe?' she asked when he drew breath.

'Yeah, it was brilliant,' he said. 'Great parties.'

'Right,' she said. 'My son's thinking of going.'

'Is he? On holiday?'

She hesitated. 'No, not really. He wants to find himself, apparently. Jake's a clever boy, he just can't seem to get started,' she added.

Joe's 'Oh' spoke volumes.

When they finally got out of the London traffic, she put her foot down and made it to the turn off for Winchester in illegal time.

'I wonder how many speed cameras we triggered,' Joe said cheerfully. 'Actually, it might be a record for the M3.'

Kate ignored his remarks and put the address into the satnav. 'Turn left,' the commanding voice instructed. And she did.

★　★　★

The house in Bishop Street was the neatest one in the road: semi-detached, a square of grass at the front, pots of daffodils and winter pansies dotting the paving-slab path to the door. Kate opened the gate and led the way, smile already in place.

'Tuck your shirt in, Joe,' she hissed at him as they got to the door. 'We're here as reporters, not for a party.'

He blushed, hastily shoved his shirt tail into his trousers and pushed his fringe out of his eyes. 'Sorry,' he said.

Angela Irving opened the door almost immediately, as if she'd been standing behind it, ready. She looked pale and serious, smoothing her shoulder-length grey hair back and taking her glasses off. She seemed to sway on her feet as she greeted them. She didn't wait for Kate to speak.

'You must be Kate,' she said.

'Yes that's right. Hello, Mrs Irving,' Kate said. 'Thank you so much for seeing me. I know it must be a difficult time for you, but I hope we can help each other.'

'So do I,' Angela said, and opened the door wide to let her visitors in. 'Go through,' she called from behind them.

Kate could hear Joe breathing through his mouth behind her and cursed the fact that she'd brought him with her.

In the kitchen, Kate's article had been laid out, centre stage on the table. Around it were piles of neatly folded cuttings, letters and an official-looking file.

'Please sit down,' Angela said, stiff and formal as she moved around the room, adding a third cup to a prepared tray of coffee and biscuits.

'I got some of my stuff out to show you. In case you were interested in seeing the history . . . '

Kate immediately picked up an article to show willing, but didn't read it. It was one she'd already scanned through at the office, but she needed time to think.

116

22

Monday, 2 April 2012

Kate

When Angela Irving had cried on the phone, Kate thought it was going to be an easy job. She thought she would be leading the conversation, but Angela's tears had dried and now Kate felt she was on the back foot. What she had misjudged was the fact that Mrs Irving was an old hand with reporters. There had been a number of interviews in the years after the disappearance — and that could play two ways. It could move things along if the interviewee knew what was expected and they could come quickly to the point.

But Kate preferred virgin territory to sloppy seconds. New subjects didn't speak in clichés or repeat well-worn quotes. And with a newbie, Kate could control the interview. She liked to listen and coax, leaning forward and maintaining eye contact when things threatened to get difficult. But Angela Irving sounded as though she had already prepared what she wanted to say.

Kate pretended to read the cutting while she watched the woman bustling around behind the breakfast bar. It all looked very business-like, but she noted the tremble in her hands that betrayed the nervous energy crackling just below the surface. She'd manage.

'Mrs Irving . . . ' she started.

'Please call me Angela. Mrs Irving sounds like you are talking to my mother-in-law,' Angela said with a ghost of a smile. 'Now,' she added as she poured the coffee, 'what do you want to know?'

Kate smiled at her apologetically and tried to match her matter-of-fact tone. 'Everything, Angela. If that's all right.'

'Of course,' the older woman said quietly and sat down.

When she didn't speak, Kate leant forward and asked, 'Are you OK, Angela?'

She shook her head.

'Sorry, I thought you would ask me a question and I'd answer it, like the other reporters did,' she said. 'I thought I'd be fine. But it's just that 'everything' sounds so overwhelming. I'm not sure where to begin, now.'

Her eyes filled with tears and Kate reached out to touch her arm in sympathy and relief.

'I'm sorry, Angela. I didn't mean to overwhelm you. Let's just take it a bit at a time. Why don't you tell me about your nursing? My mum was a nurse. Where did you train? In Hampshire?'

It was not information that Kate really needed, but she wanted to get Angela talking and relaxed before they broached the minefield of the abduction. The early stages of an interview were crucial. Get it wrong and you risked being shown the door with a note-book full of nothing.

Angela smiled properly for the first time,

118

perhaps thinking she was being let off the hook.

'It was all I ever wanted to be, a nurse. Used to run doll hospitals for my friends' toys. I trained not far from here, in Basingstoke. Where I had my babies . . . '

She faltered, then squared her shoulders. 'Well, two of my babies. Louise was nearly born in Germany, where we were stationed in the seventies. Nick was in the army — but you knew that. But we came home for her birth.'

Kate nodded, urging her on.

'Where were you in Germany, Angela? Was that after Alice disappeared?'

The name hung in the air between them.

'Yes. We went after the police stopped asking their questions,' Angela said. 'Nick said we needed a new start and there was a posting offered by his regiment. Compassionate grounds.'

Kate took a sip of her coffee to allow Angela a moment to collect herself.

'That must have been incredibly difficult, leaving your home and families at a time like that,' Kate said gently.

'It was,' the older woman said. The anguish of those weeks had clearly never dimmed. Kate could see the pain on her face. She was ready to talk.

'Tell me about that day, Angela. Tell me about the day that Alice was taken.'

119

23

Angela

She'd been waiting for this moment. Dreading it, but wanting to tell her story again. The pain of experiencing that moment of loss made Alice seem more real to her.

She told Kate Waters how quiet the evening had been, how Alice had been brought into her private room by a nurse to have a feed, and then Nick had taken Patrick home when their toddler son got tired and started whining.

'We'll leave you girls to it,' Nick had said, kissing them both and hoisting Paddy on to his shoulders.

The kiss and her brother's wails had made Alice stir and Angela had picked her up and brought her back to bed. She'd tried to feed her, but the baby had refused to latch on to her breast, fussing and snuffling before going back to sleep.

Angela hadn't worried too much — Alice was her second baby and there were no first-timer fears to deal with. She knew that the drugs she'd had for the delivery were probably still making her baby drowsy and that she'd feed later, when she was ready.

She re-swaddled her new daughter in the soft white hospital sheet to keep her warm and secure, put her back in the cot by her bed and gathered her soap bag and towel. She padded down to the showers, walking slowly and deliberately.

'Nick said I looked like John Wayne when I'd got out of bed earlier,' she told Kate. She'd giggled, she remembered, because he looked happier than she'd seen him for ages. Maybe having Alice would help them rebuild their relationship, like Nick said. Perhaps they were turning a corner, she remembered thinking as she struggled down the corridor.

The reporter was looking at her.

'Sorry,' Angela said. 'It just hurts so much to remember.'

Kate stroked her arm. 'Take your time, Angela,' she said. 'I know it must be very hard for you.'

'The thing is, I can't remember if I looked at my baby again before I left her in the room,' Angela said, and her voice faltered.

Kate Waters looked up from her notebook and met her eyes. 'Did you see anyone in the corridor, Angela?' she said gently.

'I think there were a couple of visitors — people on their way out of the ward — but I didn't take much notice. I wanted a quick shower before Alice woke for her feed.'

She'd stood under the hot water for what felt like two minutes, but the police said was more like ten. Time did strange things in hospitals. Sometimes it stretched minutes into hours and sometimes it vanished altogether.

And when she trudged damply back to her room, the baby had gone.

Her kitchen was silent. All she could hear was the tick of the electric clock. Angela looked down at the table. She could feel the surge of panic as if for the first time, the hot prickling of her skin, the sudden nausea, the paralysis. She clenched her fists in her lap and went on, desperate to get to the end without collapsing.

'I was telling myself that a nurse must have taken her. I was trying to stay calm. I remember saying out loud, 'She's been taken back to the nursery.' I thought I called out, 'Nurse!' But the staff told the police that they heard me scream and came running.'

'The baby,' she'd said to them. 'Where is the baby?' and she'd known from their pale faces and the way they turned to each other, as if lost, that they didn't know. No one knew. Except the person who'd taken her.

She told Kate about the frantic search of all the rooms and wards, which produced nothing but general terror. No one had seen anything. It was evening and the first-time mums had been curled against their stitches and cramps, gazing fearfully at their new sons and daughters, while the old hands gossiped and clucked with each other on the subject of childbirth. Curtains between the beds in the wards had begun to be drawn to allow some sleep and the visitors had almost all been ushered out.

'And while all that was going on, someone came into the room. Just walked in and took her.'

24

Monday, 2 April 2012

Kate

Kate wrote quickly, taking it all down in shorthand, while never taking her eyes off the woman across the table. She hardly needed to ask a question, just the occasional nudge when more details were needed. Angela's narrative started to slow when the story reached their return home from the hospital.

'It must have been very hard to come back to an empty nursery,' Kate said.

Angela nodded dumbly. 'We stood in Alice's room for a long time. But she wasn't there. She'd never been there. There was just a cot and a mobile of zoo animals. I felt so empty inside.'

'What were the police doing to try to find her, Angela?' Kate said.

'All the usual things,' Angela said, her voice exhausted by the tale. 'Searches, news conferences, chasing all over the country.'

'No real suspects?' Kate asked. 'There must have been loads of people walking about the hospital.'

'There were, but no one saw anything,' Angela said. 'It was like she'd disappeared into thin air.'

She waited a beat and added, 'You know, of

course, they came to the house after a couple of weeks and asked about my feelings towards Alice.'

'Your feelings? Why? What was that about?' Kate said, knowing full well what it was about. 'How awful for you.'

Angela looked grateful for the comment and nodded. 'I thought so, too. But I think one of the nurses must have said something about me. I was so drugged up after the birth I didn't know what I was doing, really. Maybe I didn't appear maternal enough. The police kept asking why I had left her alone.'

'What did you say?' Kate asked.

'I said she was asleep and I thought she was safe.'

'Of course,' Kate said. 'God, if your baby isn't safe in a maternity hospital, where would she be?'

Tears were running down Angela's face and Joe fished a packet of tissues from his bag and offered them to her.

'What do you think happened to her, Angela?' Kate said.

The older woman wrapped a tissue round her knuckles and closed her eyes. 'Someone took her. In the ten minutes I was out of the room, someone came in, lifted her out of her cot and took her away.'

'Who do you think would have done such a thing?' the reporter asked.

'I don't know,' Angela breathed. 'You hear about sad women and evil men taking children. But I don't know who took her. I would give anything to know.'

The two women sat in silence for a moment, focusing on their drinks.

To Kate's astonishment, Joe suddenly spoke. 'Why do you think the building-site baby is Alice, Mrs Irving?'

Kate bit back her annoyance. She'd wanted to ask that question, but she couldn't say anything to Joe in front of the interviewee. She tried to give him a warning look but he was staring at Angela intently, mirroring Kate's approach. And Angela was looking at the youngster kindly.

'Did you have any links to Woolwich?' he continued. 'People who knew you?'

'I wish I could say yes,' Angela replied. 'But I have never been to Woolwich. All I can say is that I had a feeling when I read the story in the newspaper. A strong feeling that this was about Alice. I know it sounds a bit crazy, but there it is,' she said.

Kate groaned in her head. No connections, no leads. It didn't sound likely that this was the baby in Howard Street.

But she didn't want Angela to see her disappointment. She touched her arm again. 'It doesn't sound crazy at all,' she said.

25

Monday, 2 April 2012

Emma

It's been two weeks and no one has come to my door. I spend a lot of time — far too much time — looking out of the window, watching for my accusers to arrive. The police, I suppose, but there are other possibilities. Funny, when I think about the police I have an old-fashioned image of a bobby striding up the path, an arrest warrant in his hand. Like they were then.

Sometimes I wish they would just come. Put me out of my misery. But no one has. I stand by the window and try to force myself to go back upstairs to work. My body won't obey. I am rooted to this spot. My place of shame. Back to the beginning.

Paul is worried about me. I can see it in his eyes, hear it in his voice.

'When did you last see Dr Gorgeous?' he asked me this morning. Our little joke. Dr Gorgeous is Dr Brenton — my wonderful GP — but giving him a funny nickname makes it easier to talk about my 'condition'.

'Not for a while, I suppose,' I said. 'Maybe I'll make an appointment.'

'Good idea, Em. You've been so much better

126

lately, but perhaps your pills need tweaking.'

That's the way we talk about my anxiety. Like it's a headache or something. Nothing to be ashamed of.

I'm not going to call the surgery. I'm not being difficult, but Dr Gorgeous likes to talk about my feelings when I go to see him for a repeat prescription and I'm not up to that at the moment. Last time I had a bad day, he said he'd like me to see someone — 'a specialist', he said — but I told him I didn't need to. I'm happy seeing him because I only have to sit chatting for the allotted eight minutes and he gives me a prescription.

A specialist would want to know about my relationships. How I feel about Jude and my absent father.

I'd have to tell him I'd gone looking for my dad as a teenager — but I can't say that. Because I can't tell the whole story. One thing would lead to another and it would mean unpicking the web.

I try it out, just in case. I can hear myself saying, 'It began with Will. Well, it began before that, but the arrival of Will started the unravelling.' But that is as far as I get before I am in the danger zone.

The day I decided to begin the search for my father, I'd had a row with Jude. Our life had been turned upside down by Will. Jude had become completely obsessed. He'd taken over her life. And so, my life. We couldn't do anything or go anywhere without asking Will what he thought or if he wanted to come too.

There was a lot more singing in the bath, I remember, the smell of her Aqua Manda bath oil making the air thick outside the door. But I'd learnt to ignore her calls to come in — peace offerings I was happy to reject. He was all she talked about. I wondered how many of her clients were still in prison because of her ridiculous fixation.

I told Harry, and she said Jude was acting like a groupie. I didn't like it. Didn't like her calling my mum that. It was all right if I said mean things, but not anyone else.

I didn't tell Harry that I'd heard Jude telling our new flatmate — Barbara from her office — how she'd first slept with Will at a May Ball. Barbara said it sounded romantic, but I thought it sounded cheap. My mum was too old to be talking like that.

Jude was changing. She'd been so serious and focused on 'the important things in life' and I'd assumed I was included in that category. She certainly had big plans for me — cabinet minister, surgeon, Nobel prize-winner were all bandied about in a jokey way, but I knew she expected a lot.

We had what Jude liked to call an 'adult relationship'. That meant we talked about politics and new books and films she'd seen, and she told me about her legal cases and the terrible situations people were forced into by authoritarian states. We didn't talk about pop stars or boys or spots. That was my other world. In my bedroom or the phone box. The kitchen was where I interacted with my mother.

But suddenly she wasn't interested in me any more. She was busy shaving her legs and searching for matching underwear in her chest of drawers, scrabbling through layers of faithful old pants and tired bras.

One night, she presented herself in the kitchen for inspection in a new dress, while I was doing my homework.

'What do you think, Emma?' Jude had asked me.

'Aren't you a bit old to be going out without a bra, Mum?' I'd said, using the forbidden M word. I hated her at that moment. She looked so beautiful and happy and it had nothing to do with me. 'The woman up the road — the one Will likes — never wears one and she looks awful,' I added.

'You little bitch,' Jude had snapped at me. She'd never used that word to me before. Never had to, I suppose. I was changing, too.

After Jude left, slamming the door behind her, I headed for the telephone box at the end of the road. It was almost eight o'clock and the box lurked in the dark pool between two streetlights. It was lit only by an ancient light bulb that cast a nicotine-yellow pall over the interior, and stank of pee and joints. The concrete floor seemed permanently wet and stained in the corners as if the last user had just zipped up his jeans and left. But I loved that phone box. It was my private space. There was a phone at home, on the wall in the hallway, but every conversation felt like a public event with Jude listening and even joining in if she felt like it.

129

I lined up my coins on the metal shelf, picked up the receiver and began dialling.

I asked Harry's father if I could talk to her. I was always polite, using my most suitable-for-adults voice. He hated me disturbing her when she was doing her homework, but I would pretend I was calling about some schoolwork.

He used to say he didn't know what we could have to talk about after being at school together all day. But he always gave in.

I'd hear the sound of Harry's feet thundering downstairs and then her voice, high and cross. 'Dad, stop listening to my calls. This is private.'

I told her about Jude calling me a bitch and Harry was thrilled. She loved a bit of other people's trouble.

'I'm sick of Jude and Will,' I said.

'Yeah,' she said, but I knew she had misgivings. The trouble was she was secretly — or sometimes not so secretly — in love with Will. She said he was sexy.

'Harry! He's so old,' I said, outraged when she first told me. I didn't tell her that the word 'sexy' made my stomach go all watery. I was trying to hate Will for barging into our lives, but I still liked it when he winked or smiled at me. I couldn't help it.

The pips crashed into my thoughts, signalling that another three minutes had passed, and I pushed the remaining ten-pence piece into the slot so we could discuss Harry's social life. I just tagged along.

I remember she'd nicked a five-pound note from her dad's trousers to buy a new top. Her theft was all in aid of impressing Malcolm Baker, her latest crush. He had apparently smiled at Harry on the bus and her heart was clearly set on slow-dancing with him at the youth-club disco.

For me, romance stayed in the pages of my notebooks and diaries. I hadn't ventured into love — or lust — in the flesh, uncertain of my looks and charms and unwilling to test the waters. There had been some smudged innocent kisses behind the youth club, informed by the stories in *Jackie*, but I preferred to write about longing and imagined lovers. There was safety in my stories. And less saliva.

And I'd had Harry's terrifying lecture on losing your virginity. I'd asked her what it was like when she told me she'd done it with Malcolm Baker's friend after the Christmas disco.

'Did it hurt?' I said.

'Agony. Bloody agony, but it gets better,' Harry'd said, puffing on a No. 6 on the top of the double decker. I knew she'd probably only done it once, but let it go. She liked being my older, more sophisticated friend.

'Agony? Really? God, maybe I'll wait a bit longer. Do you want one?' I'd offered her a cheese and onion crisp and we'd moved seamlessly on to our favourite flavours.

Harry'd rung the bell and skipped down the stairs to get off the bus. She looked up and waved as the bus lumbered off.

Harry had long thought my failure to get a boyfriend was down to having no dad.

'Where are the men in your life, Emma? No wonder you are shy around boys,' she'd said when we'd last broached the subject, months before.

It had been her idea to bring up the subject at home, so I had. I tried to keep calm and pointed out that half my DNA was my mystery father's. Jude had reacted with horror.

'But you've got me!' she'd cried. 'And he wouldn't be interested.'

She'd pointed out that he probably had another family by now and I would be making problems for him if I turned up. 'He'd have to explain you to his new wife.'

That night, the night of the row, Harry said, 'Sod them, Emma. You need a proper parent. Let's go and find your dad.'

And I agreed.

★   ★   ★

We waited until the next time Jude was out and went up to her room to look through her things for letters and photos of old boyfriends. I was so worried she'd catch us, I stood by the door while Harry did the digging around. I was nagging Harry to put everything away when she found a scribbled note at the back of Jude's 1968 diary. It said Charlie and there was an address in Brighton.

'We should go there,' Harry said. 'It's around the right time and it's not too far,' she added, practical as ever.

It was all moving too fast for me, but I'd agreed to start down the path and it felt too late to turn back now.

26

Monday, 2 April 2012

Emma

I'm supposed to be polishing the book I'm editing but I keep drifting away from the sentence I'm reading. My boss has emailed to say the subject is about to be exposed in a Sunday paper as a coke head and I need to get a wiggle on so the publishers can sell the serial rights to the press.

I've emailed back to say I'll get it to her by the end of tomorrow, but I can't concentrate. It's as if my eyes keep sliding off the screen. I get up, make myself a cup of tea and sit down again, determined to get on with it. But my tea goes cold beside me and my screen locks while I sit wondering if everything would have turned out differently if Harry and I had found my father, back in 1984. If the story had ended in Brighton.

But of course it didn't.

I almost laugh when I remember how it began — like some silly schoolgirl adventure — but there is nothing to laugh at, really.

Harry had it all planned. We forged a note for school, saying I had a dentist appointment in the afternoon, and she pretended to be ill.

'Since we're in different classes they shouldn't

133

put two and two together,' she said. 'I'll say period pains because Mrs Carr hates talking about that stuff.' Poor Mrs Carr, she was about a hundred years old and being Harry's form teacher must have been a terrible cross for her to bear.

Harry had chosen a Thursday because it was double Games, so we could leave at lunchtime. And there we were, at the railway station, about to make it all real.

I can see us standing there. Two kids. I'm the one not talking, concentrating on the plan and trying not to think what I'll say. So many questions running through my head, making me feel faint.

Harry said this was just the first step and not to build my hopes up. I said I wasn't, but it was hard not to.

The thing was, my dad had existed in my head for so long, it was hard not to think of him as a real person. I used to wonder if I looked like him, examining my features in the mirror and wondering which bits of me were his.

Some people say I look like Jude but I've never thought so. Her friends said we had the same eyes. Well, we both have blue eyes.

I didn't know how I felt about finding my dad. Excited, but really, really scared. I didn't tell Harry. She used to pull this face when she thought people were being immature.

I was so frightened that he wouldn't want to know me, like Jude said, but I let myself imagine him hugging me, like in those stories about people being reunited. Like in *Heidi*. When I thought about it I felt tingly and wanted to cry, so I wrote about it in my diary. It made me feel better when it was written down. Safe on the page.

Harry never did 'safe'. She loved a bit of excitement, a bit of trouble. And it was OK, normally, because I just watched and was the shoulder to cry on when it all went wrong. Like when she started seeing that horrible biker in the precinct. Her parents went mad and her dad went to see the biker at his house and said he would go to the police if he went near his fourteen-year-old daughter again. Harry cried for two days.

But that day in January 1984, that Thursday when we bunked off school, was all about me. Harry said it was my 'big day', but I think I'd have preferred double Games.

On the train to Brighton, I remember we got out our school packed lunches, hers white sliced bread with ham and coleslaw, mine a house brick of homemade wholemeal with hummus, and we fell silent. We were really doing this and it made us a bit giddy.

'What if he's fat and bald and drinks out of cans?' Harry said.

'What if he's a millionaire? Or a biker?' I said.

Harry gave me a look.

'What if he has ten children and lives in a council house?' she said.

Harry could be quite conservative, despite her reputation as a rebel — I think it was her mum's influence. Jude said Mrs Harrison was 'all fur coat and no knickers'. I wasn't sure what it meant at the time, but it made me laugh.

135

Anyway, I didn't say, 'What if he doesn't want to see me?' but I was thinking it and I threw away my sandwich in the bin in the toilet.

When the train pulled into the station, I didn't want to get up. My legs were all jelly and Harry pulled me out of my seat and linked her arm through mine.

'Come on. Let's go and see who lives there. We won't say you're looking for your long-lost dad until you're ready. And if we don't like the look of them, we'll go and get some candy floss on the pier. OK?'

I nodded.

* * *

The address was a big house in a posh street, set back from the sea front. But it wasn't like the other houses. The windows were boarded up and the front garden was all overgrown and full of empty bottles.

'No one lives here, Harry. Let's go,' I said, so glad the ordeal was over before it had begun. But she was having none of it.

'Don't be wet. We've come all this way. We should at least knock.' So she did, with me shivering at the gate, ready to run away at the first sign of trouble. 'There's no answer,' she shouted back to me. And she was about to turn away when the door opened and a tall man stood there, rubbing his eyes like he'd just woken up.

'Yeah? What do you want?' he said.

'Do you know Jude Massingham?' Harry said, straight out.

He looked at her and laughed. 'Jude Massingham? Christ, that's a blast from the past. Must be more than ten years ago. God, maybe twenty? She was my mate Charlie's woman. Who are you, then?'

The man was quite thin and wearing tight black trousers and a thick brown belt with a fancy buckle resting below his belly button. You could see through his shirt — it was that really thin material, even though it was freezing — and he'd got a medallion thing on a leather thong round his neck.

He knew Charlie. *He knows my dad*, a voice was whispering in my head.

Harry was chatting away, telling this stranger that I was Jude's daughter and looking for my dad. And then he looked down the path at me and I wondered what he was thinking. None of us said anything for a moment. Finally he said, 'I'm Darrell, by the way. You'd better come in.' And we did.

I can still smell that house: years of patchouli oil overlaid by grime, suffocating and musky like a hippie's old Afghan coat. And it was so dark I kept stumbling over shapes. I wasn't sure if they were human and I was frightened.

'Electric is off again,' he said. 'Someone forgot to pay the bill.'

'Why are the windows boarded up?' Harry asked.

'Keeps the marauders out,' he laughed. 'It's a squat, love.'

'Oh. Never been in a squat before,' Harry said conversationally. All that time, I'd not uttered a word. I couldn't think of a thing to say except, 'Do you know where my dad is now?' I kept saying it in my head. Trying out how it felt.

He took us for coffee in the café up the road so we could talk, and I couldn't stop looking at him.

When the waitress brought the order, he pushed my cup across the table and said, 'Emma. That's a lovely name. I remember your mum very well. She was so beautiful. I always fancied her, but she was Charlie's bird.' I don't know why but I started crying and Harry got all embarrassed.

'Stop it, Emma,' she said, handing me a wad of napkins from the dispenser. But I couldn't, so I went and stood on the pavement with her while Darrell paid.

'Come on,' he said to me outside, taking my hand. 'Let's go for a walk and talk about Jude for a bit.'

Harry gave me a look. She was being dumped and was very unhappy about it. Normally, it was me who got left while she disappeared off with her latest boyfriend.

'See you back here, then. We need to get the four o'clock train home,' she hissed at me.

'I'll have her back in time,' he said and led me off.

27

Monday, 2 April 2012

Kate

When they left, Angela kissed both of them goodbye. The intimacy had taken Joe by surprise, but Kate had expected it. They'd been privy to Angela's deepest feelings and thoughts and she had felt that, in that moment, they were close friends. Pink-faced, Joe had pulled back awkwardly from the embrace, but Kate had hugged Angela back.

'Thank you so much, Angela. I know how hard this must have been, but you've been brilliant,' she'd said at the door. 'I'll call you later to sort out when the photographer can come. Take care of yourself. And, remember, if any other reporter calls, *No comment.*'

Angela had smiled, the catharsis of confession still washing over her. 'You were the first to call me, Kate, so I'm happy to only speak to you.'

Kate had considered offering money to ensure exclusivity on the drive down. If the building-site baby did turn out to be Alice Irving, it would be a big story and others would go after it. She'd brought a blank contract with her, just in case, but within minutes of sitting down opposite Angela, she could see that even mentioning

139

payment would kill the relationship. This woman wasn't interested in making a buck. She wanted to know what had happened to her baby. End of.

She'd have to trust her.

In the car, Joe didn't say a word. The chirping silenced by proximity to personal tragedy.

'You all right?' Kate asked. 'That was a great talk, wasn't it? But there is nothing screaming that it is the right baby yet. God, I hope it is Alice.'

'Yes,' Joe agreed. 'How will she cope if it isn't? Poor woman . . .'

Kate reached over and squeezed his hand. 'It might be Alice, Joe, but it's still a very long shot. We shouldn't get too excited until the police have done DNA tests on Angela and the baby's remains. If there is a match, we'll know they are related.'

Joe nodded.

It's really shaken him, Kate thought. 'Come on, let's go and have a cup of tea and call Bob Sparkes. Get this story moving.'

★ ★ ★

He sounded distracted when he answered the phone. 'Sparkes,' he announced.

Kate grinned. This man-of-few-words thing was becoming almost a parody.

'Bob, it's Kate. I'm in Winchester. Been to see Angela Irving,' she said.

The detective's tone changed immediately. 'Hi, Kate, good to hear from you. How was she? What did she say?'

140

'She's convinced the body is Alice. But it's a gut feeling. Nothing concrete. She can't think of any links to the area where the body was found.'

'Poor woman,' Sparkes said. 'You can't blame her for wanting it to be her baby after all these years of not knowing. Any news on forensics?'

'Nothing yet. What we need is to get the Met to look at Angela's DNA. I was going to call the detective in the building-site-baby case to suggest it, but I was wondering . . . '

'What were you wondering, Kate? I can hear a favour about to be asked,' he said and laughed.

'It would have so much more weight if you called. They'll hate a reporter suggesting it. And it was you who put me on to Angela in the first place. And Alice was taken from your patch . . . '

There was a Bob Sparkes silence — the sort that went on so long she thought the line had been cut.

'I could only do that if Mrs Irving contacted me to ask about the discovery,' he said carefully. 'Don't want to tread on any toes.'

'I'll call her now and give her your number,' Kate said quickly before he could change his mind.

'Not my mobile,' he said. 'Tell her to come through the switchboard. Don't want any calls at two in the morning.'

'No. How is Eileen?' Kate asked, trying to sound genuine. Bob Sparkes's wife didn't really hold with twenty-four-hour police work, according to the crime correspondents' gossip.

'Eileen? Oh fine, you know. Fed up with my working hours. But then, so am I,' he said.

141

'And Bob,' she added quickly, 'anything on DI Rigby?'

'Oh yes, sorry, meant to say that he's alive and kicking and running a classic-car club near Esher.'

'Brilliant. Don't suppose you've got an address?'

'You know I can't give out that sort of info, but I'm sure a reporter with your resources can find him.' She could hear the smile in his voice.

'Will do,' she said. 'Thanks so much for looking it up for me.'

'Right, I'll be in touch after I've heard from Angela Irving.'

The line went dead.

'Bye, then,' Kate said.

She dialled Angela's number immediately to tell her the news and urged her to ring DI Sparkes as soon as possible. The older woman sounded excited and grateful and Kate tried to keep her adrenaline from rising.

Her next call was to Terry. She knew if she didn't check in, he'd call her when she least expected it. She wanted to be prepared, on the front foot.

'Kate, where are you?' It was always his first question, even when he knew perfectly well where his reporters were. The tone was always accusatory, as if they had disappeared without warning.

'Winchester, Terry. I've been following some leads — I told you.'

'Oh, yes, yes,' he said. Her news editor was unhappy — he'd clearly just had a tense conversation with the editor about the state of the news list. She cursed her timing.

'Where's the evidence this is the Irving baby?' he said. 'It's pure speculation, isn't it? Look, Kate, I need a splash, not a punt. This isn't going to get the readers clicking on the website. Forget it. It's not our kind of thing any more. Royals and celebrities are all that matter now. It's what the readers want.'

She let him blow himself out. Interrupting meant the rant would go on longer. When he finally stopped, she said, 'Come on, Terry, this could be a fantastic story — the *Post* solving the forty-year mystery of a missing baby. And we've got exclusive access if Angela turns out to be the mum. The readers would love it. Let me write it and then see what you think. Is that OK?'

Playing the submissive card at the end so the news editor thinks he's still in charge was an old trick. But it always worked.

'OK, OK. Are you on your way back?'

'Just setting off, but it'll take a couple of hours and I've got a door to knock on the way — a copper from the original inquiry. So no point coming back to the office. I'll write it at home and send it overnight.

'Good luck with the list,' she added. 'Put Madonna's veiny hands on it. That's always a winner.'

Terry half laughed. 'Yes, yes. But do me a favour — ring your woman at Kensington Palace. See if there's anything going on that might make my news list look better.'

'On it. Call you in a bit,' she said.

'That sounded a bit hairy,' Joe said. 'Are we in trouble?'

'Don't be daft,' Kate said. 'We've got what could be a great story. We just need to let Terry get used to the idea. Right, I need to make a call to a contact.'

She dialled Flora's mobile. 'Hi Flora, it's Kate. How are you? Just thought I'd give you a bell to see how things are. Seems a while since we spoke.' *Blah blah.*

Her royal contact sounded pleased to hear from her. Flora loved a chat and the chance to catch up on media gossip. Kate imagined her dropping in titbits on the state of an editor's marriage during office time with Prince William.

She listened attentively as Flora complained about a headline in the *Sun*, told her about one of the minor royals becoming more regal than the Queen, and, with a little prompting, tipped her off about the sacking of a royal servant.

'Selling stuff on eBay. You wouldn't credit it, would you?' Flora said, her indignation making the line squeak in sympathy.

'No, absolutely. What did she steal? Any Vermeers? No, well, difficult to smuggle out in your handbag,' Kate said, keeping her tone light. Didn't want to scare her off. 'What a shock for everyone. Who is investigating? When is she likely to be charged?'

When Flora's story had been completely combed through, Kate thanked her and promised her a lovely lunch before hanging up.

'You little beauty,' she crowed, forgetting Joe was sitting next to her. He looked alarmed.

'Sorry, not you. I've got a present for Uncle Terry.'

28

Monday, 2 April 2012

Angela

It was funny, but it was the young lad, not the reporter, who'd asked the question she'd been dreading. Why she thought Alice was the baby on the building site. She couldn't explain it rationally — there was nothing to link her or her baby to Woolwich — and she thought they'd write her off as a fantasist. But they hadn't.

'Joe, my work-experience boy,' Kate Waters had said dismissively when they'd arrived. But he'd been the one to really test her. Angela had answered all the other questions before.

She'd faltered when Kate had said she wanted to know 'everything', suddenly back in the room with the detectives, but had pulled herself together quickly enough. That was the problem with inviting reporters in, wasn't it? You never knew what they'd burrow into. She'd decided to mention the police decision to investigate her before anyone else did. It was in the coverage from the time, so she was sure the reporter would have read about it.

Anyway, she had nothing to hide.

The police had been frustrated about the lack of leads, that was all. They turned to her when they couldn't find anything else. That's what Nick had said before they came. But neither of them were ready for what happened.

They'd rung before calling round to the house and Nick had come through from the hall after he'd put the phone down on the nice inspector.

'They want to come and talk to us, Angie. Something and nothing, I expect,' he'd said, but she knew he was worried.

'What do you mean, something and nothing?' she'd asked. 'Is there some new information? Have they found something?'

'No, love,' Nick had said, taking her hand. 'Inspector Rigby said he wanted a quiet word with us.'

When the officer arrived, he'd brought two of his men with him, and while Angela and Nick sat with him in the sitting room, the others searched the house. Angela had sat in stunned silence while Inspector Rigby put his questions, unable to respond.

'Mrs Irving, when did you last see Alice?' he'd asked. It was the first time for ages that he hadn't called her Angela and Nick had reacted immediately. On the defensive. The wrong move.

'What sort of question is that?' he'd asked, too loudly. 'You know exactly when Angela last saw the baby.'

'Calm down now, Mr Irving,' Rigby had said. 'We just want to be absolutely sure we have all the details right. You see, we only have one witness and we need to check everything.'

'One witness? There were eight or nine people who came running when Angela called.'

146

'But that was after you said the baby had been taken, wasn't it?' the detective said to Angela. She didn't look up.

'*Said* the baby had been taken? What the hell does that mean?' Nick shouted. 'The baby disappeared. Someone must have taken her. What are you suggesting, for Christ's sake?'

Angela had reached out to take her husband's hand, willing him to stop asking questions she didn't want to hear answers to.

Nick looked at her for the first time. She wondered what he saw, what he was looking for.

She knew she was weeping, but it was as if she was watching herself react. It was like the moments in her hospital room after Alice went. She'd felt completely detached after the nurses had come running. Shock, it had been diagnosed, but it had not played well with the police.

'Why isn't she crying?' she'd heard a WPC whisper to a colleague at the door of her hospital room. 'I'd be doing my nut if it was my baby that'd gone.'

But Angela couldn't play the part. All her energy was diverted to continuing to breathe, to just staying alive. But no one seemed to understand that. And now here were the police, suggesting she might have actually got rid of her baby herself.

'Inspector,' she managed to say, and he leant forward in his chair.

'Yes, Mrs Irving?'

'Inspector, I last saw Alice in her cot when I went for a shower. I told you that when you first

147

came to the hospital.'

He nodded. 'And why did you leave your baby on her own, Mrs Irving?'

He'd never asked her that before. *What kind of mother are you?*

'A shower. I went for a shower. She was asleep,' Angela had stuttered.

The detective looked across at Nick. 'What time did you and your son leave the hospital?' he said.

'Why do you keep asking the same questions?' Nick said. His voice was quieter now, his anger burning out. 'Why?'

Inspector Rigby rubbed his hands on his knees. 'We need to be sure we're not missing anything here. You wouldn't forgive us if we did.'

Angela had nodded. She wouldn't have been able to forgive that.

'Mrs Irving,' the inspector said, calling her back to the questions. 'What would you say were your feelings for Alice?'

There was silence in the room apart from Angela's ragged breathing.

'I don't know what you mean,' she said finally. 'How did I feel about my baby? I loved her.'

'Loved?' the policeman said.

'Love her. Why are you trying to confuse me?' Angela said.

'And you, Mr Irving? How did you feel about Alice?' Rigby said. Tone even. No drama.

Nick slumped into his chair. 'The same. I'm sorry, Inspector. I am so tired; I can't think straight.' His voice was flat and exhausted and

148

Angela reached out to touch his hand.

The inspector cleared his throat nervously.

There's more, she thought, gripping the sofa edge as though she was about to fall.

'I understand there have been problems in your marriage,' he ventured.

Angela looked up. 'All marriages have problems,' she said and dropped Nick's hand.

'What sort of problems have you been having?' DI Rigby asked gently.

'You had better ask Nick,' she said and closed her eyes.

She could hear her husband's voice as if in another room, stumbling as he told how he had betrayed her.

'It was a mistake, Inspector,' he was saying. 'A terrible mistake. A fling. It meant nothing.'

She realized he was using exactly the same words he'd used when she'd confronted him.

He'd stumbled then, too. He'd talked her round. Persuaded her they could repair the damage.

And she'd been too frightened of the alternative to say no. Their lives were so entwined; she couldn't see a way to disentangle them. The loneliness of an existence without Nick yawned at her and she set about the task of burying her outrage and hurt. She never used the woman's name, not even in her private thoughts. She was faceless — she'd never seen her and that helped — and nameless. A nobody who had tempted her idiot husband after a night's drinking with the boys.

She would never have known if she hadn't

taken his jacket to the dry cleaner's. Out of habit, she'd turned out the pockets and found part of an empty Durex packet.

'It was only once, Angie,' he'd wept. 'I was drunk and stupid. Please forgive me. I love you and Patrick so much.'

'Let's have another baby,' he'd whispered in bed a few weeks later. 'You'd like that, Angie, wouldn't you? It'll bring us close again.'

And Alice was conceived. The sticking plaster for their marriage.

The trouble was she didn't know if he'd done it before — or would carry on doing it. *A leopard never changes its spots* kept coming into her head when he got home late or popped out for an hour. But if he did it again, he was more careful.

Angela had opened her eyes as Nick came to the end of his confession. The inspector was sitting on the edge of his chair, weighing every word.

'Why didn't you tell us about this earlier, Mr Irving?'

'I couldn't see it had anything to do with Alice,' Nick said.

'And the woman with whom you had the fling, as you call it?'

Angela closed her eyes again.

'Marian,' Nick said.

'Surname?'

'I never knew it,' he said. 'I told you, it was a drunken mistake. She is nothing to do with us and our baby. Why are you asking this? Why are you digging all this up?'

150

'We need to know the full background, Mr Irving,' the detective said. 'We need to know everything.'

29

Monday, 2 April 2012

Kate

Len Rigby was gardening when Kate and Joe arrived at his house, on his knees, grubbing up the weeds and furtively flinging slugs into his neighbour's privet hedge. He looked up, blinking into the sun, when he heard his name called.

'DI Rigby?' Kate said, leaning over the low brick wall.

'Who wants to know?' he growled, trying to heave himself upright with the help of a window sill.

'Let me help you,' she said, already opening the wrought-iron gate to walk up the path. 'I'm Kate Waters, from the *Post*.'

'Are you indeed?' he said, adding, 'I can manage, thank you,' as she got nearer.

Kate ignored him and offered her hand.

'I'm hoping you can help me with one of your old cases, DI Rigby. I promise I won't take up too much of your time.'

He laughed as he allowed himself to be steadied by Kate, adding, 'Time is what I've got plenty of. I'll get Mrs Rigby to make us a drink.'

He led Kate and Joe through to the conservatory at the back of the house and disappeared to announce their presence to his wife.

'Now then, what do you want to ask me about?' he said as he lowered himself into a rattan chair.

'Alice Irving,' Kate said. No point beating about the bush. DI Rigby was a straight-up-and-down bloke, she could see.

'Ah,' he said, taking a cup from his wife and placing it carefully on the matching side table. 'Thanks, love.

'Baby Alice. Basingstoke Hospital. Vanished without trace. Never found,' he said, reeling back to 1970. 'Very strange case,' he added.

'Strange how?' Kate asked.

'Well, there were no witnesses apart from the mother. In a busy hospital like that. I remember we talked to over a hundred people who were in the building that night — mums, visitors, nurses, cleaners, doctors, auxiliaries, maintenance men — but no one saw anything. So we only had the mother's account to rely on for timings of when the baby disappeared. I always wondered about her. Angela. She was a bit of a cold fish and her husband had been playing away.'

'Really? I never read about that in the cuttings,' Kate said, leaning forward.

'We never made it public,' he said, slurping his tea. 'We kept it quiet while we checked out the husband — Nick, isn't it? — but we never got anywhere. He and Angela both stuck to their testimony like glue. And, of course, there was never a body. Is that why you're here? Has something new turned up?'

'Possibly,' Kate said carefully. 'A baby's

153

skeleton has been found on a building site in Woolwich and I'm looking to see if there could be any connections.'

'Right. Woolwich,' he said, rolling the word round his mouth. 'No, can't think of any connection off the top of my head. Well, it has a military connection — the husband was in the army, you know. But all this is a lifetime ago and at my age I'm losing my marbles rapidly.'

'I'm sure that isn't true,' Kate said and grinned at him.

'Well, I think I might still have some of the paperwork in my study — don't tell the wife, I promised to clear all my police stuff out,' he said, grinning back. 'Shall I have a look? Have you got time?'

'Definitely,' Kate said.

The study was all about cars. Photos of expensive bodywork, chrome detail and race tracks were everywhere. Joe pointed at one and said, 'That's Goodwood, isn't it?'

Len Rigby went over to examine it. 'Yes, that's it. Go every year to the Festival of Speed. Have you been?'

'Yes, my mum gets invited and I blag a ticket,' Joe said. 'Love it.'

'We don't want to take up too much of the inspector's time, do we?' Kate said pointedly to her sidekick.

'No, well. Let's have a look at the stuff I kept on the Irvings,' the DI said, and winked at Joe.

It was a slim file of handwritten notes and Kate lowered her expectations immediately.

'Right,' Rigby said. 'What have we got?'

He leafed through quickly — too quickly for Kate's liking — but stopped halfway and pulled out two sheets.

'These were notes I wrote up after we found out about the husband's affair,' he said. 'Nick Irving said it was a fling and that he didn't know the woman's full name when I questioned him in front of his wife. But he did. He rang me the next day and told me. He didn't want Angela to know. We checked her out — the other woman — where's her name? Marian Laidlaw. That's her.'

Kate wrote it down, checking the spelling. 'And what was she like?' she asked.

'My sergeant saw her. Says here she was a pleasant, decent woman of thirty-five. Older than Nick Irving but a nurse, like Angela. The fling had gone on for a while, according to her. There'd been talk of Nick Irving leaving his wife, but then it had ended. When Angela found out.'

'A nurse?' Kate said, her pulse quickening. 'Bloody hell. Did she know Angela? Did she work at the Basingstoke hospital?'

'No, sadly not,' the detective said. 'We got all excited, like you — thought we'd found ourselves a proper suspect — but Miss Laidlaw had a cast-iron alibi. She was on duty on a geriatric ward in Southampton — miles away and with dozens of witnesses. Another dead end.'

'Interesting, though,' Kate said.

'Len, dinner's on the table,' his wife shouted through.

'Well, I think I've told you everything I know,' DI Rigby said.

'You've been brilliant,' Kate said and shook his hand firmly. 'I don't suppose I could borrow your notes for a couple of days? Promise I'll return them . . . '

'Len!' The voice was more insistent now.

'Coming, love,' he called back. 'You can photograph them, but I can't let them go. And anything I've said you'll only use as background? No quoting me. Understood?'

'You have my word,' she said, and Joe started copying the pages on his phone.

30

Monday, 2 April 2012

Emma

I've got out my old diaries from the suitcase under the spare bed. It's the first time in years I've looked at them, but the baby has made me want to check how it all started. In case my mind has been playing tricks.

They're cheap, thin exercise books filled with tiny writing. My teenage years. Funny how I divide my life into blocks of time. Like I was different people. I suppose I was. We all are.

When I read them now, I want to weep for her — for me — and the girl I might have been.

She was so young and innocent — nothing like the thirteen-and fourteen-year-olds I see on the bus, shouting and swearing, frightening old ladies. Teenage Emma scribbled away about her life as if she were Jane Austen, recording conversations and rivalries at school and home, observing people around her. And occasionally, she described her feelings — like when she saw a boy in town she liked. She used words like 'dreamy'. And that's what they were, these boys — fodder for imagined romances and happy-ever-afters. Poor Emma. Outside her books and diaries, the world wasn't like that, even if it looked like it for a bit.

Darrell Moore was her — my — first *coup de foudre*. She would probably have called it love at first sight. Whatever it was, it was devastating, literally. Not devastating as in the opposite of awesome, as used on the news to describe minor events. But devastating as in overwhelming, savage, shattering. I couldn't think straight.

The diary says we went for a walk — with hearts round the words — and I remember him stroking my hair, squeezing my shoulders and putting his arm round me as we walked along the promenade that first time. I loved it. I didn't want him to stop. I wanted him to touch every inch of my skin. He was so lovely, he took my breath away.

I was so dazzled by Darrell that I almost forgot why I'd come to Brighton. We were on our way back to the station when I asked him if he knew where Charlie was.

He said he had no idea, hadn't heard from him in years. Even joked about him becoming a stockbroker. I didn't understand why it was funny when he said it — I didn't know Charlie had been a musician when he met Jude. Darrell told me Charlie had written a song about her. About her eyes. My eyes, Darrell said, and he kissed me. I wrote in my diary that it was my first proper kiss. A sweet kiss.

He asked me to come and see him again. I wrote that I would've done anything he asked at that moment. And I would. I was thirteen and had just been kissed for the first time. I couldn't see anything wrong in it. I was in love.

158

But Harry reappeared, furious at being abandoned, and grabbed my arm to take me home.

I remember we walked away, me looking back as Harry frog-marched me off. Darrell stood in the middle of the pavement, surrounded by shoppers and holidaymakers, looking at me until we turned the corner and I burst into tears again.

Harry was telling me to pull myself together — I expect she was a bit frightened about the state I was in. She'd never seen me like that. I'd never been like that. Normally, I was the sensible one, soothing and calming her when she was upset or angry, but she was the nurse that day.

She went to the toilet on the train and got some loo roll to mop me up, but it was as if something had broken free inside me.

Harry thought I was crying because it'd been a disaster — she hadn't seen the sweet kiss on the lips — and she tried to help by saying horrible things about Darrell.

'He smells,' she said. 'Like stale bread. I don't think he washes.'

I told her he didn't know where my dad was and pretended to go to sleep so I wouldn't have to talk.

Harry let it go — she got bored easily, luckily — and started talking about the man at the sweet stall who'd chatted her up.

He'd had horrible spots but she got a free candy floss.

31

Monday, 2 April 2012

Jude

The kettle was boiling furiously — she'd forgotten to close the lid again — and she turned it off at the plug. She'd been like that all day, losing things, putting things in the wrong place. Her head was full of Will.

'For goodness' sake,' she said loudly. 'You're too old to be getting in a state over a man.' And she laughed, light-headed with the feelings that were re-emerging.

'I wonder what he looks like now?' she thought for the umpteenth time, smoothing her hair and holding her head high to stretch the creases in her neck.

She dialled Emma's number for the tenth time and put the receiver down before it connected. She desperately wanted to talk to someone about Will, but, after last week, she knew her daughter wouldn't want to hear about it. But Emma was the only person who knew Will as she did. *She'll have got used to the idea by now*, Jude told herself as she picked up the phone again.

'Emma, it's me,' she said. 'How is the work going?'

'Oh. Hello. I was going to ring you to thank

you for lunch last Sunday,' Emma said.

'I'm sorry I said that about you getting ill, Em,' Jude said. She needed to make the peace as quickly as possible so they could move on to Will.

'That's OK,' Emma said, her voice lighter. 'I'm sorry I was so moody. I've been a bit tired.'

'You're probably working too hard. Anyway, it was good to see you. And to share my news.'

Emma's silence was as loud as a clanging bell, but Jude ignored it, chattering on determinedly about Will's call, where she might meet her ex-boyfriend, what she might wear, what they might talk about.

When Jude finally drew breath, Emma said, 'I wonder what he looks like now?'

'I was just thinking the same thing, Em,' she'd gushed. 'He was always so handsome, wasn't he? We were all in love with him, weren't we?'

'Umm, well, I wasn't,' Emma said so quietly that Jude had to strain to hear her.

'What did you say?'

'I said I wasn't,' Emma repeated, more loudly.

'Oh, Em, you were. You were always there, hanging on his every word. You even went to that party with him. Don't you remember?'

She could see Emma, all eyes and jailbait legs, standing in the doorway of the kitchen, drawing Will's attention away from her. Jude got in a huff about it sometimes and Will had laughed her out of her jealousy.

'Well, he certainly made a big impact on me,' Emma said. 'He did that.'

'There you are,' Jude said.

161

'Any adult man would have done,' Emma said. 'If you remember.'

'Oh God, let's not go down the long-lost-daddy route, Em. Will was not your father.'

'No,' Emma said. 'He wasn't.'

She hesitated, and Jude waited for her to say it.

'And he made you throw me out when I was sixteen,' Emma said.

'He didn't,' Jude snapped. 'It was my own decision, based on your behaviour. You were impossible to live with and it was driving a wedge between us.'

'Between you and me, or you and him?' Emma said.

'Both. You were trying to force him out with your lies and tantrums.'

'*Lies?*'

'Saying you'd seen him chatting up other women. Trying to destroy our relationship. You can't deny it, Emma.'

'I'm not denying it. I did see him chatting up that woman down our street.'

Jude was furious all over again — with her daughter and herself. 'It was all perfectly innocent,' she hissed. 'She denied it completely.'

'Well, she would, wouldn't she?' Emma said.

'Look, I know I wasn't the perfect mother, but you weren't the perfect daughter, either.'

'But you were the adult, Jude,' Emma said, their discussion returning to well-worn lines. 'Anyway, I'm just surprised you want to see him again now. He did leave you.'

'Things are different now,' Jude said firmly, as

162

if closing the subject. But a voice whispered in her ear, *And I am so lonely.*

I should have carried on working. Stupid to have retired early.

She'd given up being a lawyer when her parents died and left her a bit of money. 'I'm sick of it all,' she'd said. 'I'll be a lady of leisure instead. I'll go to afternoon concerts and museums.' But she hadn't got into the swing of having spare time. She chafed against it constantly. Against life, really.

'Well, it's up to you, Jude,' said Emma. 'But be careful.'

Afterwards, the phrase echoed in Jude's head. But she silenced it. *Things have changed,* she told herself.

32

Tuesday, 3 April 2012

Emma

My head is full of Will Burnside and I find I've doodled a stick man on my notepad. My pencil has gouged deep into the paper, as I re-run my final days in Howard Street. The house reeked of disappointment. It seemed to drip down the walls and taint the food.

I can remember the hiss of the whispers between Jude and Will, the staccato urgency of phone calls and the closing doors. My exclusion. How could Jude say I was in love with Professor Will?

The drawing is on the same sheet as the reporter's name. Kate Waters. I trace over the letters with my pen as I think about how I can talk to her without showing my hand. I need to know what she knows. Maybe put her off the track. Away from me.

I could mention the drug addicts, I think, and stop drawing.

I scroll down through the chapter I'm working on and write down the first name I come to.

'Hello, I am Anne Robinson and I used to live in Howard Street.' I try it out. 'Did you know there was a house of drug addicts in the street? I think the baby belonged to one of them.'

It sounds stilted and scripted so I have another go, trying to make it sound more natural. 'Hello,' I say again, sounding even more forced.

'Oh forget it,' I say and throw my pen across the room.

But I know I'm going to do it. It's a good idea. She'll go looking for the sad kids. Since Jude mentioned them, I've tried to remember them — I think they must have lived at number 81 — but I can only recall them as a group, not individuals, with their dirty hair and stick-thin arms tattooed with needle tracks. 'The living dead,' Will used to call them.

What if she asks questions? I think, biting the skin round my fingers. I start writing down details I remember. There was a girl called Carrie. They were there for years. Or it seemed like years. They'd gone before I left, in 1985, I think. The landlord cleared them out early one morning. All their stuff was on the pavement — smashed cups, spilled bags of pasta, stained sheets and old jumpers. The addicts didn't take anything with them. It all stayed until the next time the bin men came round and was shovelled aboard the lorry. I'd forgotten all that until today. Packed it away with everything else.

OK, I've got my story. I chivvied myself back to the task in hand. I dialled the number for the *Daily Post* and waited.

'*Daily Post*, how can I help you?' a woman chirruped.

'Er, can I talk to Kate Waters, please?' I reply, already sounding like an imposter.

165

'Putting you through.'

'Hello, Kate Waters,' a voice says. And it begins.

My carefully crafted opening sentence vanishes from my mind and I stutter, 'Hello, is that Kate Waters?' even though she's just said so.

'Yes.' The voice is crisper now.

'Sorry, it's just I've never spoken to a reporter before,' I burble.

'That's OK,' she says. 'How can I help you, er . . . ?'

For a second I can't remember the name I've chosen, then blurt, 'Anne. Anne Robinson.'

'So, Anne, how can I help you?'

'It's about the baby on the building site,' I say, and I hear an 'Oh' under her breath. 'You see, I used to live in Howard Street.'

'Did you?' she says. 'When was that, Anne?'

'Well, early seventies to mid eighties. I read your story the other week and I thought I'd ring you.'

'I am so glad you did, Anne,' she says. She's using my name all the time and I keep thinking, *Who's Anne?*

'How old were you then? Did it jog a memory, Anne?' she adds.

'Sort of,' I say. Mustn't sound too sure. 'I was in my teens when I left. We rented, my mum and me.' *I'm telling her too much. Adding details that aren't on my pad. Need to keep to the plan.* 'It's just that there used to be a house full of drug addicts down the road — number 81, I think — on heroin and stuff — and I wondered if they could be connected to this. To the baby.'

166

'Right. That's so interesting. What number did they live at? Did you know any of them? Can you recall any of their names?'

The questions pile up in front of me and I sit and breathe deeply while she carries on digging into my lies.

'I think one was called Carrie,' I offer. 'But I didn't talk to them. No one did, really. They got thrown out by the landlord when the neighbours complained about the mess and the smell.'

'Which neighbours?' Kate asked.

'I'm not sure,' I say.

'Actually, it's brilliant that you've rung,' Kate Waters says. 'I'm tracking down people who lived in Howard Street in the seventies to ask them if they remember anything. Any births or disappearances.'

She's beginning to talk about what she knows and I push for more information. 'Tracking who down? Who have you found?'

'Hold on,' she says. 'I've got a list. Would you mind if I read it to you to see if you recognize anyone?'

'Course,' I say. 'It's such a mystery, isn't it . . . ?'

'Absolutely. The police seem to have no idea what happened,' Kate says and I breathe a little easier. But then she adds, 'I'm pursuing quite an interesting line at the moment. A bit of a long shot, but could be an amazing story.'

'Really?' I say, my voice all squeaky. But she interrupts, reading the list of Howard Street inhabitants before I can ask another question.

Jude is on the list and I hesitate — just for a

167

beat — before saying 'No.' I hope she doesn't notice and I distract her with a bit of info about Mrs Speering and ask her if she's been to Howard Street.

'What? Oh yeah,' she says. 'I've been there couple of times — I'm going later, actually. To the pub there.'

'The Royal Oak,' I say.

'That's it. Your old local, I imagine,' she says, and I mutter something about being under age.

She laughs and goes back to the names, and when she gets to the end, she says, 'That's funny. There's no Anne Robinson on my list.'

'No, well, like I said, I was just a child so I wouldn't have been on the electoral register,' I say quickly.

'Course. But you said you lived with your mum, didn't you? She'd be on the list, wouldn't she?'

'Umm, yes.'

'Let me have another look. No, no Robinson.'

'It's my married name,' I blurt. I look at my pad, searching my script for answers, but there's nothing left to say.

Must end this quickly before she asks any more.

I wrap my fist in my cardigan and bang on the desk.

'Oh, there's someone at the door. Look, I'll have to go . . . '

'But Anne,' she says, 'I've got loads to ask you. Can I have your number and I'll ring you back?'

'Sorry, sorry, I've got to go,' I repeat weakly

and put the phone down.

I write down everything she's said and start to plan what I'll say the next time I ring.

33

Wednesday, 4 April 2012

Kate

It took two days for Sparkes, Angela Irving and the officer on the case to speak and for Angela's DNA test to be booked.

'It's only three phone calls,' Kate said to Joe. 'How can it take this long to make an appointment?'

Her frustration was amplified by the cat-and-mouse game she was playing with the news editor and his sudden interest in putting Kate on every story that landed on his desk.

She had managed to kill off three of Terry's ideas before Bob Sparkes finally left a message on her mobile. 'Contact made with Angela Irving and have passed on her details to the London boys. Speak soon.'

Before she could call him back, Angela phoned. She was so agitated she forgot to say hello.

'Kate, I'm coming up to London tomorrow. I said I'd rather come to them than do it here. They want to test me to match against Alice . . . the baby.'

'Hi Angela,' Kate said, trying to sound neutral. She knew that, despite herself, her feelings for the bereaved mother had been affected by the new information from DI Rigby. He'd talked about an Angela she hadn't known and the words 'cold fish' had stuck in her head. 'It's great that they are doing the tests, but let's not get too far ahead of ourselves.'

'Yes, sorry. But I can't help it. You can't imagine what it feels like, after all these years, to be so close to finding out.'

'Of course. But the news may not be good, Angela,' Kate said.

Angela paused. 'I know. I'm trying to keep calm. But it is so hard. And I'm not even sure what would be good news. Whatever the results show, it'll be bad news, really, won't it? If it *is* her, my baby is dead. And if it isn't, I am still in this terrible limbo. But there may be some hope. Oh God, I can't think straight.'

'Of course, you can't. You must be going through hell,' Kate soothed. 'It must be so emotional for you. And your husband.'

'Nick? Oh yes, he's as anxious as I am,' Angela said.

Kate noted the change in tone. 'Is your husband coming with you tomorrow?' she asked.

There was another pause. 'I haven't asked him yet. I think he'll be too busy,' Angela said.

She hasn't told him, Kate thought. *How interesting.* She moved the conversation swiftly on. 'Who did you talk to in the Met, Angela?'

'A DI Sinclair.'

'And how did he sound when he spoke to you?' Kate wondered how seriously the Met were taking this new lead.

171

'Friendly. But he didn't give anything away. Just said they would do swab tests and come back to me.'

'Nothing about any forensics so far?'

'No. I'm not sure they've even started, to be honest. That's what DI Sparkes said. He's a nice man,' Angela added.

'He is. So would you like to meet afterwards for a coffee?' Kate said. *Keep her close. Just in case.*

'Lovely, thanks. The appointment is at ten. Mr Sinclair said it would only take a few minutes.'

'But they'll want to talk to you about Alice as well, Angela. It won't just be a mouth swab. It would be a good idea to take all the documents you've got. Everything helps.'

'Yes, I will. Shall I give you a call when I've finished?'

'Great. I'll come and meet you.'

★   ★   ★

When Kate rang Bob Sparkes back, he answered immediately.

'Kate,' he said. 'All sorted?'

'Yes thanks, Bob. Angela is coming up to town tomorrow. She's in a terrible state. I hope they're nice to her. What did DI Sinclair say when you called him?' she asked, throwing in the name to show she was on the case.

'Not very hopeful. He thinks it's pretty impossible — identifying an infant after what is probably decades underground is incredibly difficult. Newborn babies don't have fully

172

formed bones so there isn't much material to test for DNA. And what there is might be too degraded to be useful. And with a newborn you know that he or she won't be on the database and so we are straight into the imprecise world of familial DNA, trying to find parents from, effectively, half a profile. It really doesn't look likely that a match will be found.'

'Have they done any tests yet?' she asked.

'The basics, but lots more to do. He did say there were what looked like shreds of paper and a plastic carrier bag sticking to the remains, so it can't be earlier than the sixties — that's when plastic carriers first appeared in the UK — but nothing more concrete on dates. Look, don't get your hopes up on this one, Kate. Let's see.'

She refused to join in with his negativity. 'Of course it's an outside chance but I've got a feeling about this, Bob,' she said, and heard him laugh at the other end of the phone.

'You've always got a feeling, Kate. Speak to you soon.'

And he was gone.

'What did he say?' Joe asked.

'Hey, are you earwigging on my every conversation?' she snapped.

'Couldn't help overhearing. And I *am* working on the story with you,' he said. *He's learning*, she thought.

'OK. In a nutshell: the Met hasn't started the full forensics yet; the copper with the file thinks it's an impossible case; babies are difficult to test; blah blah. Onwards and upwards, I say.'

Joe smiled and nodded.

173

'Look, while the detectives are buggering about with the DNA, why don't we look at the Howard Street residents from the sixties and seventies?' Kate said. 'I had a funny phone call the other day from a woman who called herself Anne Robinson. Pretty sure it wasn't her real name, but she said she lived in Howard Street around the right time and there was a house full of drug addicts in the road. She wouldn't leave a number or anything, but it's worth checking out. We have no idea what happened to that baby or who was living round there. And we can get out of here for the rest of the day.

'Thought I'd show Joe some old-style investigation tricks, if you don't need me,' she called across to Terry.

'Yeah, yeah, fine,' he said, waving her goodbye. 'Don't lose him . . . '

★ ★ ★

Parking near Woolwich Library was murder, but Kate finally found a space and reversed, badly, into it. *I hate bloody parallel parking,* she screamed in her head, and tried to have cooling thoughts before peeling herself off her seat.

'Come on,' she said to Joe, who was scrolling through Facebook on his phone. 'We're going to look at something made of paper for a change.'

In the reference section, he trailed behind her, eyes still fixed on his phone, as she asked for old electoral registers for Howard Street.

The librarian sniffed at the request — *They must train them to do that,* Kate thought — but

174

brought her the voters' lists for the area from 1960 and 1970 without any further comment.

'Thanks,' Kate said to her departing back and pulled the bulky, unbound documents towards her. The pages had curled at the edges over the years and she wondered when they had last been turned.

The residents' names were listed by road and house number and she went straight to Howard Street and the terrace where the baby had been found.

'We're looking specifically at numbers 61 to 67, Joe. The houses that backed on to the building-site area. Oh, for God's sake, put that phone down . . . ' she hissed.

He did as he was told and sat expectantly at a Formica table. Kate knew she was still glowing from her *Top Gear* rush-hour-parking challenge. It had triggered a flush and she could feel every inch of her skin pulsing with heat.

'Are you all right, Kate?' Joe said. 'You look a bit red.'

'I'm fine. Bit hot in here, that's all,' she said tetchily.

'Oh, right,' Joe said.

She knew what he was thinking. Menopause. And for menopause, read old, irrational, past it, a woman. She bridled, furious that he should judge her professionalism on her oestrogen levels. He probably couldn't even spell 'oestrogen'. But the lecture would have to wait. She had work to do. She forced a smile and thought cold thoughts to make the flush recede. She'd read about it in a Well Woman leaflet once. Nonsense, but anything was worth a go.

She pushed the 1960s towards him. 'You do this lot. Write down the names and dates of everyone who lived in the terrace. And at number 81 — the drug den. Then we'll look for where they are now when we get back to the office.'

She pulled the 1970s towards her.

After ten minutes, they had a list. It was shorter than Kate had expected — the folk of Howard Street had been long-term residents in the sixties and the transition from family homes to rented bedsits and flats had taken a few years after that.

'How many have you got?' she asked.

Joe counted them slowly. 'Twelve,' he said. 'Nobody moved in or out. Married couples, I think, with adult children, maybe.'

'Great,' she said. 'Any names we know? Laidlaw, for instance?'

'No. One of the families was the Smiths, at number 65.'

'Damn,' she said, too loudly, alarming the man reading *The Times* at the next table. 'Sorry,' she mouthed.

'Any more unusual names?' she asked Joe. 'Smith is a nightmare.'

'Speering, Baker and Walker,' he reeled off.

'Right,' she said, checking her notes. 'I've got two of the same families in the early seventies. But everything was changing. Look, there are six different names for number 63 by 1974 — and they are all singletons. People moved on every couple of years.'

'The people at 81 don't look very interesting,' Joe said. 'It's the same couple throughout the sixties.'

'And then no names on my list. The woman who rang in said they were squatters or something, so there's unlikely to be an official trace. We'll ask around. We've got our hands full anyway.'

Joe ran his finger down the page. 'There are loads of them. How will we find them?'

'We don't need to find all of them. Just some. You'll see. Find one person and they'll lead you to others. Have a little faith, Joe.'

Kate tidied up her careful notes and Joe photographed the pages with his mobile phone.

34

Thursday, 5 April 2012

Kate

Angela looked different somehow when she emerged from the revolving doors. She looked older.

'The tests have all been done. Now we just have to wait,' she told Kate. 'I feel completely drained.'

Kate slipped her arm through Angela's and squeezed it. 'It's a big thing to do, Angela. You are being very brave. Come on, let's get you a coffee and you can tell me all about it.'

Joe offered to carry her bag of documents and led the way round the back of Westminster Abbey to the café Kate had picked earlier.

Angela slumped down in her seat and wrapped her hands round her cup to warm them.

'Have I done the right thing, Kate?' she said finally. 'I'm not sure I want to know the answer now. I'm scared.'

'It is going to be difficult, whatever they find,' Kate said, leaning forward. 'But at least there is a chance the waiting will be over.'

Angela nodded. 'Yes, that's true. I need that to be over. It is killing me. Slowly.'

Joe pushed a pack of biscuits across the table

towards her. 'Have one of these, Angela,' he said.

He doesn't know what else to do, Kate thought. *Hasn't done grief before, I suppose.*

'Thanks, dear,' Angela said and took one. 'I'm sorry I'm being so negative,' she added.

'You're not, Angela,' Kate said. 'What you are feeling is perfectly natural. I don't know how you've kept going over all these years. You are amazing.'

Joe nodded enthusiastically from the other side of the table and Angela half smiled.

'Shall I tell you what Joe and I have been doing?' Kate said, moving things along.

'Yes, do,' Angela said and picked up the biscuit from her saucer.

'We've been looking at the people who used to live in Howard Street, where the baby was found,' she said.

'From the sixties and seventies,' Joe chimed in.

'Will you have a look at the list of names we've got, to see if you recognize any of them, Angela?' Kate said. 'You can say no,' she added.

She pushed the list across the table. She had included Marian Laidlaw, Nick Irving's girl-friend. Kate wanted to see if Angela had known her.

Angela seemed happy to be distracted from the gathering gloom. She scanned through the names quickly and then went back through slowly, her mouth working silently as she tried them out.

'No, nobody,' she said, looking up. 'I am so sorry.'

'Well, it was worth a try,' Kate said, swallowing her disappointment with a mouthful of coffee.

179

'Anyway, what else did the detective say?'

Angela talked about the differences in dealing with the police in 1970 and 2012 and Kate drifted back to the names.

'Walker,' she said out loud, stopping Angela dead and making Joe slop his coffee into the saucer.

'Walker?' he said. 'What do you mean?'

'Sorry, thinking out loud. I spoke to a Miss Walker in Howard Street the first time I went there. Old lady with a horrible dog. She could be one of the Walkers who used to live at number 61.'

The other two looked at her.

'Drink up,' she told Joe. 'We'll go back. And we can drop you off at the station, Angela. What time train did you plan to catch?'

Angela took hold of her arm. 'Please can I come with you? I want to see where the baby was found.'

Kate nodded. 'Of course. Sorry, I should have thought. I don't suppose we could do some photographs there, Angela? We'll need them for the story if the police tests are positive and we might not have time on the day.'

Angela looked doubtful.

'And it could prompt someone to phone in,' Kate added.

That clinched it and Angela nodded her assent.

Kate put a quick call in to the picture desk as they walked back to her car.

★ ★ ★

Mick the photographer rang her while she was driving, but she didn't want to put him on loudspeaker. His use of the f word was legendary and she suspected Angela was not the sort to be impressed by casual swearing. *Let's not scare anyone off*, she thought, handing her phone to Joe to deal with.

'Hello, Mick,' he chirped. 'Er, how's what hanging?'

Kate pulled a 'You boys!' grimace in the mirror, hoping to catch Angela's eye.

'Yes, we're on our way now. Howard Street. OK. See you there,' Joe said, muttering, 'I will,' before turning the phone off.

'You will what?' Kate asked.

'Nothing,' Joe said, his cheeks glowing. 'Just Mick mucking about.'

★ ★ ★

Miss Walker was out and the machines on the building site had been silenced.

'Lunchtime,' Kate said. 'Let's go to the pub and wait for Mick — he won't be long.'

The bar at the Royal Oak was three deep in damp donkey jackets and a forest of arms was waving at the staff.

'We'll never get a drink,' Kate said. 'Let's sit down and hope the rush is over quickly.'

Joe laughed. 'I bet I can get us one,' he said. Finally in his element.

'OK, off you go. What do you want to drink, Angela?'

'An orange juice, please,' she said, tucking her

181

coat under her as she perched on a stool.

'I'll have a fizzy water — and bring some crisps. You must be starving, Angela,' Kate added.

Joe threw himself into the throng and five minutes later emerged with a tray of glasses and three bags of ready salted.

'I'm impressed,' Kate said and Angela laughed with her. 'Now, for lesson two in Being a Reporter . . . '

'Actually,' Joe said, 'it was easier than I thought. The landlord spotted you and served me first.'

Kate grinned and raised her glass to the man behind the bar. He bowed back at her.

When Mick bowled in, he clocked them and stopped at the bar first, slopping his pint as he set it down on the teetotallers' table.

'Hi Kate,' he said. 'How's it going?'

Kate introduced Angela and he shook her hand warmly.

There was a silence while he took a long draught of his beer, then the conversation restarted. Kate kept glancing at the door behind Angela to keep an eye out for John, the site manager. They'd need his help to do the photos on the spot where the baby was buried.

John strolled through the door ten minutes later and nodded to Kate when she stood to greet him.

'John!' she called. 'Good to see you. Can I get you a drink?'

He nodded. 'Wouldn't say no,' he said. 'Saw your story.'

'Yes. Peter's a lovely bloke,' she said. 'How is he doing?'

'OK, I think. He was happy with what you wrote,' the site manager said and Kate smiled.

'I'm really glad. Look, I wondered if I could ask another favour . . .'

It took two shandies and a packet of peanuts to persuade him, but finally he agreed. 'You can have five minutes before the work begins again,' he said. 'And I mean five minutes.'

She squeezed his arm. 'Course. I'll just get my photographer.'

Mick hated it when she called him 'her photographer'.

'I'm not your fucking monkey,' he hissed when she returned to the table. And she smiled apologetically at Joe and Angela in case they'd heard.

'Not in front of the children,' she hissed back as they walked to the door.

★ ★ ★

Angela had posed nervously in the churned mud, beside the police tape around the site of the grave. Kate had expected her to cry, but she had just stood there, her hands clutched in front of her, her eyes wide and never still.

Mick talked to her as he took the pictures, calming her and reassuring her that it would all be over soon.

But Kate knew it wouldn't. There was a long road ahead. She watched the scene, noting the anguish on Angela's face, her hair blown about,

183

the mud streaks on her tights, the wary glances at the tape that marked the baby's last resting place. These were the details the readers would want to know about, that would bring them straight to the spot where Kate stood. She wouldn't be able to write it yet, but she had it all in her head.

John appeared from his Portakabin after fifteen minutes and shouted for them to stop. 'The machines are starting up. You need to go.'

'Just one more, mate,' Mick called — the traditional cry of the photographer — and fired off more shots of Angela bending to reach through the tape to touch the earth.

'Now, please. Mate,' John shouted again.

Kate went over to Angela and took her by the arm to steady her as they walked across the deep ruts. Joe followed behind with her handbag. Like a funeral cortège.

35

Tuesday, 10 April 2012

Angela

It'd been a difficult and long weekend, but they had weathered Easter as a family and it was over now. Nick would be back at work today and she could stop tiptoeing around the house. He'd shouted at her on Saturday, as she knew he would, when she finally told him about going to London and having the DNA test.

'What, you sneaked off without telling me?' he'd roared. She hoped the neighbours were out.

'Stop shouting, Nick,' she'd said. 'The neighbours will hear. Look, you were so busy and worried about work, I didn't want to add to your stress.'

He'd looked at her, trying to detect the lie, but she'd kept her wifey face on.

'I don't want you getting all het up again,' he said. 'I'm saying this for your own good, Angie.'

Normally, she'd have smiled at him and thanked him for being so caring. But she couldn't. Everything was churning in her head, the hope and the hurt and betrayal rising to the surface after so many years.

'I won't get all het up, Nick. But this is something I have to do. For Alice.'

185

At the mention of her name, Nick had closed down and disappeared into the garage, emerging only for silent meals.

Angela had cleaned the house to vent her fury, wielding the hoover like a weapon, crashing it into skirting boards and doors, leaving chips of paint in her wake as she thrust her way through the rooms. In her head she was screaming her accusations: *You never wanted Alice. She was the price you paid for being unfaithful. That's what you felt.*

I bet you saw that woman again.

She hated herself for thinking it, but her internal rants almost always ended with that. She couldn't help it. It was always there, waiting to torture her. She'd never said it out loud to Nick. What would she do if he admitted it? Better not to know.

They'd slept back-to-back on Saturday night, not even saying goodnight. She'd lain awake, trying to quell her thoughts, and had finally drifted into troubled, sheet-twisting sleep. When she'd dredged herself awake, Nick was lying beside her, eyes open, studying the ceiling.

'Hello, love,' she'd said through force of habit.

He'd grunted.

'Patrick is bringing the children round this morning so we can give them their Easter eggs. I thought we could take them to the park,' she said, determined to wear him down.

Nick grunted again, still looking at the ceiling.

'What are you thinking, Nick?' she said.

'That this will never be over,' he said, his voice flat. 'That it will never go away.'

'*It*? Do you mean our daughter?' she'd said, sitting up.

Nick had rolled away from her, but she couldn't let it go.

'She *is* our daughter. And I need to know, Nick, if Alice and I can count on you.'

'For God's sake, Angie, what does that even mean? Whatever the police say, it will be bad news — either it isn't Alice and you will be devastated, or it is and our baby is dead. Look, Angie, it won't bring her back. We don't need tests. Our baby is dead and gone. You know that in your heart of hearts, don't you? We don't need graves and bones and policemen. It's too late for that. We need to let it — her — go.'

'You may feel that, but I need to know, Nick. I need to know for certain where she is, so that I can find some peace and say goodbye properly. The fact that you don't want to makes me sad, but it won't stop me,' Angela said, hugging herself against the growing storm.

'I know you never felt the same as me about Alice,' she went on, and felt him stiffen beside her.

'What do you mean?' he said. But she knew he knew. They hadn't had this row for a long time, but its legacy was as instantly toxic as a nuclear winter.

'I'm not discussing it, Angela. It was forty bloody years ago. It was one night and I've said I was sorry. There is nothing else I can say. Making me suffer won't bring Alice back. It wasn't my fault. I wasn't the one who left her on her own.'

Her gasp of pain silenced him. He knew he'd gone too far. Way too far. He reached for his wife's hand, unclenching the fingers of her fists.

'God, Angie, why do you do this? Make us say things we'll regret? You know I don't blame you. Of course I don't.'

'I know,' she said. But she didn't. After all, she *had* left Alice on her own.

The shouting was over in seconds — it always was, that was their way — but the silence lasted much longer. These rare rows left them both shattered and unable to think about anything else.

It was Angela who got out of bed first, pulled on her dressing gown and went to make tea.

★　★　★

By the time Tuesday came, a grumpy peace had been declared — the grandchildren had forced them to put on brave faces. Nick had held her hand when they walked to the playground down the road and she'd made him his favourite dinner.

'Bye, love,' he'd said that morning and kissed her on the top of her head.

'I'll call you later,' she'd said.

She tried to sit still and read her magazine. But she couldn't move on, getting stuck on the same sentence, the same words, over and over again. She made cups of tea that grew cold in a row beside her. She felt she could hear her heart beating.

She hadn't told Nick when the DNA results

were due — she'd been vague. She needed to deal with them herself, first.

They'd said it would normally take two days for the results. The police. But Easter would delay things. There was nothing they could do about bank holidays. But they must ring today.

She checked again to make sure her phone had not switched itself off or gone to Silent. The blank screen looked accusingly at her. She rang Kate.

'Hi, just wondered if you'd heard anything,' she heard herself say.

Kate hadn't, but said she would call and try to get a steer on how things were going.

Angela sat with the phone in her hand.

When it rang, five minutes later, she yelped and cut off the call by fumbling and pressing the wrong button. It rang again immediately.

'Kate? Sorry about that. What did they say?'

'They say they'll probably — and they wouldn't promise more than probably, Angela — have a result tomorrow,' Kate said.

Angela gripped the phone tighter. 'They said it should take two days, Kate. They've had five! Did they say if there were any indications yet?'

'No, they're keeping everything close to their chests, I'm afraid. Look, I know how horrible this must be, but we have to sit tight, Angela.'

Angela knew it made sense, but the idea of sitting tight for another day made her feel sick.

'Why don't you go and do something? Go to the shops or see a friend,' Kate said. 'Just make sure you have your phone with you all the time so I can contact you.'

'Yes, maybe. You will ring as soon as you hear, won't you? Promise me,' Angela said, hating herself for sounding so needy. So desperate.

'Of course,' Kate said.

36

Tuesday, 10 April 2012

Kate

She was scrabbling in her bag — 'the bottomless pit' as it was known by Steve and every photographer she'd worked with — for a pen that worked when the phone rang a second time.

Bob Sparkes's name flashed up and she threw her bag to the floor.

'Bob,' she said, too loudly.

'Sorry, caught you at a bad time? Shall I call back?'

'No, no,' Kate said. 'Sorry, all a bit frantic here. How are you?'

'OK. I've just had a heads up from DI Sinclair. It's a match.'

For a split second, she wasn't sure what she'd heard.

No preamble, no foreplay. Straight to it.

'Bloody brilliant!' she crowed. 'Bloody buggering brilliant!'

'Yeah. That about sums it up,' Sparkes said, his voice quickening despite himself.

'Don't come the world-weary copper with me, Bob Sparkes,' Kate said. 'You are as pleased as I am. Oh my God, wait until I tell Angela! I'll go down to Winchester right now and tell her. I'll take Mick. We want a photo of the moment she finds out.'

'Hang on, Kate,' Sparkes tried, but she wasn't listening.

'We can run it in tomorrow's paper. ALICE FOUND AFTER 40 YEARS. OR THE MOMENT A MOTHER FOUND HER BABY . . . '

'Kate!' Sparkes tried again.

'Sorry, Bob. What were you saying?'

'I was saying that you need to hang on. The DI is not going to tell Angela until tomorrow. He wants to wait for all the paperwork to arrive on his desk and then go in person down to Hampshire.'

'You said it was a match.'

'It is — the lab phoned him this morning to tell him — but he's a bit of a jobsworth and wants all the results in writing before he pronounces. That will be tomorrow.'

'How ridiculous!' Kate snapped. 'What would happen if I rang him and said I'd heard the DNA samples matched . . . '

'He'd know we'd spoken and I would get a major rocket,' Sparkes said calmly. 'I'm trusting you to keep this to yourself for another day.'

'But in twenty-four hours he'll be telling everyone,' Kate said. 'We'll lose the exclusive, and it has been all our hard work to find the link with Angela.'

Sparkes didn't respond. She was furious, but she knew she couldn't burn Sparkes by revealing him as her source. He was one of her best contacts and she needed him. She'd think of another way to force the Met's hand.

'Right,' she said, neither confirming nor denying her intentions. 'I'm so grateful for the call, Bob. I owe you big time,' she went on, hurrying him off the line. 'I'll keep you updated.'

★　★　★

Terry was in his goldfish bowl, the glass-walled cupboard where staff could watch him bollocking others with the Mute button on.

Kate slipped in quietly and sat on the naughty chair opposite her boss.

'What do you want?' he said without looking up.

Bugger, he's grumpy, she thought. *Post-bank-holiday blues that are going to last all week . . .*

'I've got a cracker of a story,' she said and he looked up.

'OK, you've got my attention, Kate,' he said.

'It's the baby buried on the building site.'

He sighed. 'Oh, that,' he said.

'Don't sigh, Terry. There's been a break-through, but I've got a problem and I need your wise head,' she said.

Terry nodded his wise head and closed his laptop. 'Go on, then.'

Kate paused. *Make him wait*, she told herself, counting to five like the host of a bad quiz show.

'The baby is Alice Irving. They've found her after forty-odd years. I've just had a tip-off.'

'Fuck!' Terry said. His highest compliment.

'Quite,' Kate said.

'We need to make some space in the paper. Where's the mother?' Terry said, his eyes bulging

193

with excitement as he got out of his chair to perch on the desk, practically knee-to-knee with Kate.

'Hang on, what's the problem?' he added, suddenly remembering how the conversation had started.

'Well, we have to sit on it until tomorrow or I'll lose my best contact.'

There was a beat of silence, then Terry breathed, 'Christ all bloody mighty.'

He got off the desk and paced the tiny room while he digested the implications. 'How many people know? Coppers and lab people. Must be a dozen, at least. It'll leak. Too good a story not to leak.'

Kate nodded. She knew it was what he'd say.

He stopped pacing, and when he got back on his perch, he looked businesslike.

'Right. How do we get it confirmed without your contact being fingered? Pity Gordon has gone — he'd have sorted this out. I can't even ring him at home — he's taken Maggie to the Costa del Sol with his redundancy money.'

'I'm working on it, Terry. I think Angela is the key. I'll go back down to Winchester and get her to talk to the copper who is holding the info.'

'Good. You can do it, Kate. My star reporter.'

Kate smiled — modestly, she hoped — but inside she was fizzing with pleasure. 'Thanks, Terry. But let's not tell the editor yet.'

Terry's happy face disappeared.

'What?' Kate said.

'I'd love to give him some good news this morning, that's all.'

'He'll do his nut if he thinks he's got the story and then we have to pull it.'

'Yeah, yeah,' Terry said. 'Ring me every hour. And refile that backgrounder you and the Boy Wonder have been working on.'

She rose quickly, relieved it had gone so well, and Terry came round to hug her. Kate went scarlet at the unexpected grapple with her boss. He was not normally a demonstrative man — that had been beaten out of him by executive bullies years ago, she suspected — but he was clearly as excited as she was.

She hoped the Crime man hadn't seen the encounter. He'd make hay out of that. Then she remembered he and the hay had gone. She almost missed him. He'd have said, 'Snogging the boss? Is it pay-rise time?'

Yeah, worth at least an extra two per cent. You should try it, she told his empty chair.

37

Angela

She felt chilled when she saw Kate Waters' car pull up outside. She'd heard it before she saw it. Alert to everything as she waited.

Oh God, it's bad news. It's someone else's baby. She wouldn't have come if it wasn't bad news, she told herself, resting her forehead against the window as she watched the reporter walk up the path and waited for Kate to notice her. When she did, Angela saw her face transform. The reporter smiled and waved.

Angela shouted through the window, 'Is it Alice? Is it her?' But the double-glazed unit stopped her voice dead. She ran to the door and swung it open.

'Is it Alice? Is it her?' she shrieked, and Kate guided her back into the hall.

'Angela, come and sit down,' she said. She looked nervous, but not sad. What did it mean? Angela tried to read her face but couldn't focus on it properly. She noticed there were other people in her hall — the young lad, and the nice photographer from Howard Street. He was shaking her hand and saying something, but Angela couldn't hear him. He and Kate led her

196

into the sitting room and settled her on the sofa. It all seemed to take so long before Kate sat beside her and took her hand.

It's going to be bad news, she thought.

'Angela,' Kate said quietly. 'We've got some news. I wanted to come and tell you face-to-face.'

Angela waited. She could no longer speak but her brain was screaming, *Just tell me!*

Kate moved slightly back from her as she realized Mick was taking pictures of Angela from across the room.

'The police have got the results from the DNA tests, Angela. I haven't had it officially, but I've been told they are a match.'

'*Alice.*' Angela breathed in the name. 'It's Alice.' She didn't hear anything else Kate said. Her head was full of her child. *I've found her.*

She could feel Angela trembling when she took her hand again.

'I'm so pleased for you, Angela,' she said, and the two women sat looking at each other, eyes locked together.

Angela felt she could have sat like that all day, but Mick said, 'Can you look at me, love?' and she turned her face to his camera, not knowing whether to laugh or cry.

Kate stood up to let him get his pictures and went to perch on the arm of an armchair. Joe was standing near the door. He kept looking at Angela and then away again, as if he couldn't bear to see her.

When Mick put his camera down, Kate went back to the sofa.

'You need to ring the officer on the case, Angela,' she told her. 'He said the results would be back by today, didn't he? So you can ring him and ask. He must tell you.'

Kate sounded worried and Angela wondered if she was being told the whole story.

'Is there a problem?' she asked.

Kate looked down at her hands. 'The thing is, Angela, I've been told very much off the record that there is a match, so I need to get it officially before I can write the story. Do you see?'

Angela nodded. She wasn't really sure she did see, but she wanted to help the reporter. She'd found Alice.

'What do you want me to say to DI Sinclair?' she asked.

Kate wrote down the questions to ask and said Angela should insist if the officer wouldn't give her answers.

'You have a right to know. You are Alice's mother and you have waited long enough,' she said.

Angela picked up the phone and dialled the direct line she'd been given.

The detective answered straight away and Angela tried to play her part.

'Hello, DI Sinclair, it's Angela Irving.'

'Mrs Irving, how can I help you?' he said, all businesslike.

'I'm sorry to bother you, but you said you would have the results today and I am going out of my mind, waiting.'

'I know it must be very difficult for you,' DI Sinclair said, his voice softening. 'But I'm just

198

waiting for the results to be typed up.'

'But when will that be?'

'Tomorrow, I hope,' he said.

'I don't think I can wait until tomorrow, DI Sinclair. It is making me ill, the wait,' she said. 'I've waited too long already.'

Kate pointed to the next question she'd written down for Angela.

'Do you know what the results show?' she asked obediently and DI Sinclair hesitated.

'Yes, Mrs Irving. I've had a verbal report from the technicians, but I like to have all the paperwork in front of me before I release the information. And I'd planned to discuss it with you and your husband, face-to-face. I'm sure you can understand my caution.'

'Please tell me what you know, DI Sinclair. I'm begging you.'

There was a silence. Angela looked at Kate and held her breath.

'It's a match, Mrs Irving,' he said finally.

'A match,' she said out loud for Kate's benefit and the reporter punched the air like a tennis player at Wimbledon.

'Yes. The DNA sample we took from you matches the DNA from the remains. The baby's skeleton, I mean.'

'So it is Alice,' Angela said, and started to cry.

'As I said, Mrs Irving, I haven't had it in writing, but yes, it does appear so. I'd still like to come and see you and your husband tomorrow to discuss the results and how we will take the case forward. I'd like to bring a family liaison officer as well. So that you always have a point of contact. Is that OK?'

'Of course, of course. Thank you so much for telling me. I don't know what to say. Please come. What time do you want to come?' she said, falling over the words.

'I'll be with you at nine thirty if that's OK,' he said. 'I'm glad the waiting is over for you. I'll see you tomorrow morning.'

Kate's feet were still dancing when Angela put the phone down.

'Well done, Angela! You did so well!' Kate said. 'Tell me everything he said.'

Angela looked at her, hollow-eyed, the initial euphoria of getting the news draining away rapidly.

'My baby is dead,' she said.

38

Wednesday, 11 April 2012

Emma

I hear the news on the radio. The newsreader with the posh voice, Charlotte someone, says that a missing baby has been found after decades and I freeze. On a building site in Woolwich, she says. A baby called Alice Irving, she says. Taken from a hospital in 1970. And I stare at the radio. This is all wrong. The baby has a name. And a mother.

There's a clip of the mother, saying how relieved and devastated she is. I stand listening in the kitchen and crying with Mrs Irving. I'm as relieved as she is. But for different reasons.

Nobody will be coming to my door. No reckoning. Not yet.

Later, when I go to buy a pint of milk at the corner shop, I see the headlines in the papers and buy the one with the exclusive interview with Alice Irving's mother. I try to read it as I walk home, but I keep stumbling and bumping into garden walls so I put it under my arm in the end. Don't want to look like a mad woman.

At home I read every word, poring over the details, reading some bits out loud. I can't quite take it in, but I feel a sort of euphoria rising in me. Maybe everything is going to be all right.

39

Wednesday, 11 April 2012

Jude

She heard the news on the radio as she waited for the kettle to boil. She was only half listening as she wrote a shopping list in her head, but the words 'Alice Irving' stopped her at natural yoghurt. She turned up the volume until it shrieked in her ears and her neighbour thumped on the wall.

40

Kate

Simon the editor stopped at her desk as soon as he arrived that morning.

'Well, you must be pleased with yourself, Kate,' he said, grinning his yellow smile. 'Great interview and most-read story online.'

She grinned back at him, happy to be back in the sunlit uplands of the editor's favour.

'And you,' Simon said, turning to the hovering figure at his elbow. 'Your first front-page by-line.'

Joe looked as if he might burst with pride. Kate had given him an additional reporting credit — his name in italics at the end of the story where it turned to pages four and five — but the back bench had bumped his name up to join Kate's on the front page. She'd ground her teeth over it when she'd checked the page proof, but she understood. Joe Jackson was the editor's golden child.

'Right, what's today's story, then?' Simon asked. 'What are the police saying? Any leads on who took her?'

Joe looked like a rabbit in the headlights.

'We're talking to the cops, Simon,' Kate said. 'And we've got a second bite at the Angela

203

Irving interview. LIFE WITHOUT ALICE,' Terry called across as he stood to join the impromptu news conference.

'Sounds good,' the editor said and walked off.

Joe looked at Kate and beamed. 'Thank you for giving me a by-line, Kate,' he said. 'I really didn't do much.'

She grunted. Then relented. 'You did a good job, Joe. Now let's stop the back-slapping and find out what happened to baby Alice.'

★ ★ ★

DI Sinclair was not a happy bunny when she called him.

'Did Mrs Irving ring you yesterday, Miss Waters?' he asked. 'Your story was completely premature. I've only just got the file.'

'I called her, DI Sinclair. We'd already done a story with her and I knew the results were due yesterday.'

'Did you ask her to ring me?'

'DI Sinclair, do you really think a woman who has waited forty-odd years to find her child needs telling? Angela Irving was desperate to know.'

'Yes, OK. I just wasn't ready and the press office has been inundated.'

Kate's mouth twitched but she stopped herself from smirking. He'd be able to hear it in her voice.

'It's a big story, DI Sinclair. Anyway,' she said, moving things out of the danger zone, 'what next? Are you setting up a murder inquiry?'

'Not necessarily. We don't know how the baby died yet. We may never know. We haven't got much to work with and the forensic team is only just starting on the other material from the scene. We'll know more in the next few days.'

'So you don't know when it was buried?'

'Not yet. Investigation ongoing.'

'OK. And when are you talking to Mrs Irving?'

Kate knew he'd already been to the house, but wanted the officer to feel he was in control of some information.

'Saw Mr and Mrs Irving this morning. They're helping us with our inquiry.'

'Any links with south-east London?'

'None we can see at the moment. But we're looking. It was a long time ago and people's memories are not what they were.'

'Tell me about it,' Kate joked. 'I can barely remember what I did yesterday let alone in the 1970s.'

'I can't believe that, Kate,' he said, and she ticked the fact that they were now on first-name terms.

'I'll let you get on — I know you must be busy — but thanks so much for talking to me. And let me know if I can help in any way. When you want to put out a public appeal for information.'

'Thanks,' he said. 'I'm planning a press conference, but I'll let you know when.'

'Great,' she said. 'Is there a direct line I can contact you on if we hear anything at the paper? People might contact us direct.'

He gave her his mobile number and told her to call him Andy.

'Speak soon, Andy. Thanks a million,' she said. As soon as the line went dead, she turned to Joe. 'He's onside. Let's get on with it. Where's that list of names from Howard Street? The police must be all over it by now. And let's not forget Marian Laidlaw. Where is she now?'

41

Wednesday, 11 April 2012

Kate

It was Groundhog Day at the Royal Oak. Dolly was still singing, pleading with Jolene over the speakers, and the same backs were facing out from the bar. Kate found herself being treated as a regular by the workmen, who nodded silently at her. She wanted to talk to the landlord again, but she'd have to wait until things quietened down. He noticed her and called across the heads, 'The usual, Kate?' and she laughed and called back her order.

'Can we have a word in a minute?' she asked as he put the glasses down on the bar.

'Sure. But my missus still isn't here. She's the one you should be talking to. She hears everything.'

She and Joe took the same table as last time and he scrolled on his phone while she watched the faces around her. She loved spotting the tell-tale details — the stained trousers that spoke of neglect, the love bites that told of teenage lust, the disguised shaking hand, the blank eyes, the back-combed hair of someone clinging to their youth.

'Kate,' Joe said suddenly.

'Yes, Joe,' she said, turning her attention back to him.

'Miss Walker. We still haven't seen her.'

'Yes, let's do that,' she said, putting down her half-finished drink. 'I wonder if the police have talked to her yet.'

★   ★   ★

They had. Miss Walker was fizzing with excitement when she let them in.

'I had two police officers here. Telling me about them finding Alice Irving. I can't believe it. That little girl buried in Howard Street all those years.'

'Do you remember the case, Miss Walker?'

'Oh yes. Well, they reminded me a bit, but I knew who they were talking about.'

'How do you think Alice ended up here?' Kate said.

'I have no idea,' Miss Walker said. 'Complete mystery, the officers told me.'

Joe sat forward and handed her his phone. 'These were people who lived here in the sixties and seventies, Miss Walker. One of the families is called Walker — are they relatives?' he said and showed her the list.

She put on smeared glasses and peered at the screen, but then handed it back. 'Sorry, I can't read that,' she said.

Kate fished out her notebook. 'Luckily, I used paper,' she said, raising a triumphant eyebrow at her colleague.

Miss Walker pored over the names. 'Oh yes,'

she said. 'This is my aunt and uncle. They lived at number 61 for years. My dad's brother and his wife. We lived the other side of the South Circular — over in Charlton. But I lived at number 63, Howard Street for a few months in the eighties.'

'Wow,' Joe said. 'So you must know all of these people on the list?'

Kate sat back and watched. He was doing well.

Miss Walker read slowly, her hand straying to pat Shorty at her side.

'Well, I knew all of the families in the terrace from visiting my auntie. I used to go most Sundays for tea when I was young. And a couple of the tenants' names ring bells, but they came and went so quickly you didn't really get a chance to get to know them.'

'Are you still in touch with any of the people on the list, Miss Walker?' Kate asked. 'We'd love to talk to them about the area as it was then. They may know something.'

'Oh, well. My aunt and uncle died a long time ago. And they didn't have any children. The Smiths had a son who was older than me, but they all moved north, as far as I know. There are Speerings and Bakers who still live round here. I see June Speering, as was, in the Co-op most weeks. And her daughter, Sarah.'

Joe was scribbling the names in his notebook.

'Who owned the houses in the seventies, Miss Walker?' Kate asked. 'When they were flats and bedsits.'

'Please call me Barbara, dear,' Miss Walker

209

said. 'A horrible man bought them. He was full of himself. Boasted how he knew everyone who was anyone. Mr Soames, he was called — like in the *Forsyte Saga*.'

'Not a fan then, Barbara?' Kate asked.

Miss Walker blinked. 'No,' she said, her voice tight. 'He was vile. Thought he was God's gift. He came round regularly. Chatting up the girls in his bedsits. Pretending to be Mr Charming. But he sent his blokes round to collect the rent every week. God forbid you got behind with your payments. They used to break up your furniture. And worse.'

'Sounds appalling,' Kate said. *Bet he'll have lists of tenants and their details*, she thought. 'Where is he now?' she asked.

'God knows. Dead, I hope,' Miss Walker said.

'Goodness. What did he do to you?' Kate said.

'Nothing, nothing,' Miss Walker said nervously. 'Anyway, he sold the houses before the prices went up. I bet he's furious he didn't wait,' she added.

Kate looked at her watch. 'We'd better get off, Barbara — got lots to do.'

'Thanks, Barbara,' Joe said. 'You've been a great help. Must be funny living at the centre of the story.'

'Yes. And we've had sight-seers. A woman who came and stared through the fence was the first, but there've been others.'

'I bet,' Joe said, putting on his coat.

'Come any time,' she said as they left. 'I enjoy a bit of company.'

42

Thursday, 12 April 2012

Jude

She hadn't gone out for a couple of days. She felt adrift from reality, as if in a dream. She needed to find an anchor. Collect her thoughts. Needed to think. To make sense of this news.

Jude put on CDs of her favourite albums — the vinyl originals long gone — and ignored the frantic thumps on the wall from the flat next door. The music helped her remember. It was the soundtrack of her youth. Of her twenties. Of her love affair with Charlie.

She'd met him when she was twenty-eight, living in London and working for a publishing house. She hadn't kept any photographs — she'd got rid of them when Emma started asking about her father, thinking, stupidly, that removing the evidence would solve the situation — but she could still conjure up that face.

He was a musician, feckless but beautiful, and she'd fallen for him like a ton of bricks, despite warnings from friends that she would get hurt. She was a sucker for a pretty face, she told them. And anyway, she was lonely.

She'd thought London — and publishing — would be full of exciting, clever, creative men, and at first glance they were, in their King's Road uniforms. But it turned out being hip was a facade. Beneath the sharp jackets and drainpipe trousers, they were still children of the postwar era, tied to the apron strings of their mumsy mums at home. Turned out they were looking for a woman to make the bed as well as jump into it and she wasn't interested.

She'd kept the sexual wolf from the door with one-night stands and willing men friends before she met Charlie. He was only five years younger than her, but he seemed to come from a completely different era — and he definitely was not looking for a mother figure. He was living in a squat in Brighton and she'd met him at a pop concert in Hyde Park. The Rolling Stones, just after Brian Jones died. She'd been queuing for a drink and there he was, long hair, lopsided smile, beautiful hands, and, if she was honest, not that interested in her. Definitely a challenge and, so, irresistible. She had to have him.

She'd become obsessed with him. Spending money on him, paying his fares up to London, dressing him like a mannequin, taking him to the theatre, lending him books by Mailer and Updike, and hanging on his every drawled word.

Of course, Charlie was, as predicted, unfaithful. All the time. It went with the territory of musicians, apparently. Didn't mean anything, he said. So, girls and groupies. But Jude stuck to him like glue.

'He makes me laugh, he makes me feel good,' she'd told friends. 'He's fun and I love him.'

And she did love him. He was the first man

since Will at university who'd made her feel alive.

But she didn't take him home to meet her parents. She didn't need their disapproval to sour her happiness. She'd tell them when she was ready. When everything was settled.

Because she'd decided to marry Charlie, whatever it took. Her biological clock was ticking and she needed to bind him to her — that was all. He needed to appreciate what he'd got in Jude.

She knew Charlie thought marriage was square — 'It's what old people do. We're free spirits, Jude,' he'd said — but after a year she decided to force the issue. Get pregnant. Forget the shame. He'd marry her.

She'd dropped her contraceptive pills down the sink each morning and when she missed a period she told him he was going to be a father. He looked as if he was about to cry.

'Pregnant? How can you be? You said you were on the pill,' he'd said.

She'd lied easily, telling him that she must have forgotten to take one or had an upset stomach. And she'd told him she was happy about the pregnancy. She'd hoped he would be, too. But it wasn't that simple for Charlie.

He'd looked as if he was about to bolt for the door, saying he wasn't sure if he was ready. He'd even suggested that she get rid of the baby.

She'd burned with indignation at the thought and shrieked, 'Absolutely not! I'm keeping this baby.'

For the hundredth time, Jude wondered what

213

her life would have been like if she'd followed Charlie's suggestion. If she'd got rid of her baby then. If she hadn't talked him round, telling him he'd make the most brilliant father and kissing him into submission.

Too late for all that 'what if', she told herself. She'd won the initial battle with Charlie and had to live with the consequences.

He'd taken a while to get used to the idea, but there were days when he stroked her stomach and joined in her chatter about names and the Future. But he went away more and more. On tour, he said. She wasn't sure if he was lying, but decided she didn't want to know. He always came back to her, and she'd convinced herself he'd settle down when the baby was born.

43

Thursday, 12 April 2012

Emma

I feel stronger this morning. Better than I've felt for weeks. I don't know why, but I reach for the phone and ring Jude to tell her.

'Hello, Jude,' I say.

'Oh, two phone calls in just over a week. I am honoured,' she says. 'You sound good.'

She doesn't.

'Is everything OK with you?' I say. I don't really want to hear about her problems. I don't want to lose my high.

'Yes, yes,' she says. 'So, why are you so chirpy?'

'I just feel happy today,' I say. I don't mean to, but I find myself going straight to the news that has lifted my mood. 'You know that baby I told you about, buried in Howard Street? It's been identified as a little girl who went missing forty years ago,' I say. 'Alice something . . .'

'Irving. Alice Irving,' Jude says. 'Yes, I heard on the news. She went missing before we lived there.'

'Oh, do you remember the case? I couldn't believe it when I heard it on the radio.' I'm sounding manic. I try a deep breath.

'Nor me. Unbelievable,' she said, but there's

215

no mania in her voice. No emotion at all.

'So it can't have been the drug addicts,' I say.

'Looks unlikely,' she says. 'It happened so long ago, I expect they will never find out the truth.'

'Oh no, the police have got new methods now, Jude. They've managed to match the DNA after all this time, haven't they?'

'Well, so they say,' Jude says. 'Why are you so pleased about it?'

'I'm not,' I say. 'Just interested.'

Jude clearly isn't as she changes the subject. To Will, naturally. She is obsessed all over again. And I feel my mood dip.

'I haven't heard back from him,' she says. 'Do you think I should ring him?'

'No.'

It's the wrong thing to say and Jude's voice hardens. 'Well, I'm going to. I don't know why I asked you, really. You only think of your own feelings. You have got a husband, a job, colleagues, friends. Who have I got? A daughter I barely see. I need someone in my life. I'm lonely, Emma.'

It is a big admission from my mother and I try to be sympathetic.

'I'm sorry. I didn't know you felt like that. I would ring you more often, but we always seem to end up arguing. Don't you ever see any old colleagues from work, or friends?'

'They're all busy with their own families — or dead. I'm getting to that age where it seems as if practically everyone I know is dying. I wonder when it will be my turn.'

'Why? Are you feeling ill?'

'No, just old today. But don't you worry about me.'

And I feel a flicker of intense irritation. She is manipulating me. I know it, she knows it, but I can't stop it happening.

'What about joining a club or evening class?' I say, desperately grasping for ways to draw her out of her gloom.

'Not interested,' Jude says. 'Why would I want to do basket weaving or line dancing? I need someone to talk to and make me laugh. And take care of me.'

'But surely there is someone better than Will Burnside?'

'There isn't. I've looked,' she says. 'And Will was the love of my life. You know that. Anyway, you haven't done any better.'

'What's that supposed to mean?'

'Well, marrying someone old enough to be your father — what a cliché.'

I don't rise to it. I hunker down to absorb the blows. And that makes it worse. Jude has always hated my silences. She's got the bit between her teeth now, dragging up all her past hurts and accusations. 'You'll end up as his carer,' she shrieks at one point. And I realize we'll never get past her disappointment in me.

'Look, I've got to go, Jude. Sorry I've upset you again. I'll call you again soon.'

I wait till the line goes dead before I put the phone down.

44

Thursday, 12 April 2012

Jude

She sat looking at the phone for a minute, finishing her last rant in her head.

I should never have had you. You've been trouble from the start.

It had all begun to go wrong when Charlie came home from the tour. She'd stood at the door with Emma in her arms to greet him.

She'd longed for the moment when he'd come back to her — had planned the big reunion — but it didn't go to plan.

She thought he would turn up with roses and an engagement ring, but he brought nothing but a bag of dirty clothes and stories about drunken nights. And when he'd reached to take the baby, she hadn't been able to let go of her. She was the bargain they'd made, but Jude needed reassurance that Charlie was playing by her rules.

Jude had swallowed her disappointment and tried to involve him in her new domesticity, letting him change Emma and make up her feed. But she didn't let him hold the baby for too long. He had to earn that privilege.

'She's asleep, Charlie,' she'd say when he reached for Emma. 'Don't wake her up.' She'd seen the hurt in his eyes, but she couldn't let that sway her. She had to be careful with her daughter.

She'd held on to Emma all that first evening. Keeping the baby between her and Charlie.

He hadn't asked about the birth when she'd told him on the phone that Emma had been born. He just wanted to know about the baby.

'Who does she look like, Jude? Has she got your beautiful eyes?'

But sitting across from her for the first time, he'd wanted to know everything. She'd told him how she'd wanted a natural birth, with no doctors sticking metal instruments up her. She'd decided to give birth at home with a friend who was a doula.

He'd made a face. It was all a bit too visceral for him. He hadn't been to any of the classes or read any of the books. *Too busy being a rock star*, she thought.

He'd shied away from the gory details and focused on what a doula was.

She'd explained that doulas had helped women with labour throughout history. They were often sisters or aunties. But her doula was someone she'd met through NCT classes. *National Childbirth Trust, Charlie.*

'Sounds cool,' he'd said.

And when he'd yawned and suggested bed, she'd made him sleep on the sofa — so he wouldn't be disturbed by the crying.

The next morning, he'd come in with a cup of tea and sat on the bed.

'I'm sorry I wasn't here for you, Jude,' he said.

'But I am now. OK?'

And she'd said yes, hoping he'd talk about marriage. But he'd hugged her and tried to get in under the covers. She'd pushed him away, saying Emma needed feeding.

'For God's sake,' he'd said after two weeks, when the tension threatened to suffocate both of them, 'What's going on here?'

He was standing by the window, looking out, not at her.

'You've changed, Jude,' he'd said. 'You're so uptight about everything. Paranoid. I'm not even allowed to hold my own baby. It's like I am nothing to do with her. As if she's just yours.'

She'd put Emma down in her carrycot and tried to keep her voice level. 'I'm sorry, but I've had to do everything else on my own. I'm not sure if you are here to stay.'

He shrugged, his back still turned. 'You are treating me like a stranger. It makes me wonder if I ever had anything to do with her. Is she someone else's? Is that it? Did you sleep with other blokes?'

She could still feel the heat in her body as he screamed the accusation at her. She'd told him she'd never slept with anyone else, that Emma was his. But he wasn't listening any more. The thought that he'd been betrayed had driven reason out of his head. *It's what people do in his rock-star world,* she told herself.

'Charlie, please listen to me. Maybe if we got married?' she'd said. 'Maybe it's because I'm not sure of your commitment. Maybe that's what's come between us.'

'Bollocks,' he'd said. 'Marrying you wouldn't solve anything. It'd just bind me to this nightmare situation.'

And he'd kissed Emma and left.

★　★　★

She hadn't gone out of the house for a couple of days. Too shocked to leave the nest. But finally, she'd taken Emma to be weighed at the surgery. She didn't want any trouble about missing appointments.

Dr Grundy had been pleased to see her — he always was. Other patients complained about him, especially after his lunchtime session in the local pub. But she singled him out for appointments and, with a little careful flirting, had become one of his favourites. He'd told her so, holding her hands in his shaky grasp. He'd told her off for delivering Emma at home with a doula when she'd brought the baby to him the first time, but she'd cooed her explanations and he'd been putty in her hands. He'd tutted and signed all the paperwork.

After he'd weighed Emma on the last visit, Jude had told him she'd decided to go home to her parents and he'd looked disappointed. 'We'll miss you, Jude,' he'd said.

'And I'll miss you, too, Dr Grundy,' she'd said, and kissed his papery cheek.

It had been a hard decision, but she needed a new start. With Charlie gone, she'd have to support herself. She couldn't work and look after Emma. And she didn't want to leave her with a child-minder. She needed help.

Her parents knew Emma had been born but had chosen to stay away, signalling their disapproval of their daughter's life choices with a resounding silence. She'd go to them. They wouldn't be able to resist their first grandchild.

Her mum and dad had given her the 'more in sorrow than in anger' treatment, with a dry peck on the cheek and serial tutting, when she'd appeared at their door with a suitcase and Emma in her pram. Her mum had bristled all morning, but Jude pretended not to notice.

Lunch was hideous. There was meat — a joint of bloody beef — and her mother shrugged as her vegetarian daughter helped herself to cauliflower. 'Well, we didn't know you were coming,' she said.

A stifling silence followed. Jude struggled to fill it, talking about the baby, her job, how lovely the garden was looking.

'So, Judith, where is the father?' her mother said as she handed her the roast potatoes.

'Gone, Mum,' Jude said, keeping it simple.

'I see,' she said. 'And how long are you staying?'

'Not sure, Mum,' Jude said.

'Your baby needs stability, and she'll get little of that if you flit off again.'

'Deirdre,' her father said, a warning note in his voice. 'Now is not the time for this conversation.'

Jude gave him a tight smile of thanks.

'Well, when is the right time? She doesn't contact us for months, gets herself pregnant and throws away a perfectly good career, and then

222

turns up and we're supposed to pretend nothing's happened? For goodness sake, Judith. You can't imagine how much unhappiness you've caused. I haven't slept for months.'

Jude stabbed a potato with her fork. 'I was not trying to make you unhappy, Mum. I made the wrong decision. Can we leave it at that? There's a baby to consider now. Can I have some carrots, please?'

And, trained to be polite even in the midst of a row, her mother passed the bowl with a face like thunder.

45

Thursday, 12 April 2012

Kate

She rang DI Sinclair early that morning, eager to hear the latest in the investigation before the editor's news conference. She hoped the officer would have something for her. She and the DI were getting on like a house on fire after their shaky start. She'd made sure of that. This was a story that could run and run and she was going to keep him onside, whatever that took.

So she behaved herself, never straying from the official line. It had been a happy collaboration so far — the DI was very pleased with the response provoked by the *Post*'s story — mothers who'd given birth at the same time as Angela, the nurses who searched for her, even one of the officers who had investigated the case. Their chats had got cosier.

Kate now knew he had kids the same age as hers and supported Spurs.

'Hello, Andy,' she said. 'Sorry to be an early bird. How are you?'

'Been better, Kate,' he said, sounding weary.

'Sorry to hear that. Heavy night?'

'No. Not really.'

He hesitated, and she let the silence force him to continue.

'Look, something has come up on the Alice Irving case. Bit of a problem. Can we talk off the record?'

'Course,' she said, brain on full alert. 'Problem, Andy? What kind of problem? Is it the DNA tests?'

'No, no. The match is solid. But there is a major snag with the timeline.'

Kate pulled out her notebook. Off the record now, but she wanted to get it all down for later. In case things changed.

'Go on,' she said.

'As we know, Alice was taken on 20 March 1970,' DI Sinclair said.

'Yes . . .'

'Well, she wasn't buried in Howard Street until the 1980s. Couldn't have been.'

'What? Why? How do you know?' Kate said.

'Forensics are telling us the paper wrapped round the body was from the eighties — something to do with the ink on the newsprint, haven't got the details in front of me — and we've been looking at the history of the site. Should have done it earlier, but the DNA match blindsided us. Anyway, the houses had tiny concrete yards, not gardens, until the end of the seventies. The yards backed on to a Boys' Brigade hall and workshops. The buildings were only knocked down in 1979 when the houses were bought by a developer and the gardens extended. So the body couldn't have been buried before then.'

225

Kate swallowed hard.

'Peter, the lad who found the body, said there were concrete foundations in the garden,' she recalled. 'They were digging them up. Underneath where the urn was.'

'Did he? I'll go back to him,' DI Sinclair said, making his own notes.

'So what does this mean, Andy?' The million-dollar question.

'I suppose it means that Alice's body must have been kept somewhere else for ten years.'

'Christ. This is all becoming pretty macabre.' *Who else knows this?* she thought.

'Indeed,' he said, adding, as if reading her thoughts, 'No one outside the team knows yet, Kate. I haven't even told Angela. Want to be absolutely sure we've got everything right.'

'I'd love to write this, Andy.'

'Yes, I bet you would. Hold off until tomorrow, though, Kate. Then you can write as much as you like. I need your help getting this new timeline out there.'

'Course. Whatever we can do to help.'

Her brain was racing. *Who was living in Howard Street a decade later? Where would you keep a body?*

'Thanks for telling me, Andy. I'll sit on the info until you are ready. Let's talk later,' she said.

'OK,' he said.

★ ★ ★

She rang Bob Sparkes immediately. Her touchstone.

226

'Kate,' he said. 'I'm driving. I'll put you on loudspeaker.'

'Right. On your own?'

'Yes. Why? What's happening?'

She told him the highlights of the conversation with DI Sinclair and he left her hanging while he thought it through.

'The body could have been kept anywhere in the country for ten years. Throws the whole investigation into the air again. Could have been someone already living in the house who needed to move the body, or someone who moved in and brought the body with them.'

'Or one of the workmen working on the demolition of the Boys' Brigade hut?' Kate added.

'All possibilities. Poor Andy Sinclair. Does Angela know?'

'Not yet. Glad it's not me telling her.'

'And me,' Sparkes said. 'Keep in touch, Kate.' And gone.

Joe arrived as she put her phone down.

'You're in early, Kate,' he said. 'Have I missed anything?'

'You could say that, Joe. Sit down,' she said quietly. 'Bit of a spanner in the works as far as Alice is concerned.'

'What?' Joe stuttered, wheeling his chair closer to Kate so he could hear. 'What's happened?'

'We've got to fast-forward to the 1980s, Joe. Alice was buried in Howard Street in the eighties, not the seventies. But no one else can know yet. Andy Sinclair told me this morning but it's still unofficial.'

227

Joe rocked back in his chair. 'But she wasn't killed in the eighties?'

'No, or we'd have the body of a ten-year-old, wouldn't we?'

'Course, course,' he said. 'Just thinking out loud. So where was the body for ten years?'

'Exactly,' Kate said. 'And who buried it in Howard Street? Let's concentrate on that.'

'Well, it couldn't have been Marian Laidlaw,' Joe said. 'I looked for her last night in the records and she died in 1977.'

'God, that was young. What a bugger,' Kate said. 'Well, it was a long shot — Len Rigby said she had an alibi — but it would have been a great story if she'd confessed all these years later. So who was alive at the time?'

'Barbara,' Joe said. 'She was living in one of the houses then.'

46

Thursday, 12 April 2012

Kate

Miss Walker's flat was empty when they got there, but a note on lined paper flapped on the front door, telling callers she was out shopping. 'Back by 3 p.m.' she'd written.

'Good grief, she might as well have added 'PS: Help Yourselves,' Kate said, pulling it off the door and stuffing it in her pocket.

It had begun to spit with rain and she led the way to the pub. 'She'll be back in twenty minutes,' Kate said.

Graham the landlord laughed when he saw them. 'You can't keep away, can you?' He called through to the back, 'Toni, the press is back!'

'Your wife?' Kate asked.

'Yes, that's me,' the landlady said, emerging from the back room. 'Graham says you're a reporter,' she said, as if it was some sort of guilty secret. A species apart. Kate waited, expecting the usual snide remark. Things had changed since the days when people thought being a reporter was glamorous. Now, journalists were down there with tax inspectors and traffic wardens.

It seemed everyone was jumping up and down

about the press and their methods of getting information. But it was all about the technology, nowadays. When Kate had been starting out, her ex-Fleet Street boss had told her how to disable a public phone box so no other reporter could use it — unscrew the receiver — and once ordered her to take a hidden camera into a hospital ward to photograph a famous patient.

She hadn't done the sneaky hospital-bed photographs. She'd been frightened enough of her boss — an alcoholic whose mood for the day could be gauged by the way the office door swung open in the morning — to do almost anything he ordered, but not that. She'd taken a photo of her coat and pretended the camera had gone wrong.

But her old boss sounded like a character out of an Ealing Comedy in comparison with some of the new dark arts. Breaking into phone voicemails, bank accounts and medical records had become the norm in some newsrooms, it was said more and more loudly.

Some newsrooms. But it didn't matter who'd done what, any more. They were all guilty, as far as the public was concerned, and they all had to face the reckoning.

Kate's paper had escaped a police investigation into hacking and paying officials for information — 'It may happen yet,' Terry had said over a beer one evening, deep in a pit of despair.

'Don't be daft,' she'd said. 'I've never hacked anything — wouldn't have known where to start.' But she knew it didn't change the public opinion that all journalists were scum.

'Yes, but crème de la scum,' Mick the photographer had boasted.

The landlady kept quiet and looked at her expectantly.

'Er, yes, I'm Kate Waters from the *Daily Post*. Nice to meet you.'

'You don't look like a reporter,' the landlady said.

Kate wasn't sure what to say. She wondered what Mrs Landlord thought reporters looked like. Men, probably. Men in dirty macs rummaging through dustbins, quite possibly. She tried not to sigh. 'Well, we come in all shapes and sizes,' she said and laughed.

The landlady laughed too and stuck out her hand. 'I'm Toni. I hear you're asking about the baby in the garden. Incredible it's that little girl . . . '

Kate nodded. 'Incredible,' she echoed. 'Your husband was saying that you grew up in the street, that you might remember some of the people who were around in the seventies and eighties,' she said, shuffling round to give Toni room to sit.

'Yes, my mum and dad had the pub, and before that they lived at number 57 for years.'

'Was your maiden name Baker?' Kate asked.

'That's right. How did you know?' Toni said.

'I've been looking at the electoral register from those days, that's all,' Kate said. 'Did they sell to Mr Soames?'

Toni rolled her eyes. 'The local sleazebag. He was revolting — all hands. Always after the girls. I stayed well away.'

Kate underlined the note 'Find Soames' in her notebook. 'What about the girls you knew in the eighties?'

'I thought the baby was taken in the seventies,' Toni said.

'Well, the police are looking at a wider spread of years to be thorough,' Kate said quickly. She'd almost given the game away. Sinclair would go mad if she said anything before he gave the go-ahead.

'Right. Well, let's see, there was quite a gang. They all came to my sixteenth birthday party. That was 1985. It was a brilliant party. A disco, just down the road at the new Boys' Brigade hall. God, I can't believe that's almost thirty years ago.'

Kate smiled winningly. 'We must be about the same age, then,' she said. Kate was a good six years older, but never mind. 'Best days of my life, too. Do you remember *Jackie?* I loved that magazine, read it every week and put the posters on my bedroom walls. And the fashions! Can't believe some of the outfits I used to wear. My boys think I'm making it up.'

Toni lapped it up. 'I wore a mini skirt and fishnet gloves, like Madonna, to my sixteenth. Thought I was the bee's knees. I think I've still got photos somewhere.'

'Oh, I'd love to see them,' Kate said quickly.

'I'll get them,' the landlady said happily, getting up and disappearing through a door marked 'Private'.

'You've started something now,' the landlord laughed. 'Hope you've got nothing else planned for the day. Toni loves a trip down memory lane.'

'Oh, so do I,' Kate said. 'I've got all the time in the world.' She looked meaningfully at Joe and hoped he wouldn't get restless.

Ten minutes later Toni emerged, her arms filled with a stack of fat photo albums and several framed pictures.

'I'm not sure which ones are the party, so I brought everything,' she said. 'And these in the frames were in the same box, so I brought them too.'

She heaved them on to the table, sending up a cloud of dust. 'Haven't looked at them for ages,' she said, apologetically waving away the evidence of neglect.

The two women sat side by side on the velour banquette and began trawling through the pages, Toni pointing and giggling, while Joe looked at his phone and Graham polished the glasses behind the bar.

'You ladies want a cup of tea?' he called across when he'd finished. Joe looked up. 'Sorry, mate,' the landlord said. 'Tea for everyone?'

'Yes please, love,' Toni called over her shoulder. 'He's a treasure. Oh, I think these must be the party ones.'

Spilling out of the album were loose snapshots and birthday cards. Kate scooped up a handful of photos that had fallen on to the floor and laid them out on the table like playing cards.

'That's the gang,' Toni said, delighted. 'Look at us all dolled up. We all got together in my bedroom before the disco to do our make-up and hair. You could hardly breathe for hairspray

233

and perfume. Takes me straight back.'

Kate was scrutinizing the faces. 'Which one's you?'

Toni tapped a smiling face near the centre of the group. 'There I am. I had a feather cut then. Everyone did. We all thought we were Sheena Easton. Hideous now, but it was big then. Literally.' She smoothed her shiny bob nostalgically. 'And look at the make-up. We used to put blusher on with a trowel.'

Kate laughed loudly. 'Looks like you should all have been down at the Burns Unit. Didn't we use to put the same stuff on our lips and cheeks? I remember it was sticky and smelled of bubble gum.'

'Yes! And I had that lip gloss that tasted of strawberries. Revolting!'

'So who are the others?' Kate asked, anxious to get them back on track.

'Now then, that's Jill, Gemma, Sarah B and Sarah S . . . not sure about her — think she was only at our school for a term . . . I think that's Harry Harrison and her weird friend. They were a year below us at school, but Harry knew my brother, Malcolm. Well, she fancied him rotten — all the girls I knew did. Poor Malcolm. Too gorgeous for his own good. Anyway, Harry begged me to invite her. I think they went out for a while — oh, and then he dumped her for Sarah S. I can't believe I've remembered that — it's a million years ago. I do remember that Harry was always in trouble at school, but she was a great laugh.'

Kate was writing down names, occasionally

234

staunching the torrent of gossip and memories to check surnames and spellings.

'Don't suppose you knew an Anne Robinson?'

'Only the one from *The Weakest Link* on the telly.'

'No, that isn't her,' Kate said. 'Who still lives round here?' she asked, during a pause for a second cup of tea. 'Who can I go and see?'

'Both the Sarahs live near the industrial estate, but I haven't seen them since I had my tubes tied.'

Kate nodded with a sympathetic wince. The level of instant intimacy always astonished her. She'd met this woman half an hour ago and she now knew her reproductive history.

'Took ages to get over,' Toni said. 'They said I'd be out of bed in two days, but was I, buggery?'

'Poor you,' Kate said — the catch-all phrase for halting an interviewee in his/her unwanted reminiscences. 'What about Jill and Gemma?' She prodded Toni back on track.

'Oh, they married and moved to Kent or Essex, I think. God, I haven't thought about them for years.

'We were all so close then, but we just lost touch. I moved to west London for a few years when I got my first office job and that's all it takes, isn't it? The ground closes over you. When I came back, they'd gone and I was married.'

'I know.' Kate stirred her cup sympathetically. 'What about the others in the photo? The girl who fancied your brother?'

'Harry? Oh yes. Don't know where she went

either. Nothing would surprise me. I'm not being much help, am I?'

'Nonsense. You've been brilliant. Thanks so much, Toni. You've been a godsend.'

The landlady grinned back at her. 'Loved it. It's got my juices flowing. I think I'll try to set up a reunion. A return to 1985. I'll go on Facebook and find them all.'

'Let me know who you hear from, then,' Kate said. She would look on Facebook herself, but she knew Toni would have a better chance of finding and hearing back from the disco girls. 'And make sure you invite me. I love a boogie.'

Toni squeaked and started doing a hand jive.

47

Thursday, 12 April 2012

Angela

It was Nick who answered the door to the officers. He'd come home for lunch and to pick up a bill he'd left on the hall table. He never used to come home in the day — he preferred a packed lunch or a sausage roll from the bakery round the corner — but since the news about their baby, he made excuses to pop back. Angela suspected he wanted to keep an eye on her.

He'd cried with her when she told him they'd found Alice. He'd come home that day to find Angela sitting in a silent house. No radio or television on to keep her company as usual. And she'd looked at him and he'd known.

'It's her, isn't it? Our baby' he'd said. And he'd cried as if he'd never stop.

'I never thought we'd find her, Angie,' he'd sobbed. 'It all felt unreal, all these years. I began wondering if we'd even had a baby. I mean, I only held her once before she was gone. I thought it was my punishment for hurting you. I am so sorry, Angie. So sorry for everything.'

She'd shushed him. But she felt deeply shaken for him — it was the first time he'd said anything so nakedly honest about his feelings for their first

237

daughter. Or about his guilt. He'd never said anything like this before — not even in their darkest early days — and she wondered if she had made it impossible for him to be open with her. Her anger and all-consuming grief had filled every corner of the house. He'd had to be the strong one. But what had been going on in his head for all those years?

Angela felt she was rediscovering her husband and the marriage that might have been if . . .

She'd rocked him back to calmer waters until they both quietened.

'Now what?' he'd said, looking at her. 'What's going to happen now?'

'The police are coming to talk to us tomorrow. They're going to try to find out who took our baby, love.'

'How will they? After all this time?'

'I don't know, Nick. But at least we know where she is. Alice.'

They'd rung the children straight away, before the news leaked out. Patrick had listened in silence as his two played up about bedtime in the background.

'God, Mum. I can't take it in,' he'd said finally. 'Where was the body found? Woolwich? That's miles away. How did it get there?' he said.

Concentrating on the facts, she thought.

Louise had burst into tears, as Angela knew she would.

'How are you feeling, Mum? How's Dad? You must be in pieces,' she said. 'I'll come round now.'

Their daughter had obviously rung Patrick, because he arrived just after his sister and stood

238

awkwardly in the doorway as Louise and Angela hugged and cried again.

When they had stopped and everyone had sat down, Angela told them the story of Alice's abduction again. It was the first time in twenty years it had been mentioned in the family — Nick had told Angela to stop upsetting the children with it and she'd complied. But that night, everything could be spoken about. Apart from Nick's betrayal. She wondered if Nick might confess it to them himself. It was his secret, after all. But he didn't. Some things were probably best left unsaid.

'So it's going to be in the papers tomorrow?' Patrick had asked. 'Will we get reporters coming to the house?'

'I don't know, Paddy,' Angela said. 'I hope not, but if they do, you don't have to say anything. Just ask them to contact the police.'

'Oh Mum, this is going to be so awful for you,' Louise said. 'Do you want me to come and stay?'

'We'll be fine, love,' Nick had said firmly. 'We've coped with losing Alice all these years. We can cope with this.'

But he'd started coming home at lunchtime, pretending to have left something or that he'd just been passing. She loved him for it.

⋆ ⋆ ⋆

The family liaison officer, a sweet-faced woman called Wendy Turner, rang them each morning with an update or a question, and Nick was relaxed when he went to the door.

239

'Oh, hello, Wendy. How are you?' Angela heard him say and she poured his soup back in the pan. 'Didn't expect you, Andy. You'd both better come through. Angie is in the kitchen.'

DI Sinclair came in first and Angela pulled out a chair for him without speaking. DC Turner stood with her back against the counter.

'Sorry to come unannounced,' DI Sinclair said. 'But I wanted to bring you both up to date with the investigation.'

He sounded formal and Angela sat down across from him with Nick standing behind her, his hands on her shoulders.

'What is it?' she asked.

'Well, we've established that Alice's body was buried in Howard Street in the 1980s. We know this because of the history of the site and forensic analysis of the debris around her body,' he said.

Angela went to speak, but Nick stopped her. 'Let Andy finish, love,' he said quietly.

'I know this must be distressing for you both. But we are doing everything we can to find out what happened to Alice. I just want to reassure you of that.'

Nick spoke first. 'Thank you for telling us, Andy. Will this help you find Alice's kidnapper?'

'It might,' the officer said. 'We'll be looking at who moved into the terrace in Howard Street in the early eighties. It's at least ten years closer to today, so people's memories may be clearer.'

'Who would bury a body after ten years?' Angela said.

'We don't know,' DI Sinclair said. 'Not yet.'

240

48

Friday, 13 April 2012

Kate

Kate filed the new story about Alice at 9.07. She'd had it written the day before — as soon as she'd put the phone down on DI Sinclair. But she'd waited to phone Angela for a quote that morning: 'We don't know what to think. We are just glad she's been found,' she'd said. Kate had given the story a final tweak after the officer rang to give her the go-ahead at 8.40.

'Go easy on the headline, Terry,' she said as she re-read her copy over his shoulder. 'Let's not go too gruesome. Think of the parents . . . '

Terry had quickly typed ZOMBIE BABY RISES FROM GRAVE, laughed at Kate's expression and deleted it. 'Just kidding, Kate. How about ALICE BURIED TEN YEARS AFTER KIDNAP?'

Kate nodded grumpily. She knew he'd add *Shocking Revelation by Alice Cops* or something equivalent when she'd moved away, but watched as he clicked the copy through.

'OK, link tweeted and headline posted on Facebook, publishing on the website now. It's a good story, Kate. And exclusive for the next thirty seconds. Anyway, what the hell's gone on there? Shoebox under the bed? In the freezer?

241

What made them decide to bury the body at all?'

'Good question, Terry. Andy Sinclair says there isn't enough material to say if the body was mummified from being above ground or had been buried and dug up. A lot of this is going to be guesswork. They're concentrating on tracing people who came to live in Howard Street in the early eighties.'

'OK. Assume you are, too,' Terry said.

'Of course,' Kate said. 'Going out on it now.'

★ ★ ★

Joe had found Alistair St John Soames listed in a flat in Peckham.

'There's no Mrs Soames, unless she's not on the electoral roll,' he said conversationally as they drove past dozens of practically identical fried-chicken shops.

Kate's sons collected the names of fried-chicken shops — it had started as a joke, but they had a list of over 120 by now — but she decided not to share such family minutiae with Joe.

'Doesn't seem to have held on to his money,' she observed. 'This is where poverty lives, round here.' *Good. He might be more cooperative if he thinks there could be some cash in it*, she thought.

There were five doorbells to choose from at the address, each bearing a faded name on a piece of card.

'Can you make these out?' she said, peering at them. 'Can you see Soames?'

242

Joe's younger eyes deciphered the writing and Kate pressed the bell for Flat 4. There was silence.

She waited and then rang again. Nothing.

'Once more for luck,' she said and pressed long and hard, then did a couple of staccato dings for emphasis. 'That'd wake the dead,' she said.

There was a crackle and an angry voice barked, 'Stop ringing my bell! Who the hell are you?'

'Mr Soames? I'm from the *Daily Post*. I wondered if I could have a word?'

'The *Daily Post*? What do you want?'

'I'm doing a piece on the discovery of Alice Irving's body in Woolwich. In Howard Street, Mr Soames, and I need your help. You used to be the main property owner in the area and the locals say you are the man I need to talk to. The fount of all knowledge, they say.'

'*Flatter, flatter and flatter again,*' an old news editor used to say. '*Gets you through the door every time.*'

'Oh. Come up then,' the voice said and buzzed them in.

Kate went first.

'And we're in,' she said cheerfully.

★　★　★

The door to Soames's second-floor flat was open and he stood just inside, waiting. He was a shambling figure, with day-old bristles and dressed in a jumper and pyjama bottoms, the frayed cord holding them up dangling limply.

243

'I hope we didn't get you out of bed,' Kate said.

Soames eyed her suspiciously. 'Bit of a slow starter these days,' he said and led them into his sitting room. It looked like a burglary had taken place. A table was overturned, a spilt bowl of Rice Krispies had pebbledashed the carpet, and a landslide of books and stray pieces of paper littered the floor.

'Excuse the mess. Had a bit of an accident this morning,' the old man said, waving his hand over the disaster zone.

Kate stooped to pick up the bowl and table. 'There you go,' she said. 'Did you hurt yourself?'

Soames looked pleased at the attention. 'No, no. Just a bit clumsy when I first get up. It's my age.'

'Shall I make you a cup of tea?' Kate asked and smiled at him. He had lonely old man written all over him. A bit of a gift for her. Lonely people loved to talk.

'How lovely,' he said. 'What was your name again?'

'Kate. Kate Waters, Mr Soames.'

'Call me Al,' he said and grinned roguishly. Kate's stomach turned. *Be nice*, she told herself.

'This is Joe Jackson, my colleague,' she said. Joe was standing behind her, apparently afraid to move in case he set off another avalanche of detritus in the flat.

'Pleased to meet you,' Soames said, extending his hand. They shook and the younger man balanced himself on the arm of an overstuffed armchair.

244

'Goodness, you've got a lot of stuff in here,' Joe said.

'Souvenirs of a life well lived. And a lot of rubbish,' Soames said, standing by a mantelpiece studded with dusty ornaments and ancient 'stiffies' — gilt-edged invitations to parties long over. Kate noticed that his pyjama bottoms were coming adrift and hoped they'd stay up.

'Why don't we sit down, Al?' she said sweetly, mouthing to Joe to put the kettle on.

'Yes, of course. Where would you like to sit, my dear?' He was now clutching his pyjamas to stop them from falling down and she looked round desperately. Every seat was taken, but she moved a stack of magazines from a dining chair and brought it close to the old man's armchair. He hovered at her elbow as she arranged things, patting her shoulder as she sat and then taking his own seat. *Always the gentleman*, she thought.

'Now then. You want to talk about my properties in Howard Street?' he said, settling back to give them the benefit of his experience.

'Yes, particularly in the eighties, Al,' Kate said.

'I had five houses in that street, if I remember rightly. Dozens of others elsewhere. Quite an empire,' he said.

'Really? That's amazing,' Kate said, egging him on. 'So you must have had hundreds of tenants.'

'Of course.' Soames grinned. The rogue emerging again. 'Turned them into bedsits. Lots of lovely young girls, I remember.'

'I bet,' Kate said and Soames winked at her. A quick wink. But it spoke volumes. She felt sick.

245

A rattling of china heralded the return of Joe, carrying a tray of cups and saucers. Everything had a patina of grease on it and Kate tried to drink without her lips touching the rim of the cup.

She had been in worse homes. There was the one where she'd had to step over dog mess in the hall, and a house where a mother had served her child's tea, a fried egg, from the frying pan straight on to the arm of the sofa. *Other people's lives*, she told herself.

She put the sticky cup on the floor. 'I'll wait until it cools down,' she said. 'Have you kept lists of your tenants in Howard Street, Mr Soames — er, Al?' she asked. 'Would be great to see who was living there at the time Alice was buried. And I'd love to hear more about you in those days. Your memories, I mean.'

Soames went pink with pleasure. 'Well, if you really want to, my dear.'

'Have you got any photographs of you from those days? It would be great to see them.'

'Oh yes. I kept everything,' he said.

★ ★ ★

Kate had sent Joe out to get some sandwiches while she carried on charming the old man. It was getting on for one o'clock and she'd offered to get Soames some lunch but there was nothing in the fridge apart from a pork pie with a fuzz of mould blurring its outline and a half-empty bottle of gin.

'Haven't managed to get to the shops yet,'

246

Soames had said, and she wondered when he had last been out of the flat.

'Don't you have any help here, Al?' she asked.

'The girl in the flat downstairs sometimes pops by to see if I'm still alive,' he said gloomily. 'Lovely girl. Beautiful long hair and a darling figure.'

'Right,' Kate said. 'I meant a cleaner or someone to do the shopping.'

'No. I don't need anyone to do that. I'm fine. Been on my own for years. Since my wife buggered off, really.'

'It must be lonely, though,' she said. 'Do you have a family, Al?'

'Yes, two children. A girl and a boy. But they are off doing their own thing. Got their own sprogs now. They don't want to bother with an old fart like me. I prefer to be independent, anyway,' he said. He looked a bit teary, Kate thought, and she patted his hand automatically.

He grasped her fingers as she moved her hand away and held on tight, surprising her with the strength of his grip. 'You've got lovely eyes,' he said.

'So have you, Al. Now shall we look at those photos?'

'They're in my bedroom,' he said softly. 'Bet you go into strange men's bedrooms all the time.'

'No, not really,' she said, easing her foot off the flirtation pedal and praying that Joe would come back soon. It was all going a bit Leslie Phillips for her liking. She was pretty sure she could fight off a man of Al's age if it came to it, but she didn't fancy the skirmish.

'You stay there, Al. I'll get them,' Kate said firmly.

He told her there was an album and a carrier bag of loose pictures on top of his wardrobe, so she took the dining chair to stand on.

The bedroom curtains were still drawn so she yanked them open to let some light into the room. The pale sunlight filtering through the dusty panes revealed a scene of Dickensian squalor. The sheets on the bed were grey and stained and there appeared to be a chamber pot under the bed. She tried not to breathe through her nose as she clambered up on the chair to peer into the dark space above the wardrobe.

Al's voice suddenly came from far too close to her. 'Have you found them? I've got a lovely view from here . . . '

Kate looked down, silently cursing the fact that she'd worn a skirt, and saw him propped in the doorway, ogling her legs. *Bloody hell, he must be desperate, looking at fifty-year-old knees,* she thought. 'Think these must be them,' she said quickly.

'Let me help you down,' he said and moved towards her, but Kate stepped smartly off the chair, keeping it between her and the eager Soames.

'No, all sorted,' she said. 'Here, you carry this and I'll bring the rest so we can go and look at them in the other room. There's better light in there.'

Al Soames turned, disappointed, and shambled back to his seat.

Kate quickly got back on the chair and felt around for anything she might have missed. Her hand brushed something papery and she pulled it out. It was an old manila envelope that had become wedged between the wardrobe and the wall. It was dusty but not sealed and 'Parties' was written carelessly across the front. She took a quick look inside and saw a bundle of Polaroid photographs.

'What are you doing in there?' Soames called.

'Nothing. Coming. Just dusting myself off a bit,' she called back.

As she emerged, Joe rang the doorbell, making them both jump. Kate put the envelope down by her handbag and let him in, then got involved in the flurry of activity as he unpacked their picnic.

'Come on, let's spread the pictures from your albums on your table,' she said. 'Then you can see them all.'

She cleared the surface, heaping the detritus on the floor, and laid the photos out like Tarot cards.

'There we are,' Soames said, now standing at her elbow. He was pointing to an image of himself and another man with two girls. The men were laughing into the camera. The girls weren't.

'The lady-killers,' he said and smirked. 'We ran up quite a tally.'

'Who is the other bloke?' Joe asked.

'A friend from the old days. He lived in Howard Street, actually. Good old Will. But I lost touch with him. Oh, look at this one . . . '

The fashions changed and hair got longer,

then shorter, as the pictures progressed through the decades.

Kate was scrutinizing every picture, looking at each face for anything that might help the story.

'Tenant?' she asked, and when Al Soames nodded, she put the picture in a separate pile. He wasn't good at names but he promised to get his old rent documents back from his accountant.

'That would be wonderful,' she said to Soames. 'Could I borrow a few photos in the meantime?'

'Of course, Kate, if it would help,' he said. She'd got him wrapped round her little finger.

She piled the photos up and slipped them into the envelope by her bag.

'That way, you'll have to come back. To return them,' he giggled.

Joe caught Kate's eye and raised a sympathetic eyebrow.

'So when did you sell up, Mr Soames?' he asked, picking up the baton.

Soames stopped giggling and thought. 'Must be fifteen, maybe twenty years ago now.'

'Gosh, a long time.'

'Yes, I sold at the wrong time and got shafted by a property developer. He made a mint. And as you can see . . . ' He and Joe looked round the room. 'The wife took most of what was left,' Soames said.

Joe nodded and leant forward to show Soames he had his full attention. 'Oh dear,' he said.

'I became PNG after that,' he said, then noticing Joe's blank look added, '*Persona non grata.* No longer welcome. The party invites dried up and then time just passed . . . ' Soames grinned at Joe. 'I liked to party. And the girls were only too willing.'

'You must have had a great time,' Joe said, smiling. *Boys together,* Kate thought.

'Yes. Great. We had all the chat-up lines.' He leant closer to Joe so Kate had to strain to hear. 'And if they didn't work, there were always our little helpers.' And he laughed. A coarse, nasty laugh.

'Little helpers?' Joe asked, and Kate held her breath. A question too far.

'Just a turn of phrase,' Soames said quickly. But he winked at Joe.

49

Friday, 13 April 2012

Kate

When they finally emerged from Soames's flat, Kate and Joe stood on the pavement like competitors at the end of a race and caught their breath.

'Oh my God. That was horrible,' Joe said.

'Welcome to my world,' Kate said. 'Come on, let's get out of here.'

In the car, she sat for ten minutes, scribbling notes of the conversation. She hadn't wanted to get her notebook out in the flat — she knew Soames would clam up if he realized his words were being written down.

She'd turned her recorder on in her handbag as soon as they went through the door, but she wasn't sure what would be on the tape. Everyone was moving around, in and out of the rooms. Still, she might've got something. She'd check later.

Kate didn't rely on recorders in the normal run of things. They were temperamental creatures: buttons got stuck, batteries ran out. On one excruciating occasion, she'd taped a whole interview and, playing it back, found she had an hour of hissing static.

She preferred the ancient art of shorthand — a skill regarded as laughingly analogue by the online newbies. Kate had learnt it as a junior reporter from a former Japanese POW. He was a tiny, chirpy man whose party trick was to walk into the room and do a flying kick to switch on the light. Isaac Pitman would've had a fit, but the ninja had got her through her hundred words a minute.

She and Joe had been in the flat for two and a half hours, but her memory had become trained to recall whole conversations. It was essential for the job, but was also particularly useful at home during arguments with her sons. 'You never forget anything, Mum,' Jake had said during one of their recent rows over his future. 'You never let anything go.'

He was right. Kate could remember things people said as if they were lit up in neon in her head.

And Soames had used some wonderful phrases. In the margins of her notebook, she drew stars beside names and places dropped into the conversation.

'We liked to party . . . We had all the chat-up lines . . . And if they didn't work, there were always our little helpers,' she wrote, adding 'Drink? Drugs? Rohypnol?'

Joe had also got his notebook out and was writing in it, but with the same look of pained concentration as Kate's sons when they did their homework at the kitchen table. Steve handled the maths and science duty, she did the spellings and essays. Teamwork.

'Get down everything you remember, Joe,' she said. 'We'll compare notes later.'

* * *

At the office, she opened the envelope and pulled out a handful of pictures. Included were the Polaroids she'd found wedged on top of the wardrobe.

The images were slightly faded, the photographic paper losing its definition over the decades, but the content suddenly came into focus. Naked limbs, scattered clothing, slack, unconscious faces.

She scooped them up quickly and took them into the Ladies, where she could look at them uninterrupted.

She went through them carefully, her hands trembling, scrutinizing the faces of the women and girls. *They were all someone's daughter*, she thought. *I'm glad I only have boys. How can you protect girls from harm?*

They definitely looked drugged, Kate thought as she examined the half-open, dead eyes in the photos.

'You look so young, you're just a child,' she told one of the girls.

And there were glimpses of the perpetrator — a shoulder, a hand, the side of Soames's face, recognizable. These were trophy photos. The kill recorded by the hunter.

Kate tried to see more, straining her eyes to see something in the picture that would tell the whole story, but there was just what was there. A small square of evidence, like a tile from a mosaic. She spread all the photos out on the floor.

Nina, the news desk secretary, found her kneeling on the floor, surrounded by the images, when she swept in for a quick pee.

'Bloody hell, Kate, I nearly fell over you. What are you doing? Is it the call to prayer or something?'

Nina delighted in being the least PC person in the office.

'Sorry, Nina. Wanted to look at these pictures without anyone rubbernecking. They're a bit sensitive,' Kate said.

Nina crouched down beside her. 'Bloody hell, my knees. What's going on here?' she said.

'You may well ask,' Kate said. 'I think someone drugged and raped these women.'

'No. What an animal,' Nina spat. 'And he took his own personal photographer?'

Kate looked at her. She was right. She'd been so busy looking at the images, she hadn't clocked the obvious fact that there had to be two people involved. The photographer and the man in the pictures. This wasn't a selfie. It was posed and framed.

'Nina,' she said, 'you are a constant marvel.'

Nina looked confused but pleased. 'I help when I can. Now get me back on my feet.'

50

Emma

I woke crying last night. Not dream crying. My face was wet with real tears and I lay curled in on myself. Fighting to silence my breathing, so I didn't wake Paul next to me. Fighting not to think about my dream.

But it's hard not to. It invades my every cell. It's the same dream I've had for years.

It started when I was fifteen. I remember I used to wake up then, unable to move or breathe. Night terrors, I suppose they'd label them now. But they couldn't imagine what it was like. In the dream, a baby was talking to me, angry with me, following me on its little legs like a grotesque doll. It was banging on the door to get in. And I was holding the door closed and sobbing. I woke, as I always did, when the door began to crack open.

I can see myself then, transfixed. My chest tight and my throat thick with distress. It took what felt like ages for me to be able to move again. I had to work out where I was and convince myself that it had just been a dream and I could nail the door shut again. I remember I used to bury my face in my pillow when I heard Jude moving about in her room below mine because she'd heard me. I used to slow my breathing to pretend I was still asleep.

Sometimes it worked, but other nights, Jude's bedroom door creaked to alert me and I heard her pad in bare feet to the bathroom.

'Go back to bed, Mum,' I whispered to myself, willing her to stay away. But, inevitably, the bare feet padded up the attic stairs and stopped outside my room.

'Are you all right, Emma?' Jude said softly as she opened the door. 'I heard you crying again.'

I remember lying there with my back to her, in silence. I didn't know what to say, what to tell her. Sometimes Jude stroked my head and went away when I ignored her, but that night, she sat down on the bed.

In the end, the pressure of my mum's presence in the dark forced me to speak.

'It was just a dream. I think I ate too much dinner. That's all.'

'You hardly ate anything. You're getting thin — I'm worried about you. Will and I both are. I know things have been difficult, but you're just growing up. I wish I knew what's going on in your head. Tell me, please.'

'Nothing's wrong,' I said quickly. I hadn't realized she'd noticed so much. I thought I'd made myself invisible. 'I'm just a bit fed up with school.'

'Oh Emma, what's happening to you? You were doing so well. You don't seem to care about anything any more.'

I roll on to my back and put my hand out to

touch Paul's face. To know he is there. He puts an arm across my chest, squeezing me as he sleeps. I'd wanted to hug my mum that night, but I was afraid to.

Afraid that my body would give me away.

★ ★ ★

Paul is so worried about me he's rung in to cancel a lecture this morning.

'I'll work from home, Em. I can't leave you like this,' he says.

I try to object, but I haven't got the energy. I go upstairs and try to work, but nothing is happening. The words just jumble up and stick, like an old record, juddering in my head until I want to scream. In the end, I go downstairs to make a coffee and turn on the radio for company.

When the music stops, the lunchtime-news man announces there's been a new development in the Alice Irving case and I stand and wait, letting the kettle go cold again. I have to listen to three or four stories about the Olympics and politics and wars. And suddenly, the newsreader tells me that the baby was buried in the 1980s. Just like that. And I shout 'No!' at him. I want him to take it back. Say he's made an error. But he carries on, saying the police have 'made fresh discoveries that place the burial of Alice Irving at least ten years after her abduction'.

I don't know what to think any more. Everything is wrong. I've got everything wrong.

Paul rushes into the kitchen, making me jump.

I'd forgotten he was at home and it frightens me when he appears suddenly.

'What's the matter?' he says. 'What's happened?'

'Just something on the news. Just me being silly, that's all,' I say, trying to be soothing, but sounding too loud.

'What was on the news?' he says.

I try to lie. But I can't. There are no other words in my head.

'About a baby,' I say. 'They've got it all wrong. They're making a terrible mistake.'

'Come and sit down. You are getting yourself all upset again,' he says and takes me by the hand to sit me at the table with him. 'Now then, why are you so worried about this baby?'

I look at him and say, 'I think it's my baby.' And I watch his face collapse.

'Em, you haven't got a baby,' he says gently. 'We decided not to have one, didn't we? Because you weren't ready.'

I swipe away his words with my hand. 'Not your baby, Paul. Mine.'

'Why are you saying this? You've never mentioned this before,' he says, searching for the truth in my eyes. I am frightening him. I know I must sound mad.

'I didn't want you to know,' I say. 'No one knows.'

'Not Jude?' he asks.

'No,' I say, and I can see the disbelief creeping across his face.

'You're upset,' he says. 'I'll get your pills.'

51

Friday, 13 April 2012

Jude

She hadn't recognized his voice when she picked up the phone, and for one wonderful moment she thought it might be Will. But it was Paul. Emma's Paul.

What does he want? she thought crossly.

'Hello, Jude,' he said. *Well at least he's dropped the Judith thing.*

'Hello, Paul. This is a surprise.'

'Look, I'm sorry to ring out of the blue, but I'm worried about Emma.'

Jude sat down and gripped the receiver. 'What's happened?'

Her son-in-law hesitated, searching for the right words. 'Em is getting herself upset about the discovery of a baby in Woolwich,' he said.

'The baby in Howard Street?' Jude said. 'Yes, she told me about it. It's the road where we used to live.'

'Yes, I know,' Paul said, and stopped again.

'You are obviously trying to tell me something. Just spit it out,' Jude said. She hadn't meant to be so brusque, but he was unnerving her with these long, ominous silences.

'Sorry . . . yes, well . . . Emma says she thinks it is her baby.'

Jude gave a bark of astonishment. '*Her* baby? What a lot of nonsense! It's been named as Alice Irving.'

'No, that's right, but the police have issued new information saying she was buried in the 1980s — and it seems to have sent Emma into a panic.'

That stopped Jude dead. But only for a second.

'Have they? I hadn't heard that. But it's still nonsense. Look, Paul, you haven't known her as long as I have. My daughter has always had a tenuous relationship with the truth.'

'You think she is making it up?'

'Obviously. To be frank, she used to make up a lot of things when she was younger. Silly lies about her dad, and my boyfriend. We don't need to go into all that, but perhaps she's upset at the moment because we talked about the old days — the bad old days, in our case — when she came for lunch the other week.'

'She didn't tell me that,' Paul said.

'Didn't she? No, well, she probably doesn't want you to know what a nightmare she was when she was younger. You know we had to ask her to leave home in the end?'

There was silence at the other end of the line. 'Paul?' Jude asked.

'Yes, I'm here. Poor Emma. I didn't know that. She's never talked about her childhood, really. But you said 'we'. I thought it was just you and Emma. She said she didn't know who her

261

father was. Who else was there?'

'My boyfriend. Will. Emma must have mentioned him.'

'No, I don't think so,' Paul said.

'How strange. Well, anyway, it wasn't *poor Emma*, it was poor us. You can't imagine what it was like,' Jude said. The case for the defence. 'Why don't you get Emma to ring me?' she went on. 'I'll have a chat with her about things. Maybe I can calm her down.'

'I might suggest it, Judith. Goodbye.'

★　★　★

Jude got up and picked up a photo of Emma from her mantelpiece. She'd been two when it was taken, dressed in a little kilt her mother had brought home from a holiday in Scotland, and was beaming up at the camera. *That little face.*

When she'd dreamed of having a baby, Jude had never really thought beyond the cradle stage about the impact of having another person in her life. She'd concentrated on the image of herself as Madonna with child, until the issue was forced by Emma growing out of her arms and becoming herself.

There'd been a hint of things to come with the terrible twos — a brief, hellish period of daily tantrums while they were still living with Jude's parents — followed by the continual questions of the frighteningly bright five-year-old Emma and the pleasure of helping her discover the world of books.

Jude thought she knew her daughter, but the

mercurial change in her when she hit her teens was a revelation. Emma blossomed and grew thorns in what felt like a matter of weeks. All at the worst possible time, with Jude's affair with Will in its infancy.

He'd been great about it when there was that awful business with Darrell Moore. That had knocked Jude sideways. Em was still thirteen, just a child.

She'd wanted to tell the police about Darrell. 'He's practically a paedophile,' she'd told Will, but he had counselled against it, claiming it would be too much for Emma. Always thinking of Emma.

And she knew there would be too many questions. And once questions start . . .

Anyway, she'd found out about it before Emma could ruin her life with that sleazebag.

Will was a godsend that summer of 1984, Jude thought. *Those were the good times. Brief, but good. Emma really came out of her shell.*

She remembered the care Will had taken of her and Emma, always there for them, making them laugh, making things right. Jude had allowed herself to believe once more that he was the one, their future, but it had all gone wrong somehow. Not somehow. Because of Emma.

The switch back to glowering insolence had come practically overnight, with her daughter's moods swinging like a wrecking ball in the house.

Emma had retreated to her room, posting KEEP OUT on the door and barely speaking unless forced to. She lost interest in everything

263

— except food. She took all her meals to her room, piling her plate high and stuffing herself, Jude remembered. She put on so much weight. *Puppy fat*, Jude had called it. But it was as though it was deliberate. Sabotaging herself.

Her withdrawal had become almost total. It was a bit like Barbara. She'd gone all quiet and wouldn't say what was wrong. Will had said it was creepy and had encouraged Jude to push Barbara to find another place.

But they couldn't do that to a fourteen-year-old. They'd had to wait another eighteen months. And in that time, Jude had moved from being scared at the change in her daughter to being angry, seeing her behaviour as selfish and cynical. 'I don't deserve to be treated like this,' she told Will. 'I have every right to be happy.'

And Will agreed, telling her there was no need to take it too seriously.

'It's just part of growing up, Jude,' he'd said. 'She's testing you. It's what adolescents do. Emma'll grow out of it. We need to give her space.'

So they spent less and less time in the house, going out to the theatre and dinner and leaving the problem at home. The months passed and Jude remembered to feel guilty occasionally — when she heard Emma crying at night — but her prickly child would not allow herself to be comforted or loved. She'd stopped the binge eating, at least, but she continued to shove Jude away with her blank indifference, gradually blunting her affection.

And Will was always there as a shoulder to cry

on — 'She's just being a cow, today. Probably got her period. Ignore it, Jude,' he'd say and pull her into bed. Jude had been happy to pour all her energies into the good part of her life: Will.

Anyone would have done the same, wouldn't they?

But things had got much worse after they decided to get married. Well, she'd decided and Will had agreed in a moment of grand passion. 'Time I settled down,' he'd said as they shared a post-coital cigarette. Hardly the romantic declaration she'd hoped for, but it would do.

She'd been very nervous about telling Emma. She remembered the silence in the room when she broke the news. 'He makes me very happy,' she'd said. *Not like you,* said the hum in her head.

The news had ignited something in her daughter and the ugly silences had been replaced by slamming doors and histrionic explosions. The insolence had become vocal and challenging. Emma had started being openly rude to Will, accusing him of treating women like objects, of being a male chauvinist pig, making obscene grunting noises when he walked in the room.

Will had laughed off the insults and accusations at first, but Jude could see this new Emma made him very uneasy. As if he was dealing with an unexploded bomb.

Everything was souring. She and Will were at each other's throats, having hissed arguments in the living room so Emma couldn't hear them, and Will had started going absent for days at a

265

time and then turning up as though nothing had happened. When he presented her with the choice, 'Me or Emma,' she'd been appalled, but he explained everything so well. 'It would be best for Emma. Removing her from the situation she finds so challenging will give her a chance to mature,' he said. And it made sense when he said it. Of course, it had been Jude who'd had to deliver the message to her daughter.

'We think you ought to go and live with Granny and Grandpa for a bit, Emma,' she'd said. 'We all need a break from this situation. You do see, don't you? We can't go on like this.'

'But this is my home,' Emma had said. 'Why are you throwing me out? Is this his idea?'

'No. Well, I agree with him,' Jude had said. And when her daughter smiled that knowing smile, she'd lost her temper. 'You've forced us to do this!' Jude had shouted. 'You're driving Will away! He won't stay if he has to deal with you any more. I can't let you ruin my life. You were a terrible mistake from the start.'

She could still see Emma's face. White with shock.

52

Saturday, 14 April 2012

Emma

Harry said to meet at the usual place. She knew straight away that something was up when I rang, but didn't ask any questions. She's good like that. Instead, she said, 'Come on, Em, we'll go and sit in the park and you can tell me your news.'

I should see her more, but we are both busy. Well, that's what I tell myself, but I know I keep away because she is part of the past and I have to work to keep that separate from my present. She's met Paul a couple of times, but I made sure they were never on their own. Because she knows things and I don't want her talking out of turn.

Poor Harry, it's not her fault, and I think she feels hurt when I don't respond to her texts sometimes. Maybe it would be kinder to just cut her off completely. But I can't. On days like today, she is the only person I want to see. Paul wanted me to talk to Jude. But I can't. Not after what she said. I can feel her closing the door on me again.

I get off the Tube and walk to the little café Harry likes in Hyde Park, near the lake. She can walk there from home and it's a treat for me to

267

sit outside and feel the sun on my face.

Paul thinks I am at the doctor's. He's going to ring my mobile in about thirty minutes and I'll have to lie about what Dr Gorgeous thinks. It's OK. I know what I'm going to say. I practised on the Tube.

I'm early so I read Kate Waters' story in the paper again. The story is long now; it's getting more detailed and there are more people involved, talking and guessing what happened. But at the centre is little Alice Irving. There's only one picture ever used of her and it is so blurry and old it is hard to make out. But there is a photo of Angela Irving, the mother, standing in our garden in Howard Street.

I feel the truth fluttering so close. They must see it. Surely.

I'm about to ring Kate Waters again to see what she suspects, but I see Harry coming through the park. I'll do it later.

She hugs me tightly, then pushes me back so she can have a good look at me.

'God, Harry,' I say. 'I'm fine.'

But we both know she knows I'm not. Harry crashes down into a seat, swinging a vast handbag on to the chair next to her. 'Yeah, yeah,' she says. 'You look lovely, by the way.'

'I look like hell. I'm supposed to be at the doctor's,' I say and she raises her eyebrows.

'Why aren't you?' she says.

'Don't feel like it,' I say and pick up the laminated menu. 'Anyway, if Paul rings, I'll have to lie. OK? Oh, don't look like that. You've done worse.'

She laughs and pulls the menu out of my hand. 'Actually, I was supposed to go last week and ducked out, so I won't grass you up.'

'What was yours for?' I ask.

Harry pulls a face. 'Lump in my breast. Well, not even a lump, really.'

'You idiot,' I say. 'Go. Make another appointment.'

'Yes, yes. OK, I'll do it tomorrow. What do you want to drink?'

I watch her disappear into the café and thank God for her.

★ ★ ★

It was Harry who finally made me take stock of my shambles of a life. It was the summer of 1994 and she breezed into the pub where I was working. Pulling pints, defrosting shepherd's pies and treading water.

'Emma!' she called when she spotted me bringing a tray of food to the next table. It was so weird seeing her again. It had been years and all the context had gone, so she was familiar but a stranger — like someone famous you spot in the street and can't quite place for a moment.

And Harry didn't look like the best friend I'd last seen.

This Harry was W8 glamorous with her tailored trousers and jacket, manicured nails, straightened hair and eyes hidden by outsize sunglasses.

And I suppose I didn't look like her best friend any more. I'd grown taller, my hair was bleached blonde and cropped short, and I was stick thin. In photographs of myself from that period, I look like a heroin addict.

'Hello, Emma,' she said.

I had sort of expected her to turn up one day. Secretly hoped, I suppose. I missed her when I let myself think about my previous life. Little things would set me off — a song on the radio we used to sing together, a phrase she used to use — and I'd be stopped in my tracks. I'd be a teenager again. Just for a moment. Then I'd get back on with scraping greasy plates or pulling pints.

It was hard seeing her and remembering how close we'd been once. I held myself back from her, as if she was some sort of threat.

'Hello, Harry,' I said. 'Can't stop, sorry. Got a kitchen full of orders.'

She pushed her sunglasses on to her head and looked at me hard. 'No problem. I'll wait,' she said.

Later, when I sat with her in the park — in this park, cans of cider and bags of chips in our hands, like the old days — I started thinking she was my wake-up call.

She knew I'd gone to live with my grandparents, but I'd left without saying goodbye to her and she was still furious about being deserted when we finally met again. It was only when I told her I'd been thrown out by Will and Jude that she calmed down. That day in the park, I told her I'd left school as soon as I could because I didn't want to be tied down.

'I chose freedom instead of a degree and a

mortgage,' I boasted. 'I wanted to do what I liked and go where I wanted.'

Harry had given me another one of her looks and said, 'Then why aren't you out there, conquering the world, Emma?'

The cider and nostalgia had lowered my defences and I started to cry. Fat tears splashed on my chips. In that moment, I longed, physically longed, to be *me* again. The girl I used to be.

Harry put her arms round me and held me without speaking.

'Because I am nothing,' I managed to say.

'Not to me,' she said. And waited.

And I started to tell her how I really felt.

'Jude used to tell me I could be anyone,' I said. 'When I was little. But the reality is, I'm no one.'

The years of pub work and waitressing in the winter, changing beds and cleaning loos in the summer, dirty sheets, dirty strangers, drifting from job to job had worn me down.

'I can't get started, Harry, that's the problem. I feel like I'm in a thick fog most of the time. I can't make out what's ahead. I'm too scared to move forward. It might be worse than this. I keep telling myself: Stay where you are. This is the safest place to be.'

'What happened to you?' she said.

'There was a baby,' I said.

'Oh, Em,' she said.

'I couldn't tell you — or anyone. I did a terrible thing.'

She was silent again.

271

'I'm so sorry,' she said. 'I'm sure it was the right thing to do at the time.'

I remember being startled at the remark. How could it be the right thing to do? But then I realized she thought I was talking about having an abortion and for a moment I almost corrected her mistake. But the relief that I didn't have to explain further stopped me.

'What do you want to be when you grow up?' she said when I quietened. I rested my head on her shoulder and dreamed a future.

'I'm thinking about going to university, Harry,' I said.

'OK,' she said. 'You'll need A levels, but with your huge brain . . . '

'I'm not sure what's left of it,' I said, and she squeezed my hand.

'Loads,' she said. 'So . . . ?'

'I once thought I'd apply to do evening classes.'

'Sounds like a plan, Emma.'

'Yes, I'll be a schoolgirl again.' And I laughed, and there was something light in my head I hadn't felt for a long time.

★ ★ ★

But there is nothing light in my head now. The coffee is going cold as I struggle to tell Harry everything and nothing.

I know she'll bring up Alice Irving — the Howard Street connection is irresistible.

'What about this baby Alice story?' she says. 'We used to sit in your garden, didn't we? That last summer before you went to your grandma's. You had deckchairs, didn't you? Do you remember? We used to argue over who got the yellow one.'

'I think the baby in Howard Street is mine,' I say. 'I'm having dreams about it.' And she looks at me hard while she's thinking what to say.

'It isn't, Emma,' she says slowly, as if to a child. 'It is Alice Irving. The police tests show that. You mustn't talk like this. I can see that this story has really upset you, but don't you think it's because of your abortion? It's dragged up all those feelings you had at the time. It's completely normal. It was a terrible thing to cope with. Have you told Paul?'

I shake my head.

'Well, maybe you should. He loves you, Emma. He'll understand.'

I nod.

'But you have got to stop saying this is your baby. People are not going to believe you if you say these things. OK?'

I nod again. She's right. I'll keep quiet until people find out for themselves.

53

Angela

Asda was heaving with people throwing bags of Monster Munch into trolleys and screaming at their offspring.

'Kylie, put that down!' the woman in a Southampton football shirt shouted behind her in the queue for the till, and Angela ducked her head against the noise.

'Sorry, love,' the woman said. 'But the little bleeders need telling, don't they?'

Angela mimed that she had forgotten something, pretending to search through her trolley, and walked away from the queue. She carried on out of the supermarket and sat in the car with her eyes closed and her hands over her ears. Her sensitivity to noise had become unbearable since Alice had been found. She found everything unbearable, really. She'd thought it would be easier, knowing where her baby was after all those years, but it wasn't. It was a piece in a long-abandoned jigsaw, but there was still no picture, still no answers.

She sat on until it began to rain, then started the car and set off for home. When she drew up in the drive feeling cold to her bones, she didn't

274

remember whole sections of the journey. Nick came out to get the bags of shopping from the boot. And she remembered her discarded trolley in the supermarket.

'I'm sorry,' she said when he opened the car door. 'I didn't get anything. I couldn't bear it in there. Everyone was shouting . . . '

He put his arm round her and shepherded her to safety. 'I'll go later,' he said. 'Give me your list.'

★ ★ ★

Angela watched the television without seeing anything. Nick had been watching the sport, but the images of Howard Street, the mud and the flapping tape played over and over in her head.

'It's not getting any better,' she said when he sat down beside her.

'Louise will be here in a minute. I've given her a call.'

'You shouldn't have rung her. She's got her own life. She can't keep running round here.'

'She wants to come. She's worried about you. We all are.'

★ ★ ★

Louise came round the living-room door cautiously, as if afraid to wake her, and Angela went straight into mum mode, jumping out of her chair to greet her and offer tea. 'Or a sandwich? Have you eaten, love? You need to eat properly.'

Her daughter gave her a big hug, not wanting to let go.

'I'm fine, Mum. I'm a big girl now. I don't need you to feed me any more,' she said. 'The question is, are *you* eating properly? Dad says you are leaving your food.'

'I haven't got much of an appetite,' Angela admitted.

'Mind you, if Dad was cooking for me, I'd lose mine,' Louise said and they both smiled. 'Sausage and mash every night, I expect. I've brought humanitarian supplies — a lamb casserole. Dad's put it in the kitchen.'

'Thanks, love. You're so good to us.'

'Rubbish. You're my mum and I love you. That's all.'

Angela started to weep. The simple sentiment only amplified her feeling of loss.

Why is this not enough? You're a lucky woman. You're surrounded by people who love you. You have two beautiful children.

Louise was talking and Angela tuned back in to hear her say that she wanted to take her mother away for a weekend.

'Oh, I couldn't go away. Something might happen — the police might need me,' she said.

'I've got my mobile phone. You don't have to be here all the time. It's making you ill, Mum.'

'No, I'm fine,' she said, pulling a tissue out of her sleeve to blow her nose. 'I need to be here. For Alice.'

Louise's face stiffened. 'You need to do what's best for you and Dad, Mum. You need a break from this. The police will do their job and you need to take care of yourself. For Paddy and me. Alice is gone, but we are still here. You do see that, don't you?'

'I am here for you!' Angela shouted at her daughter. Like the woman in Asda.

Nick came back in. 'What's going on here?' he said.

'I've upset Mum. I shouldn't have come,' Louise said. 'I'm so sorry.'

'No. It's not your fault. It's me. I don't know what I'm saying or doing at the moment,' Angela said.

'I'm taking her back to the doctor's,' Nick half-whispered to Louise. 'She's not coping.'

Back to the doctor's. Dr Earnley must be dead by now. But it will just be more patting on the shoulder, more encouraging words.

'You will get through this, Angela.'

54

Friday, 20 April 2012

Kate

Toni practically shrieked with excitement when she rang Kate to say her big reunion was on.

'I've found all sorts of people online. They all love the idea and we're having a party next week, at the Boys' Brigade hall. It's going to be brilliant. We've got an eighties DJ and everything. Say you'll come.'

Try and stop me, Kate thought. 'Sounds unmissable, Toni. Who's on the guest list?'

The landlady reeled off a string of names.

'Oh, well done for finding all of them,' Kate said. 'Must have been quite a task, after all this time.'

'Yes, some of them were hard to find, but I tracked them down. Even Harry Harrison. The girl we all thought would get herself mixed up in drugs. Actually, she's done well for herself. Who'd have thought . . . ' Toni sounded almost disappointed.

'Where's she living now?' Kate asked.

'All very posh in Kensington. Mrs Thornton now. She wasn't sure about coming at first, but I laid it on thick. You know: 'Remember where you come from, Harry.' The girls won't believe it when they see her.'

Kate noted it all down.

'Ah, but will Malcolm be at the disco?' she asked, laughing.

'Oh yes. And the Sarahs. Should be a hoot,' Toni said, breathless with excitement. 'I'd better go, got loads to do. It starts at eight. See you there in your glad rags.'

Kate put down the phone and sat back in her chair.

'Who was that?' Joe asked, ever alert. 'You look really happy.'

'For a change,' Terry said as he walked by. 'Moody baggage, your boss.'

Kate was too pleased with herself to rise to the bait.

'I've been invited to a party,' she said and laughed. 'Now I need an outfit.'

The two men looked at each other, mystified.

'I thought it was a story,' Joe said.

'Of course it's a bloody story,' Kate replied. She stood up and pulled her jacket off the back of the chair. Enjoying her moment.

'Come on, tell us,' Terry teased.

'Not in the mood,' she said and swung her bag over her shoulder ready to flounce out. 'Got to go and see someone. See you later.'

Outside, she rang Joe and told him to meet her by the main doors.

'We're going to talk to Harry Harrison,' she told him. 'No driving this time. We can walk from here.'

★ ★ ★

279

The door was opened by a middle-aged woman with a cigarette in her hand.

'Hello, Mrs Thornton? I'm Kate Waters from the *Daily Post*,' Kate said.

'Really? The press? What do you want?' the woman said, her tone instantly dismissive. 'Look, I'm on my way out.'

She's lying, Kate thought. *She's only just lit that cigarette and she's got her slippers on.*

'It won't take a minute, I promise,' Kate said. 'I'm hoping you can help me. I'm trying to contact Suzanne Harrison from Woolwich.'

The woman on the doorstep narrowed her eyes and hesitated.

Gotcha, Kate thought automatically.

'Who wants to know about her?' Harry said, a little flustered.

'Look, I'm sorry just to turn up, but could you give me five minutes of your time so I can explain?'

'You'd better come in, then,' Harry said, and then spotted Joe. 'And who are you? You don't look old enough to be a reporter.'

Joe grinned shyly. 'I'm a trainee. I'll sit quietly, I promise.'

She wafted them in with her free hand, crashing the front door closed, and herded them into her designer kitchen where it appeared she had, moments earlier, been reading a paper. Kate noticed it was the *Post*'s main competitor and put her handbag down on it.

'Well, you obviously know I'm Suzanne Harrison,' Mrs Thornton said, stubbing her cigarette out in a bowl of long-abandoned granola. 'Harrison was my maiden name — and I was Harry to everyone who knew me.'

'So many names — what shall I call you?' Kate said, laughing.

'Call me Harry. Short and sweet.'

Unlike you, Kate thought. The woman at the table was tall and chic. Harry might speak in the bored drawl that moneyed people use, but the tattoo on her breastbone, peeping above the neckline of her expensive blouse, told a different story.

'Actually, you're lucky to catch me in. I'm normally at the office by now, but I'm lunching out of town today.'

'Great,' Kate said. 'Where do you work? In the City?'

'No, at Thornton and Coran — the publishing house.'

'Oh, they do a lot of the celebrity memoirs, don't they?' Kate said. 'Actually, we serialized one of your books last year — the actress who survived cancer.'

Harry smiled. 'Yeah, that's right. I remember,' she said. 'You gave it great coverage — the books were flying off the shelves. Do you want a coffee?'

Harry poured coffee from the percolator into exquisite hand-painted cups, chatting about current projects and dropping in bits of celebrity gossip as she found the matching milk jug and sugar bowl.

'So,' she said as she sat back down. 'What's all this about, then?'

'Well, I'm writing about something that

281

happened in the area where you grew up.'

Harry stirred her coffee. 'Christ, it's been a long time since I was living in Woolwich — decades. Nothing to go back for now . . . '

'No family there?' Kate asked, reaching for a biscuit.

'A mother.'

Harry's eyes slid over to Joe, who was writing in his notebook. 'What are you scribbling about? This isn't an interview.'

Kate had forgotten about her work-experience child and she hadn't noticed him get out his notebook. Fatal, bloody schoolboy error.

'Sorry, Harry. He's just making notes on how I do my job. Aren't you, Joe?'

The edge to her voice worked and he quickly put down his pen and beamed at Harry. 'Homework!' he said.

But the connection had been broken. Harry started clearing the cups, balancing the expensive china like a waitress in a beachfront café. Kate got up to help her, sliding saucers into the dishwasher as she worked out how to rebuild trust. They were running out of time.

'Look, we haven't talked about why I've come. I'm hoping you can help me,' Kate said. 'I'm doing a story about the discovery of Alice Irving's body in Howard Street. I expect you've seen my stories about it?'

The shutters fell. Harry's eyes went blank. 'No, I hadn't heard anything about it,' she said stiffly. 'In Howard Street? Well, I didn't live there. Not sure I remember it.'

'It's where your friend lived.'

'Don't think so,' she snapped.

'Toni at the Royal Oak,' Kate prompted.

'Toni? Toni Baker. God, she rang me the other day. Did she tell you where to find me? Look, I don't know. It was all so long ago. I can't really help. Must get ready. You'll have to go,' she said, picking up her handbag. 'Can you see yourselves out? Thanks.'

Kate bundled Joe out into the hall. 'I'll leave my card here on the table, Harry, in case you want to contact me,' she called back and quietly closed the door behind her.

'There we are, then,' she said as she and Joe walked back to the office.

Joe looked at her, mystified. 'Where are we? Wasn't that a disaster? She asked us to leave.'

'But what did she tell us before she asked us to leave?'

'Nothing. She said she didn't know anything.'

'Joe, for Christ's sake, don't you know anything about reading people? As soon as I mentioned the baby, she closed down. Telling a silly lie about Howard Street.'

'Oh,' he said.

'She knows something,' Kate said. 'We'll have another chance to talk to her at the disco. And Joe — don't take notes when you are trying to persuade someone to trust you. Golden rule of interviewing.'

'But you said the golden rule was to take notes every time,' he said.

Kate sighed. Baby steps.

55

Monday, 23 April 2012

Emma

Kate picked up immediately.

'Hello, it's Anne Robinson,' I say. I've closed the door of my office so I don't get disturbed by Paul.

'Hello, Anne,' she says. 'Nice to hear from you again. How are you? What are you up to?'

I'm a bit taken aback. She's talking to me as if she knows me. I look at my crib sheet for reassurance.

Number one on the sheet is *Drug addicts?*

'Oh I'm fine, thanks. I thought I'd just give you a ring to see if you tracked down the addicts in Howard Street.'

'No, drew a blank, I'm afraid. No official records for them — expect they drifted from place to place. Anyway, everything has changed a bit since we last spoke, hasn't it? The baby was buried in the 1980s, the police say.'

'Yes, I saw that.'

'So that would have been more your era. Can you think of anyone who was behaving strangely at the time? Any gossip among the neighbours about what people were up to?'

'Not that I can think of,' I say. 'People kept

themselves to themselves, really.' Well, they did.

Kate Waters sighs. 'If I had a pound for every time someone said that,' she says and laughs. 'People love to keep things secret, don't they?'

I need to move on. Number two on the sheet is *How do they know it's her?*

'I wanted to ask you how sure they are about the identity of the baby. The police, I mean. I think they've made a mistake.'

'Do you? Why? Do you know something about the baby, Anne?'

'I'm not sure,' I say. 'I just think they've made a mistake. They should look again.' I am veering off script. *Stop.*

'Do you think the baby is someone else's, Anne?'

I don't trust myself to speak, so don't answer.

Kate Waters sounds agitated. 'Do you still live in the area?' she says. 'I could pop round to see you.'

'Oh, no,' I say too forcefully. 'I live out of London.'

I can hear Paul coming up the stairs and will him away. But he doesn't stop. 'Are you on the phone?' he calls through the door and I freeze.

'Darling!'

I put my hand over the receiver and hiss, 'I'm busy.'

'Your husband?' Kate says when I take my hand away.

'Yes, I'd better go,' I say.

'Anne,' she says carefully. 'You rang me because you want to talk about the baby and I am really glad you did. If you think the police

285

have made a mistake, it is important to say so. I know it may be hard for you, but we can talk about it. I can help you. It doesn't matter what name you use. OK?'

'OK,' I reply. 'I'll think about it.'

I do nothing else for the rest of the day.

56

Monday, 23 April 2012

Jude

Jude was doing her roots — painting out the grey with a colour she'd bought at the local chemist — and thinking about which dress to wear. She might put on the black velvet one — if she could squeeze into it — but she'd have to buy tights. And nail varnish. She felt girlish for the first time in years. She was going on a date.

Will had rung again. She'd almost not picked up the phone. She hadn't recognized the number and thought it might be a cold call or a crook, trying to scam her out of her money. Well, it had been, in a way.

'Hello, my lady, how are you?' he'd said.

'Fine, Will,' she'd said, hearing the simper in her voice.

'Thought I'd give you a call to see if you've transferred your donation to the university centenary fund? We're almost halfway to the total.'

She'd forgotten. That's why he'd rung in the first place. Not for her. For money. She'd pushed the ungenerous thought to one side. 'Sorry, Will. I'll do it today. It is lovely to hear from you again.'

'Lovely to hear you, too. You don't sound a day older, Jude,' he'd said. And she'd felt happier than she had for weeks.

'Where are you living these days?' she'd asked. 'Still in Clapham?'

'No, I moved when I retired. I'm in a little village in Kent. Bucolic retreat. Dead as the grave, actually.'

'You sound in need of cheering up,' she'd said. 'Why don't you come up to town and we can go for dinner?'

He'd hesitated and she'd felt ridiculous for having asked, but before she could make an excuse, he'd cleared his throat and said, 'That would be a real treat.'

The date had been set for the following Monday at one of their old haunts in Victoria. 'Handy for the trains,' he'd said.

'Tonight's the night,' she told herself in the mirror as she fastened her earrings.

★   ★   ★

She arrived first, leaving home early so she could walk slowly with her dicky hip, but he appeared in the plate-glass window minutes later, and peered in.

God, you look old, she thought as she caught sight of his face.

He swept through the restaurant and bent to kiss her, then held her by her shoulders to get a proper look.

'Still beautiful, Jude,' he said.

'Still a smooth talker,' she replied.

'Yes, but it's all talk these days,' he said and they both laughed.

Ice broken, they cantered through decades of life during the tri-colore salad starter. Shorthanding their experiences, hooting with laughter at shared memories and skirting round the reason they hadn't seen each other for almost twenty years.

But halfway through the melanzane alla parmigiana, Will asked about Emma. She'd wondered when he'd venture there.

'So,' he said, as the waiter poured more wine, 'did Emma ever get back in touch?'

'Yes, actually. A couple of years ago. Out of the blue.'

'I see. So how is she doing these days?'

'So-so. Married to a man old enough to be her father.'

'Right,' he said. 'Working?'

'Yes. She got herself together in the end. It took a while, but she went to university in her twenties. She's a book editor. Working from home. Commercial rubbish, most of it, but she does it well.'

'Do you see much of her?'

'Yes. Well, sometimes. I told her you'd been in touch.'

'Did you?' he said, his hand jerking and flicking a gobbet of tomato sauce off his fork. He rubbed it into the tablecloth with his finger. 'What did she say?'

'Not much,' Jude said, remembering Emma's frozen expression. 'Well, it must be difficult for her. She probably still feels guilty about coming between us.'

Will carried on chewing.

Jude knew what he was thinking. Will had tried to understand Emma's moods and her descent into teenage angst, but she had been impossible to read some days.

'You used to say she'd grow out of it. But, of course, she left before she could,' she said, disarmed by the wine and his proximity.

Will looked up quickly.

'I sometimes wonder what would have happened if we'd got married back then, like we planned, Will,' Jude added. She wasn't sure what she expected him to say, but she longed for a glimmer of the intimacy they'd shared. For old times' sake.

'Hmm,' he said. 'Me too.'

She didn't believe him. He was humouring her.

He looked up and she tried to smile, but it got stuck on her teeth.

Will reached out a tomato-stained hand to pat hers. 'Look, it was a difficult time for all of us,' he said. 'I loved you, Jude, but Emma soured everything.'

'She had been gone for six or seven years when you left,' Jude said quietly.

'Well, the damage had been done, I suppose. I had to get out of there,' he said, wiping his mouth with the serviette.

'Yes,' she said. *And sleep with anyone with a pulse*, she thought.

She didn't think she'd have a pudding.

57

Tuesday, 24 April 2012

Emma

I really don't want to go.

'Stupid idea,' I told Harry when she rang last night to say that Toni from Woolwich Secondary had been in touch, but she wouldn't let it go. It's sent her off on some sort of nostalgia trip. It's something about our age, I suppose. I wonder if she wants to show them how far she's come. Show the big girls who teased her and made her life a misery. But I don't say it. She's banging on about seeing people from school on Facebook. I haven't looked. I'm more of a lurker, hanging round the posts, just seeing who is doing what. I tend not to advertise my presence. I've got nothing to say.

Emma Massingham thinks it is her baby in Howard Street would put the cat among the pigeons, wouldn't it?

I told Harry I'd only go to the disco if she went to the doctor's for her check-up. I knew she wouldn't, so there would be no more discussion. But she went this morning.

When Harry rings at lunchtime, she is happier than I've ever heard her.

'It's like a huge weight has been lifted, Emma.

291

I don't think I knew how worried I was. But the doctor is happy it's just a cyst. It's not going to kill me.'

'That's brilliant! I'm so glad,' I say.

'Anyway, you've got to come to the disco now. You promised,' she says, and I groan.

'No, really? It'll be awful. All those girls who teased us about our terrible haircuts until we cried.' I pleaded my case.

'Well, we'll have the chance to confront them about their appalling behaviour, won't we? I can't wait to see their faces when we swan in. We could stage a truth and reconciliation hearing. Where's Desmond Tutu when you need him?' Harry says, trying to wheedle me into it. I can't resist her good mood, much as I want to.

'Yes, that sounds like a fun evening. Or we could dance to terrible music round our handbags in cruel shoes?'

'Now you're talking,' Harry says. 'Start thinking about your outfit and ring me tomorrow to finalize.'

'OK.'

'Thanks for today, Emma. You always were the clever one.'

★   ★   ★

I tell Paul I'm going to the reunion and he smiles. A proper smile, not the nervous twitch of the mouth he's adopted recently.

'That's great. It will do you good to go out. You spend too much time sitting at your computer. Always on your own.'

I want to tell him I'm never on my own, but I don't.

'I spoke to Jude the other day,' he says and glances up to see how I'll react.

'Did you?' I'm astonished and can't hide it. 'Why? Did she ring when I was out or something?'

'Well, no. Actually I rang her.'

'Rang her?' I repeat.

'I was worried about you,' he says. He's sorry he told me, I can see it on his face. 'I wanted her advice.'

'Well, she'd be the last person I'd ask,' I say. *What has she told him?* The thought is rattling round my head like a runaway train. 'What did she say?'

'Not much, really. Except that she thought she'd upset you, talking about the past. When you went for lunch. Do you think she's right?'

I sigh. 'Well, you know I hate looking back, Paul. And we had a very difficult relationship.'

'She said she had to ask you to leave home,' Paul says, and I realize he has been working up to this. 'You've never told me that.'

I go and sit next to him on the sofa so he can't see my face properly. 'I don't like talking about it. It was such a horrible time. You can't imagine. I don't think I've ever got over it. I was only just sixteen.'

'Oh Emma, how could they have done that? You were still a child,' he says, squeezing my cold hand.

But I am back on full alert. '*They?*' I say.

'Well, Jude told me her boyfriend, Will, was

293

living with you both. I don't think you've ever mentioned him, either. Too many secrets aren't good for you, Emma. Keeping everything inside is toxic.'

And it's as if he's seen inside my head.

Can I tell him it all? Can I? Will he hate me for the terrible thing I did? Of course he will.

'You're right, darling. But you know now.'

He turns my face towards him gently and holds it in both hands. 'You can tell me anything, Emma, you know that.'

I lean forward and kiss him. To show I love him. And to silence him.

58

Saturday, 28 April 2012

Kate

On the night of the do, Kate pulled up in Howard Street ridiculously early. It was only seven o'clock but she'd got ready too quickly and had worried about running the gauntlet of her sons' remarks about her maxi dress, slit to the thigh, and floppy hat à la Anita Ekberg.

She needn't have done. Freddie was at the cinema with friends and Jake stayed upstairs. He was spending more and more time on the internet in his room, planning his trip.

'I've found a project in Phuket,' he'd announced a couple of days earlier.

His little brother had laughed. 'Is it to do with sunbathing?' Freddie had said. 'I could do that, too.'

Kate had sucked in her comments and carried on laying the table.

'You've put the knives and forks the wrong way round,' Freddie told her and swapped them all.

'Sorry, lots on my mind,' she'd said, giving Jake a meaningful stare. He ignored it.

'Actually, it's about coastline conservation,' he'd said to Freddie.

'What do you know about that? You were doing Law.'

'I've got GCSEs in biology and geography,' Jake had said. 'Should be fun.'

'Well, as long as it's *fun*,' Kate had muttered under her breath. But Jake had heard and taken his dinner upstairs.

Steve had gone up to talk to him when he'd got in from work.

'He's a bit hurt that you were so dismissive of his plans,' he had said.

'Oh, come on. Babying him and dressing the problem up in big words isn't going to help. He's twenty-two and he's going to become a beach bum, Steve. He needs to be challenged.'

She was glad her dad wasn't around to see his grandson opt out of life. He'd have had a few well-chosen words to say to Jake. *He'll be turning in his grave*, she thought. *Sorry, Dad*.

'OK, Kate. Let's leave it for tonight, hey?' Steve said. 'He's coming down to watch the match with me on the telly.'

She'd sulked in the kitchen while the boys cheered and jeered the footballers, stirring a cheese sauce for a future meal until it glooped out of the pan and made a mess of the hob and she dumped the whole lot in the bin.

★ ★ ★

The only person who saw her outfit was Steve, who came home early that night. For a change. They'd thought that with the boys practically off their hands they'd get more time together, doing the things that people of their age did: theatre trips, wine bars, exotic travel. But the empty spaces in their diaries — where the football training, the swimming practice, the lifts to gigs and dates used to be — gaped invitingly for a brief moment and then were filled with work instead of pleasure. Kate knew it was important for Steve to build his consulting work at the hospital and never nagged. She could hardly say anything with her own ridiculous hours, anyway.

So that night, she was surprised and happy to hear him come through the door.

Steve whistled when he saw her. 'Wow, look at you!' he said. 'What's going on?'

'I told you last night. I'm going to a party in Woolwich. I'm trying to find women who might know how Alice Irving ended up in their neighbourhood.'

'Course you did, sorry, love. Awful day. Nothing but bad news. Mrs Telling's cancer has spread. I'd only just told her she was in remission. It's so bloody unfair.'

'Oh, Steve,' she said and put her arms round him. 'How awful. It makes my day sound pathetic. I've been tinkering with a Sunday-for-Monday story about the Queen's Jubilee. Guess who's playing at the concert?'

'Is it Paul McCartney?' he said and they both laughed.

'Of course. No big occasion's complete without Macca,' she said. 'Anyway, I'm hoping I get somewhere with a real story tonight.'

'Hmm,' Steve said, rooting in the fridge for something to keep him going until dinner. 'Is

297

there any more brie?'

He had his feet up in front of the telly when Kate emerged from the bathroom, and wished her good luck in that maddeningly casual way he had sometimes when it came to her work.

'It's not about luck, Steve, it's about hard work and persistence,' she said.

'Course it is. It's just difficult to take it completely seriously when you have to dress up and go to an eighties disco. Doesn't really happen in my world . . . '

He meant that his world, the Oncology Department of Lewisham hospital, was more real, more important, somehow.

Kate bit her lip and tasted essence of strawberry. 'I'm investigating the kidnap and death of a baby, Steve. It doesn't get much more serious than that, does it?'

'Oh Katie, always on the defensive. You look brilliant, by the way.'

'Sod off. I can't be bought off with a few lame compliments,' she said. Kissing him hard.

'Hmm. Yummy. Tastes of my youth. Make sure you put that on before you come to bed tonight,' he said.

'Later,' she called as she left with a cheeky wave, tottering out to her car on three-inch platforms and clambering in quickly so next-door Bet didn't see her.

★ ★ ★

Now here she was with an hour to kill. She didn't fancy the pub in full eighties gear so

298

switched on her radio and listened to Radio 4. There was an item about global warming and some old duffer was talking over the interviewer. She smiled. It was always a challenge to control gasbags in an interview. No one liked being interrupted and it could ruin the rapport.

She'd learnt to silence people with body language — lean forward to encourage and back to halt them. She hadn't believed it when an old hand gave her the technique. But it worked time and time again.

Losing eye contact and putting your pen down were also effective, but a bit obvious. Radio reporters raised a hand to stop a long answer. Interesting how we interpret signals.

Kate jumped when Barbara Walker knocked on her window. She lowered the glass, smiling at her surprise.

'Goodness, you scared me to death — I was miles away,' she said.

Miss Walker shook her head. 'Sorry, dear. I saw you sitting there from the window and wondered if you wanted a cuppa? Bit sad sitting here on your own.'

'Love to,' Kate said and levered herself out to tower over her new friend.

Miss Walker looked up at her and then at her boots. 'Look at you. Are you going to a party? Love the platforms. Where'd you find them?'

'Age Concern,' Kate said. 'Historical-footwear department.'

'Come on then, before you fall over and snap an ankle,' Miss Walker laughed.

She made Kate put on the big hat and give her

a twirl in the front room. The fuss disturbed Shorty, who barked at them both.

'Hush,' Miss Walker said, tapping his nose. 'It's only a bit of fun. Now then, do you want a Cinzano instead of tea? Seeing as we're going all retro.'

'Have you really got some? I didn't know they still made it,' Kate said, collapsing into an armchair. 'Thank you, Barbara.'

'I'm not sure how old the bottle is, but I'll stick some lemonade in it to jazz it up. I might even have some ice. Come on, Shorty, I'll feed you at the same time.'

Kate sat back and wriggled her cramped toes, willing the blood to circulate again. Suffering for her craft, Steve would say if he was here.

She laughed out loud as Barbara emerged with a tray bearing two tall glasses, a dusty bottle of Cinzano, a can of lemonade and a bowl of ice cubes. She made a big to-do of mixing the drinks and then the two women clinked glasses and took a sip.

'Wow, I'd forgotten what this tasted like. Cheers,' Kate said. 'What did you use to do in the eighties, Barbara? John the foreman said you were a model.'

'Well, I did that part-time — amateur stuff, really, but I did some photo shoots for a friend who was a magazine photographer. I was really a legal secretary.'

'Photo shoots! How exciting. I bet you met some interesting people, heard some stories,' Kate said, taking another gulp of her drink.

'Yes,' the older woman murmured.

'And there must have been parties,' Kate said, smiling expectantly. She loved showbiz gossip, that mixture of glamour and the fabulously mundane — Hollywood and haemorrhoids.

'Lots of parties,' Miss Walker began, but tailed off uncertainly and busied herself with the tray.

'Goodness, you must have seen some things,' Kate said.

'I don't really remember, dear,' the older woman said as she stood up and made for the kitchen.

Kate sat alone and wondered what she'd said.

When Barbara reappeared, she'd put on fresh lipstick, a red gash dominating her face.

'You look nice,' Kate smiled.

'Just a bit of lippy. Gives you a boost, doesn't it?' Miss Walker said, pleased.

'I hardly wear make-up now,' Kate said. 'Too much fannying about and no one notices anyway. You get to a certain age and paff! You're invisible. People look straight through you. They look startled when you speak. My friends have all noticed it.'

'You could do a lot with your face,' Miss Walker said, reaching to brush Kate's wayward hair back. 'Lovely cheekbones. And I could get rid of those bags easy as winking.'

The women looked at each other. 'I'll get my box of tricks,' Miss Walker said, and disappeared into the hall.

The box was large and well travelled, its pink vinyl cover discoloured by its adventures.

'Come on, sit in the light by the lamp. Let me have a proper look,' Miss Walker said.

301

She got out her sponges, which looked permanently stained TV-personality orange, and began dabbing Kate's face. They smelt unwashed and Kate tried not to mind.

'Now then, look up while I do your eyeliner,' Miss Walker said, bending over Kate, her voice confident and younger, somehow.

'Lovely eyes, Kate. You need to do more with them. Now blink.'

Kate did as she was told and tried to enjoy the pampering.

'Blusher? Just a hint, I think. We all need roses in our cheeks, don't we?'

'Goodness, do you remember when we used to put it on in stripes, in the seventies?' Kate laughed. 'We looked like Hiawatha.'

Barbara laughed, too. 'I loved that look. All smoky eyes and statement lips. You can keep the natural look.'

'I bet you knocked them dead,' Kate said. 'I'd love to see a photo of you from then.'

Miss Walker hesitated, lip brush in hand. 'OK. I think I've got some somewhere. Just blot your lips on this tissue while I look.'

She brought back a handful of black and white studio shots.

'Oh my God, you are stunning in these!' Kate said, genuinely impressed. And then stopped, dead.

'I turned a few heads,' Barbara said shyly.

Kate didn't speak. Couldn't speak. She kept looking at the glossy photos of Barbara. She was one of the women with the dead eyes in Al Soames's Polaroids. She recognized the arch of the eyebrow, the hair. Kate took another sip of

Cinzano. She didn't know what to do or say. She couldn't just blurt it out. Did Barbara know?

Barbara was still chattering about her modelling days, laughing over her memories.

'They must have been falling at your feet,' Kate said, trying to keep the conversation going. 'I'd love to borrow these to show to the photographer I work with. He'll be so impressed. Who was your most famous conquest? Mick Jagger?'

Miss Walker laughed. 'Don't be daft,' she said. 'I wasn't in his league. You can take them if you like.'

'Were you living here, then, Barbara?' Kate said.

'At number 63. I told you the other day. I rented a room with shared bathroom. It was a great big place. My friend from work, Jude, lived there too.'

'Right. Who else? No men? In the house, I mean?' Kate asked.

'Jude didn't bother with men really — too much trouble, she said. Jude had her work and her daughter to keep her busy. Until Will came along . . . ' Barbara tailed off.

'Oh?' Kate said, leaning forward.

'Will Burnside,' she said, and Kate was taken aback by the bitterness in her voice.

'Who was he?' Kate asked. 'Not a favourite with you, then?'

'No. He was horrible.'

'Horrible? How was he horrible?'

'He wasn't what he seemed. I just didn't like him. But Jude did. She was absolutely smitten with him. I moved out, anyway. Changed job. Had a fresh start.'

'Was number 63 one of Al Soames's houses?' Kate asked.

And Barbara Walker closed her eyes. It was as if she had shut down. Kate sat forward and touched the older woman's arm, to remind her she was still there, and the eyes opened.

'Are you OK, Barbara?'

Miss Walker tried a watery smile. 'Sorry, dear. Memories, that's all. Can catch you unawares, can't they?'

'You look a bit wobbly, Barbara,' Kate said.

'I am,' Barbara Walker said, her voice quavering. 'You see, people are not what they seem. You see them on the street or at a party and they look like normal people, but they're not. Sometimes they're not.'

'What do you mean, Barbara?' Kate said. One minute she was sipping flat Cinzano and lemonade, the next taking confession while wearing platform shoes. No one could say journalism was predictable. She waited.

'I'm just saying,' Miss Walker said, moving Shorty on to her lap.

'But you are all upset. I think you are talking about a specific person, Barbara. Are you? It might help to tell someone.'

Me, tell me, thought Kate, crossing her fingers and legs. Miss Walker closed her eyes again, but jerked them open at a sudden tinny blast of Wagner's Ride of the Valkyries.

'Christ,' Kate said, rummaging in the bottomless pit of her handbag. 'It's my phone. I'm so sorry, Barbara.'

It took six rings to locate the phone, six

rounds of the opening bars to spoil any chance of intimacy.

'Hello, Mick,' she said when she finally answered it. 'I'm a bit busy.'

But Barbara was already clearing away the glasses. 'You'd better go,' she said. 'You're going to be late for your party.'

59

Kate

Kate found Mick leaning on the wing of her car.

'Look at you, all dolled up. On the game tonight?' he shouted as she approached.

'Shut up, Mick. What are you doing here?' she said.

'Picture desk sent me. To do pics of some reunion you're going to. Didn't they tell you?'

'No,' Kate said. 'You'd never think we were in the communication business. Look, I'm not sure what you can do. It's a bit of a fishing expedition. I'm going to this party to find people who were around when Alice Irving was buried. There won't really be anything to photograph.'

'Fucking desk. It's my day off. They never ask enough questions before they send,' Mick said, flicking away his cigarette end.

'Sorry, Mick,' she said. 'Actually, you can do something. I've been given some photos that I need copying. Can I give it to you to do?'

He hunched his shoulders and shrugged. 'Yeah, OK.'

Kate was beginning to shiver with cold. She'd left her coat in the car when she'd gone into Barbara's house. 'Let's get in the car,' she said. 'I

306

can tell you about it in the warm.'

She gave him the black and white modelling photographs of Barbara and he studied one. 'Lovely face,' he said. 'Who is she?'

Kate filled Mick in on Barbara, 63 Howard Street and Al Soames as he chain smoked, carefully holding his cigarette out of the passenger window as if it made any difference to the blue fug filling the car.

'And then there are other photos,' she said.

'Others? What, other modelling pics?'

'No, Polaroids of unconscious women — some of them young girls — that I got from Soames's flat. I think Barbara maybe among them. I haven't got them here, but I'll show you tomorrow.'

'Fuck. Have you told Terry yet?' he said.

'Give me a minute, Mick. This has just happened. I didn't know I was going to meet one of Al Soames's victims. One minute I was having my make-up done, the next this story came tumbling out. Anyway, I want to have a think about it before I tell the news desk. You know what they're like — they'll go full-steam ahead. I don't know if Barbara knows what happened to her. It could be devastating for her. This is going to take some very careful handling.'

'Yeah, you're right. Poor woman.'

'I've got to find the other man in the photos, for a start,' she said.

She wished she still smoked.

'Go on, you get off,' she said, wafting his smoke and the temptation away from her. 'I'll talk to Terry in the morning. There's nothing we can do tonight.'

Mick grinned at her. 'OK, I'm in the office tomorrow if you need me,' he said, tossing his cigarette away.

A gaggle of ageing disco divas tottered past, shrieking and clutching each other.

'Evening, ladies,' Mick called after them.

'Better go. I'm expected,' Kate said, reaching behind her for the purple felt hat.

'Go on then. Can I come? I'm a demon on the dance floor.' Mick pulled a John Travolta shape, banging his hand on the rear-view mirror and swearing.

'I can see that, Mick. But I've already got a date. You go home and ruin your fiancée's evening instead. How is the saintly Anna?'

He grinned. 'Bearing up,' he said and flicked the brim of her hat in farewell as he got out. She waited until he had driven off before readjusting the mirror to check her face. It'd do. She looked tired.

'I've peaked too early,' she said out loud.

She wondered how Barbara was. She'd offered to stay with her for a while, but she'd been shooed towards the door.

'You get off,' Barbara had said. 'I think I'll shut my eyes for a while.'

'Of course. You have a rest. But I'll call you in the morning, Barbara,' Kate had said.

'Come on,' she said to her reflection. Joe would be there in a minute and their job shouldn't take long. They only had to talk to Toni's friends and see if they could pick up some leads on who might have brought Alice here. 'Hour, tops, and then home.'

Joe sprinted into view, running up the street to show he realized he was late. 'You look like Donny Osmond in that shirt,' she said as he stood panting by the car.

'Bus got stuck in traffic and I got called an effing poofter by a drunk.'

'Never mind. I've had a bit of an evening too, but let's get in there and chat everyone up. Ready?'

He nodded and squared his shoulders.

★ ★ ★

The music almost blew her hat off as they walked through the door. Gloria Gaynor was belting out 'Never Can Say Goodbye' and the Boys' Brigade hall was heaving with sequined boob tubes and unsuitable legs in short skirts. *Oxfam has had a good week*, Kate thought.

She looked at Joe's stricken face and laughed. 'Mum heaven,' she shouted in his ear. 'You go to the bar and talk to the women there. I'll take the dance floor.'

She sashayed into the crowd, arms raised in mock tribute to the opening bars of 'Girls Just Wanna Have Fun' as Toni lurched towards her and enveloped her in a hug.

'This is brilliant!' Kate shouted. 'Fantastic job, Toni!'

The landlady gave her a double thumbs up and screamed in her ear to follow her.

They wove their way through the dancers, avoiding flailing arms, to a table near the emergency exit.

Toni did the introductions, pointing and shouting the names. 'This is Jill and Gemma.' The two brunettes bobbed their heads at her, smiling warmly. 'And Sarah B and Sarah S. And Harry.'

Kate mouthed hello to all of them. Harry raised one startled eyebrow in recognition.

'Kate's the reason we're all here,' Toni screeched. 'She gave me the idea in the first place. Come on, this is my favourite record. I want to dance all night.'

Four of the women jumped up to join her, and Kate stayed put with Harry.

They tried to talk but it was impossible, so Harry shouted, 'Ladies' toilet?' and they trooped off.

'Meanwhile, back at the youth club,' Kate said when they reached the traditional teenage sanctuary and closed the door on the music.

Harry eyed her up and down. 'Why are you here?' she hissed.

'Toni invited me. You know why I'm here.'

At that moment, the cubicle door swung open, banging noisily on its hinges in time-honoured fashion. A woman in a beautiful blue dress emerged and Kate looked at her closely.

60

Emma

Harry and I met at Woolwich Dockyard station and got a taxi to the venue. The Boys' Brigade hall had stopped being new a long time ago. It looked as if it was leaning drunkenly to the left, the roof was mossy and the paintwork was peeling.

'Can't believe it's still standing,' Harry said, paying the driver and leaping out. She'd gone for the glam-rock look and I'd opted for New Romantic. Looking through a box of old clothes in the loft, I found one of Jude's old dresses with a thousand buttons — it hung off me, way too big, but I could've sworn I'd worn it before. I got Paul to help me. He kissed me when he'd finished and said, 'You look fantastic, Em. Go and have a lovely time with the other ravers.'

'Thanks for the buttons,' I said, slipping my coat on and picking up my keys. 'Don't wait up. I'll be late.'

'OK, bye,' he called, switching on the television.

★   ★   ★

311

The disco is in full swing and the music hits me like a brick to the head, so I can't see or hear anything for a few seconds. Harry pinches my arm to get my attention, her eyes shining. 'It's like stepping back in time,' she shouts. 'But we're legal this time. Bacardi and coke?'

'No, Dubonnet and bitter lemon, or that horrible sweet cider. I want to be able to taste it on the way back up.' We are both lighter than we have been for years, kidding around like teenagers.

Toni and her gang gather around us immediately, eager to hear where we've been all these years.

I've decided beforehand what I'll say about my life story. *Keep it short and sweet, Emma,* I told myself. *Let's keep the grime and degradation to a minimum. We don't want pity. Or judgement.*

And it all seems to go well. I let Harry do the talking — well, she tries, but it is hard to make herself heard over the thunderous clamour of a hundred voices singing along to Wham! — and the girls are rapt. They keep touching us, as if we are aliens. Hilarious, really, but if I'd stayed living round here I might be doing the same thing. Might have been one of them. A middle-aged, restless mother with a little job at Tesco's and kids who don't ring.

Finally, we get our drinks, and when some of the others get up to dance I try to talk to Harry, but it's hopeless and in the end I head off to the loos. I've often wondered why so much of my adolescence was spent in stinking public lavatories, but it all becomes clear when I get in and shut the door. It was the only place we could hear.

I go into one of the cubicles, crouching on the child-sized loo and reading the obscene messages scrawled at head height. Apparently, a girl called Maz is working her way through the ranks of the Boys' Brigade, marking them off on the wall as if she's a con doing time. Perhaps she is.

I store the info to tell Harry, but when I come out of the cubicle, she's there. She's talking to a woman I've never seen before. Our age, but I don't think she's from our school. I decide to save Maz for later.

The woman is Kate Waters. I feel like someone has hit me in the stomach when Harry introduces her. I hear myself gasp and turn it into a cough so she won't know. But she is looking at me as if a spotlight has been turned on. I wait for her to expose me. Even though I know she doesn't know my real name. My mask feels so flimsy I can sense it slipping away. But Kate Waters shows no sign of recognition.

I try not to react when she mentions Alice Irving. Move the conversation to a safer place.

'That must be interesting, being a reporter,' I can hear myself saying. *God, I'm so obvious. She must know. She must see right through me.*

If she does, she doesn't show it. She goes along with my little game. She is a laugh, actually — she knows all about Malcolm Baker and Sarah S, even though she's only just met us. Toni must have told her. Funny, that, a bit like me and my books. An instant expert on someone else's life. Dangerous to think you know too much, sometimes, because who really knows someone else? You can scratch the skin, but you never get to the meat of someone else. Into their bones.

61

Saturday, 28 April 2012

Kate

God, she's slim, Kate thought when she saw her. *Wish I could lose some weight.*

'Emma,' Harry said. 'I didn't know you were in here. I was waiting for you at the table.'

'Sorry, I needed a quick pee. These long drinks go straight through you.'

'Hi, I'm Kate,' she said.

'Hi. Kate? I don't remember a Kate in my class. Were you in the year above? Toni's class?' Emma said.

'No, she's a reporter,' Harry said. 'Kate Waters.'

'I was talking to Toni about the Alice Irving story — the baby found in Howard Street — and she invited me to her reunion,' Kate explained.

The woman reacted to the news by avoiding eye contact.

Hiding, Kate thought. *But hiding what?*

'That must be interesting, being a reporter,' she said.

Kate looked at her. Classic distraction technique, she noted. She'd expected a comment or a question about Alice. That was the most interesting thing she'd said, wasn't it? It was

315

what everyone who lived round here was talking about. Not that she was a reporter.

'Er, yes, I get to meet all sorts of people. How about you? What do you do?'

'I'm a book editor,' she said.

'Em works on celebrity memoirs,' Harry chipped in.

'Like a ghost writer?' Kate said.

'No, someone else is the ghost. I sit in my spare room and polish other people's stories for them.'

Kate smiled. 'I seem to be doing a lot of that as well.' It was a bit of a struggle, but she pushed on with the small talk. 'What a great job. Have you done anyone good?'

Emma named a couple of well-known footballers and her current film-star project as she rummaged in her handbag for her make-up and Kate made all the right noises.

'Must be fascinating seeing behind the public face,' she said.

'Yeah, fascinating and a bit scary at times,' Emma said.

'Scary?'

'Well, knowing what people are really like and then having to write them up as someone different. To match their public persona. It's a bit of a responsibility when you suspect someone is a violent thug, say. Is it your lie or their lie?'

'God, that must be very difficult. Have you ever turned a commission down?'

'No, I need the money,' Emma laughed. A brittle laugh.

'Must be funny seeing all the old faces here

tonight,' Kate said, moving on quickly.

'Yes, it's been years. Decades.'

'You moved away, then?'

'Well, not far physically,' Emma said, exchanging a glance with Harry as she emerged from a cubicle, tucking her shirt in. 'Our lives went in different directions, I suppose.'

'What's it like coming back?' Kate said.

'Odd. A bit like being in a dream,' Emma said. 'I look round the room and see faces I almost know. Familiar but I can't quite place them. Then they say their name and they come back into focus. Do you know what I mean?'

Kate nodded, enchanted by the description.

'Harry persuaded me to come. She has far too much influence on me. Don't you?'

Harry smiled at her friend. 'Does you good to get out. And this is brilliant,' she said.

Kate smiled mischievously and added, 'I wonder if Malcolm is here.'

Both the other women laughed.

'Bet he's got a toupee and a gold medallion off the market,' Harry said.

'Bet he's got a mistress and a midlife-crisis Harley,' Emma said. 'Let's go and find him. Meet back here in half an hour and report.'

Kate opened the door to let the party back in and shooed them out. 'See you later. Good hunting.'

317

62

Saturday, 28 April 2012

Kate

She edged round the room to the bar to see how Joe was doing. He was leaning on the sticky counter, deep in mimed conversation with the barmaid, a woman in shoulder pads with too much hairspray.

'Lemonade, please,' Kate ordered, spotting a bottle behind the bar.

'Hi, Kate,' Joe mouthed, looking pleased with himself. She pointed to the exit and picked up her plastic cup to lead the way.

'How're you doing?' she said as they perched on a low brick wall in front of the hall.

'Great, thanks. Told people I was your son.'

Kate tried not to mind. 'Good thinking,' she conceded. 'And?'

'Rita behind the bar has been filling me in on all the gossip.'

'Good. What've you got?'

'Loads on Harry. Seems that's all anyone wants to talk about. It's the first time anyone has seen her since she was a scruffy little troublemaker. They can't believe she's done so well.'

'I've just been chatting with her in the Ladies.

318

Bit awkward at first, but she's relaxed. But what about the baby? Are there any rumours?'

'No, nothing about a baby. No pregnancies that ended suddenly, no married women having affairs, no whispers. Complete mystery, Rita says. I asked about Barbara Walker's house, number 63. She said she remembered there was a lawyer living there as well. A clever woman called Jude.'

'Judith Massingham, Barbara's housemate,' Kate said.

'And a daughter,' Joe added.

'Yes. Barbara said there was a child. But she wouldn't have been listed on the electoral register. What did Rita say about her? Did she know her?'

'Oh yes. Rita was at school with her. She's here tonight. Emma, she's called.'

Kate clutched his arm. 'Emma? I think I've just met her. You little genius, Joe. I'd kiss you, but it could be construed as sexual harassment these days.'

Joe beamed with pleasure. He wasn't sure exactly what he'd done right, but it didn't matter. He'd done good. The boss said so.

Kate left her drink on the wall and marched towards the door. 'I'm going to the Ladies,' she called back over her shoulder. 'See you later.'

Harry and Emma were already there, reapplying lipstick in the smeared mirror.

'Well?' Kate said. 'Millionaire or dosser?'

The reflections of the two women looked at her and grinned. 'Bald, beer belly and five kids,' Harry said.

'Serves him right for breaking your heart, Harry,' Emma added.

'Did he marry Sarah S?' Kate asked.

'No. Blimey, you know all our secrets,' Emma said.

'Well, some of them,' Kate said and got her own lipstick out.

63

Saturday, 28 April 2012

Emma

We're on our way back out on to the dance floor — just like we always used to, me following Harry, jigging up and down in readiness — when Kate taps me on the shoulder.

'Can we have a quick chat, Emma?' she shouts in my ear. She sounds nervous. And I wonder if she has guessed who I really am.

'Shall we go outside?' she says, and I follow her instead of Harry, to the door, past the red Formica table where we'd picked up a name badge, now littered with crumpled plastic cups.

We sit on the wall at the front, watching the smokers waving to passing cars while our ears retune.

'What a brilliant party,' Kate says. 'Must be just like the old days.'

'Yes. Weird to see us all back in the hall as adults. Like one of Dennis Potter's plays. The one where the adult actors play children.'

'*Blue Remembered Hills*,' Kate says. She's seen it too. 'It was a really dark play,' she adds. 'One of the children died.'

We sit silently. I'm thinking about the baby and reach for my stomach. And it's as if Kate is

321

reading my thoughts, because she starts talking about Alice Irving.

'It was just down the road that they found her. In the garden of the terrace where you used to live, Emma. Have you seen the stories I've written in the paper?'

'Yes,' I say. 'I saw them.'

'I'm trying to find out what happened to Alice,' she says. 'The police think that she must have been buried when you and your mum were living in that terrace.'

'I can't believe that,' I say. 'I talked to my mum about it. She can't believe it either.'

'Well, it happened,' she says. And she turns to sit sideways so she can see me properly. 'What was it like, then? How old were you? You must have been thirteen or fourteen in the early eighties.'

I nod.

'Do you remember those days?' she says. Insistent. 'Must have been hard living in a shared house at that age. It's when you need a bit of privacy, isn't it? You had your mum and Barbara Walker living there. Hard to keep anything private — or secret — when people are living on top of each other.'

'You'd be surprised,' I say. I didn't mean to say it out loud, but it just came out.

'How do you mean?' she says. 'I used to hide the books we were all reading secretly at school — *The Carpetbaggers*, I seem to remember. What sort of things did you keep hidden?' Like she knows.

I don't know what to say without betraying myself.

'Emma, was there anyone you think might have had something to do with burying the baby?' she asks. Her voice is all soft and hypnotic. Willing me to speak.

The word 'baby' is ricocheting round my head. *Baby, baby, baby.*

'I don't want to talk about it,' I say. 'It upsets me too much.'

'What does?' she says.

'The baby,' I say.

'Alice?' she says.

'No. My baby,' I say.

I start rocking gently on the wall. Soothing myself, like my mother used to do.

'Your baby?' Kate asks. 'What do you mean?'

I think I wanted her to ask. I wanted to tell. I wanted to let it out. She could be my razor blade.

'I got pregnant when I was fourteen,' I say.

'God, you were still a child,' she says, and she takes my hand as if in absolution. I thought when I finally confessed there would be shouting and recriminations, but the world doesn't stop turning. We are still sitting on the wall and the smokers carry on waving to drivers.

'Shall we go somewhere to talk?' she says. 'You must be getting cold. The Royal Oak is just round the corner.'

I shake my head. I can't bear the thought of other people.

'Or we could sit in my car?' Kate suggests, as if she understands. Maybe she does. I don't know why, but I trust her.

In the car, she starts with gentle questions,

asking if anyone else had known. Had Jude or Barbara known?

I shake my head.

And she says, 'How did you keep it a secret? You must have been so scared.'

There's no judgement in her tone, just empathy. She isn't telling me to stop talking about it, like Harry. She doesn't think I'm mad.

I want to tell her about the lies and hiding my pregnancy in big jumpers, and I know she will listen.

64

Saturday, 28 April 2012

Emma

'At first, I couldn't believe it,' I say. 'I told myself you couldn't get pregnant from one time. Told myself periods came and went at my age — all the agony aunts in the magazines said so. Told myself I'd counted the weeks wrong. Told myself I was putting on weight because I was eating too many sweets. Told myself the fluttering in my stomach was anxiety over exams.

'But my body was telling another story.'

Kate puts her head on one side. 'Oh Emma,' she breathes.

'When the sickness started, I thought I had food poisoning. My mum had had it once and I'd looked after her. But mine didn't get better and I was retching most mornings, turning on the taps in the bathroom so no one could hear me and spraying the room with deodorant so they couldn't smell my disgrace.'

I turn to Kate. I need her to know that I wasn't a stupid girl. I was a bit of an innocent about boys and sex, but I wasn't stupid.

'I know it's hard for anyone else to believe — especially now, when sex is everywhere — but even though I knew what was happening, I thought I could will it away. I didn't consider an abortion or drinking gin in a hot bath. That would've meant admitting it was real.

'I believed I could stop it by the power of thought. I would 'get better', as if it was just an illness. I hadn't even worked out when the baby was due to be born. It wasn't going to happen.'

Kate shifts in her seat beside me and rummages in her bag for a tissue and hands it to me. I hadn't realized I was crying.

'But Emma,' she says, 'how did no one notice what was going on? It must have been so obvious.'

'Well, they didn't. I didn't let them. I led a double life: Emma the schoolgirl and Emma the girl who'd got herself in trouble.

'But it couldn't last. The truth was battering down the door, demanding to be acknowledged, like a mad woman in the attic. I suppose it was a kind of madness.'

'You must have been out of your mind with worry. And at that age. How did you cope?' Kate says.

'I don't know, now. But it's when the Dread started, that overwhelming feeling that the world is about to end.'

'But what about when your pregnancy started to show?' Kate says.

'That was the worst part,' I say. 'I couldn't bear to look at myself in the mirror. My stomach wouldn't stop growing. I wrapped it tightly in scarves and I wore big jumpers and I stayed in my room, away from friends and family, saying I needed my own space. I was terrified they would see and know.

'Sideways, I was sure you could tell, so I became obsessed with always standing head on with my mum and I stopped hugging her. I could see she was hurt when I pushed her away, but I couldn't risk it.'

I can't stop talking now. Now that I've started. And I tell Kate how I took my meals upstairs. 'Jude wasn't happy, but her boyfriend, Will, told her not to make a fuss. He was glad to get me out of the way. And as my stomach grew, I piled more food on my plate to throw away later, so I'd have an excuse for my weight gain.'

I was so resourceful. My quick brain spotting the dangers. I almost feel proud of my child self. I would have got an A grade for deception.

Kate is nodding and never takes her eyes off me. I know she wants to ask lots more questions about how I got pregnant and what happened to my baby, but there is too much to tell. I have to let it out a little at a time or it will flood out and drown me. I feel dizzy. As if my head is going to explode.

'What happened when you went into labour, Emma? You couldn't hide that,' she says.

'No, it was like a nightmare,' I say. 'But I was on my own. It happened so quickly, the actual birth. I'd had some pain in my back for a day or so and then I wet myself and my stomach went rigid. It was my body, but not my body, if you know what I mean. It just went out of control and every time the pain came, worse and worse, I held on to the edge of the bath and shouted

327

myself hoarse. I thought I was going to die. I remember calling for my mum, knowing she wasn't there. Knowing I was alone. I had to be. No one could know.'

Kate is gripping my hand like I gripped the bath. And the deep-buried memories are crowding in on me, banging on the door to get in.

I can see myself, as if through a window. When the thing slithered out, shiny and steaming in the cold bathroom, I lay in the mess of blood on the lino beside it. It just grew cold beside me.

It wasn't like it said in the pamphlets. While other girls at school were secretly reading the one copy of Fear of Flying, I'd been looking at booklets about placentas and cords, stolen secretly from a hospital waiting room. The words made me want to throw up but I read on, just in case.

In the bathroom, I cut the cord with scissors from the first aid kit and wrapped it and the other stuff that had come out of me in a copy of the Sunday Times from the box beside the front door. I turned on the taps of the bath and climbed into the lukewarm water, watching the shreds of blood move around me.

'It's the silence after the shouting I remember,' I tell Kate.

'I'd been lucky. Jude and Will were at work. It was just me and the thing. I don't remember looking at it, but I must have done. Like when there is something scary on the television and you watch through your fingers so you don't see

328

the full horror. I've got no memory of its face. I don't even know if it was a boy or a girl.'

'Oh my God, is this the first time you've told anyone this?' Kate asks.

'Yes,' I say. 'I tried to tell Harry once, but she didn't understand what I was saying. And I couldn't tell anyone else. You see, I did something terrible.'

'What did you do, Emma?' she says gently. 'Did you do something to your baby?'

'I buried it,' I say.

65

Emma

Kate stops talking when I say I buried the baby.

I can hear my voice, as if it is someone else's, telling her that burying the baby was easy.

'It was like burying my pet rabbit when I was nine,' I'm saying. 'I wrapped it in newspaper and a carrier bag so you couldn't even tell what it was. I dug a hole in the garden and put it in and just scraped the dirt over it. It only took a few minutes and it was gone.

'I dragged the big pot that my mum had planted with daffodils over the top. You could see the little green tops, just poking through. Then I walked back to the house.'

I remember thinking that all I had to do was throw away the bloody towel I used and it would be as if nothing had happened. Everything back to normal. I was so young. I didn't know that nothing was ever going to be normal again. I remember I put my hand on my empty stomach and it felt like a balloon at the end of a birthday party, soft and puckered. I twisted the loose skin through my jumper to see if it was still me. To feel something. Anything.

'Stupidly, I'd thought the danger would end

when I'd given birth,' I tell the reporter. 'I'd had it all planned.' I almost laugh at the naivety of it now, but, then, I was so alone.

'When I finally accepted that there was going to be a baby, I'd decided I was going to leave it at the local maternity hospital for a nurse to find and look after. I'd seen it on the news, how the nurses gave abandoned babies names — Holly if it was at Christmas, or after the policeman who found it, that sort of thing — and held them tight in their arms. And loving families adopted them and everything turned out fine as far as the public was concerned. Happy endings all round.'

I tried to see my life in terms of a heroine in a novel. Everything clean and tidy. No loose ends.

'I was convinced it was going to be so easy. I was going to pop the baby out like in the drawings in the pamphlets, wrap it up in a white blanket I'd bought secretly in Boots, and lie it down quietly in the toilets and walk away. People are in and out of toilets all the time. It wouldn't take five minutes for the baby to be found.

'But I hadn't needed to do that. I'd used newspaper and the Boots carrier bag to wrap it instead.'

'Oh Emma,' Kate says. 'And you've kept all this inside until now. Until Alice's body was found.'

'It's my baby in the garden!' I hear myself shout. 'My baby!'

I can see Kate is shaking and she's gripping the steering wheel to steady herself. I'm frightening her. I'm frightening myself. I sound mad. I must stop this.

'I need to go home, Kate. I must tell Harry where I am. She'll be frantic,' I say.

Kate's face is pale and she speaks to me as if I'm a patient in a hospital. Low voice, calming rhythms.

'I'll drive you home, Emma. You must be tired and too raw to think straight. You need time to gather your thoughts.'

It all sounds so comforting and normal. Gather your thoughts. That's what I should do. It's what Paul says when he is worried about something. But I don't need to gather mine. They have been there for years.

★ ★ ★

Harry is standing on a chair, scanning the dance floor when we go back in, plucking at her hands and looking anxious.

'Where the hell have you been?' she shrieks as soon as she catches sight of me. 'Disappearing like that. I've been looking for you for half an hour.'

But she shuts up when she sees my face. I must look awful because she takes my arm and leads me back outside and whispers, 'What's happened, Emma? Where've you been?'

'I've been to talking to Kate, that's all. I'm sorry I worried you,' I tell her, trying to keep my voice steady.

'What about? What have you been talking about?' she says.

'It doesn't matter now. I'm a bit tired, Harry. I'm going home. Kate's going to drive me.'

Harry looks across at Kate. She's talking to a young bloke near the car, giving him some money for a taxi. 'Have you upset her?' she shouts at her and the bloke looks frightened, as if she's accusing him.

'No, she hasn't, Harry,' I say. I want it all to stop. Can't face any more emotion. 'It's all been a bit much tonight. Seeing everyone. Lots of memories, not all good.'

She squeezes my arm. 'Sorry, Emma. I shouldn't have made you come. I'll go home with you.'

I shake my head. 'I'm fine.' The strands of the story are still working themselves out in my head and I can't share them with anyone else just yet, not even my closest friend. Harry would get upset and angry for me and I'd have to deal with her emotions as well as my own. She wouldn't understand why I had chosen to tell a stranger my secrets. But it felt so safe. I was almost anonymous.

'I'll call you in the morning,' she calls after me, waving miserably as we pull away.

It's a long way home, snaking through dark streets, then out into the dazzling lights of the dual carriageway.

We don't speak much. I give directions. Left here, carry on over the roundabout. But Kate and I are both deep in our own heads. Me, reliving my shame. And haunted by the Dread.

★ ★ ★

The house is in total darkness when I get in. Paul hasn't left the hall light on. I stand in the

333

dark for a while, unable to put one foot in front of another, the thoughts crowding in on me.

'Emma, are you OK? What are you doing down there?' Paul calls, his voice sleepy.

'Nothing. Just taking my coat off,' I call back. 'Go back to sleep.'

I turn on the light and have to close my eyes to protect them from the dazzle. I open them slowly, testing the glare. Everything looks exactly as it did when I left this evening. Paul's jacket hanging crooked on a hook, unopened junk mail on the table, my shoes lined up by the mat. But everything has changed.

I have told. The police will come now. I need time to think. To plan.

I feel like one of those wildebeests tiptoeing to the edge of the river while the crocodiles wait round the bend, jaws braced. I think about running away. Hiding. But I pull myself up short. *At your age?* I tell myself. *Don't be ridiculous.* It's time to face it all.

I make a grown-up plan. I'm not going to let this sleeping dog lie.

66

Saturday, 28 April 2012

Kate

Kate got lost as she drove home. She missed her turning but didn't realize until twenty minutes later when the landscape turned leafier instead of neon-lit.

'Shit,' she yelled at the road ahead. She pulled over into a lay-by but couldn't let go of the steering wheel. She looked at her whitening knuckles as if they belonged to someone else.

Kate could still see Emma's face, bright with shock in the darkness of her car, her trembling lips making her trip over her words when she told her story.

When she shouted that it was her baby . . . Kate thought. It had really frightened her. The noise and the pain in her voice — that was real. But was her story?

Reporters were often the first call for the delusional or attention-seekers. The sad people who want to be part of the news at any cost.

Kate shivered. Her head was all over the place, scrambling over the questions and answers, looking for what she must have missed.

'Two babies? Two bloody babies? It can't be,' she said out loud. 'What the hell do I do now?'

It was all happening so fast. She felt she was losing control of the situation. Of the story.

When Kate had first read the tiny cutting about the baby's body, she'd hoped she'd be able to write a moving piece about a forgotten child and the personal tragedy behind its death. A Saturday read, she'd thought. A chance to get away from the treadmill of online news. But disturbing the surface had triggered an eruption of unexpected secrets.

She ought to be thrilled to have landed such a huge story, but Kate felt caught up in the torrent of information.

She knew she was the keeper of secrets: the drugging and possible sexual assault on Barbara Walker, the teenage pregnancy of Emma Massingham, the adultery of Nick Irving. She was entrusted with their hidden stories because she had asked the right questions. But what could she tell? Could she tell anything?

What she ought to do, she knew, was ring Terry to bring him up to speed, but that would mean letting go of the minute amount of control she still had. It would be snatched from her, dissected, discussed, pawed over by people who had never met Barbara, Angela or Emma.

That's journalism, Kate, she could hear a former boss saying. *You're there to tell their story, not to be their mother. You get too close.*

But you had to get close to get the full story. The college lecturers who taught Media Studies to kids like Joe Jackson banged on about objectivity and balance, but she'd like them to sit down with a rape victim or the mother of an

336

abused child and remain unaffected. Without empathy, without feeling someone's pain, how could you tell a story like that and capture the truth of the situation?

The problem came when you couldn't tear yourself away from the feelings and start writing.

She needed a moment. She needed an adult voice to tell her everything was going to be OK. *I need my dad*, she thought, and almost laughed. *Pull yourself together, for God's sake.*

She phoned her husband's mobile and crossed her fingers he would still be up. Steve answered immediately.

'Hello, Katie,' he said. 'Is everything all right?'

She burst into tears. She hadn't known she was going to, but the sound of his voice triggered a release of the emotions she had been keeping in check all day.

'What's happened? Are you OK?' Steve said, anxiety rising in his voice. She never cried.

'Everything's fine. Sorry, love, it's just been an incredibly stressful day and it was so brilliant to hear you.'

'So brilliant that it made you cry?' Steve laughed. 'I have that effect on far too many people.'

She calmed down and told him what had happened, listening carefully for his reaction, alert for censure. She needed his reassurance that she hadn't gone too far.

'You must talk to the police, Katie,' he said. 'This is getting way beyond an investigation by a reporter.'

He was right. Of course he was right.

'OK,' she said. 'I'll do it now.'

She looked at the display on the dashboard. It was just before midnight. Could she ring Bob Sparkes? Eileen would kill him. She dialled the number and held her breath.

He picked up on the second ring. Police training. His voice was blurry with sleep as he said, 'DI Sparkes,' but he clicked into gear as soon as she spoke.

She heard him put his hand over the phone and say, 'It's work, love. I'll go downstairs.' Eileen neutralized.

'Kate, it's the middle of the night,' he said as he walked downstairs. 'This had better be important.'

'It is, Bob. I'm sorry it's late, but I had to talk to you.'

'Go on then,' he said.

'I've just spoken to a woman who says she had a baby when she was just fifteen. In 1985. No one else knew. She hid the pregnancy. She was living at 63 Howard Street and she buried it in the garden.'

'The same garden that Alice was buried in?'

'Yes.'

'Christ. Do you believe her?'

'It sounded very real, Bob,' Kate said. 'But we only have her word.'

'So was it Alice she buried? Did she take her?'

'She can't have done, Bob. She wasn't born when Alice was taken.'

'No, of course not. Sorry, it's the middle of the night — brain not working. But she could have buried her in 1985. She could have found her

338

body and buried it.'

'A fifteen-year-old? Really? I don't know what to think, Bob,' Kate said.

'Well, how likely is it there were two babies buried in that garden? For goodness' sake, ring Andy Sinclair now, Kate. Don't try to work it out yourself. This is too complex. Ring him now, or I will.'

Kate clutched the phone tighter. 'I will, Bob. Thanks for listening to me.'

'Text me after you've spoken to Andy.'

He doesn't trust me to call it in, Kate thought as he hung up.

★ ★ ★

DI Sinclair wasn't asleep. Kate wondered if he was still at work when he picked up his phone with a crisp 'Sinclair'.

'Andy, it's Kate Waters,' she said. 'Sorry to bother you at this hour.'

'That's OK, Kate. You're working late. But so am I. Catching up on paperwork. You didn't wake me.'

She told him exactly what she'd told Sparkes and he let her come to the end before he spoke.

'Who is she, the woman who says she buried the baby?' he said.

'Emma Massingham — well, that's her maiden name. She's Emma Simmonds now.'

He scribbled down Emma's name and address, checking the house number twice.

'Did you tape the conversation?'

'My tape was running — I switched it on while she was talking — but I haven't listened yet.'

'Please do that now,' he said. Kate pulled the recorder out of her bag and rewound. The sound wasn't great, but Emma's voice was audible. She put the recorder to her phone so DI Sinclair could hear.

'It's my baby in the garden! My baby!' the voice shrieked.

'She sounds distraught. What state was she in when you left her, Kate?' he asked.

'Calmer but fragile,' Kate said.

'And do you think she's telling the truth about her pregnancy?' he asked.

'I don't know, Andy. I mean, how can she be? There can't be two babies, can there?'

'Extremely unlikely. She may be an attention-seeker, Kate. It happens. Look, leave this with me, but you need to come in and make a statement tomorrow — God, today — and keep that recording safe.'

'What are you going to do, Andy?' she asked.

'I'm going to talk to my boss. What about you?'

'I'm not writing anything, if that's what you're worried about.'

'I am,' he said. 'This is clearly a vulnerable woman. We mustn't push her over the edge.'

Kate swallowed hard. She'd pushed her, hadn't she? Was this 'dabbling her fingers in the stuff of people's souls' — the Press Complaints Commission's verdict on the media's treatment of Princess Diana?

'Will you let me know what you decide to do,

340

Andy? Please,' she said.

'We'll speak tomorrow. I'll ring you. Good-night.'

67

Sunday, 29 April 2012

Jude

Emma didn't ring before she appeared. She just turned up at the door at the crack of dawn. Said she knew Jude would be up.

'Lucky I'm a creature of habit, then,' Jude said, her voice prickly. She'd wanted to sound pleased, but her nerves got the better of her. *Why has she come?* was rattling round her brain. She had to practically beg her daughter to visit usually.

She ushered Emma in and hurried into the kitchen to make her a cup of coffee. She hadn't even waited for the kettle to boil, slopping warm water on to instant coffee in her haste to hear what was coming.

She plonked the cup of greyish liquid down beside her daughter and stood over her, unable to settle anywhere.

'Sit down, Jude, for goodness' sake,' Emma said. She looked different today. No soft edges. No blurred eyes.

Jude perched on the arm of a chair. 'Look, I can see you are working yourself up to say something, Emma. Just say whatever it is,' she snapped. 'Is there a problem with Paul?' she asked, trying to keep the anticipation out of her voice. 'I told you he rang me, in a state about the things you were saying. About the baby in Howard Street. I told him it was nonsense. Is he leaving you? Is that what this is about?'

'No, of course not. He loves me,' Emma said quietly.

And Emma had looked at her. Fixing her with her eyes as if she was seeing her for the first time. 'I want to talk about what happened when I was fourteen, Jude.'

Jude's stomach turned. 'For goodness' sake, Emma. Do we have to revisit that again?' she said. 'I'd have thought you would want to put it behind you, not pick over it obsessively. It was a nightmare. Let's not go there.'

Emma's gaze didn't falter. 'It was,' she said. 'But did you never ask yourself why my behaviour was impossible? Why I changed from being the good daughter?'

'Hormones and adolescence. You were a difficult teenager. You just had it worse than others,' Jude said, her pat response, and started knitting her fingers together.

'No,' Emma said firmly. 'Something happened to change me.'

'What? What happened?' Jude said.

'I was raped.'

There was a beat before Jude spoke. 'Oh God, why are you saying this? Is this another one of your stories?' She closed her eyes against the answer.

'Will did it,' Emma said, as Jude knew she would.

She tried to keep control of the outrage screaming in her head and stay calm.

'Of course he didn't. Don't be ridiculous, Emma,' she said. 'Will was very fond of you. He couldn't do enough for you and he put up with all your nonsense. You are obsessed with him. You are not well. Have you taken your pills today?'

Emma didn't react, she simply carried on, her eyes burning into her mother's. 'He raped me on July 21, 1984. In his car, Jude. Do you remember his car? That red Cavalier with the black stripe down the side and the traffic-light air freshener hanging from the mirror. Do you? I'll never forget it.'

'Of course I remember it. I was in it hundreds of times. So were you. That doesn't mean anything.'

Emma's expression didn't change. Her refusal to react was scaring Jude.

'But that time was different. You weren't there. He'd told you a lie, Jude. Said he was going home to collect something. But he collected me instead. And after it was over, Will took me back to the bus stop at the end of Howard Street and told me not to say anything. He said I had made him do it and that you would blame me. That you would never forgive me.'

Jude sat forward in her chair with her hands pressed over her eyes, as if to blot out her daughter's face and the words coming out of her mouth.

'Emma, you know this isn't true,' she said from behind her hands. 'You just want to hurt

344

me because Will has come back into my life. You're jealous because you had a crush on him. You always did. You tried to split us up before, with your nasty lies about him and the woman up the street. This is just another invention. Stop this.'

But Emma went on. Unstoppable now.

'Afterwards, he said I had led him on.' And she laughed. A low, mirthless sound. 'I was fourteen and a virgin. I didn't lead him on.'

Jude raised her head wearily. 'Why would he do it, Emma? He had me,' she said.

'Perhaps he did it because he could,' Emma said, her anger finally breaking through. 'Perhaps he enjoyed the risk of being caught. Some men get off on that. Or on a whim, or as a power game. I wouldn't begin to seek his reasons. He was a twisted man. A monster, Jude. *Your* monster.'

Jude thought she was going to throw up. 'You don't know what you are saying!' she shouted. 'You're frightening me. I want you to go.'

Emma stood and picked up her coat. 'All those years you blamed me for driving him away, but I saved you from him,' she said and laughed again bitterly. 'You could have married a rapist.'

After she slammed the door behind her, Jude tried to get up, but her legs failed her.

The anger she'd felt when Emma was making her accusations had disappeared, and now she was too shocked to feel anything at all.

Why would she say such things? she said to herself. *Lies. Awful lies.*

But she was thinking back to that summer. The summer when Emma had disappeared and a sullen stranger had replaced her.

68

Sunday, 29 April 2012

Kate

She was cooking breakfast — a Sunday ritual — when Emma rang. She pushed the spatula into Steve's hand, dripping fat on his newspaper, and said, 'Got to take this. Sorry.'

'Emma, are you OK?' Kate said. 'How are you feeling?'

'Not great. How about you?'

'It's not about me. I was so worried when I left you last night. I think what you told me shocked us both,' Kate said. 'It is an extraordinary story.'

'I'm sorry if I scared you,' Emma said. 'The thing is, I've kept things hidden for so long, I think I just needed to tell someone.'

Kate hesitated, torn between returning to the story and whether to tell Emma she'd informed the police about the confession. She knew that could be the end of any trust between them. She'd see what Emma had to say, first.

'What are you going to do next?' Kate asked.

'I'm not sure. But I need your help,' Emma said. 'Can we meet?'

Kate walked back into the kitchen, where Steve was flipping bacon like a pro.

'How many eggs, Katie?' he asked.

'I've got to go out, love. I'm really sorry,' she said.

Steve pulled a face and put the pan back down on the hob. 'For God's sake, this is your day off. The one day we can spend as a family. Is it too much to ask for one day together? I'd hoped we could sit down today and talk to Jake properly.'

'He's not even awake yet. We can do that tonight,' Kate said. 'It's an emergency. Honestly.'

'It's always an emergency, isn't it? You can never put us first,' he said.

'That's not fair,' she said, knowing it was. 'Anyway, Freddie will be pleased. He'll get double bacon and egg.'

Steve was very unhappy, she knew. But what else could she do? She put on her coat and shouted, 'Call you later' from the door.

Steve didn't respond.

'Bye, then,' she said into the silence.

★ ★ ★

Emma had instructed her to meet her at North Greenwich Underground station and said she'd tell her more when she got there.

Kate arrived first and sat in the car park, wondering what she was getting herself into. She was going out on a limb. A very creaky limb. She still didn't know what to make of Emma. She'd been caught before. Just the once, but it still rankled. The fantasist who'd persuaded Kate that she and her illegitimate baby had been abandoned by a famous businessman. She and the paper had spent a couple of thousand putting the mother up in a wonderful hotel and travelled halfway across the world to gather evidence before the grubby truth had emerged.

Kate had got hold of the baby's birth certificate and found another man's name was on it. She should have done it earlier. A call to the man named as the father had revealed that the woman was a serial con artist and Kate had had to confess all to Terry. Luckily, they'd caught the lie before publication.

Her comfort was that the woman had gone on to persuade another paper to actually print her story. Egg on someone else's face, but Terry still dragged it up if she got too out of line.

It was tricky, but Kate felt she was edging towards some sort of truth about the Alice Irving case. She couldn't stop now. She would see what Emma had to say. And keep her fingers crossed.

Emma was so bundled up in a hat and scarf that Kate almost missed her.

'Kate,' Emma said when she was practically next to the car window.

'Sorry, Emma, I don't know where my head is today,' she said and smiled.

'Can we sit in your car again?' Emma said. 'I need you to come somewhere with me.'

'To Howard Street?' Kate said.

'No. To see the father of the baby.'

Kate stared at her. This was deep water she was getting into. This wasn't just about her and Emma and the phantom baby any more.

'Does he know about the child?' she asked.

'No. He forced me to have sex,' Emma said. 'He wasn't interested afterwards.'

349

'Who forced you?' Kate said quietly. 'Was it Al Soames?'

'Al Soames?' Emma said and looked out of the windscreen. 'No, course not. He was the landlord when we were renting in Howard Street. How do you know his name?'

'I went to see him to ask about the tenants in his houses around the time the baby was buried,' Kate said, unsure how much detail to divulge. 'He gave me some photos of naked women by mistake. They looked drugged.'

'Naked women?' Emma said. 'In black and white Polaroids?'

Kate risked a look at her. 'Er, yes. Have you seen them?'

'I don't know. But there was one in Will's desk. A photo of Barbara, who lived with Jude and me for a while. I found it when I was messing around in his office at the university.'

She closed her eyes as if searching for that moment.

'Will was in the library, sorting out some photocopying, and he'd promised to buy me an ice cream when he finished, to celebrate the end of school for the summer. I was swinging round on his chair, singing 'Wake Me Up Before You Go Go'.

'A glass of water on the desk crashed over, and I saw the water was seeping into one of the desk drawers so I pulled it open and used my school cardigan to soak up as much as I could. The damage wasn't too bad and I was about to shut the drawer but then I saw the photo. Of Barbara. And stopped. I remember wondering why Will had a picture of Barbara.'

Kate listened intently. *Will and Al Soames* was playing in her head. This couldn't be just coincidence. They were in it together.

'I pulled it out to get a better look,' Emma was saying. 'She looked so strange. It was her, but not her, if you know what I mean.'

Kate nodded.

'Her eyes were half closed and I suddenly realized she didn't have anything on her top. I could see one of her nipples and I dropped the picture as if it had scalded me. I felt sick and frightened. I knew I shouldn't have seen it, but I couldn't unsee it. I picked up the photo and went to put it back so no one would know. But I knew.'

'What happened when Will came back? Did you confront him?' Kate asked.

'I was fourteen, Kate. And he was my mum's boyfriend. I didn't know what to say. I was embarrassed and frightened about what Jude would say if she found out.'

'Did she? Did you tell her?' Kate said. And Emma shook her head.

'Will told me not to. We were sitting outside later, Will and I, with cornets, sitting in the garden in Howard Street. His arm was flung behind his head and he was gazing at the sky, and I asked him if he was in love with Barbara. He laughed and said it was a funny question. But he went a bit quiet. So I told him I'd seen the photo. I said I'd spilled the water by accident and seen it. And he said Barbara had sent it to him. She'd been a bit of a nuisance, throwing herself at him behind Jude's back. And since she'd left she had started trying to get him to leave Jude.

'And he told me not to say anything because Jude didn't know and it would upset her.'

'And you never did?' Kate asked.

Emma shook her head again. 'I couldn't. Will made sure I would keep quiet.'

'How, Emma?' Kate said. 'What did he do to you?'

The only sound was Emma's breathing.

'Was it Will who raped you?' Kate said.

'Yes,' Emma said and pulled the scarf up over her mouth.

'But you could have told someone,' Kate said. 'Why didn't you tell anyone what he'd done?'

'Because I didn't know he'd raped me. I know it sounds crazy now, but he told me he'd had sex with me because I'd made him want me. It was my fault. It was me who had done a terrible thing, not him.'

'The bastard,' Kate blurted.

'A very clever bastard,' Emma replied. 'He made me believe I'd been the instigator. I was fourteen. I'd only kissed one bloke before. I didn't know anything. So when he told me I'd thrown myself at him he must have known I would believe him. I wrote in my diary that I was 'dirty' and I told myself that the baby had been my punishment.'

Kate started the engine. 'Where are we going, Emma?' she said. 'Where is he?'

69

Emma

I thought I'd feel better when I'd told Jude. I thought she would acknowledge her guilt. But of course, she didn't. She denied it. I'd expected her to argue at first, but I thought, in her heart of hearts, she would know. She'd see the truth when I laid it out in front of her. But no. Will still has that hold over her.

But I've started now, so I must go on. And Kate is going to help me.

As we drive out of the car park, she says it could get ugly if we confront Will, but I say it couldn't get any uglier than it is.

'I deserve this moment,' I say. 'And so does he. I don't want to go to the police yet. I don't think they'll believe me — and if they don't act, it'll be over, won't it? I won't get a second chance.'

Kate nods. I think she's on my side.

'We need a confession,' I say. 'Fronting him up' is what Kate calls it.

Kate gets an address for Will from a colleague and we drive out of London. I've already decided what I'll say and I'm practising it in my head.

I need to eat something or I might faint, I think. I can't remember when I last ate. I feel dizzy at the thought of seeing him, but I know this is the right thing to do.

I wonder what he'll do when he sees me. The spectre at the feast. I wonder if the shock will kill him? For a second, I fantasize that he'll have a heart attack, right there in front of me. But I want my moment with him.

I've waited twenty-eight years for this. My mouth waters and I feel dizzy again. There is this image of an avenging angel in my head. The beating of strong wings, the rush of heavenly winds. Stop it. I need to get a grip.

★ ★ ★

His cottage is like a picture on a biscuit tin. Roses round the door, the whole thing. *How inappropriate*, I think as Kate knocks.

And there he is, Professor Will. Smiling a welcome to her, a stranger, and then spotting me.

He masks his shock well, turning on the urbane charm and saying, 'Well, this is a surprise. How are you, Emma? What are you doing here?'

'I want to talk to you, Will,' I say.

'What about?' he says. 'I'm not sure we have anything to talk about.'

He is nervous now. A neighbour passes his gate and calls, 'Hello, Professor Burnside' to him and he quickly ushers us out of public view. *Doesn't want a scene*, I think.

He leads us into his chintzy sitting room. There's a cup and saucer on the coffee table,

354

brown toast and honey, and the Sunday supplements spread out on the sofa.

He sits down, crossing his legs to reveal yellow socks and tanned calves.

'So, Emma, who is this with you?' he says, as we perch on the armchairs.

'A friend, Kate,' I say — I don't want him to know she's a reporter and Kate has agreed not to say anything. 'She drove me down here,' I add in explanation.

'Hello, Kate,' he says and waits for one of us to speak. Smiling all the time.

The tension is making me feel ill and I force myself to speak.

'I came to talk to you about what happened when I was fourteen.'

'Goodness! This isn't going to be a short visit, then,' Will says. 'Do you want to talk about your vicious lies or your screaming fits? They are all still quite vivid in my memory.'

'No, about how you raped me,' I hear myself say.

It is as if the world has stopped. None of us move or even breathe. The word 'raped' seems to echo round the room, bouncing off the sprigged wallpaper and shepherdess ornaments.

The colour has drained from Will's face, then floods back as he half rises from his seat to protest.

'*Rape?*' he says, as if he's just heard the word for the first time. 'What are you talking about? This is preposterous!'

He realizes he is shouting and sits back down again.

'Dear me, Emma. You really are not well, are you?' he says, back in control.

I look at him and he looks back. Challenging me to repeat the allegation.

'You raped me, Will,' I say. 'You picked me up in your car when I was walking home. You had sex with me and said I made you do it. That I led you on. But I was a child, Will.'

'Hardly, Emma,' he sneers. It is a mistake and I see Kate rock forward, outraged.

'A child, Will,' I repeat loudly. 'I was fourteen.'

'Emma,' he says, 'please calm down. You and I both know that you were a very troubled girl. And it appears you still are. I want to feel sorry for you, but if you are going to make up this sort of slanderous nonsense, I may have to act.'

'*I* am going to act,' I say, because I am. It is part of my plan now that I've seen him. 'I'm going to the police.'

'Well, it will be your word — the word of a deranged woman with a history of mental problems — against mine,' Will says, his tone a shade harder. 'You may want to reconsider.'

'No,' I say. 'It is time.'

He turns to Kate and does this two-adults-with-a-difficult-child look, radiating weary empathy. 'I don't know what she's told you, Kate,' he says, 'But it is all lies. She has mental health issues — did you know that? Had to be sent to live with her grandparents. She's making the mistake of her life.'

'It sounds like *you* were the mistake of her life, Will,' Kate says. 'She was the daughter of your girlfriend. She trusted you like a father.'

356

And I want to hug her.

Will drops the charm offensive immediately.

'Rubbish! This is total rubbish!' he says, uncrossing his legs so quickly he bangs into the coffee table and upsets his cup. 'Look, I never wanted to have to say this, but your friend was no innocent flower. She'd had an older boyfriend in Brighton. She told me. It was all part of her Lolita act. She was begging for it.'

Kate nods to herself. I think she has heard what she's come to hear. She believes me. My avenging angel.

'Of course, having sex with a fourteen-year-old, with or without her consent, is a crime. But I'm sure a man of your education knows that,' she says and he shuts up. 'And Emma had a baby, Will. *Your* baby,' she adds. It comes out almost as an afterthought and Will does a sort of double take.

'There was no baby. I lived with her and her mother. There was no baby. More lies,' he says, but his nerve seems to be failing. 'Lies,' he repeats, as if he has run out of words. He looks smaller now on his big sofa, with his ridiculous yellow socks.

'Actually, you are wrong. You have misjudged Emma,' Kate says.

'Just like Jude and I misjudged you,' I add. 'But I know who you are now. I won't listen to any more of your vile excuses. You will have to tell them to the police instead.'

Kate takes my arm and we walk to the door with Will ranting about legal action behind us.

70

Kate

Kate and Emma sat in stunned silence for the first half of their journey back to London. But finally, Kate spoke.

'Are you OK?'

'Yes,' Emma said. 'Are you?'

'I feel a bit wobbly, to be honest. What an animal.'

'My mum wouldn't agree with you. She didn't believe me when I told her. She still thinks the sun shines out of Will. I wish she had been there with us. Heard him. Seen the real Will.'

'Are you really going to go to the police, Emma?' Kate said. She sounded worried. 'The problem is that there's no evidence, is there? Look, I believe you, but he's right. It will be your word against his. It could be bloody.'

'There's the baby. His mark will be on it,' Emma said.

★ ★ ★

Kate dropped Emma off round the corner from her home.

'Paul will be home from the university library

358

by now,' Emma said. 'I don't want to have to explain you. Not yet, anyway. Thank you, Kate. Thanks for coming with me.'

Kate squeezed her arm. 'You were so brave, Emma, but think carefully about the next steps. Ring me if you need help.'

As soon as Emma disappeared from sight, Kate rang Terry's mobile. It was nearly lunchtime and she still hadn't told him about Emma's confession or her summons to the police station. She decided the confrontation with Will Burnside would remain between her and Emma. At least for the time being. She didn't want to complicate things even further.

'Kate? What's up?' Terry said. 'Thought you were off today.'

Ten minutes of tense conversation later, he sighed. 'Bloody hell, Kate. What a mess,' he said. 'So we've got a woman who thinks she gave birth to Alice Irving?'

'No, Terry. She says it is her baby — a different baby — buried in Howard Street. Look, I'll come to the office so we can talk about it properly before I have to give a statement. OK?'

'Yes, I'll have to call Simon and tell him what's happened. Hopefully he'll be on the golf course and won't want to come in. Maybe we can sort this out ourselves.'

★ ★ ★

The editor looked like a man in a hurry when he burst through the office door in pink slacks and toning jumper. 'Had to drive myself,' he complained. 'My driver's at his mobile home in Frinton. Come on, let's get this over with.'

Terry had clucked round him, sending out for a double espresso and apologizing for the umpteenth time for breaking into his Sunday. Kate had sat quietly with her notebook and tape recorder in her hands.

Finally, they all sat in the editor's office and Kate recounted her interviews with Emma for the fifth time.

Simon and Terry listened to her tape twice, Terry cocking his head to catch every spit and cough.

'She sounds in a terrible state, Kate,' he said. 'Is she making this up?'

She shrugged. 'I only have her word for it,' she said. She couldn't be more definite than that.

'We've been here before, Kate, haven't we?' Terry said.

She knew he'd bring it up. The blot on her copybook. The fantasist who'd almost convinced her.

'For goodness' sake, Terry. That was years ago. We all learnt several lessons,' Kate snapped. 'I've told you I only have her word for it. I'm not asking you to splash the story without checking it. Let me go and talk to the cops. I'll find out what they know. DI Sinclair has asked me to come in at two.'

Terry and Simon looked a bit stunned by her outburst. *Wait until you hear the rest*, she thought.

Then she told them about the photographs.

360

The editor's eyes practically popped out of his head when she handed him the bundle of Polaroids.

'Christ, get the lawyer up here,' he said.

The duty lawyer, a barrister who topped up her huge salary with the occasional weekend shift on the newspaper, took her time to climb the flight of stairs from her floor. She listened without comment as Kate repeated her story and then advised she should reveal the photos to the police as soon as possible.

'They will want to know how the Polaroids came into your possession, Kate,' she said.

'They were in a bundle of photos that Mr Soames gave me,' Kate replied crisply.

Well, it was almost true, and Soames would be in too much trouble to protest.

'Right,' Simon said. 'Kate and the lawyer to the police station, Terry. And keep me updated.'

Kate excused herself to get ready. She had something to do before she left. She went off in search of her favourite photographer.

Mick was alone in the monkeys' room, a windowless space left over by the architects between the newsroom and the fire escape, where the photographers hid from the picture editor. He was playing Candy Crush on his phone. Barbara's photos were on the table in front of him.

'Are you winning, Mick?' she said. He paused the game and looked up. 'Course I am,' he said. 'Boss thinks I'm doing GVs for the Property section. Knocked off a couple of high rises and a bridge and now I can do as I please for the rest of the day without him on my back. Fancy some lunch? There's a new place just opened up the road.'

'Would love to, but I'm a bit busy with this story' she said. 'Sorry it was a waste of your time last night, Mick.'

'No problem. I was only down the road, really. Did you get to the disco? What time did you get home?'

'About one in the morning, in the end. The party went on late and then there were developments.'

Mick nodded and picked up his phone. She could see he was itching to resume the game. 'Poor you. But worth it, hey?' he said.

'Have you finished copying that photo? I'll take it back to Barbara if you're done.'

Mick put down his phone and put the black and white model shots of Barbara in a plastic sleeve.

'What about those Polaroids you mentioned last night. Can I have a look?' he said.

'Sure,' she said, fishing them out of her bag. 'And can you do a quick copy of them? I've only got half an hour before I've got to leave for an interview with the police.'

Mick raised an eyebrow. 'Finally caught up with you, then? Well, let's have a look.'

She handed him the pack of photos and he shuffled through them quickly. 'God. Grim. Bloody hell, there's Barbara,' he said and Kate felt a rush of relief. She hadn't imagined the resemblance.

'Look,' Mick said, pulling one of the studio shots out. 'You can see it, plain as day. I'll copy them all now.'

'Thanks. And Mick . . . '

He grinned, knowing what she'd say next.

'No chatter, OK?' she said. 'The police don't know about the photos yet. I'm taking them with me later.'

Mick winked at her. 'They'll piss their pants when they see these.'

Kate tried to grin back. They might. Or she could be in deep trouble for holding on to them — never mind how she'd got them in the first place.

'I'll be back in a minute to fetch them,' she said.

'You looked bloody brilliant last night,' Mick suddenly added.

'Sod off,' she said and left the room.

71

Sunday, 29 April 2012

Kate

They'd been ushered through to an interview room when she and the newspaper's lawyer had arrived and Kate sat drumming her fingers on the table in front of her. The lawyer cleared her throat and she stopped. 'Sorry nerves,' she said.

Andy Sinclair smiled his apology for keeping them waiting as he entered.

'Thanks for coming, Kate,' he said. 'It's important we get your statement. Have you brought the tape?'

They sat and listened to Emma's misery in silence.

'Have you spoken to Emma yet?' she asked as he bagged the tape up and labelled it.

'No. We're talking to a psychologist about the best approach. And listening to this in full, I am sure we don't want to rush into something and have it blow up in our faces. She needs careful handling.

'Now, then . . . ' he got down to business.

Kate took a breath and related her conversations with Emma on the Boys' Brigade wall and in the car for Sinclair's tape.

It was a strange feeling, being on the other

side of an interview, and she interrupted Sinclair a couple of times to rephrase questions for him.

'Thanks, Kate. Think I've got this,' he said and grinned. *Still friends, then*, she thought.

He asked why she'd been at the reunion in the first place. 'You're not from round there, are you?' he asked.

'No, I was working — trying to find people who lived in the area and might have known something about how Alice ended up in Howard Street. About who might have taken her.'

'Right. So you dug out your eighties disguise and headed in there?' he said. 'Very resourceful.'

'I thought you might be there, too,' she said.

'Spangles aren't really my thing . . . ' he said. And they both laughed, breaking the tension in the room.

'Now then, moving on . . . ' he said. 'What else do you know about the Massingham household at 63 Howard Street?'

Oh dear, can-of-worms time, Kate told herself. *Keep to the simple stuff.*

'What you know, I imagine,' she said. 'Emma lived there with her mother, Jude Massingham, and another lodger, Barbara Walker. Barbara lives over the road now. Number 16. You went to see her — or one of your blokes did.'

'Yes, that's right,' he said and underlined something heavily in his notes.

'Barbara said there was a boyfriend there all the time. Jude's boyfriend. Will Burnside,' Kate offered, spelling the surname for the officer.

'Right, thanks for that,' Sinclair said, flicking through the file. 'OK. We know the house

365

belonged to a man called Alistair Soames. He's got form. Sex offender. Minor stuff. Touching women on the Tube — hands up skirts, that kind of thing. Put on probation in the late seventies, it says. Just before he bought the Howard Street houses.'

'A convicted sex offender?' Kate said. 'I went to see him a couple of weeks ago.'

Sinclair's eyes widened.

'He lives in a seedy flat in south London,' Kate said. 'I tracked him down to see if he knew anything about the case.'

'Bloody hell, Kate, is there nowhere you haven't been?' Sinclair said.

Kate glanced quickly at the lawyer, who gave an almost imperceptible nod. She was sure Andy Sinclair had clocked it.

'The thing is, Andy,' Kate began, 'Soames gave us some photos from the eighties — to help identify people — and there was an envelope of Polaroids.'

He looked interested.

'The pictures are of women and girls who look like they've been drugged,' she said. 'You can see Soames in some of the pictures.'

Sinclair pushed his chair back and whistled softly to himself. 'And I suppose you still have these photos?'

Kate reached into her bag and pulled out the envelope. She spread the Polaroids on the table.

DI Sinclair and Kate studied each face carefully, reverently. Giving the victims the attention they deserved.

Kate was wondering if he would recognize

Barbara and she searched for her in the pictures. But another face came into focus. She stabbed her finger at a photograph and twisted it round to see it better.

'My God, it's Emma,' she said. 'Emma,' she repeated. She looked away to compose herself.

Sinclair had picked up the picture and was studying it. 'This is our girl?' he said.

'Yes, I am sure. I spent most of yesterday evening looking at her. 'Sorry,' she said and blew her nose.

She was sipping a consoling cup of tea when a young copper put his head round the door.

'Sir, there's a woman — actually a couple — to see you. They're in the front office.'

'What's it about, Clive?' Andy Sinclair said. 'Can it wait?'

'Not sure, sir. Says it's about the baby.'

Kate and Andy both snapped round to look at him properly.

'Who are they?' Sinclair asked. 'Names, Clive.'

'Emma and Paul Simmonds,' he said, consulting a piece of paper in his hand.

'Bloody hell,' Sinclair said. 'Put them in Interview Room Nine. And give them a cup of tea or something. I'll be there in five minutes.'

Kate looked at him. 'She's come to you. She's got something to say. God, don't suppose I could . . . ?' She'd heard of colleagues being allowed to watch interviews through one-way mirrors.

'Forget it, Kate. This is a police matter,' Sinclair said. 'We'll talk later.'

She picked up her things and started

367

shovelling them into her bag.

'Hang on, leave the Polaroids. We're going to need them,' he said.

72

Sunday, 29 April 2012

Emma

Paul is next. He needs to know. I can't let him find out when the police come. It wouldn't be fair.

I don't take my coat off when I get in. I ask him to come for a walk, to the park down the road, telling him I need some air.

'You do look pale, Emma,' he says. 'It's a bit blustery outside, but it'll blow the badness out.'

We walk without saying much; he occasionally points out the freshly planted flower beds and dogs chasing sticks. When we get back to the park gates, we buy a coffee from the kiosk and sit on a bench.

'Better?' he asks.

'Yes, thanks,' I say. 'I need to tell you some things, Paul. Things that are going to come out about me.'

He looks so worried, I want to stop, but I must say it all now.

'Paul,' I say, 'I had a baby.'

'But — ' he starts to say, but I hush him.

'Just wait, Paul. I know you think I am making this up. But I'm not. I had a baby when I was fifteen. No one knew, because I hid my pregnancy. But I gave birth. And I buried the baby in our garden in Howard Street.'

Paul puts down his coffee and takes my hands while I tell him about Will. He is pale and he doesn't move once while I talk.

At the end, he sits still, like a statue.

'I'm so sorry,' I say. 'I didn't mean to bring this sort of unhappiness into your life.'

He looks at me with tears in his eyes.

'Emma,' he says, 'I want desperately to believe you. But these are the most serious allegations. And if they are wrong . . . If you are mistaken, in any detail, there will be big consequences. You do know that, don't you?'

'It is true, Paul,' I say. 'I promise.'

And he puts both arms around me and rocks me. I fold myself into him like a child and he comforts me.

'Emma,' he says at last, 'what is going to happen now?'

'I don't know,' I say. 'It is up to the police. I want to go and see them. Will you come with me?'

★   ★   ★

Paul and I sit for ages in the police-station waiting room for the right officer to be found.

We'd walked up the steps arm in arm as if we felt strong, but I could feel the tremor running from me to Paul and back again. He smiled at me when we got to the door.

'It's going to be all right, Em,' he said and I nodded.

It's funny. I always imagined the police coming to my door. Here I am, coming to theirs.

At the front desk, we give our names and ask to speak to DI Sinclair. He's been quoted in all the stories about Alice as the man in charge. The young officer on duty tells us to take a seat and Paul sits next to a man who looks like he's been beaten up. He's drunk and bloody and crying. Paul gives him tissues to mop the mess and tries to speak to him, but he's too out of it to hear him.

I sit, jiggling my knee in time to my internal music.

When we're called over to the desk, Paul pats my shoulder and we stand.

We walk what feels like miles, the constable's big feet making an echo chamber of the corridor. Everything seems exaggerated — the time, the sounds, the glare of the lights. I dig my nails into my skin beneath my handbag. *It's going to be all right, Em* is my mantra.

The young officer can't tell us anything but he offers us a drink and brings thin plastic cups of sweetened tea that neither of us can stomach. We wait in silence, each caught in our own bubble. We have said all there is to say to each other.

'No more secrets,' I'd said to Paul and he'd said, 'No,' and looked away.

Now I have to tell my secrets to DI Sinclair. I wonder if they will believe that the baby didn't breathe? Maybe they'll think I killed it. They might lock me up straight away.

The detective comes in quietly and introduces himself. Not as old as I expected. Chubby face.

371

All polite. He puts his reading glasses on when he sits down and opens his folder. I can see the corner of a photograph poking out from under documents. He notices me looking and closes the file.

'Mrs Simmonds,' he says, 'can you tell me why have you come here today?'

I'm ready.

'To tell you that the baby you found in Howard Street is not Alice Irving. It is my baby. The baby I had a week after my fifteenth birthday,' I say. My prepared statement.

He looks at me carefully. Like Kate did. Weighing me up. Weighing my words.

'When was your baby born, Mrs Simmonds?'

'April the first, 1985. I had the baby on my own, in the bathroom at home, 63 Howard Street.'

'That must have been a frightening ordeal,' he says. But I know he doesn't believe me. He's play-acting concern.

'Did anyone know about your pregnancy or the birth?'

'No, I was too frightened and ashamed to tell anyone. I hid it all,' I say.

'Right. When did you bury your baby?'

'The same day,' I say.

'And how did your baby die?'

Paul suddenly speaks. 'You don't have to answer that question, Emma.'

'It's OK, Paul,' I say. 'I want to tell the police everything I know. No more secrets.'

I turn back to the policeman and say, 'I don't know. It never made a sound when it was born.'

I am back in the smothering silence of the bathroom and I clench my fists against my thighs.

'Mrs Simmonds, we have DNA evidence that this baby is Alice Irving,' he says, too gently, as if he is talking to a child. *Be careful with the mad woman*, he must be thinking.

'Then you must have made a mistake,' I say. 'There cannot be two babies.'

DI Sinclair rubs his head. His hair is very short and he's got little blond prickles on his scalp. I wonder what they feel like when you rub them. I'm drifting. *Must focus.* I twist the skin on my stomach.

'As you say, it would be against all odds,' he says. 'Are you all right, Mrs Simmonds?'

'Yes, thank you,' I say and sit on the front edge of my chair to show I'm listening to him.

'My wife has had a very traumatic experience,' Paul says and I silence him with a look.

'It's fine, Paul.'

DI Sinclair clears his throat. *Must be finding it hard to ask the next one.*

'I think you spoke to a reporter last night, didn't you?'

I nod. I feel sick. *He's talked to Kate. Why didn't she tell me? She's lied to me.* And I fumble with the idea that no one can be trusted.

'You told the reporter that you had done something terrible. What was the terrible thing you did, Emma?' he says. 'Did you have anything to do with burying Alice Irving?'

Him using my first name catches me off-guard and I almost don't hear the accusation that

373

follows. Then it crashes in on me.

'No, of course not. It isn't Alice. Why won't you believe me? The terrible thing I have tortured myself with since the age of fourteen is that I had sex with my mother's boyfriend. And I believed I made him want to do it.'

He raises an eyebrow.

'He said I had seduced him and if I said anything about what we'd done, my mum would hate me for ever,' I crash on, my words spilling out into the room. 'But I didn't. I know that now. He raped me and he made me feel I was to blame.'

He glances up at me as I recount the loss of my virginity and I wonder if he has daughters.

'You are saying you were raped?' he asks.

'Yes, Will Burnside raped me,' I say.

It is all said. No going back now.

The officer scribbles it down in his notes.

'And you claim that he is the father of the baby you say you gave birth to?' the officer asks, and I nod.

There is a pause as he finishes his notes and I close my eyes. When I open them, he has pulled out the photos from the file and put them in a stack, face down on the table.

'Mrs Simmonds,' he says, all formal again, 'I would like to show you some Polaroid photographs that have come into our possession as part of another inquiry. Can I ask you to look at them to see if you recognize any of these women?'

I don't understand and I look at Paul. He doesn't understand, either.

374

DI Sinclair turns them over and spreads them out so I can see the images. I can't make them out at first. They are bits of things. People. They are bits of people. A leg, a breast, a cheek. But gradually, they come into focus and I put the pieces together. I look at the faces — the eyes are open, but they are not seeing. They look blank. Dead eyes. Like Barbara's face. Like the photo in Will's drawer. These are the photos Kate got from Al Soames.

I look up at DI Sinclair. 'What have these got to do with me?' And I hear Paul's gasp.

I follow his eyes to a photo in the middle and I know immediately it is me.

And I reach out to take it, to gather her in. I have the dead eyes of the other girls and, for a moment, I'm glad. *At least she didn't know,* I think. I don't want to put the photo down. I can't bear the idea that strangers will see me like this. Exposed.

I want to be the keeper of my last shred of dignity. For a bit, at least. He should allow me that.

I look at it again and I shudder when I notice the hand in the corner of the photo. A man's hand, touching Emma's face. My face.

I can't stop looking at the image, but DI Sinclair is speaking and Paul is crying.

'Is this you?' the DI asks gently.

'Yes,' I say. 'Where did you find this? Who took them?'

'We are investigating that. But can you tell me if you know a man called Alistair Soames?'

'Yes,' I say. 'Al Soames was the landlord of our

375

house in Howard Street.'

And I see his face in my head. I feel his hand brushing my breast. At a party. The party Will took me to when I was fourteen and Jude had food poisoning.

I taste vomit at the back of my throat and swallow hard, trying to remember more about that night. *How did I get home?* I'm shivering.

And DI Sinclair is talking to me, but I can't hear what he's saying. I must remember. I play memory games, trying to kick-start my brain. But I can't remember anything about the end of the evening.

'Did he take the photos?' I say, interrupting the DI.

'As I said, Emma, I can't give you any more details at the moment. But I will be talking to you over the next few days as things progress.'

It's a policeman's answer. Saying something, but nothing.

'What about my baby?' I ask. 'What are you going to do about my baby?'

He plays for time, shuffling his papers, so I repeat my question.

'We'll check the DNA results again, obviously' he says. *He doesn't believe me.*

'You should take mine,' I say. 'My DNA sample. To compare.'

'Yes, of course,' he says. 'I'll just ring down and get someone to bring the swab kit. Can you wait here for a moment?' he says and makes his farewells. Very grateful for us coming in, etc.

★ ★ ★

After the test, we find ourselves outside in the sunshine.

'He didn't believe me,' I say.

'I believe you,' Paul says.

73

Sunday, 29 April 2012

Emma

Kate was waiting for me in the coffee shop across the road. She'd texted me to say she was there, but I'd had to explain her to Paul. He was horrified I wanted to talk to a reporter and wanted to come with me if I insisted on going, but I said I knew what I was doing. That I trusted her. In the end he gave in, telling me to be very careful what I said. He would wait for me, and if I wasn't back in twenty minutes, he'd come and find me.

As I turned to go, he caught hold of my arm. 'Are you absolutely sure you need to do this?'

It had taken another five minutes to convince him, and now I'm late. Kate looks as though she thought I wasn't going to come and is beginning to put her coat on when I finally walk through the door.

A waitress appears as I sit down and we have to order before we can even say hello properly.

The young girl writes down 'Two white coffees' with agonizing precision, repeating the three words as she does so. I'm willing her to go. And when she turns away, Kate says, 'Sorry, Emma. What happened at the police station? Are you OK?'

I've picked up a sachet of sugar from the bowl in front of me and am fiddling with it, like a child.

She's spoken to DI Sinclair. Everyone is talking about me. Too many whispers. I can't trust her.

I tell her what she probably already knows. And wait.

'DI Sinclair said he showed you the photos, Emma,' she says. 'I didn't know you were among the images. I swear to you. It was only when I was being questioned by Andy Sinclair this afternoon that I spotted you. I was going to call you as soon as I came out, but you turned up at the police station before I could.'

She's seen me. Seen Emma.

She's still saying sorry when I tune back in and I don't know whether to believe her any more. But I need to know more, so I'll play along.

'It was a terrible shock to see myself,' I say, sugar spilling from the ripped packet in my hand.

'It must have been,' she says.

'DI Sinclair asked if I knew Al Soames. He must think he took them.'

'But how could he?' Kate says, and I tell her about the party.

'It was Jude's idea,' I say. 'She asked Will to take me, to cheer me up. I was so excited. Jude let me wear her favourite Laura Ashley. It was midnight blue with a tiny sprigged pattern. Low at the front and tight in at the waist, with a thousand tiny buttons down the back. I

379

remember I twirled like a ballerina to make the skirt stand out and we both laughed.

'The party was like in a film with champagne and famous people and Will was urging the waiters to refill my glass. It felt like the best night of my life.

'Will introduced me simply as 'my friend Emma' and I remember a couple of men winked at him and laughed. I wondered what the joke was.'

I know now.

'Then a man kissed me on the cheek when Will introduced me. I wasn't expecting it, but he looked familiar. I was about to ask a question when his hand brushed one of my breasts as he let go of me. It was like an electric shock and I must have gone bright red because Will steered me away, apologizing.'

'Al Soames?' Kate says and I nod. I don't tell her that Will said I was looking very tempting and I got that watery feeling in my stomach again.

'He took me outside for some air,' I say. 'And the door beside us suddenly crashed open and the man with the wandering hands came out. It was then I recognized him. I'd only seen him once or twice at the house — and I was shooed out of the room by Jude each time because he wanted to talk about the rent — but I noticed his funny bumpy skin. I remember turning to Will to say, 'Look, it's our landlord,' but Will was acting as if he hadn't recognized him.'

'What happened then?' Kate says, insistent now.

I realize that my memories of the party are like one of those home movies, where a jerky camera records slices of the action, then breaks off suddenly before picking up again at another point. There are gaps. Gaping holes.

'I don't know,' I say. 'I can't remember anything after that. Not even getting home. But Will rang the next morning to say I'd done him proud.'

'Oh God,' Kate says. 'Do you think it was at that party that Soames drugged you and took the picture?'

'It isn't Soames in the picture,' I croak and concentrate on drawing a cross in the sugar on the table. 'It isn't his hand on my face.'

Kate nods. 'Soames boasted about going looking for girls with a friend.'

'It's Will,' I say. 'The hand in the photograph belongs to Will Burnside. I recognize the ring on his thumb.'

'Christ, Emma,' she says, too loudly, and people turn to stare.

I start to cry as the waitress reappears with our order. She stares at me as she puts the steaming cups down and backs away as if my misery is catching. Heads turn again. Must be thrilling for them to have a bit of drama with their coffee.

Kate reaches across and stills my hand, crunching it down on the crystals of sugar.

'Have you told the police this, Emma?'

'Not yet. I wasn't sure. I've told them he had sex with me in his car. That he threatened me if I told anyone.'

Kate is nodding slightly faster. She's excited, I

381

can see it. I have to remember she's a reporter, not my priest. She hasn't taken a vow of silence.

'I think I understand why he did it now. I have spent years trying to work out how I earned his contempt. But I think it was self-preservation. He didn't want me to tell anyone I'd seen the photograph in his drawer. I thought he wanted me to keep quiet about it so poor lovesick Barbara wouldn't be humiliated. But, of course, there were dozens of Barbaras.'

'And you could expose him,' Kate says.

'No one could know about his little hobby, so he had to make sure he'd shut me up properly, didn't he? Had to shame me into silence.'

I sit there and think about Will. I try to recall his face as he looked back then, but I can't. It's a blur now. I try to remember how he treated me after the party, after he and his friend had posed me for the Polaroid. Had he been different? Had there been any looks or innuendo the next time he'd come to the house? But he hadn't changed. Because he'd always been like that. He'd deceived us all. The monster in our midst.

The trust I'd put in him. Clever Will — the master manipulator. How he must have laughed afterwards. At my gullibility. My innocence.

I wonder what he felt when he saw me afterwards. Did he see the naked me, at his mercy? Did he keep that image in a corner of his head, to be pulled out whenever he wanted it? Did he do that when he was sitting across the table, at Sunday lunch, with my mum there?

I try to stop myself thinking like this. But it rolls over me, crushing me. And I think about

382

the baby. I start to sing a lullaby in my head. A lullaby that Jude used to sing to me.

'I think it's best if I go home,' I say.

'Will you be all right?' she says.

I think she really cares. 'I'll be fine. Paul is waiting for me up the road.'

She puts a five-pound note on the table and signals to the waitress, safe behind her counter, that we are leaving. I stand on shaking legs and she leads me out by the hand.

74

Monday, 30 April 2012

Will

He'd taken a shower after Emma and her friend left. Soaping away the accusations under hot water. He'd be all right, he thought. He enjoyed sailing close to the edge, always had.

He particularly liked a challenge when it came to women. *Nothing should be too easy*, he'd told himself as he got dressed again. *Jude was too easy. I just had to show up.*

It had been like that at university with women throwing themselves at him — Jude had told him one night that she had 'queued' to be with him. He'd laughed.

'I was a spotty undergraduate and you were a goddess. I should have been queuing for you,' he'd said. Smooth. And she'd taken off her dress. Worked every time.

In truth, he'd never been a spotty undergraduate. His skin had survived adolescence largely unscathed and his looks had grown into his gangly frame. His seriousness at school, mocked by his peers, had somehow become an attractive depth at college. He'd suddenly found that he just had to be Will and he was adored. He'd loved being adored.

When he walked into a room, people turned to look at him and moved towards him, twitching with anticipation like iron filings round a magnet. They wanted to be near him. They wanted people to see that they were near him. The Golden Boy. It could have gone to his head — well, it did, obviously, but he didn't let it show.

But it was frighteningly fragile, this adoration. People were fickle. You couldn't trust them. So he'd made it seem as if he didn't realize how brilliant he was. He'd laughed at himself and pointed out his flaws to anyone who would listen — 'Made a mess of that last essay. How did you do?'

It made him even more attractive. Tutors and fellow students were charmed by his modesty and tumbled over themselves to reassure the Golden Boy that he was brilliant. Then he tumbled them into bed. Even the tutors succumbed. Indeed, they were sometimes easier to seduce than the undergraduates. *Dear old Dr Foster didn't wait until I'd closed the door before flinging himself at me. Heady days.*

He'd left Cambridge with a double first to become a rising star at a Russell Group university and had revelled in it to begin with. His department won grants and prizes, he published regularly and was feted in his field, and the perks included dalliances with a healthy handful of undergraduates each year.

The fallow years came when he emerged from that man-boy stage and his freshness started to curdle.

He'd discovered, at thirty-nine, that he was not the only wolf in the pack. Academia was full of Wills. He'd kept up his body count of willing girls, but they no longer queued.

Sometimes he had to offer an A grade to clinch the deal. It was a colleague in the Sciences who told him about Rohypnol — joking but not joking, he realized. The colleague could get the drugs from a friend in the business, he told Will. They'd come on the scene recently and were proving popular with older men who had to try harder to get laid.

'It's ten times more effective than Valium,' his colleague had said. 'You can't taste it or see it in a drink and it makes them act totally plastered in about twenty minutes. Best bit is that they don't remember a thing in the morning.'

He was nervous the first time he used it, planning how he would explain things if it went wrong, if the girl woke up or remembered what had happened. But he didn't have to.

It wasn't as satisfying, obviously, with your conquest semi-comatose, but it did the job. And no one was any the wiser the next day.

He'd met Alistair Soames in Howard Street. Al was the landlord of Jude's house and had come to collect the rent one night. The Barbie doll owed money and was hiding in her room, and Will had been left talking to Al for half an hour while Jude pretended to search. It turned out they had a couple of friends in common and Al had made him laugh with his stories about his array of weird tenants. Will had liked him immediately.

386

The two men had arranged to meet for a drink the next night in a Chelsea pub. They'd drunk flat beer and then gone back to Al's nearby flat to talk until midnight about work, sex, the property market, sex and the future.

'I've had a bit of trouble with the ladies,' Al had confessed as the whisky loosened his inhibitions. 'And the police. Need to be more careful these days.'

And Will had told him about his little helpers.

Al's eyes had lit up. 'They don't remember anything?' he'd asked. 'Maybe slipping them something to keep them quiet is the way forward. Look, we should team up. I've got the contacts and the party invites, you've got the know-how, Will. Perfect combination.'

It had been fun picking victims — they went for a variety of ages and types just for the challenge — and dangerous. Thrillingly danger- ous. Barbara had been a mistake — she hadn't drunk enough of her drink for the drug to work properly and they hadn't noticed in their haste — but she hadn't told anyone. He'd made sure of that.

And Emma. Well, the risk had been worth it.

He wondered if she'd made up the pregnancy. He'd definitely worn a condom for the photo session — he always did to cover his traces — but he couldn't remember now if he'd worn one in the car. Or if Emma remembered the photo of Barbara. Didn't really matter, now.

No one will believe her, even if she does go to the police. Not with a history of mental illness. Sad woman, he thought.

He poured himself another cup of Earl Grey and allowed himself a stroll down memory lane. A frisson of nostalgia. Pity he hadn't kept any of the photos.

75

Tuesday, 1 May 2012

Angela

The weekend with Louise had started disastrously. Her daughter had booked them both a spa break, telling Angela she could have a massage and they could just relax, away from everything. But the place was full of hen parties, with shrieking women in the jacuzzi and drinking games in the lounge.

Louise and Angela had retreated to their overheated twin-bedded room when it all got too much and pretended to read their books while they waited for their treatments. Angela had noticed that her daughter's bookmark didn't move over the whole two days they were there. It still stuck out an inch from the cover. But she had been no better, hiding her thoughts behind the beach novel she'd brought with her.

She didn't tell Louise she'd cried during the massages; the soothing hands of the beauticians had made her feel suddenly defenceless and she'd felt she had to apologize. Everyone was very understanding when she explained — a bit too interested, in one case, and Angela had found herself telling all the details of Alice's disappearance as she lay naked on a table.

By the Sunday night, both of them had been ready to go home, but they'd paid until Monday morning and so they stayed. Angela was so glad they had because, with the bridal mobs gone, they could sit together and talk.

Louise had told her mother what it had been like growing up in a family tainted by tragedy. She'd held nothing back for the first time, even admitting that she'd hated Alice at times for ruining everyone's happiness.

'I know she was just a baby, Mum, but I never thought of her like that. I never knew her. There were no pictures. She was just this black cloud hanging over everything. No one could talk about it in case we made you cry. I am glad she's been found, but she's still making you cry.'

Angela had been mortified. She'd been so bound up in her own feelings and her determination to protect her children from them that she hadn't noticed their unhappiness.

'Your dad said I shouldn't talk about it, after a while, because I was upsetting you and Patrick,' she explained. 'I wish I'd known how you felt. I'll try not to cry any more, Lou. You're right. We need to get on with our lives now. We'll have the funeral for Alice as a family — is that all right?'

Louise had nodded and reached for her mother's hand. 'Of course, Mum.'

'And then I'll concentrate on the future,' Angela had said. 'On you and Patrick and the grandchildren.'

★　★　★

Angela's head had been clearer when she came home and she had started talking to the local vicar about a funeral service for Alice and thinking about hymns and readings. She felt better than she had done for weeks and Nick had stopped fussing over her every move.

'You look well, love,' he'd said that morning. 'Do you fancy going out for something to eat tonight? It's been months since I took you anywhere.'

And she'd smiled at him and said yes.

But an hour later, DC Turner rang. Angela had answered the call and mouthed 'Wendy' at Nick. She'd been glad to hear from her — she wanted to ask the officer about when they could have Alice's service, but DC Turner cut her off.

'Have you had anyone from the press on today, Angela?'

'No, Wendy. Why, what's happened?'

'Andy Sinclair is on his way down with me. We'll be there in half an hour, so sit tight. It's probably best if you don't answer the phone until we get there.'

'My God, what's happened?'

'Let's talk about it when we arrive, Angela. Is Nick there?'

'Yes.'

'That's good. See you soon.'

They'd sat and waited in the living room, watching for the car. And when DI Sinclair and DC Turner knocked, Angela was too shaky to stand.

Nick ushered the officers into the room and

Wendy went immediately to sit with Angela and took her hand.

DI Sinclair looked tired and depressed. He slumped down on the chair by the window and looked at her and Nick. 'I'm sorry to have kept you waiting,' he said, 'but it was important to talk to you in person.'

No one spoke and he cleared his throat.

'I've got some difficult news. There's been a significant development in the investigation. A woman came forward yesterday to claim she is the mother of the baby found in Howard Street. I honestly thought she was an attention-seeker, but the initial tests we have run on her DNA show a match.'

'No,' Angela whispered and put her other hand out for Nick, to steady herself.

She watched as the colour drained from her husband's face.

'I cannot believe this. How could this have happened?' Nick was saying. 'Whose mistake is this?'

'Nick, don't,' she said.

'We're not sure yet, Nick. Mistakes in this sort of testing are rare. We're trying to sort it out as soon as possible.'

'But when will you know for certain?' her husband asked.

DI Sinclair spread his hands helplessly.

'I see,' said Nick.

'But you will tell us as soon as you do know, Andy,' Angela said.

After the officers had gone, they sat at the kitchen table and stared at each other.

'It must be a mistake,' Nick said. 'We need to sit tight until they sort it all out.'

'No, she's gone,' Angela said. 'Our little girl has disappeared again.'

76

Kate

The results of the new DNA tests would probably come back today, she knew. DI Sinclair had pushed them to the top of the pile, anxious to get things back on track, he'd told Kate after his interview with Emma.

He'd phoned her to check if Soames had anyone living with him. 'I'm sending my blokes round there now, Kate. Just want to know if there are any complicating factors.'

'No, there's an ex-wife and two estranged grown-up children. But he's Billy No Mates,' she'd said.

'How did it go with Emma?' she'd added. He'd be expecting her to ask and she wanted to keep her own meetings with Emma quiet.

'Poor woman was all over the place,' he'd said. 'Shaking with nerves. Her eyes kept drifting off somewhere.'

'Come on, Andy, wouldn't you be all over the place if you'd been raped and had a baby when you were still a child?' Kate had replied.

'She says she had a baby, Kate. But we both know it is unlikely to be true,' he'd said. 'I mean, it's a bit of luck for her story that no one else

394

knew about it. A teenager having a baby and no one noticed? Really?'

'It happens, Andy,' Kate had said. 'There have been cases where it has happened. People can do the most extraordinary things.'

'OK, OK, but the body is Alice's — the scientists say so — and that's what I'm focusing on. We can't get distracted by this sort of attention-seeking. We get it all the time in our job, Kate.

'And if you want my advice,' he'd added, 'don't get involved.'

But she was already involved.

★ ★ ★

It was Angela who broke the news to her on the Tuesday. DI Sinclair had rung her to warn her that there was a new line emerging in the investigation and to prepare her for media calls.

Fortunately for Kate, Angela didn't think of her as the media.

'Kate,' she said, close to tears, 'something awful has happened. The DNA tests have linked a woman in London with the baby. DI Sinclair says she came forward to say the baby was hers and they thought she was a time-waster. But it now looks like she was telling the truth. They're re-testing my samples, but I think I've lost Alice all over again,' she wept.

'It is all such a mess,' Kate said. 'I'm so sorry, Angela.'

'The police can't seem to get anything right,' Angela cried down the phone. 'They got the timeline wrong and now they say it's somebody else's baby. I don't think I can cope with much more . . .'

'Come on, Angela. Is Nick with you? That's good. Now, when did Andy Sinclair say he'd ring you back?'

'In the morning. I don't know what to think any more.'

'I know,' Kate said. 'I'll get off the phone in case he's trying to get through, but ring me as soon as you hear anything.'

She didn't call Sinclair. He'd know immediately that Angela had called her and might order her not to speak to Kate again. It had happened in the past. She would bide her time until he called the Irvings with any updates.

Kate sat in the goldfish bowl in silence while Terry ranted. It did him good to let it all out, she knew. He bottled too much up and something eventually had to give. He'd had a bad week, he said, and she was 'the tin fucking lid'.

'It's still a brilliant story, Terry,' she said and then let him have his tantrum.

'I knew Emma wasn't making it up,' Kate said.

'No, it seems she wasn't,' Terry replied. 'Damn her. OK, what can we write?'

'Just that DNA tests are being re-run at the moment. We won't get a sniff of the results until tomorrow morning. And if we say they are re-testing, we'll be alerting everyone else. Why don't we wait and run the results exclusively?' Kate urged.

'OK,' he said grumpily.

Joe was waiting at her desk. He'd watched the

show through the glass and was desperate to be in on it. 'What did Angela say? What did Terry say?' he asked.

'Angela's been told Emma's DNA matches the baby.'

'No! What about Angela's DNA? Have they got it wrong in the lab?'

'Must have. Poor Angela is in pieces. They're re-running the tests and Andy Sinclair is going to call her back when they've got the result.'

'So it isn't Alice,' Joe said. 'What a story.'

'And you thought it was going to be boring when I gave you that first packet of cuttings,' Kate said.

'Well . . . '

'It's never boring,' she said.

'Is that Golden Rule Number Two?' he asked and grinned.

'Write it down. I'm ringing Emma now,' Kate said.

The mobile number went straight to voicemail and she left a message, urging Emma to call back.

There was nothing to do but wait, but Kate couldn't sit still.

'I'm going round to Emma's house,' she announced to Terry. Joe picked up his notebook and followed her out of the newsroom.

★ ★ ★

They knocked over and over again, peering in through the windows at the front and side, but there was no sign of life. Kate stood indecisively at the gate.

'She's not here,' Joe said.

'Yep, worked that one out, Joe,' she snapped.

'What shall we do now?' he asked. Like a lamb to the slaughter.

'How the hell should I know?' she barked at him. 'Stop whining, for God's sake.'

He'd looked away, pretending not to care. Like Jake had done that morning as he left for the airport. She'd let him kiss her goodbye and then said, 'I expect we'll hear from you when you need money.'

Steve had nudged her hard to shut her up. 'Keep in touch, Jakey,' he'd said, but their son was already walking through the door.

'Why on earth did you say that?' Steve had said.

'You baby him,' she'd said. 'He needs a dose of the real world, not to be humoured.'

But Kate had texted Jake from the car: 'Come home safe. Love you, Jake, m x'. But he hadn't replied.

★   ★   ★

'Hello there!' a voice hailed her from down the street and an officious-looking woman hurried up to them. 'Are you looking for the Simmonds?' she said.

'Er, yes, I was hoping to catch Emma in,' Kate said.

'She was on the Tube this morning with my husband. He told me when he rang to say he'd got to work. I'm Lynda, Emma's friend, by the way.'

'Oh, pleased to meet you,' Kate said, registering that some wives required their husbands to clock in and out. 'Did she say where she was going?'

'No, Derek said she was very distracted, hardly said a word. Mind you, the Metropolitan Line is extremely crowded at that time of the morning. It's a funny time to travel if you don't have to.'

Kate pulled an understanding face.

'Perhaps she is having one of her bad days,' Lynda added disloyally. 'She can be quite odd sometimes.'

'Right,' Kate said and, thanking her for her time, pulled Joe towards the car.

'Where's Emma going?' Joe said as he did up his seatbelt. 'Just asking, not whining,' he added.

'Sorry, Joe. Having a bad day myself. No idea.'

She drove back towards the office in west London and let Joe talk about his ambitions and a reality TV show he'd watched the night before.

Where are you, Emma? she thought. She pulled over when her phone pinged. 'Bet that's her,' she told Joe.

When she looked, the text was from Jake. 'Shit,' she said. The last thing she needed was more grief from her son.

'Love you, too, mum. Sorry to be such a crap son, x' Jake had texted.

She felt like bursting into tears, but forwarded it to Steve instead. He texted back immediately: 'x'

Joe sat patiently until she'd finished. 'I've been thinking. What about Emma's mum?' Joe said. '*Why* don't we go and see her? We haven't talked to her, have we? She might know where Emma is.'

'Good call, Joe,' she said. 'Find me an address.'

77

Tuesday, 1 May 2012

Kate

The traffic was horrendous, but they finally pulled up outside the converted house where Jude lived.

Kate tried Emma's number once more as she locked the car, but there was still no answer.

'Come on,' she said.

She and Joe were buzzed straight in when they pressed the bell — no questions asked — and they trooped up the stairs.

An elderly woman in clothes that were slightly too young for her was standing at her open door.

'Oh! Who are you?' she said. 'I thought you might be my daughter.'

'Ah, sorry, no, Mrs Massingham,' Kate said.

'It's Ms Massingham, actually.'

'Right, well, I'm Kate Waters. I'm a reporter for the *Daily Post*. I've been talking to your daughter, Emma, over the weekend about the Alice Irving case and I need to find her again.'

'Has Emma talked to you? Never a good idea to talk to a reporter. I used to be a lawyer and I always told my clients to avoid the press like the plague. No offence . . . '

Kate laughed unconvincingly. 'Good advice in

some cases, I imagine. But the stories I've been writing about Alice have uncovered some important facts.'

'Hmm,' Jude Massingham said. 'But not the truth, I think. Slippery thing, the truth.'

'Er, yes. There have been some setbacks in the investigation — the police would be the first to admit that.'

'Would they? That was never my experience,' Jude said with a tight smile.

'Look, something has emerged this morning that I want to tell Emma, but she's not picking up her phone,' Kate said, trying to move the conversation on to firmer ground.

'I've no idea where she is,' Jude said. 'I'm not her keeper. What has emerged?'

'Can we come in, Ms Massingham?' Kate said. 'It's a bit public here. Don't want your neighbours overhearing things.'

'Oh, all right,' Jude said. 'Mind the step.'

They sat in a tight group in and on the two armchairs. No drinks were offered.

'Right,' Jude said. 'What has happened?'

'I don't know if Emma has told you, but the police have done some new DNA tests.'

'No, we're not really talking at the moment,' Jude muttered.

'Well, the tests show there is a match between Emma and the baby on the building site.'

'No,' Jude blurted and held her head in her hands. 'It can't be. How could she have had a baby without me knowing?'

'She hid it from you, Ms Massingham. And from your boyfriend, Will Burnside.'

'What has she told you about him?' Jude said quietly, the tension in the room thickening.

'Exactly what she told you.'

'I didn't believe her. I said terrible things to her. Said she was ill and jealous,' Jude said, almost to herself.

'But she was telling the truth, Ms Massingham. Did you really not suspect anything?'

The older woman shook her head. 'No, of course not. Do you think I would have turned a blind eye to something like that? You don't know what it was like. I loved Will. Adored him. And it is hard to imagine that the man you love could do something so despicable. Could you believe that of someone you love, Miss Waters?'

Kate instantly pictured Steve confessing and shook her head.

'You see how difficult it would have been? It still is. I need some time to think about this. And to talk to Emma.' She seemed to be talking to herself.

Kate leant forward to ask another question, but Jude suddenly exclaimed, 'I knew it couldn't have been the Irving baby.'

'How did you know?'

Jude looked flustered. 'Well, that baby disappeared ten years before they say the body was buried. The whole police investigation has been cack-handed, if you ask me.'

'But the match with Angela Irving,' Joe said. 'What about that?'

'Lab cock-up,' Jude said. 'I used to hear about it happening from colleagues with criminal practices when I was working. Test tubes in

403

wrong racks, contamination from other samples, that sort of thing. There's always room for human error.'

'But there are lots of checks and balances to the process,' he said. 'I've been reading up on it. It's really interesting, actually — '

'I'd like to tell Emma,' Kate said, cutting him off. 'I'm a bit worried I can't get hold of her. Her friend Lynda said she was on the Tube into town this morning.'

'Was she? How odd. She never comes into town if she can help it. Too many people,' Jude said and fell silent. 'I suppose we could ring her husband,' she offered. 'He'll be at work. I've got a number for him. Emma wrote it in my address book in case of emergencies.'

She dialled slowly, punching the numbers deliberately, and waited.

'Paul, it's Jude. I'm trying to get hold of Emma. Do you know what she's doing today? Right. Well, she's not. She was seen on the Tube this morning. Right. Well, if she calls you, will you tell her to give me a ring? Yes, and you. Bye.

'He thought she was working at home this morning. Sounded a bit rattled when I said about the Tube. She's not in great form at the moment. As you probably know,' Jude said, her tone accusatory, her voice shaky.

When Kate and Joe got outside, Kate's phone rang.

'It's Andy Sinclair,' he said. 'I'm trying to reach Emma Simmonds. She seems to have disappeared. You don't know where she is, do you?'

78

Jude

When the phone rang late that night, Jude snatched it up. 'Emma?' she said.

'Jude, it's Harry,' the voice said. 'Sorry to disturb you, but I'm worried about Emma.'

'We're all worried about her,' Jude said. 'I've had the press here asking for her, too.' Jude felt shaky and she sat down too quickly on her chair, jarring her elbow and dropping the phone. 'Sorry,' she said when she put it back to her ear. 'Have you heard from her?'

'No, she's vanished. Paul just called me to say he still can't get hold of her. He thinks she's turned off her phone.'

A dark curl of dread twisted itself round Jude's heart.

'I need to know what's been happening, Jude,' Harry insisted. 'Paul won't tell me.'

'Emma's been to see the police, Harry. To tell them the baby in the garden of Howard Street was hers. That she was raped by Will and got pregnant,' Jude said, hardly believing what she was saying.

'Will?' Harry shouted down the phone. 'Will Burnside? Are you serious?'

405

'Yes. I can't believe it either,' Jude added.

'Oh my God,' Harry said.

'Did you know she'd had a baby Harry?' Jude asked. 'You two were thick as thieves. Did she tell you anything?'

'Not until much later. And then I got hold of the wrong end of the stick. She was trying to tell me, said she'd got pregnant, but I thought she'd had an abortion. I didn't press her. Not like that reporter.'

'The reporter came here today, Harry. Do you want to speak to her? I've got her number,' Jude said, longing for someone else to take control of the situation.

'No I don't,' Harry snapped. 'What gives them the right to meddle in people's lives like this? How is this news? This is a personal tragedy, not some story for everyone to gawp at. Emma must be in pieces.'

There was a terrible, echoing silence. Jude listened to the static on the line. 'Harry?' she said finally. 'Are you still there?'

'Yes. I'm here. Can I come round? Now?'

'Yes,' Jude said. 'And I'm going to ask Kate Waters to come too. She's very much a part of this and Emma seems to trust her, whatever you may think. She was the one she told . . .'

'OK,' Harry said. 'Give me half an hour.'

Jude called Kate immediately. She couldn't think about anything but Emma. What was she doing? Where was she? What had she driven her to?

★ ★ ★

406

Kate arrived just after Harry had pulled up and buzzed Jude's bell. When Jude opened her door, she could see that the reporter had pulled her jeans on under her nightie and put a coat on top in her haste to get on the road.

And Harry was talking frantically into her phone.

'It's Emma,' she mouthed, and Jude took a deep breath to calm her fear about what was coming next. 'Emma, stay there. I'm coming to get you. Promise me you'll stay there.'

When she hung up, Harry turned to Kate and said, 'We're going back to Howard Street. She's gone to the building site.'

'How did she sound?' Kate said.

'How do you think?' Harry snapped.

The three women got into Kate's car. London was almost empty: the normally congested roads rang with the sound of the engine, the street lights bouncing off the road surface all round them; they didn't talk again until they pulled up outside the building site.

'Do you want me to come with you?' Kate asked.

'Not really, but I think you'd better. I might need back-up,' Harry said.

They found Emma sitting on an upturned bucket in what had once been the garden, surrounded by heavy clay clods and lit by the security lights she'd triggered. She looked up when Harry called her name, but didn't rise from her seat.

'I've been trying to think about what happened. Trying to make sense of it,' she said. 'I

407

thought I'd come back to where it began. With the baby . . . '

'I've been trying to persuade her to come away,' a woman's voice came from the gloom.

'Barbara?' Kate said. And the older woman walked into the glow of the arc lamps.

'I saw the lights go on — I'm not sleeping well,' she said. 'And John has been saying there have been problems with kids getting into the site, so I came over to see. And found her. Found Emma.'

Jude looked in disbelief at her old friend. 'What are *you* doing here?' she said. It all felt like a strange dream.

'I moved back to Howard Street, Jude. After we'd lost touch.'

After you made a play for Will, Jude thought automatically, then stopped herself. That was what Will had said. But he had lied about everything, hadn't he?

Harry had crouched down beside Emma and touched her arm. 'You're cold, Emma,' she said. 'We need to get you in the warm.'

'I live just across the road. We can go there,' Barbara said and Jude stiffened. She'd wanted to take Emma home with her, but it was out of her hands.

Emma let herself be led to Barbara's flat and sat beside a sleeping Shorty on the sofa. She looked numb, her eyes frozen with shock.

'Do you know everything?' she whispered to Harry.

'We don't have to talk about it now, Emma,' Harry said.

'I tried to tell you once. That day when you turned up in the pub.'

'I remember. I didn't listen, did I? I jumped to conclusions. I'm so sorry, Emma. But why didn't you tell me at the time? When we were kids?'

Jude had to lean forward to catch the answer.

'I couldn't then. Will said everyone would hate me.'

The two friends put their arms around each other. Jude struggled to stay in her seat. It should have been her comforting her child, but Emma hadn't reached for her.

When they finally let go and sat leaning against each other, Kate turned in her seat to face them.

'The police will get Will for what he did,' she said, trying to steady her voice. 'To you, Emma. He may think he's untouchable after all this time, but there is evidence now — photographic evidence — and I'm sure Soames will have no hesitation in taking him down with him. I've met him. He's a scumbag,' she added.

'She's right,' Harry said. 'We'll have the bastard's head on a stick.'

'And for what he did to you, Barbara,' Emma said. 'I know he did the same to you.'

Jude stared from her daughter to her former friend.

'How do you know?' Barbara whispered. 'Did he tell you?'

'No, I saw your photo in Will's desk. I thought you were asleep, but it had been taken when you were drugged. I was too young to know what people were capable of then. I asked Will about it and he said you had sent it to him because you wanted him.'

Barbara gasped.

'He raped me the next day. To shut me up,' Emma said. 'He must have known that I could be shamed into silence. I believed him when he said everyone would blame me. I didn't know any better.'

Jude squeezed her eyes shut. It'd all been lies. His lies, her own lies. She'd done this. She couldn't blame Emma or Barbara any more. She'd brought this man into their lives. She was guilty of this. Everything was unspooling in front of her.

79

Kate

Emma shook her head when Kate told her she ought to ring DI Sinclair. That there was news about the tests.

'I know what the result will be. I don't need to ring him,' she said. 'I put my baby in the ground, under the urn. I don't need him to confirm it.'

Kate rang him instead, to tell him she was with Emma in Howard Street and to alert him to Will Burnside's second victim, Barbara.

'I'm coming over now, Kate,' he said. She couldn't tell if he was angry that she'd got there first. Didn't matter, did it? As long as Emma was safe.

★   ★   ★

When he arrived, with his sergeant, a woman in her thirties, they all crammed into the front room and the dog was put in the kitchen.

'Now then,' DI Sinclair said, 'this is all getting very complex, but I would like to start with the baby. It's where all of this began for my investigation. OK?'

Emma nodded and the others sat back, out of

411

the detective's gaze.

'I think you probably already know, Emma, that a match has been found between you and the baby's body uncovered on the Howard Street building site?'

'Kate told me the test results had come back,' she said.

'I'll discuss that with you later,' he said to Kate, raising his hand to silence her explanations. 'Later . . . We are waiting to verify Angela Irving's DNA results, but it looks like there must have been an error in the tests,' he said. 'I'm talking to Mr and Mrs Irving in the morning. What I would ask is that you do not reveal the results of your test to anyone, Emma, until all results are in and we can make a proper statement.'

He looked over at Kate, to underline his meaning.

'This is a very sensitive matter, especially for the Irvings. They have waited a long time to find out what happened to their child and we must be fair to them,' he added.

Around the room, heads nodded in unison. 'So we understand each other?' he asked. 'And that obviously includes you, Kate.'

'Of course,' she muttered crossly.

'It's late,' DI Sinclair said. 'I think we should meet again in the morning. Could you come to Woolwich police station tomorrow, Mrs Simmonds? And you, Miss Walker? I understand you both have matters you want to discuss with regards to Professor Burnside. We need to do this properly, not on this ad hoc basis.'

412

Emma and Barbara said they would and Kate avoided his eyes.

'Perhaps we could have a quiet word, Kate,' he said. 'Outside.'

She followed him out, leaving the women to say their farewells.

'You've completely overstepped the mark, Kate,' DI Sinclair said as soon as they reached the pavement. 'You've put this investigation in jeopardy with your cowboy antics. It was not up to you to tell Emma Simmonds about the DNA test results. It could have caused all sorts of damage.'

Kate knew she'd only told Emma the results were in, but DI Sinclair wasn't interested in excuses. She should try to defuse the situation by apologizing, but the stress of the evening had left her raw and ready for a fight.

'I have only done my job, Andy. This is what I'm paid to do. I've followed up leads and chased down people who might be able to help with your inquiries. And I've passed them on to you when asked. My paper has done everything it can to help find out what happened to Alice Irving. Hardly my fault you got the tests wrong . . . '

'I'll be speaking to your editor,' DI Sinclair said, turning on his heel and marching off into the night, his DS scurrying behind him.

'Bugger,' Kate said out loud. 'Another contact bites the dust.'

80

Kate

Joe was hard at work when Kate arrived in the office the next day, focusing on his screen with the sort of attention that gave her an instant headache. She was too tired and dispirited to bother asking him what he was doing. She slumped down in her chair and waited for the next bollocking.

It only took thirty seconds to arrive.

Terry beckoned her over. The slow, angry-finger beckon.

'Right, my star reporter, where are we then?' he said, his tone laced with sarcasm. 'Have you stood this story up yet?'

'Well — ' Kate started.

'Yes or no?'

'No,' she said. 'And I think Simon is going to get a complaint from the police. I got a rocket from my contact on the case last night and was told not to write anything until an official statement is released. I think our love affair is over.'

'Great,' Terry said, winding himself up. 'So we haven't got the exclusive I promised Simon? And he's going to get an earful from the Commissioner? Brilliant. Bloody brilliant.'

She thought about saying sorry, but it wasn't what he wanted to hear.

'I'll try another route,' she said and slunk back to her desk.

Joe looked up. 'Shall I get you a coffee, Kate?' he said and she could have hugged him.

'Yes, my lovely boy. Have I told you I'm going to adopt you? And get a brandy too, if they've got one.'

She switched on her screen to appear in work mode and got her notebook out.

I wonder what Simon will say? she thought, the threat of redundancy fluttering at the back of her mind. *He'll back me, won't he?*

Joe returned with caffeine but no strong liquor. 'They were all out of brandy,' he said.

'What are you looking at?' Kate asked when he screwed his eyes firmly back on his computer.

'A thing about DNA,' he said. 'It's really interesting. Did you know if you test the mitochondria, our DNA can be matched with our ancestors? Well, through the maternal line to our great-grandmothers. And if you do y-str profiling, you can do the male line. It's fascinating.'

'Fascinating,' Kate said. 'Haven't you got a story to get on with?'

'No, you don't understand. All our closest relatives — parents, aunts, uncles, brothers, sisters, cousins, grandparents — will match. They share the same DNA markers.'

'OK. So what you're saying is more than one person could match the baby's DNA?'

'Yes, I think so,' Joe said. 'That's what it says on Wikipedia.'

415

She leant over his shoulder and read the entry for herself.

'Not two babies, then,' she said, grinning from ear to ear. 'Two relatives.'

She rang Andy Sinclair's mobile, but he didn't pick up. *Still sulking*, she thought.

Bob Sparkes answered immediately. 'Oh dear, Kate. Not DI Sinclair's favourite reporter, I hear.'

'You hear right. Has he called you? He threw a hissy fit last night and marched off,' she said.

'Not the description he gave me, but he is extremely fed up with you. And they are having to run all the tests again because they keep getting the same results. He's under huge pressure. Cut him some slack, Kate.'

'Cutting slack won't solve this case, Bob,' she said and he laughed.

'You just can't leave things alone, can you? Like a terrier with a bone.'

'That's what makes me a good reporter, Bob. Anyway, Andy won't take my calls. But I've got something to suggest. Can I run it past you first?'

'Go on, then,' Sparkes said.

She told him about Joe's discovery, omitting the fact that the information was on Wikipedia, and waited for him to digest it.

'So both Angela and Emma could be related to the baby?'

'Could be, if I've understood the science properly . . . '

'I'll ring him now,' Sparkes said and rang off before Kate could ask him to call her back immediately.

She took a mouthful of coffee, swilling it round thoughtfully. Joe perched on the edge of her desk.

When the phone trilled, she gulped and spluttered and pointed to Joe to answer.

'Hello, DI Sinclair, I'll just pass you over,' he said, handing it to Kate.

'Hello, Andy. Sorry, just choking on my coffee. Look, I'm so sorry about last night. It was all very stressful and I probably over-reacted.'

DI Sinclair cleared his throat. His turn. 'Yes, well, I probably came over a bit heavy-handed. Let's put it behind us, shall we?'

'Yes, let's do that. Thanks for ringing me. I really appreciate it.'

'Bob Sparkes has just told me your suggestion,' DI Sinclair said. 'I wanted to let you know that our forensic team is already comparing Emma and Angela's DNA as a check on false positives. That would confirm their shared ancestry. And we're about to talk to both women to try and establish a link. So please do not get in contact with either of them until we have done so.'

'Oh God, Andy, Emma is Alice, isn't she?' Kate said, the idea suddenly bursting in on her.

81

Wednesday, 2 May 2012

Jude

DI Sinclair was on his way to Pinner.

Emma had called Jude in a panic. 'He's just rung to make sure I'm home. I think he's coming to take me away. To lock me up. I just wanted to tell you.'

'Why would he want to lock you up?' Jude had said. 'Try to stay calm.'

'I buried the baby without telling anyone. They might think I killed it,' Emma had sobbed.

And Jude had run down the stairs to find a cab. She had to be with Emma now.

★ ★ ★

She arrived just after the detective. He looked exhausted. Nearly as exhausted as Paul looked. Emma had packed a small bag in readiness and was sitting holding her husband's hand.

'I'm glad you are here, too, Ms Massingham,' DI Sinclair said to Jude. 'I called your home but there was no answer. I need to talk to both you and Emma.'

'Why?' Emma said. 'Jude didn't know about the baby.'

418

'Not your baby, Emma,' he said. 'Alice.'

Jude knew immediately it was all over. The detective's face was set. There'd be no dancing round the facts. Or new lies. The truth could no longer be many things.

So she told the story of how she'd lost Charlie's baby at five months. How she'd fallen, tripped over the flex of her hairdryer in the bedroom as she rushed to get ready for work and crashed face first on to the floor. There was no one there to help as she grasped her stomach and tried to will away the burning pain, and the blood, lots of blood. She went and sat on the toilet as waves of agony took over her body. She'd flushed away all that came out of her, unable to look into the bowl and acknowledge that her pregnancy was over. She'd rung work from the payphone in the hallway of her rented flat and said she was ill.

'I was going to tell Charlie that night, when he rang,' she said. 'But his first words were so loving, calling me his angel and asking about the baby. And I said, 'We're fine,' and the lie was told. There was no going back.'

Emma wouldn't look at her, but the detective held her gaze steadily.

'Go on, Ms Massingham.'

'I decided to pretend to lose the baby later. After he'd promised to marry me. He should have married me, then none of this would have happened,' Jude said, but the detective's expression didn't alter.

'I made layers of padding out of an old foam rubber cushion, adding layers and wearing

419

bigger maternity clothes. I told Charlie on the phone about how my legs were aching. I think I believed I was still pregnant.'

'And your boyfriend? Didn't he suspect anything?' DI Sinclair asked.

'He was a musician and away in Europe, on tour with his band. And the dates kept being extended, so he didn't see me for months.'

'What did you tell your friends and family, Ms Massingham?' Andy Sinclair asked.

'My parents stopped talking to me when I told them I was having a baby. An illegitimate baby was too much for them to bear. What would they tell their friends at the golf club? But I kept on working — I needed the money — and when I got to seven months, I took maternity leave. I told them I had to leave early because my blood pressure was up and I'd been told to put my feet up for the baby's sake. The girls at work were disappointed. They'd wanted to have a party for me . . . ' Jude looked across at her daughter. *What are you thinking, Emma?*

She told the detective she'd rung the surgery to tell them she would be away, abroad with Charlie for a while. So no more antenatal appointments were necessary.

And she'd waited at home and tried to work out what she was going to do. She could still summon up the dulling panic that had invaded every moment as D day approached. Charlie was coming home in two weeks, expecting to find her heavily pregnant, about to deliver their child. He'd know as soon as he held her, wouldn't he? Wild ideas presented themselves in the middle of

420

the night. She'd say it was a tumour and hadn't wanted to tell him. He'd be too shocked to question it. Wouldn't he? She'd say the baby had died. Too many questions — and then he'd leave her.

'I couldn't bear the thought of him leaving me. I had to give him a child.

'I went to Waterloo station and caught the first train south that came up on the board. I was out of my mind, I didn't know where I was going — I just needed to find a maternity hospital.'

She remembered that someone had stood up to give her a seat and she had smiled her thanks, lowering herself down like a pro.

'I got off at Basingstoke,' she said.

'Had you ever been there before?' DI Sinclair asked.

'No, I had to ask the way to the maternity hospital.' Jude took a deep breath and, in her head, walked back through the hospital doors.

She took the lift, avoiding eye contact with the other people crammed in with her. They had bunches of flowers, presents in baby and stork wrapping paper, held toddlers by the hand. They were excited, laughing. No one seemed to notice her.

But she realized she'd picked the wrong time. She needed to come at the end of visiting time, not the beginning. There were too many witnesses now. She left the hospital and sat in a nearby park for an hour, growing cold as the weak spring sun began to disappear.

Back in the lift, this time she was alone. The doors opened on the post-natal floor and there were the same people, flowers and congratulations delivered, on their way home now. She'd bought some flowers from a seller on the street outside and clasped them to her stomach.

When the lift doors opened, she saw a woman come out of her room halfway down the corridor. She had her wash things and a towel in her hand. She walked away from Jude without seeing her.

Jude paused, pretending to look in her shopping bag. The woman might have forgotten something. She might come back. But she didn't. She went into the bathroom at the end of the corridor and closed the door. Jude couldn't move for a moment, transfixed by terror at what she was about to do, but then she heard a baby cry in the woman's room.

I can do this, she said in her head and moved, as if in a dream, through the door. The baby was snuffling in its cot. She walked straight over, picked it up, all wrapped ready, and put it in her shopping bag. And walked away. She took the stairs this time. Nobody used the stairs.

On the train home, a woman said companionably, 'When's yours due?'

'Not long now,' Jude said, and went and stood near the doors, where there was more noise to drown out the baby if it cried. But the baby didn't make so much as a murmur.

Back in her room, she unwrapped it, like a present, and sat looking at her sleeping child for the first time. It was a girl.

'Hello, Emma,' she said.

82

Wednesday, 2 May 2012

Angela

The doctor had given her some pills to dull the shock but she kept jumping up every time a car passed the house. DI Sinclair had phoned to say he'd be there in twenty minutes. He'd sounded sombre and tired and she'd let him go without any further questions.

Nick came downstairs and paced round the room.

'Angie, we've got to prepare ourselves for the worst,' he said. 'The police have got it wrong. There's nothing we can do to change it. I think he's coming to apologize, don't you?'

'Let's see, Nick,' she said. Her head was buzzing again. Filled with Alice.

* * *

Nick opened the door before DI Sinclair could knock. 'Come in, Andy,' he said.

Angela stood at the window, looking at the detective's car. There were three people in it.

'Aren't your colleagues coming in?' she asked.

He hesitated. 'No, not at the moment.' The officer cleared his throat. 'Angela, Nick,' he said.

423

'I've got some news for you. I'm not sure how to tell you, to be honest.'

He was perspiring, the beads of sweat on his forehead winking in the light.

'That you've made a mistake?' Nick said. 'We thought that was it.'

'Well, no,' the detective said. 'The thing is . . . Look, we have found Alice. But she is not the baby on the building site.'

Angela gasped.

'Angie,' Nick said, his voice shaking, pulling her close. 'Tell us, Andy. Just tell us what you've found.'

'Alice is alive,' DI Sinclair said.

'*Alive?*' Angela and Nick both shouted, the sound bouncing off the window.

'Yes.'

'How can she be?' Angela said, frantically looking around the room for her child. 'Where is she?'

'She's here,' DI Sinclair said, his voice catching with the emotion of the moment. He'd never cried on a job, even when he'd been breaking terrible news. But the tension was unbearable.

'Where? Where?' Angela shrieked.

'She's in the car,' he said.

Angela was out of the front door before they could stop her, running to the car and stopping beside it, her hands spread on the passenger window.

The woman looked back at her: dark hair like Paddy, Louise's chin. And she put her hands up to mirror her mother's.

83

Emma

Angela and I cannot stop looking at each other. Even when DI Sinclair is talking to us, we look at each other, drinking each other in. She looks like me. I look like her.

I feel like I'm in some sort of surreal dream. I haven't stopped thinking of Jude as my mother, but I feel like I might love this stranger, too.

DI Sinclair had wanted to wait before reuniting us. He was worried that it would be too much for everyone. 'You are in a fragile state, Emma,' he'd said after Jude was taken away to the police station. 'There's a lot to take in. Why don't we give it a day so you can prepare yourself?'

But I wouldn't let him leave without me. I was terrified that Angela would reject me, but I had to see her. To be sure.

In the car, I kept thinking that all this time I've been looking for a father and I should have been looking for my mother. Paul sat beside me in the back of the car, holding my hand but unable to speak.

And when I saw her burst out of the front door and run towards the car, I knew it was her.

425

I wanted to touch her to see if she was real and I put my hand up to hers at the window.

But I'm not sure what will happen now. The euphoria has faded to a pleasant hum in my head, but there are spikes of fear in my stomach. I'm still afraid. Afraid of how it'll turn out. Maybe I'll lose everyone. Jude will go to prison for what she did, and Angela . . . may not want me.

'Alice,' she says as if she can read my thoughts, 'I've never stopped thinking about you. Never.'

'She hasn't,' Nick says. My dad. He keeps looking away, as if I'm too much to take in. But Angela doesn't.

'I thought we'd be safe in a hospital,' she says. 'But we weren't. When I got back from the shower, I knew as soon as I came into the room that I was alone. There was a silence so unnatural I felt faint and had to grab the door. Everything was wrong, but I couldn't see how. I went over to your cot and there was just a slight dent in the white cotton sheet to show that you'd been there. I put my hand in your cot — I couldn't believe you'd gone — I searched every corner in case you were hidden somehow, and I felt your warmth for the last time.'

My mother weeps.

'I couldn't remember if I'd looked at you again before I went out. I shouldn't have left you.'

I reach out and take her hand. It is the first time we've touched. Her hand is soft and warm and I squeeze it.

'It wasn't your fault,' I say.

426

84

Wednesday, 16 May 2012

Emma

Two weeks later, I'm sitting in the waiting room of a magistrates' court with Mick and Kate. Mick has put on a terrible, stained tie as a nod to the occasion and brought an Egg McMuffin in his pocket — 'Bit late up this morning,' he explained.

'Don't worry, I'll be ready,' he said to Kate when he finally swallowed the last mouthful. 'I'll go outside for the arrival. Can't wait to see his face.' Kate's in a severe black suit and white shirt. She looks like an undertaker's receptionist. She's up and down all the time, talking to DI Sinclair in the corner.

Her story about Angela and me caused a huge fuss when it came out. She'd had to write it carefully, she said, leaving out anything that might identify Will as the rapist and hedging round Jude's role. There was a line saying, 'Police have arrested a 73-year-old woman as part of their investigation.'

'I don't want to be responsible for their trials collapsing,' she told me. 'There'll be plenty of time to tell that part of the story later.'

The day after Angela and I met for the first

time, the *Post* put our reunion on the front page and on three more pages inside there were pictures of us with our arms around each other. It was the first time we'd held each other; we'd needed Mick to give us permission, almost.

'Come on,' he'd said when we hovered nervously near each other, neither ready to make the first move. 'You've waited forty-two years for this. Give her a hug, Angela.'

Mick clicked away for ages, but when he stopped, we couldn't let go.

Joe had cried and Kate put her arm round him. Everyone seemed to be hugging.

★　★　★

But there's no happiness here. This is where my misery started. And where it will end. It'll be the first time I've seen Will since that day at his house. I wasn't going to come, but DI Sinclair said Will was going to fight it all the way. I suppose I knew he would. His arrogance wouldn't let him do anything else. Kate said she'd heard he was putting all the blame on Soames. Soames's face was identifiable in the photographs. He was the one with the record of sex offences.

I couldn't let him think I would back off. So I've come. To show him I'm still here. Like Banquo's ghost.

He arrives with a swagger.

'I have come to protest my innocence,' Will says on the steps of the court, turning his best side to Mick's camera.

I can feel every inch of my skin, as if I'm on fire, as I stand up from my seat and face my attacker. He looks startled and his public face disappears. He is just a frightened old man.

Jude isn't here. She's retreated from me, from everyone, since she was arrested. She seems to have shrunk in the days that have followed her confession and she's refusing to eat.

Barbara is staying with her while she is on bail. To look after her — picking up where she left off all those years ago. I've told Jude I don't hate her. But I think I do. I've tried to understand why she took me from the hospital, what drove her. I've tried to put myself in her desperate shoes. But all I can think of is Angela's face when she found me gone. And her years of agony.

When I asked Jude how she could have lived with herself, knowing what they were going through, she said she forced herself not to think about them.

'They had other children,' she said, as if that made it all right. I wanted to scream at her, but there was no point. She is shielded by her self-obsession. Her sense of entitlement. Whenever she wanted something, she took it, whatever the consequences, because she felt she deserved it.

I now see why she threw me out without a backward glance. She had to have Will. I was collateral damage.

Angela won't talk about her. Won't speak her name. She says she wants to concentrate on the future, not the past.

We speak on the phone every day with a growing familiarity and I wonder if I'll ever call her Mum. Not yet. She still calls me Alice and then corrects herself. I feel like I am two people now. Emma and Alice. I'm going to see my brother and sister next week. I think I'm ready now and Angela wants us to meet. I'm not sure how they feel about it. About me. The shock of my reappearance must be taking its toll on them as well. I'm the missing child who caused so much unhappiness to their family. Angela says they are thrilled I have been found, but she wants everyone to be happy. I need to take it a step at a time.

I sit back down with Kate and catch my breath after Will goes into court. I feel elated and destroyed by the confrontation, shaking with the effort.

'You did brilliantly,' Kate says. 'All over, now.'

Well, almost.

85

Tuesday, 26 March 2013

Emma

I started calling the baby Katherine after the police interviews, because she was a person at last. I'd named her for Kate. Without her, I would still be in hell.

Paul calls her Katherine as well. Naming her means we can talk about her and grieve for her. My child. I hadn't realized how much I missed her. She was a physical presence in my life for such a short time — like Angela with me — but she's been part of me ever since, my ghost child.

I had to wait another week to hear what the police would do. It was DI Sinclair himself who rang. He said I would be formally notified but he wanted to tell me there was no evidence that I had harmed my baby and he was recommending no further action. He said it wouldn't be in the public interest to pursue me after twenty-seven years for the technical offences of failing to register a birth or to notify the Coroner. I tried to say thank you, but I couldn't get the words out and Paul took the phone from me to thank him instead.

It felt as if everything was going to be all right, like Paul said.

But we couldn't say goodbye to Katherine properly until the end of the trials. Jude's first. It was over before it began, really. A guilty plea, a psychiatric report which said she knew that what she was doing was wrong, and a prison sentence.

She looked at me as she was led away, but she didn't look like Jude any more. She looked like a husk. I nodded to show I'd seen.

She's asked me not to visit her in prison. She said it would be too upsetting for both of us. So I am writing to her instead.

Then Will. A horror story. DNA tests had to be done again on my little girl's tiny bones to show that Will Burnside was her father. They hadn't damaged her, the police said when I asked. They've been so gentle with me and her.

When I finally took the stand, in January, my legs were shaking, but I wanted to be there. To bear witness. Will's barrister accused Barbara and me of inventing the whole thing, laying bare my mental health problems with fake concern and alleging we were vindictive whores. Well, he didn't use those words, but we all knew that's what he meant.

'I'm an innocent man,' Will said when he got his turn, switching on the charisma as if it was a button on a remote control.

'Hardly innocent,' the prosecutor said. 'You have admitted to having sex with a number of women, including former students.'

Will didn't miss a beat.

'They were willing partners,' he said to the jury, taking off his glasses. 'But sometimes women throw themselves at you and then

432

complain afterwards if you don't answer their letters or stay in touch.'

'But some were girls, Professor Burnside, not women, weren't they?' the prosecutor said. 'Miss Massingham was fourteen, wasn't she?'

He couldn't deny it. Katherine had told her story.

'Those I had sex with wanted it,' he said and tried to make eye contact with the jurors. 'They were begging for it.'

'Hard to beg for it, Professor, if you are drugged,' the prosecutor said.

'It was a different time, then. There was a lot more sex going on. Experimentation with drugs,' Will said.

But he must've known he was fighting a losing battle. The jury didn't know, but Alistair Soames had already admitted his part and given the detectives chapter and verse on their use of Rohypnol. The friend who'd supplied it was long gone, DI Sinclair told me. An accidental overdose. Well, what goes around . . .

When the jury went out, Will's bail was revoked and he was taken down to the cells under the court to await the verdict. It was a bad sign. He came back to hear the jury foreman pronounce the word 'Guilty' over and over, and the life sentence had silenced everyone, but he looked at me once as we all stood to allow the judge to retire. A look of pure hatred.

I simply looked away. He was nothing to me now.

86

Monday, 1 April 2013

Emma

There were three of us at the funeral. Me, Angela and Kate. It was what I wanted. Paul and my dad, Nick, would wait for us at home.

The funeral director had helped me choose a casket for the child. My child. A tiny, woven willow coffin with a simple plaque bearing the name Katherine Massingham.

I'd decided I would do it properly, but I couldn't bear the thought of putting her back in the cold earth. Angela had suggested a cremation and then scattering her ashes together. I loved the idea of her being carried by the wind and we'd talked about taking her down to the coast — to Dorset, we thought — when everything was over.

We held hands as we waited for our turn at the crematorium. There was a big funeral before ours, with flowers and undertakers in top hats and tailcoats, like at a wedding.

I hadn't wanted a hearse — it was too lonely for my little one to travel like that — so the undertaker brought her in a car and handed her carefully to me. She was almost weightless and I was immediately back in our garden, the carrier bag in my hand, held away from me as if it was toxic. It was twenty-eight years ago today. So long ago, but it was as if it had happened yesterday.

The man with the top hat under his arm took the lead and we followed him into the chapel, my mother and me, carrying my baby in my arms for the last time.

Acknowledgements

My husband, Gary, children, Tom and Lucy, and my parents, David and Jeanne, for their encouragement and love; my sister, Jo Wright, and friends Rachael Bletchly and Jane McGuinn, who have listened, read and cheered me on.

My experts: Colin Sutton for his invaluable guidance and humour on police matters, Dr James Walker, independent forensic DNA expert, and my brother, Jonathan Thurlow, who stopped me making a terrible footballing faux pas.

My wonderful agent and mentor, Madeleine Milburn, for the calm advice and occasional much-needed glasses of fizz.

And special thanks to my brilliant editors at Transworld and Berkley. Producing *The Child* has not been without its moments and Frankie Gray and Danielle Perez have urged me on, mopped my brow and stayed with me during the delivery of my difficult second baby — I mean book.

We do hope that you have enjoyed reading this large print book.

Did you know that all of our titles are available for purchase?

We publish a wide range of high quality large print books including:
Romances, Mysteries, Classics
General Fiction
Non Fiction and Westerns

Special interest titles available in large print are:
The Little Oxford Dictionary
Music Book
Song Book
Hymn Book
Service Book

Also available from us courtesy of Oxford University Press:
Young Readers' Dictionary
(large print edition)
Young Readers' Thesaurus
(large print edition)

For further information or a free brochure, please contact us at:
Ulverscroft Large Print Books Ltd.,
The Green, Bradgate Road, Anstey,
Leicester, LE7 7FU, England.
Tel: (00 44) 0116 236 4325
Fax: (00 44) 0116 234 0205

Other titles published by Ulverscroft:

THE WIDOW

Fiona Barton

Jean Taylor's life was blissfully ordinary. Nice house, nice husband. Glen was all she ever wanted: her Prince Charming. But then everything changed. The newspapers found a new name for Glen: MONSTER, they shrieked. Jean was married to a man accused of the unimaginable. And as the years ticked by, with no sign of the little girl he had been suspected of taking, their lives were constantly splashed across the front pages. But now Glen is dead, and Jean is alone for the first time — free to tell her own story on her own terms . . .

FRIEND REQUEST

Laura Marshall

When Louise Williams receives a message from someone left long in her past, her heart nearly stops. Maria Weston wants to be friends on Facebook. But Maria Weston has been missing for over twenty-five years. She was last seen the night of a school leavers' party, and the world believes her to be dead. Particularly Louise, who has lived her adult life with a terrible secret. As Louise is forced to discover the truth about what really happened, the only thing she knows for sure is that Maria Weston disappeared that night, never to be heard from again, until now. . .

99 RED BALLOONS

Elisabeth Carpenter

Eight-year-old Grace is last seen in a sweet shop. Her mother Emma is living a nightmare. But as her loved ones rally around her, cracks begin to emerge. What are the emails sent between her husband and her sister? Why does her mother take so long to join the search? And is there more to the disappearance of her daughter than meets the eye? Meanwhile, ageing widow Maggie Taylor sees a familiar face in the newspaper. A face that jolts her from the pain of her existence into a spiralling obsession with another girl — the first girl who disappeared . . .